D. S. Gregory

Christian Ethics

The true moral manhood and life of duty - a text-book for schools and colleges

D. S. Gregory

Christian Ethics

The true moral manhood and life of duty - a text-book for schools and colleges

ISBN/EAN: 9783337368876

Printed in Europe, USA, Canada, Australia, Japan

Cover: Foto ©Andreas Hilbeck / pixelio.de

More available books at **www.hansebooks.com**

CHRISTIAN ETHICS;

OR, THE

True Moral Manhood and Life of Duty.

A TEXT-BOOK

FOR

Schools and Colleges.

BY

D. S. GREGORY, D.D.,

PROF. OF THE MENTAL SCIENCES AND ENGLISH LITERATURE IN UNIVERSITY OF WOOSTER.

PHILADELPHIA:
ELDREDGE & BROTHER,
17 North Seventh Street.
1881.

J. FAGAN & SON,
ELECTROTYPERS, PHILAD'A.

PREFACE.

THIS volume had its origin in the demands of the class-room. It seeks to present that most important of all sciences,— the science of right and noble living,— from the point of view of the enlightened Christian conscience, so as to set before the youthful mind the highest attainable human life and mission. It aims to embody the great principles concerning the nature of the true moral manhood and work, and the mode of attaining the former and performing the latter, in such a form that they may be understood by students of average intelligence in our schools and colleges; and to give to the whole such a unity and natural order that the entire system may be most readily retained in the memory and made a life-long possession and guide. While no truths have been excluded simply because they are old, and no statements introduced merely because they are new, and while no effort has been spared to make the presentation of the subject such as is warranted by the moral facts of man's nature and of the world, it has still been the constant endeavor to present the old truths in new aspects and relations, so as to awaken mental activity, to fix the attention, to arouse enthusiasm, and to incite the student by this practical and living interest to the formation of the noblest character and the accomplishment of the highest work of life.

A glance at the printed page will show the intelligent teacher that the aid of the compositor has been freely invoked to remedy the defect —so common in the text-books on this and kindred subjects — of covering up the main truths in the mass of details and obscuring the connections of the parts by want of proper and logical division and arrangement. By reason of this defect, the student is often required to spend the greater portion of his valuable time in trying to ascertain what are the main points in the discussion, and what is the connection existing between them, and even after he has succeeded in this profitless task finds himself unable to retain the subject permanently in the memory. To remedy this defect, the type has been made to perform an important office, in giving to the various divisions and subdivisions their proper relative degrees of prominence, in bringing out the connections of the subject, and thus preparing the very page to do a work of discrimination and instruction.

It is hoped that the features which have been introduced to adapt the volume to the class-room, may likewise commend it to the professional man and the man of business, who equally with the student need to keep freshly in mind, in this busy age, the science of the best and noblest life of duty.

The writer would acknowledge his obligation to the various authors whose names are mentioned, or whose works are cited, in the pages of this volume, — a debt often the greatest to those from whom he has felt constrained to differ most widely. Especially is his grateful acknowledgment due to the able men — now venerable or sainted — who led him, in his student years, in the higher walks of science and theology; and most of all to his college instructor in metaphysics and ethics, whose valuable counsel, generous encouragement, and unselfish friendship have always been of the highest service.   D. S. G.

UNIVERSITY OF WOOSTER,
Wooster, O., April, 1875.

CONTENTS

INTRODUCTION.

NATURE OF THE SCIENCE.

PART I.

THEORETICAL ETHICS. THEORY OF THE LIFE OF DUTY.

DIVISION I.

The Nature of the Moral Agent.

CHAPTER I.

General View of the Personal Agent.

SECTION I. — The Active Being.

SECTION II. — The Springs of Action.

1 *   v

CHAPTER II.

Special View of the Moral Agent.

SECTION I.—Elements of the Moral Nature from the Theories of the Moralist.

SECTION II.—Elements of the Moral Nature from Consciousness.

DIVISION II.

The Nature of Virtue, or the Dutiful in Conduct.

CHAPTER I.

The Supreme End of Virtuous Action.

SECTION I.—Theories of the Supreme End.

SECTION II.—The True Theory Established.

CHAPTER II.

The Supreme Rule of Rightness.

SECTION I.—Unsatisfactory Theories of the Supreme Rule.

CHAPTER III.

The Requisite Moral Reconstruction.

SECTION I.—The Moral Disorder of Man's Nature.

SECTION II.—The True Scheme of Moral Reconstruction.

PART II.

PRACTICAL ETHICS. DUTIES IN THE LIFE OF DUTY.

DIVISION I.

Individual Ethics. Duties toward Self.

CHAPTER I.

Duty of Self-Conservation.

SECTION I.—Self-Preservation.—Life.

SECTION II.—Self-Care.—Health.

SECTION III.—Self-Support.—Well-Being.

CHAPTER II.

Duty of Self-Culture.

SECTION I.—Physical Self-Culture.

SECTION II.—Spiritual Self-Culture.

CHAPTER III.

Duty of Self-Conduct.

SECTION I.—Self-Control.

SECTION II.—Self-Direction.

DIVISION II.

SOCIAL ETHICS. DUTIES TOWARD MAN-KIND.

CHAPTER I.

General Ethics. Duties toward Men in General.

SECTION I.—Duty of Social Conservation.

SECTION II.—Duty of Social Improvement.

SECTION III.—Duty of Social Direction.

CHAPTER II.

Economical Ethics. Duties in the Household.

SECTION I.—Duties of the Marriage Relation.

SECTION II.—Duties of the Parental Relation.

SECTION III.—Duties of Master and Servant.

CHAPTER III.

Civil Ethics. Duties in the State.

SECTION I.—Duties of the State.

SECTION II.—Duties of the Citizen.

DIVISION III.

Theistic Ethics. Duties toward God.

CHAPTER I.

Supreme Devotion of the Intellect to God.

SECTION I.—The Binding Force of the Duty.

SECTION II.—The Range of the Duty.

CHAPTER II.

Supreme Devotion of the Heart to God.

SECTION I.—The Binding Force of the Duty.

SECTION II.—The Range of the Duty.

CHAPTER III.

Supreme Devotion of the Will to God.

SECTION I.—Obedience toward God.

SECTION II.—Worship of God.

SECTION III.—Acceptance of the Divine Scheme of Moral Reconstruction.

TO TEACHERS.

IT is suggested that the teacher may use this volume in any of the three following ways:

First, omitting *Theoretical Ethics*, or the theory of human duty, he may take his pupils over *Practical Ethics*, with its view of the practical duties of life. This will meet the wants of the younger and less mature pupils who may attempt the study of the subject.

Secondly, with a more mature class of pupils, he may use the whole work, with the view of having them master the entire system of Ethics, Theoretical and Practical, and make it their own for life. In such use of the text-book, the attention should be especially directed to the paragraphs in the larger type, as containing the substance of the whole, and to the connection of all the parts in one complete system.

Thirdly, for the advanced classes, the teacher may, if he has the leisure, use the matter printed in the larger type as a syllabus in connection with which to deliver lectures of his own.

xii

INTRODUCTION.

NATURE OF THE SCIENCE.

I. Definition.

Ethics, or Moral Science, is the science of man's life of duty, or of what man ought to do in this present world.

Ethics is a Science.—Ethics belongs to the genus, or class, *Science,* since its aim is to ascertain, classify, and rationally explain a certain group or range of facts. The statement of its aim shows it to be in its method an inductive science, in the same sense in which psychology and the physical sciences are inductive. In all these sciences an element of deduction is always joined with the prevailing and fundamental element of induction before the complete scientific result is reached.

Ethics is the Science of Man's Life of Duty.—That which distinguishes the facts of this science from those of all other sciences is, that they are the facts of human duty, or obligation; in short, everything in the nature, relations, and actions of man, of which either *ought* or *ought not* can be predicated.

The science of morals finds its one great subject in the life-task, or mission of duty, appointed for man to fulfil in this world. It investigates and treats all the facts of human duty as they are connected with this appointed task. Theoretically, it aims to ascertain the principles of the true moral manhood and the complete moral task; practically, it aims to direct men to the attainment of the true moral manhood and to the accomplishment of the complete moral task. It is, therefore, evidently a science the knowledge of which is of the utmost practical importance to every man.

Other Definitions Tested.—Ethical writers have defined this science from various points of view. The science which treats of morals, the science of right. *Haven.* The science of moral law. *Wayland.* The systematic application of the ultimate rule of right to all conceptions of moral conduct. *Hickok.* The science which teaches men their supreme end, and how to attain it. *Hopkins.* That science which teaches men their duty, and the reasons of it. *Paley.* A code of rules for the regulation of conduct among men as they should be. *Herbert Spencer.* The science which proposes to direct and regulate human actions as right or wrong. *Fleming.* The science of the moral. *Wuttke.* The scientific presentation of human action. *Schleiermacher.* The rational explanation of our moral actions, moral nature, and moral relations. *Calderwood.* Some of these various definitions may, with proper explanation, be made to cover the exact ground of the science of morals; but most of them, as will appear by examination, are too general, or incomplete, or tautological; some *too general,* as Schleiermacher's, which ignores the differentia of the science; others *incomplete,* as Dr. Hickok's and Herbert Spencer's, which cover only the ground of practical morality; still others *tautological,* as the comprehensive one of Calderwood.

The Name Selected.—The science of human duty has been variously designated: Ethics, Moral Philosophy, Moral Science. According to the best usage these names are equivalent. *Ethics* has been selected for convenience, and will be used interchangeably with the others.

Ethics is of Greek origin (Ἠθική from ἦθος, custom, habit. disposition), and originally applied only to individual conduct or manners; but its application has been extended by usage to the whole range of morals private and public.

Moral Philosophy is of Latin origin (Moralis Philosophia), and the designation *Moral* (*moralis* from *mores,* manners, customs,) was limited, like the corresponding Greek expression, to individual conduct, and has been extended in like manner in its application.

Moral Science is perhaps the name most in accordance with the present modes of English thought. *Moral Philosophy* was used by the early English writers to denote the science of mind as distinguished from the physical sciences; but the prevailing tendency among later writers was to confine it to its own proper sphere of morals. In past usage a still later tendency has been to name the mental and spiritual sciences, *Philosophy,* and to confine *Science* rather to the sciences of material nature; to say intellectual philosophy, moral philosophy, etc.; and astronomical science, geological science, etc. The present tendency is to apply *Science* to both these departments of being, since the sciences of spirit and of matter are now both regarded as equally *sciences of obser-*

ration; to say mental science or moral science, as freely as science of optics or astronomical science.

II. Relation to Psychology.

1st. Place in the Scheme of Psychological Sciences.—The facts of human duty from which the science of ethics is constructed are chiefly drawn from the examination of conscience, or the moral faculty, and of virtue, or the right in conduct. So far as ethics treats of conscience it is therefore a psychological science; so far as it treats of the right it is not a psychological science. In view of its twofold subject and nature, ethics may be classed with æsthetics as a *Mixed Psychological Science.*

Its relations to the other sciences of the soul may be seen from the following *Scheme of Psychological Sciences:*

A. The Pure Psychological Sciences.	Science of Intellect,
	    " Feelings,
	    " Will.
		On Simple Faculties.

B. The Mixed Psychological Sciences.	Æsthetics. or the Science of Taste and of the Beautiful. Ethics. or the Science of Conscience and of the Right.	On Complex working of Faculties.

Pure Psychological Sciences. — Psychology, or the science of the human soul, often ambiguously styled mental philosophy, treats of the soul in its three faculties: the Intellect, the Feelings, and the Will. Upon these faculties are founded the three psychological sciences: the Science of the Intellect, the Science of the Feelings, and the Science of the Will. All the facts out of which these three sciences are constructed are drawn from the soul itself, and they are therefore designated the *Pure Psychological Sciences.*

Mixed Psychological Sciences. — The two sciences of æsthetics and ethics are not purely psychological. Æsthetics is the science of the faculty of taste, or of man's æsthetic nature, which is a complex of intellect and feeling, and is so far psychological; but it is also the science of the beautiful, as a quality in objects, and is so far not psychological. Ethics is the science of the moral faculty, or of man's moral nature, and is so far psychological; but it is also the science of virtue, or the right in conduct, and is so far not psychological. In their second aspect both these sciences are termed *Metaphysical*, because they aim to treat in a scientific way the principles or laws which underlie and condition the phenomena of the beautiful and the right. They may therefore be properly termed mixed psychological sciences.

2d. Demand for Correct Psychology. — It is obvious, from the foregoing considerations, that a science of morals is impossible without a correct knowledge of psychology in general, and a correct knowledge of the psychology of man's moral nature in particular.

The psychology of the moral nature has been so imperfectly treated, or so entirely neglected in the text-books on psychology, that undue prominence must necessarily be given it in any treatise on morals which aims to be at all intelligible and satisfactory.

The Imperfect Treatment of the psychology of the moral nature will hardly be denied. In the many valuable works on general and special psychology accessible to American students, there is scarcely to be found a complete and satisfactory discussion of the phenomena of conscience and of the feelings and will, so intimately connected with moral action.

The Denial of the Moral Nature with its intuitions of right and duty has in certain quarters been still more fatal to scientific ethics. It is a well-known fact that the empirical school of philosophy — which has of late numbered among its adherents the boldest, if not the ablest, speculative minds of the day in the British Islands, and among them John Stuart Mill — begins with denying all the intuitions of the soul, and declaring that all so-called intuitions in every department of knowledge are derived solely from experience. It persistently refuses to recognize the nobler and more important part of man, and by so doing eventually blots the idea of right out of its system of things and puts expediency or utility in its place.

If there is to be any solid basis for ethical science, it becomes necessary to investigate carefully the main facts of conscience, and of the feelings and will in their relations to human action in general, and to moral action in particular.

3d. Correct Psychological Method. — As an inductive science, ethics must observe, systematize, and explain the facts of man's moral consciousness. The mode of inquiry, so far as ethics respects these facts of consciousness, is the introspective, or reflective. Internal perception, or the power by which the soul takes cognizance of its own acts and states, is the instrument of observation in this science, as external perception is in the physical sciences.

The Facts of Consciousness. — It is to be noted that the facts of consciousness, from which the inductions of ethical science are made, may be found not only in the present mental state of the investigator himself, and in his past mental states as recalled by memory, but also and more especially in what he discovers of other men's thoughts and feelings as expressed in their words and actions.

To be Studied in the Complete Man. — As man's reason may be studied best not in the idiot nor in the undeveloped child, but in the man of fully developed intellectual power, so man's moral nature may be studied best not in the brutalized or undeveloped man, but in the man of fully developed moral power and character. In this view the *Sacred Scriptures*, irrespective of their inspiration, may have for the moralist the highest value as giving expression to human consciousness when morally enlightened in the highest degree. Paul's testimony concerning any principle of morals is of vastly greater value, irrespective of his inspiration, than the testimony of Cicero, and that for the simple reason that Paul's moral condition was vastly higher than that of Cicero.

By the Scientific Method. — A rigid application of the scientific method of psychology to all these facts of the moral consciousness is necessary in order to arrive at the truth concerning man's moral constitution.

III. Relation to Theology.

1st. Distinction between Ethics and Theology. — *Ethics* is the science of human duty: *Theology* is the science of God and the mutual relations of God and man. If the two sciences are constructed from the facts of nature, we have *Natural Ethics* and *Natural Theology:* if from the facts of divine revelation, we have *Revealed*, or *Theological*, *Ethics* and *Revealed Theology.* By comparing the definitions of the two sciences, it appears that the sphere of ethics is much narrower than that of theology, covering the single relation of man to God as his lawgiver and governor. Comparing the practical fruits of the two, theology aims to produce religion; ethics, morality.

The Different Spheres.—Revealed theology, according to Dr. Hodge, is "the science of the facts of divine revelation, so far as those facts concern the nature of God and our relation to him, as his creatures, as sinners, and as the subjects of redemption." It thus involves a scientific view of the nature of God and of many relations both of a present and a future world; while ethics involves the single relation of duty to God as the moral governor. The sphere of ethics is but a small part of the greater sphere of theology.

The Different Fruits are seen in *Religion*, the appropriate practical fruit of theology, which takes into account the nature of God, and all the relations of God and man; and in *Morality*, the appropriate practical fruit of ethics, which has regard exclusively to the relation of man to the will of God as his lawgiver.

2d. A System of Christian Ethics proposed.—In man's present condition a complete system of ethics cannot be constructed from the light of nature alone. It is therefore proposed to construct a system of Christian ethics, as distinguished from natural ethics on the one hand and from theological ethics on the other.

Christian Ethics is the system of morals reached by the scientific investigation of the moral consciousness of man as enlightened, elevated, and purified by the Christian religion.

Natural Ethics Impossible.—It would be equally impossible to construct a complete system of natural ethics in heathendom and in Christendom.

Among the heathen, man is degraded and his moral nature, like his intellectual, only imperfectly developed; so that it is impossible to gain from such a wreck of man a full view of what the moral agent should be.

In the Christian nations, Christianity has unfolded a vast range of new duty and motive to the moral agent, and has cleared the views and elevated the moral standard of the individual and of society. From a system of ethics designed for the regulation of conduct in Christian society, it would not only be eminently improper and unphilosophical, but utterly impossible, to exclude those great moral principles that have come from Christianity, but which are accepted and fully approved by the most enlightened conscience.

Theological Ethics not Advisable.—A system of theological ethics is, of course, possible; but for the purposes of the ordinary instruction of the class-room it is not advisable. Many minds are open to the reception of Christian ethics, that would be closed against a system of morals drawn directly from the Sacred Scriptures. Christian ethics is fitted, moreover, to strengthen and to give a more practical bent to those who already accept revealed ethics.

IV. Divisions.

A system of Ethics properly consists of two *Parts*, the one Theoretical, the other Practical.

Theoretical Ethics investigates and arranges the principles which mark out and govern man's life of duty, or that life-task which he ought to fulfil. In other words, it aims to construct the theory of the true moral manhood and the complete moral task.

Practical Ethics applies the principles of duty to the regulation of human conduct in all the various relations of life. Or in other words, it aims to direct man to the attainment of the true moral manhood and the achievement of the complete moral task.

The Common Distinctions. — There is a sense in which ethics is wholly a *practical* science: it is a science pertaining to practice and for the sake of practice. But Practical Ethics, as here considered, is so called because it actually applies the principles of the theory of morals to the regulation of man's conduct in the various relations of life. Theoretical and Practical Ethics are also named Pure and Applied Ethics, since the former treats of the fundamental principles of the science in themselves considered, and the latter applies them to the regulation of conduct.

Relation of the Two Divisions. — A distinguished British writer cautions his readers against supposing that there is any such connection between Theoretical and Practical Ethics as is to be found between theory and practice in art, where the one is in order to the other and prepares for it. In opposition to this view, the truth is that the relation between theory and practice is precisely the same in ethics as in the arts. (A correct theory of ethics must lie at the basis of all correct moral practice.) In any helpful treatise on moral science, the theory must be constructed with wise reference to its application to practice in regulating human conduct.

NOTE.

As one important aim in the study of a system of ethics is to grasp and retain that system in the mind, the student will find it a profitable exercise to prepare a careful *Outline Analysis* of each Part, Division, Chapter, and Section, arranged in such a form as to show the relation of all the various subjects considered. Whatever is thoroughly mastered in this way will not easily be forgotten.

The following analysis of the *Introduction* may serve as a guide in this kind of work:

ANALYTIC SYNOPSIS FOR REVIEW.

Introduction to Christian Ethics.

Nature of the Science.

I. DEFINITION.

II. RELATION TO PSYCHOLOGY.
      1st. Place in the Scheme of Psychological Sciences.
      2d. Demand for Correct Psychology.
      3d. Correct Psychological Method.

III. RELATION TO THEOLOGY.
      1st. Distinction between Ethics and Theology.
      2d. A System of Christian Ethics proposed.

IV. DIVISIONS: THEORETICAL AND PRACTICAL.

CHRISTIAN ETHICS.

PART I.

THEORETICAL ETHICS.

Definition and Division.

Theoretical Ethics is that part of Christian Ethics which aims to construct the true theory of man's life of duty from his moral nature and the nature of virtue, or the dutiful in conduct.

It thus appears that a twofold investigation must precede and prepare the way for the construction of the theory of duty. Theoretical Ethics will therefore be treated under three *Divisions*:

Division I. Investigation of the Nature of Man as a Moral Agent.

Division II. Investigation of the Nature of Virtue, or the Dutiful in human conduct.

Division III. Presentation of the Philosophy of Man's Life of Duty.

Preliminary Explanation of Terms.—Before proceeding to the proposed investigations, a brief explanation of some of the more common expressions made use of in ethical discussions will be helpful.

Ethical View of Man.—Ethics regards man as essentially an agent, or active being; as a creature of reason so made that he sets before himself, either consciously or unconsciously, a divinely ordained end which he feels himself bound to attain; as able to attain this end by his own voluntary activity as a free, rational agent; and as recognizing the existence and claims of a divine law which points out the way in which the divinely ordained end is to be reached.

The Moral and Right.—The conduct, or activity, by which, in accordance with this law, man voluntarily realizes this end, is the morally good: that by which he fails of this is the morally evil. The moral, or the right, is found, therefore, in conformity of the conduct to the appointed end and law: the immoral, or the wrong, in a corresponding want of conformity.

Moral Agency and Moral Action.— Man's moral agency is his agency so far as it relates to this end of life under the moral law. His moral action comprehends all such action, and such only, as has reference to this moral end and law; or, in other words, all such action as is either right or wrong, or of which it may be said that it ought to be done, or ought not to be done.

Morality.— In ethical discussions the term *morality* is used as a general term embracing both the morally good and the morally evil, both the right and the wrong. *Moral conduct* may mean conduct morally good or conduct morally bad. The *truths of morality* include the truths concerning vice as well as those concerning virtue.

Duty and Ought.— The words *duty* and *ought* need no extended explanation for the present. Even a child understands that duty is what one is morally bound to do, or what ought to be done. The thoughtful man necessarily and consciously connects these ideas of duty and obligation with the grand moral end, or task of life, which is the complete duty.

These preliminary statements are to some extent necessarily anticipative. Their full meaning and the reasons for it will appear more clearly in the further progress of the discussion of Theoretical Ethics.

DIVISION I.

NATURE OF THE MORAL AGENT.

Definition and Subdivision.

DIVISION I. treats of the facts of man's nature as a moral agent, or of conscience. It aims to investigate, arrange, and explain the facts.

By man as a moral agent is meant man as a personal agent endowed with a moral nature, commonly called conscience, that fits him for a mission of duty.

Man is first an agent and then a moral agent, first active and then morally active. He must be understood as an agent or active being in order to be understood as a being morally active. For convenience and clearness, the subject will be treated in two *Chapters*:

Chapter I.   General View of Man as a Personal Agent.
Chapter II.   Special View of Man as a Moral Agent.

Reason for this Treatment.— Much of indefiniteness, ambiguity, and even positive error, has found its way into ethical discussions, from the simple lack of a clear understanding and full statement of the elements of human agency. It is obvious that any so-called system of ethics, which has not a correct and consistent theory of human action at the foundation, must be, to say the least possible, radically defective. It is for these reasons that such prominence is here given to the consideration of the subject of man's personal agency.

CHAPTER I.

GENERAL VIEW OF THE PERSONAL AGENT.

Elements of Human Agency.

IN order to a clear knowledge of man as a personal agent, it is necessary to take a general view of what may be called the elements of human agency.

Human action requires a personal actor, origin, movement, and aim. Hence are deduced the essential elements of human agency.

The Elements Deduced. — Action, in the sense in which the term is used in ethics, properly originates only in a personal, self-active agent. Hence the nature of the agent, or active being, must be considered. In order to the origination of action there must obviously be some starting-point, or power of beginning, or spring of action, in the agent. Hence the springs of action must be considered. Man has the power within himself, in his own free will, of deciding along which of the various courses of action presented he will move. Hence the arbiter and executor of action must be considered. The action of a rational being is not purposeless, but must take some rational direction, so that reason, in revealing the various possible ends, and in deciding upon the particular end to be pursued in the movement originated by the will, becomes a guiding power in action. Hence the guides of action must be considered.

The essential elements of human agency will therefore be treated in the following *Sections*:

Section 1.   The Active Being.
Section 2.   The Springs of Action.
Section 3.   The Arbiter of Action.
Section 4.   The Guides of Action.

SECTION I.

The Active Being.

Statement and Subdivision.

The first element to be considered is the general constitution of the active being who is to be the moral agent.

The human agent consists of spirit and body. As a spirit embodied he is linked with God. Under God's government in this present world, he is in a state of probation and development for an endless future.

These facts are all essential to any complete view of man as an active being, and they furnish the proper *Topics* for investigation and discussion.

Topic First. Man a Self-active Spirit. — Man's activity as a spiritual being is self-determined, constant, progressive, and immortal. All these aspects of his spiritual activity are essential to any complete view of human duty, and they accordingly furnish the proper *Subjects* for consideration.

Subject 1st. Man Self-active. — Man is by his very constitution self-active. He is conscious of his active powers, and of his freedom to exert them on the various objects appropriate for them.

Action Defined.—An *act* or *action* is the exercise of power by any agent. A *human action* is an action by a human agent in the full possession and exercise of intelligence and will, or the faculties proper to man as a reasonable being.

It is obvious that the word *action* is to be understood negatively as well as positively. There are acts of omission, or of refraining to exert power when its exertion is called for, as well as acts of commission.

When *act* and *action* are distinguished, the former is individual, the latter collective, or applicable to a course made up of many actions. So *act* is applied chiefly to internal or psychical activity; *action* to external or bodily activity.

In common speech a distinction is made between thought, word, and act; but, in the sense in which *act* is used in ethics, to think and to speak are no less acts than the doing of any outward deeds that may be in one's power.

Man Consciously Self-active.—"As the lamb frisks," says Dr. McCosh, "and the colt gambols, and as the child is in perpetual rotation, so man's internal powers are forever impelling him to exertion, independent altogether of any external object, or even of any further internal ends to be gained." "I know myself as a force in energy," says Sir Wm. Hamilton. And again: "Human existence is only a more general expression for human life, and human life only a more general expression for the sum of energies in which that life is realized, and through which it is manifested in consciousness. In a word, life is energy, and conscious energy is conscious life."

Man Consciously Free in Action.—With this consciousness of self-action is always involved a consciousness, on the part of the agent, that his action, in its normal forms, is determined by himself. He is not impelled unconsciously by some extraneous force toward some end, but is himself conscious of the end, and directs himself toward it. He himself thinks, feels, and wills. He himself acts by his own choice and determination. He is free to turn his powers toward whatever object he may wish, and is conscious that in his experience he actually does this.

Fundamental Forms of Human Action.—There are certain forms in which it is universally admitted that man as a rational agent exhibits and unfolds his life. He is an intelligent, or knowing spirit; a sensitive, or feeling spirit; a choosing, willing, or determining spirit: knowing, feeling, and willing are therefore forms of human action.

Combining the foregoing distinctions, we reach the following:

Scheme of Action.

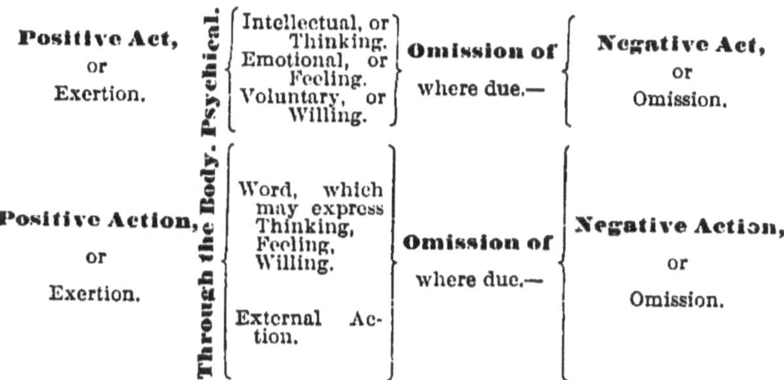

Subject 2d. Man Constantly Active.—There is reason for believing that man never for an instant ceases to act. The

bodily senses rest; the soul probably never rests, but is always consciously active. The acts of the agent are thus seen to be numbered only by the separate instants of his entire existence.

Views of the Authorities.— Plato, Descartes, Leibnitz, Kant, Hamilton,—almost all the greatest investigators of the soul,—have held this view.

The Soul is always Active when we are Awake.— It is comparatively easy to show that the soul is always consciously active when man is awake. Let any one turn attention to his soul, even in his dullest moods, and he will find some train of thought passing within. He will be able to trace back his way, by the laws of association, from image to image and from thought to thought, till memory fails him. Were memory a perfectly faithful servant, man might doubtless go all the way back to the moment when the soul began its being and action.

The Soul is probably always Active when we are Asleep.— The argument against activity of mind in sleep is substantially as follows:—" I do not recollect such constant and conscious activity, therefore there is no such thing." It is a sufficient answer that conscious activity and recollection of it are not the same thing, and do not always go together. In somnambulism the mind is vastly more active than when awake, new powers are temporarily acquired by it, and the body is in a state of high activity and under perfect control of will; yet waking always cuts the consciousness in two, so that there is never any recollection of the experience. In dreaming, the mind is consciously active. Many dreams are actually remembered; much dreaming, of the existence of which we have good evidence through others than the dreamer, is actually forgotten. In incipient slumbers—between waking and rest—if gently disturbed, Sir Wm. Hamilton found himself conscious of beginning a dream, which could often be traced back to the time of complete wakefulness. In deep slumber, if suddenly awakened, he always found himself in the midst of a dream, which could sometimes be traced far back. The watcher with the sick, while undisturbed by sounds foreign to the patient, is awakened by a groan or a sigh or a difficulty in breathing, or a very slight noise in connection with the object of his watching. A man can appoint his hour for waking and waken himself at just that hour. These clearly ascertained facts go far toward proving that it is the body only that is inactive and asleep; the soul is awake and active. The extended observation and experiment of Hamilton, and of M. Jouffroy, a sketch of which is given in the *Metaphysics* of the former, go very far toward establishing the constant conscious activity of the self-active spirit, and thus toward doubling the activities which the future may somehow recall for man.

Subject 3d. Man Progressively Active.—Man is not only essentially self-active, but development and progress are the law of his activity. His powers of action unfold and increase in the variety of their uses and in their capabilities by exercise. To his development and progress no definite limit can be set. His life may therefore in the future rise to a power and greatness altogether beyond any possible conception he can now form.

Progressive Development.—There is an outward and visible development. Human life begins with infancy, proceeds through childhood and youth to manhood and age. There is likewise a marked and corresponding progress in the inner life, in all the forms of the activity of the soul. The first waking of the intellectual life of the infant may be seen in the recognition of pain, as shown in its cry; the first waking of the emotional life may be found in the instincts which direct to the securing and swallowing of the food provided by nature; the first waking of the voluntary life may perhaps be seen in the determination to live, shown in following out the natural instincts. Out of such a feeble, flickering life is developed the strong man with his powers full-summed, and available for noblest purposes. Even the position of the strong man is but the vantage-ground for a development vastly grander, and an increase in power vastly more rapid. From the infant soul, capable only of a wail, the human being may grow through the years into a Moses, or a Luther, or a Newton, capable of comprehending a destiny of immortal glory, of rejoicing with unspeakable joy of hope in the prospect of it, and of directing all the powers of the being to the securing of it; or into an Alexander, or a Napoleon, capable of fashioning a plan seemingly glorious, but in reality dark and fatal; of exulting in it, and of perishing in its attempted accomplishment.

Law of Progress by Exercise.—That man's faculties increase in power only by being exercised is a familiar principle, applicable to the powers both of body and soul. The infant grows into the muscular artisan or the athlete by long exercise of the bodily powers, and into a Bacon or a Milton by long exercise of the spiritual powers. It is also an acknowledged principle, that the exercise which is to make the strong man, physical or intellectual, must be vigorous as well as persistent. The listless use of the powers weakens rather than strengthens. The child will never become a Hercules by dreamily swinging on a gate in the May day sunshine, or a Butler by an existence made up of sleep and novel-reading.

Progress Indefinite.—No possible progress of a finite being can ever make that being infinite. Man can never become God — must always remain at an incomprehensible remove from God. Yet no definite limit can be set to his progress, no point of attainment can be fixed upon, even by the loftiest imagination, beyond which there is not possible a career of progress greater than all that has gone before. Time and opportunity are the only limits to human development and growth.

Subject 4th. Man Immortally Active.

—Man as an agent has an endless existence before him,— i. e., his unceasing activity will continue everlastingly. His life must therefore in the future rise to a power and greatness altogether beyond his highest possible conception.

In what sense Immortal.—Nothing in the universe save God himself is necessarily self-existent. If man's active being, his soul, is to exist forever in its career of activity, it must be because God wills to preserve it in immortal existence. Spirit is as truly created being as matter, and is as truly dependent on Omnipotence for its continuance in being. Man's soul, if immortal at all, is immortal because God has willed to preserve it forever in being.

Proof of Immortality.—That there is a life after the death of the body cannot therefore be made certain without some revelation from God of his will to that effect.

Revelation of Immortality in Man's Nature.—God has indicated his purpose of immortality in man's nature, as that nature expresses itself in the consciousness of the race. Among the forms of the argument from this source are those drawn from the belief, from the longing, and from the moral expectation of mankind.

Universal Belief.— The argument may be stated thus:

Whatever all men everywhere and always have believed is in accordance with truth.

All men everywhere and always have believed in the doctrine of the future immortal life.

Therefore the doctrine of the future immortal life is in accordance with truth.

This statement assumes, first, the fact of such universal belief; and, secondly, that the very belief contains in itself an assurance of its truthfulness. The second assumption must be admitted by those who

3 *

recognize the hand of Divine Wisdom in the constitution of man. The first assumption must be justified by an appeal to facts. These two assumptions admitted, the conclusion must follow. The existence of this universal belief of immortality becomes the Maker's revelation that he designs the soul to be immortal.

Universal Longing.— The argument may be stated formally:

Every universal instinctive and practical longing or pre-assurance of man is destined to be satisfied.

Man has such a longing for immortality and such pre-assurance of it.

Therefore this longing is destined to be satisfied by an immortal life beyond this present existence.

The force of the argument evidently depends upon two assumptions: first, that man has such a longing; and, second, that the existence of this longing involves the certainty of its satisfaction. That there is such a desire, instinctive, practical, universal, few will venture to deny. It is implied in the universal belief of immortality. That the law of satisfaction, implied in the second assumption, is universal, has been admirably shown by Coleridge in his *Aids to Reflection*, and by Chalmers in his *Natural Theology*. Says the latter, "For every desire, or every faculty, whether in man or in the inferior animals, there seems a counterpart object in external nature. . . . . . There is light for the eye; there is air for the lungs; there is food for the ever-recurring appetite of hunger; there is water for the appetite of thirst; there is society for the love, whether of fame or of fellowship; there is a boundless field in all the objects of all the sciences for the exercise of curiosity,—in a word, there seems not an affection in the living creature, which is not met by a counterpart and a congenial object in the surrounding creation. . . . Nature abounds not merely in present expedients for an immediate use, but in providential expedients for a future one; and, as far as we can observe, we have no reason to believe that, either in the first or second sort of expedients, there has ever aught been noticed which either bears on no object now or lands in no result afterwards." These two assumptions admitted, the conclusion must follow. The very longing for immortality becomes an intimation of the will of the Creator that the soul is to be immortal.

Universal Moral Expectation.—The argument may be stated formally:

God will complete, either in the present or in the future, the work of rendering exact justice to those under his moral government.

There are manifold promises and beginnings of the work of his justice left incomplete here.

There must therefore be a future existence in which to complete this work of justice.

The two assumptions in this argument are: first, that this universal expectation exists; and, second, that in its very existence is found a warrant for its realization. Both these assumptions have sufficient ground for support in the nature of conscience as the voice of God in the human soul.

These are only some of the forms in which the argument from God's revelation of his will in man's nature may be presented. Bishop Butler, in his *Analogy*, gives almost demonstrative force to the argument as drawn from man's present state as one of discipline and probation for a future condition.

Revelation of Immortality in the Scriptures.—But while the consciousness of immortality is God's revelation in man of the Divine will concerning a future existence, the Christian doctrine of immortality, in its completeness and full glory as held in lands familiar with the Bible revelation, rests on the solid basis of that revelation. The teachings of the Scriptures, in bringing "life and immortality to light," commend themselves to man's consciousness the more powerfully because the revelation is substantially the same in both Scriptures and consciousness.

We find that the doctrine was taught by divinely authenticated messengers, first in the Old Testament, and then still more clearly in the New Testament. (Hodge, *Theol.*) In the New Testament, God himself, in the person of his Incarnate Son, has spoken to man the doctrine of the future life; and has in the highest sense "brought life and immortality to light," by bringing back that Incarnate Son from the life beyond the grave in his resurrection from the dead; so that the truth of the Christian doctrine of man's immortality is established by the proofs of Christ's Divinity and of his resurrection.

Immortality of Progression.—The longing of man is not simply for immortality, but for a great immortality. "Our intellectual powers grasp infinity. We are conscious of a boundless capacity of research, knowledge, and progress, and our curiosity grows faster than its gratification, our sense of ignorance faster than our knowledge. In no department of life do we ever reach our aims or embody our conceptions." (*Peabody.*) The Miltons and the Newtons, while they have yet caught only glimpses of the world of beauty and of truth; the Brewsters and the Faradays, while they have yet caught only glimpses of the ineffable glory of the better life, pass away; and they pass away with their great souls longing for the ever nearer and grander views of beauty and truth and holiness in the presence of God. The very existence of such longing for a great future life, and of such faith in it, gives promise of the satisfaction and the indefinite progress, just as the simple desire for future existence gives promise that man shall live forever.

The enlightened human consciousness, as expressed in the Scriptures, more clearly holds out like hope for the life to come, in the "far more exceeding and eternal.weight of glory" into which Paul hoped to be introduced through the blessing and instruction and discipline of the life that now is.

Bearing of these Considerations.— It will at once be evident that the elements of constancy, progressiveness and immortality in man's activities are all-important elements. No true and adequate conception of the agent or of his life-task can be gained without giving them a prominent place.

Topic Second. Man a Spirit Embodied. — Man is a spirit embodied. His self-active spirit lives its earthly life in a material body. The body is to be considered as the spirit's earthly home and working-place, its medium of communication, and its instrument for its work.

Man's earthly mission of duty would be impossible without the body, and cannot but be greatly modified by it. Hence these various relations of the body to the activity of the spirit furnish important *Subjects* for consideration.

The Body Ignored or Despised.—False theories concerning the body —such as that it is the source and cause of all sin — have led mankind generally in the past ages to ignore it in all ethical discussions. It has been looked upon as something to be despised and mortified, rather than as an instrument "fearfully and wonderfully made" by God himself for a wise and beneficent end. In the reaction against this error, the tendency of the irreligious materialist of the present day is doubtless to ignore the spirit, or make it a mere transient force-manifestation of organized matter, and so to exalt the body above it; but Christian moralists have at the same time been brought to see the necessity of taking a correct and adequate view of the mission of the body as subservient to the spirit.

Considered in the Present Life only.—The body will be considered only in its present relations to the soul. Aside from the teachings of revelation, man might possibly be led by reason to conclude that there will be a spiritualized body to correspond with the conditions of the immortal existence of the future life; but the range of our investigations does not necessarily require any consideration of the subject, as it can have only a comparatively slight bearing on the great questions of present duty.

Subject 1st. The Spirit's Home and Working-place.—The body is not only the home and citadel of the soul, to fix its place and to give seclusion, security, and proprietorship; but it also furnishes its necessary point of departure in its action in its present condition, and its chief working-place. From the vital connection of soul and body, the condition and efficiency of the former must, to a greater or less degree, depend upon the state of the latter.

The Body is the Physical Basis of the Soul in its Life-work.—The self-active spirit is conscious that it inhabits a physical and material structure which has life and force, and which is its own body. This body is the physical basis of the soul's phenomenal existence. If the soul is to dwell in a material universe and fulfil its mission in such a universe, it must have a body suited to such a habitation—a substantial body. In a material world the spirit must have some point of departure in its activity. The body is such a point. It is the place for carrying out every purpose of the mind and every end of living; and, the Creator being judge, it is the best place for the well-being and manifestation of the soul, else would he not have embodied the soul.

A sound Spirit in a sound Body.—It is a fact, that in our present state the powers of the soul are in general developed along with the powers of the body. After the body is completely developed for all its functions, it passes through certain stages of growth, increasing in size and strength. During the same period the soul is also unfolded and matured. One power after another is brought forward as the body is prepared for its use. It is natural, therefore, that there should be a very close sympathy between body and soul. The former depends upon the latter for much of the exercise of its energy and activity. Everything that introduces disorder into the body deranges or modifies the action of the soul. It is a general principle, that a sound and properly developed human body furnishes a fit place for the proper existence and right action of a human spirit.

Marked Exceptions.—But while this is a general truth, it is a well-known fact, that many of the grandest workers and thinkers the world has ever known have accomplished their missions with, and even in spite of, mean or diseased or shattered bodies. There is therefore no such absolute dependence for soundness and power of the spirit upon the body as the materialist would have men believe.

Subject 2d. The Spirit's Medium of Intercourse.—The body through the senses furnishes the spirit which inhabits it with its indispensable medium of communication with nature, and with other embodied spirits like itself. Hence, by the modifying power of man's material structure, arise the various earthly relations which express themselves in the several stages of life, in the difference of the sexes, in the variety of temperaments individual and national, and in all the forms of social relation and activity.

The Organ of Communication.—The body, as the physical basis on which the spirit develops itself to its full power, is the perfectly answering and absolutely subserving organ of that spirit in its communications with the material universe and whatever is embodied in it. In man's present condition a body with the five senses is necessary in order to any easy and perfect communication between one soul and another, and between any soul and external nature.

Stages of Life.—Resulting from the soul's embodiment there are stages of development (as already noticed) in the life of the spirit, running partially parallel with those of the body. First, comes childhood, in which the body is as yet master over the spirit. The spirit is dependent on outer, sensuous, and spiritual influences, and is rather guided than self-guiding. (Secondly, comes youth, or the stage of transition to majority, in which the spirit is still struggling, with the aid of educators, for control over the body.) Thirdly, comes the period of manhood, or of majority, in which the agent has become completely master of himself and able to control the body and make it subservient to the purposes of the soul. Fourthly, comes old age, which in man's normal condition would doubtless exhibit a growing power of the spiritual and an increasing pre-occupation with the supernatural,—but which in man's fallen state often witnesses a return to the condition of youth, or even childhood, in which the body again becomes master of the soul.

The Differences of Temperament—which have been defined to be " the different tempers of the spirit in its bearing toward the outer world "—are also determined by differences in the embodiment of the spirit, or, in other words, by differences in bodily peculiarities, as will be shown subsequently. Similar to these, and also dependent on the bodily structure, are the *national*, or *race peculiarities*, which fit different nations for playing such different parts in the history of the world.

Social Relations.—The differences of sex, and the social relations hence arising, have their origin in like manner in connection with the embodiment of the human spirit. It is apparent that this embodiment furnishes the basis of all the various social earthly activities of the spirit. The family with its ties and its work, and the state with its connections and its mission, rest upon it.

Subject 3d. The Spirit's Instrument for its Work.— The body is the instrument in connection with which and through which the spirit must accomplish its work in the world. It is through the body that the active spirit moulds material nature, secures and holds dominion over it, and uses it for its own ends; it is through the body likewise that it reaches, moulds, and controls other human beings. In short, in man's present condition and place of abode, without the body the life-work would be impossible; and, other things being equal, the most perfectly furnished and developed body prepares for the largest and most perfect life-work.

Connections of Spirit with Body.—The action of the spirit is vitally connected with and, in general, dependent upon the nervous system as centring in the brain; the nervous system is vitally connected with the circulation of the blood as centring in the lungs; the circulatory system is vitally connected with the respiratory system, by which the blood is purified, by being brought in contact with the air, and with the nutritive system by which the blood is manufactured from the food. The condition of the body, therefore, determines in general what a man's working power is.

The Perfect Instrument.— In short, the body is the instrument for carrying out every purpose of the mind, and every end of being; and, the Creator being judge, it is the best instrument for the well-being and manifestation of the soul. The ideal is the perfect soul in the perfect body. Every departure from this normal condition must hinder the efficiency of the human agent.

So much time has been given to the consideration of the body of the human agent, because no true view of man's work in this life can be gained if it be forgotten that he is a spirit embodied, and so subject to the conditions, limitations, and relations of time and space on this material globe.

Topic Third. Man Consciously Linked with God.— The consideration of the agent as spirit and body suggests and presses for answer the question, *What is the relation of this* *embodied spirit, with his so grand capabilities and his endless existence, to the Infinite Spirit?*

Man is linked with God in his origin, in his activities, and in his immortal destiny. He is made to know God, and to work out his immortal destiny under God.

Subject 1st. Man made to Know God.—Man was made to believe in the existence of God and to acknowledge him as the Author, Sustainer, and End of his being; to recognize God as his Lawgiver and Moral Governor, and to acknowledge his responsibility to God.

Belief in God's Existence.—Says Dr. McCosh, "The idea of God, the belief in God, may be justly represented as native to man. He is led to it by the circumstances in which he is placed calling into energy mental principles which are natural to all. He does not require to go in search of it: it comes to him. He has only to be waiting for it and disposed to receive it, and it will be pressed on him from every quarter; it springs up naturally, as the plant or animal does from its germ; it will well up spontaneously from the depths of his heart; or it will shine on him from the works of nature, as light does from the sun."

But while the belief in God is native, it is not a *special intuition* in the strict sense, as Kant taught. The majority of philosophers and divines in all ages have held that the truth is rather, that "the common intelligence, combined with our moral perceptions and an obvious experience, leads to a belief in God and his chief attributes." The *facts* relating to God furnished by observation and experience are the facts of the universe material and spiritual, and especially of man himself with his material and spiritual being. The common sense, or reason, of man furnishes the *intuitive principles* of causation, of design, of moral obligation, and of the infinite,—which rise up spontaneously in the soul when the facts concerning God are presented. It is through the intuitions and the facts that man reaches the idea of God and the belief in God.

Progress to full Belief.—Into the full idea of God enter the elements of cause, personality (including intelligence, will, and separate existence), infinitude, and moral authority. To reach faith in all these, man does not need to pass through all the intricacies of the argument of Natural Theology: there is a simple process suited to all men, and which may be described as the course along which the race of man has always advanced to belief in God.

First Step.— Man opens his eyes upon the universe in which he lives. He sees all around him things changing, new beings coming into existence. He learns that he has himself recently sprung into being. Upon a wider observation and knowledge, History assures him that the race of man has come into existence within a few thousand years; Geology assures him that all the extant genera of plants and animals on the globe are of comparatively recent origin; on every hand evidence comes to light which leads him to think that the whole universe some day began to exist. In the presence of this vast and varied beginning of beings, including himself, the intuition of *causation* springs up spontaneously in the human soul. Every effect must have a cause, and an adequate cause. This vast system of effects must have an adequate cause, an exceedingly great and powerful cause, practically an *Infinite Cause*. Man's nature is so made that this conclusion is inevitable and irresistible alike with the ignorant man and the sage.

Second Step.—In the progress of observation man sees that this vast system of the universe is full of the evidences of design. As far downward and upward as the microscope and telescope will carry him, appear wonderful adaptations of organs to their special purposes, of parts of beings to each other, of each part of the world to all its other parts; wonderful adaptations of means and systems of means to the accomplishment of certain ends,—the hand answering to its mission of work, the eye responding to the light, the man rejoicing in the beauty and glory of the globe as made for his abode; systems upon systems of worlds circling in one great harmony in immensity. In the presence of this vast array of design the intuition of *design* springs up spontaneously in the soul. Design must originate in a designing mind. It has intelligence in it to conceive some plan, and will in it to carry out that plan. Only mind or spirit thinks or wills. The great cause of this universe which is so full of design must therefore be a mind or spirit,—a *Personal Cause* present and working throughout the universe. Man's own nature again renders the conclusion irresistible.

Third Step.—As his observation and experience advance, man turns his thoughts inward upon himself. He finds himself finite and dependent in his intellect, his affections, and his will. There are powerful forces of evil and destruction on every hand; darkness and mystery gather around him; his richest treasures are snatched away from him; his most cherished plans end often in failure and disappointment. In his helplessness and dependence the intuition of the *infinite* spontaneously springs up within him. An irrepressible longing takes possession of him for some infinite intellect, heart, and will on which to rest and depend. That longing takes shape and finds voice in *prayer*, which is the instinctive going out of the human soul toward the Infinite Spirit for light and love and strength. He cannot live in the truest, highest sense without believing in and resting on the infinite, Personal Cause, as his *Helper* and *Friend*, the object of supreme devotion. His own nature leads him irresistibly to the infinite God.

Fourth Step.—Advancing still further, man observes his moral nature and experiences. He finds himself possessed of the ideas of right and wrong, of obligation, of merit and demerit, of responsibility. There is something within him that is able to urge him on with an imperative *ought*, and to hold him back with an equally imperative *ought not*. He judges intuitively that to love God, to care for his own being, and to love his neighbor, are right and binding. He discerns thus a rule of action, a law within him. Intuitively there springs up the conviction that there must be a lawgiver, a *Moral Governor*, who has authority over him, and has made conscience the representative of that authority. The conviction grows in intensity and breadth, with widening observation and experience, until the Infinite Personal Cause and Helper becomes also the *omnipotent, omnipresent*, and *omniscient Judge*, who will inevitably reward the righteous and punish the wicked. Man's nature presses him irresistibly to the conclusion.

Somewhat in this way along the track of reason, the race moves on irresistibly to its idea of God and its belief in God. So the human soul cries out after the living God; while its sense of having sinned against that God prompts it to seek to make some *expiation*, some *atonement*, and pushes it on to despair, until God's word reveals to it the true Atonement. So it results that all men everywhere and always have naturally come to believe in God.

Theism the only adequate Theory of the Universe.— It belongs to Natural and Revealed Theology to unfold fully the argument for the *Being* of God: it is sufficient, here, that it be seen that the doctrine of Theism, or of a personal God, the infinite Author and Moral Governor of the world, is the only one that meets the wants of man's nature as a personal spiritual agent. Theism alone furnishes an adequate solution of the great problem of the universe,—accounting for its origin, its continuance, its immensity, its infinitude of truth and goodness and power. Theism alone furnishes man the God on whom, in his helplessness and dependence, he can rest. Neither Fatalism, Materialism nor Pantheism is a solution of the problem of the universe or of man; they alike ignore the grandest of all facts, the facts of spirit with its free moral action, and reject those clearest intuitions of the soul, the existence of spirit and the principles of causation and design.

Man has but to open his eyes and see the impress of God, and the conviction will grow upon him with the cumulative argument; but to be able to say with the atheist and the fool "there is no God," "we must," says Dr. Chalmers, "have roamed over all nature, and seen that no mark of a divine footstep was there; we must have searched into the records not of one planet only, but of all worlds, and thence gathered that, throughout the wide realms of immensity, not one exhibition of a living and reigning God has ever been made. For man *not to know of a God*, he has only to sink beneath the level of our common nature; but *to deny him*, he must be a God himself."

Subject 2d. Man in a State of Probation under God.— There are abundant indications that man's present state is one of trial and preparation for a future and higher state. Some of these indications are found in the law of progress impressed upon his being; in the arrangement of the government of the world to call out his co-operation in the work of his own development; and in the grand moral possibilities in work and character constantly set before him.

1st. The Law of Progress.—The law of development and progress, that has been written in his being, indicates a future and higher state of development and progress.

This has already been shown in the consideration of man's immortal activities. The thoughts presented there apply with equal force here.

2d. The Government of the World.—The arrangements in the constitution of the world and the moral government of God are such as are fitted to secure man's own consent and co-operation in his training for a higher future state and mission.

The Arrangement of the World.—This world is so arranged as to make man dependent, to the largest degree possible, upon his own exertions for his possessions, attainments, and position, and so to give him the best training for a greater future. God has given *nature* into his hands as a great storehouse of food, of treasures, and of materials for his wealth and comfort, and of forces to be used as his aids and agents in his work: but the price of the food is the ploughing, sowing, and reaping; the price of the treasures and materials is the mining and manufacturing; the price of the forces as agents is the enterprise and the inventive genius to harness them to his engines and his machinery. God has opened before man a *vast world of truth and beauty* with which he may fill and enlarge and glorify his spiritual being: but the price of the spiritual elevation is the docile, studious, diligent spirit. God has opened the way for man to *large influence and exalted position in society*, so that in these free Christian lands, the lowest and last may become the highest and foremost, and mould the destiny of nations and ages: but the price of the influence and position is the noble purpose and the high endeavor. With man's own consent and co-operation everything will combine to elevate and give power and fit him for a higher future destiny. The world is thus manifestly a training-place for higher work.

3d. The Moral Possibilities.—The choice between the evil and the good to which man is constantly called, the grand mission of duty and the boundless possibilities in moral attainment that are constantly set before him, indicate trial and preparation for a higher coming work and glory.

It has already appeared that man's moral nature gives him assurance of God's government over him and of his own future existence: his present condition, as peculiarly one of moral discipline, in which the good and the evil, the highest and the lowest, the noblest and the basest, are kept before him as the objects of his choice, assures him that he is passing through a probation with reference to a future existence. It is in accordance with this view, that provision is everywhere found for rewarding virtue and punishing vice; for drawing toward virtue by the happiness which results from it, and driving from vice by the misery it brings; for disciplining to power and perfection in virtue by the resistance of allurements to wrong, by the difficulty in doing right, by the call for resolution in self-denial and self-restraint, by all the varied chastisements of God summoning to submission and resignation, and by the vast and varied arrangement, not to save man from dangers, but to lead him to go triumphantly through them. At the same time, the call to a grand mission of duty — having reference, in his present relations, to God, to himself, and to his fellow-man—which comes up from the soul itself as the voice of God, is accompanied with the assurance that here the moral destiny of man is to be decided for all the future; that this is the moral training-place for immortality, where man is to fit himself, as saint or sinner, to be a being of virtue or of vice, of blessedness or of woe, forever.

SECTION II.

The Springs of Action.

Statement and Subdivision.

The second element to be considered is the springs of action.

For man as an agent there are certain starting-points of action. These are found in his natural relation to the good. The *good* in its various forms exists around and within the self-active agent. He has a *conscious need* for that good. Hence arises action in view of the good. The good as the *object* of action, and the conscious need for the good as the *cause* of action, constitute the springs of action, or motive principles, and furnish the proper *Topics* for investigation and discussion.

Starting-point of Action.—All action must have some point of beginning. The point of origin in human action is furnished in the twofold fact that there is such a thing as good and evil, and that the soul has the capacity of appreciating their nature and of seeking or avoiding them. The good and evil furnish the object of action; the capacity for appreciating them furnishes the proper starting-point, or spring of action.

Ambiguous Use of Motive.—Both the objects of action and the causes of action are generally included under the term *motive*. Edwards defines *motive* to be "the whole of that which moves, excites, or invites the mind to volition; whether that be one thing singly or many things conjointly." This definition is broad enough to include all objects, occasions and causes of action, both external and internal, even to the will itself; but it presents man too much as passive rather than as self-active. Besides, it is too general to be of any great service in clear thinking and reasoning,—at least without constant explanation and qualification. The object of action needs to be kept distinct from the cause of action.

Distinction of Cause and Object of Action.—The *cause* of human action is found in the self-active being exerting himself in some of his powers or faculties and producing an effect, an action. The *object* of action is found in something material or spiritual, which may be wholly inert or passive in itself, but which, by appearing to the soul as good or evil, affords an occasion for the active being to exert his powers. The *gold* which the thief takes is the inert and passive object of his action; the *avarice*, or thieving propensity, in the soul of the man himself, is the cause of the action. The presence of the gold merely furnishes an *occasion* for the working of the propensity.

For the sake of distinctness, the object and cause in their relation to action may be called the *motive object* and the *motive cause*.

Topic First. The Good as the Motive Object in Action. —The motive object, or that which either furnishes the occasion for the agent's action or invites him to action, is found in the good. *The good* includes the agreeable or useful, the perfect, and the right. The evil, which is but the negative of the good, includes the opposites of these.

The Perfect.— The propriety of the distinction of the good into the agreeable and the right will readily be admitted. The *perfect*, or the quality of completeness of being in any object, or the exact fitness of anything to its end, is added for the sake of increased clearness and definiteness. That there is ground for this distinction appears from the fact that there is an attractiveness in the perfection of anything, of a fruit, or tree, or animal, or man, or of an action, entirely different from that which is found in rightness, or in agreeableness in the ordinary sense of pleasurableness. The justness of the distinction will be more easily recognized in the use of the words *happiness, holiness,* and *righteousness.* Moreover, it will be found, in the treatment of the next *Division* of Theoretical Ethics, that an entirely distinct class of moral theories has been based upon the perfect as a form of the good furnishing an end of human action.

The Evil.— It is both convenient and customary to use the term *good* in a generic sense as including both the good positive and the good negative, or the evil; just as the term *moral* is used in a generic sense to signify both the moral and the immoral.

The good in its three phases may be either external to the agent, as a quality in things, character, or action; or internal to the agent, in his own experience, character, or conduct.

Taking both its positive and negative forms, the good includes, therefore,

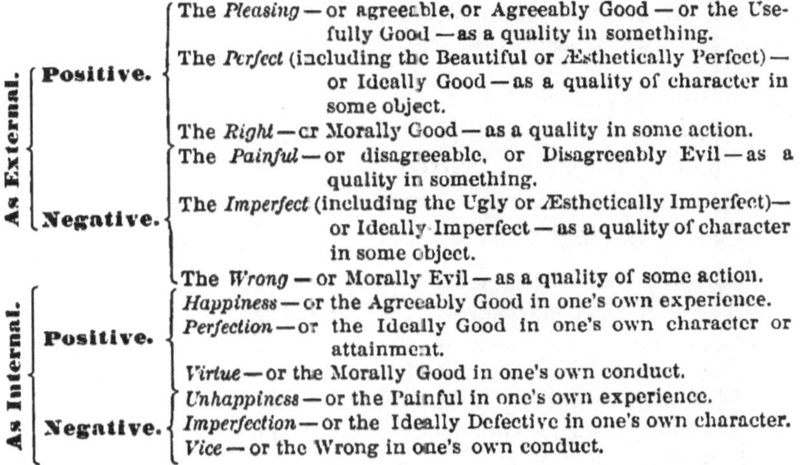

The Good not an Abstraction. — It is necessary to keep clearly before the mind the fact that the good always appears in some concrete form. "Virtue has no separate existence in some ethereal sphere, but it has a reality in the voluntary acts of beings possessed of intelligence, conscience, and will." Goodness as external to the agent always appears as a quality in some object, character, or action; as internal to the agent, it always appears as a quality in his own experience, character, or conduct. The good in the highest sense can only be found in *God*, who embodies Infinite Goodness in all its forms.

No other Forms of Good. — The mere statement of the forms of the good, as given above, shows that these cover the whole ground of objects of action. Everything that can furnish the agent occasions for action, or invite him to it, and everything that can repel him, may be grouped under the divisions enumerated.

Good External and Internal. — Proper regard to the distinction between the good as *external*, or as a quality of the objects, men, or actions brought before the soul; and as *internal*, or as an experience or quality of character or of conduct in the agent himself, — will remove the ambiguity which attends the usual method of treating the good as *purely external* and *objective*, and will prevent the common failure in clearness which results from not distinguishing between these two forms of the good. The gold which is sought as a means of increasing happiness is an external good; the happiness sought by its aid is an internal good. The holy or perfect character, which we recognize in a Job, is to us an external good; the holiness, or perfection, which we may embody in our own character, is an internal good. The virtue, which, as embodied in a

Daniel, wins our moral approbation, is to us an external good; the virtue which we embody in our own conduct is an internal good.

While the good, in all its phases external and internal, furnishes the motive object of action; *the internal phases* — happiness, perfection, virtue, and their opposites — furnish what are more properly termed the *ends* of action, or that for which, in the highest sense, the action is done.

Ends of Action.— The action of a rational being must have end, as well as origin and movement. The possible ends of action are happiness, perfection, and virtue, as good to be sought; and unhappiness, imperfection, and vice, as evil to be shunned. The good (including the evil) as internal properly furnishes all the possible ends for the sake of which human action should be performed. The external good furnishes only the object in the narrow sense, or the occasion of action. Both the end and the occasion are included under the object of action in the wider sense.

Topic Second. The Motive Cause in Action.—The motive cause, or cause which moves to action, is found in the agent's own self-active nature.

The fundamental facts concerning the moving forces of this self-active nature, and the classification of these forces as springs of action, are the *Subjects* which require consideration.

Subject 1st. Fundamental Facts of Human Action.

1st. Basis in practical Need for the Good.—The foundation for action, as has been seen, is laid in the conscious practical need for the good in its various forms. Man is made for the good, as the good is made for man. There is implanted in the agent's nature a tendency to exert his powers in view of the good.

This practical need is the *starting-point* of action.

The Need for the Good.— It is universally admitted that there are certain native wants or appetencies of the soul, and certain aversions or inappetencies. The good is fitted to satisfy the want; the evil is fitted to call out the aversion. Without these native wants positive and negative — better called *needs*, because man has them in his nature whether he is conscious of them or not — there would be no starting-point for action.

The evidence of design and plan in the works of the Creator nowhere comes out more clearly than in the fitness of the good to meet the needs of the human agent. Man was made to enjoy the agreeably good in objects, to be the perfectly good in character, and to do the morally good in conduct, and to shrink from suffering, being, or doing the evil. Separated from the good he is every way wretched; in the enjoyment of it he is happy.

Native Tendency to Action.— There is accordingly found in the agent a natural tendency to exert all the powers under his control to secure the good for the satisfaction of his needs, and to avoid the evil. This tendency has manifested itself in all ages and in all men, and has given rise to all the work ever accomplished in the world.

2d. Basis of Action in the Intellect.— The intellect furnishes the medium of connection between the good and the various needs of the agent. It is the power by which the agent discerns both the good and the needs, and also the fitness of the good to supply those needs. It therefore prepares the way for the action which seeks to secure the good to satisfy the needs.

Without the intellect to perform this office, there can be no *origination* of rational action.

Intelligence Essential.— It is an admitted principle in psychology that there can be no action of the feelings and the will without the previous or concurrent action of the intellect. "A man does not feel except he knows or apprehends some object which excites feeling. He always feels about or with respect to something cognized." Porter, *Human Intellect,* p. 43.

3d. The Movings to Action in the Feelings.— When the agent by his intellect perceives any form of the good and its adaptation to his needs, the real impulses to action appear. These impulses are the *Sensibilities,* or *Feelings,* which are the true springs of action.

Distinction of Intellectual and Active Powers.— The *feelings* and the *will* make up what are familiarly known as the *active powers* of the soul, as distinguished from the *intellectual powers.* It is not meant by this distinction that the intellectual powers "are a whit less energetic than those specially denominated *active,*" but that the former have only an *intellectual* or *speculative* energy ending in knowledge, while the latter have a *practical* energy, and therefore have in view some ulterior end in

their action. (Hamilton, *Met.*) The intellect is thus excluded from
the strictly active powers, which therefore include feeling and will.

The Active Powers distinguished.—The active powers may be divided
into the springs of action, or the feelings, and the arbiter and executor
of action, or the will. The former furnish the impulses from which all
action originates; the latter wields and directs all the powers of the
agent in that action.

General Relation of Powers to Action.—The cognitions of the intellect
lead to feeling only as they are cognitions of the good in some form.
The knowledge of truth and fact can therefore lead to action only as
some quality is seen in them which fits them for satisfying some want
of man's being. The springs of action are therefore never touched
except through the native need for the good; or, in different phrase, an
agent never acts unless there is first awakened in him an *interest* in the
object or end of action. The agent as a rational being exerts his will
in the presence of the impulses, or motive springs, or feelings, which
arise from the apprehension of some good by the intellect.

Subject 2d. Classification of Springs of Action.

1st. Principles of Classification.—The feelings as springs of
action are divided, first, according to the general relation of
the action to the good. Man was made with two fundamental
needs: the need of *giving out* from his own being and resources
toward the good; and the need of *drawing in* to himself from
without to replenish his own being and resources. The first
of these needs expresses itself in the *Affections*, or giving
powers; the second, in the *Desires,* or craving powers. These
two forms of feeling embrace all the immediate springs of
action.

The feelings are divided, secondly, according to the special
relation of the action to the three forms of the good. There
is obviously a form of feeling — both as affection and desire —
corresponding to every form of the good which the soul is
capable of cognizing. There are feelings connected with the
agreeably good, with the ideally good, and with the morally
good, and with their opposites.

The feelings are divided, thirdly, according to the different
beings with whom the good is viewed as being connected. As
man is by his nature not merely an individual and isolated

being, but also a social, moral, and religious being, there must be a corresponding subdivision of the feelings, as they have reference to the individual who cherishes them, to society, or to God.

As man is at once animal and rational, some of these feelings are instinctive, and implanted chiefly for the purposes of the body, or the animal nature; others are intelligent, and given chiefly for the purposes of the higher nature, or spirit.

2d. General Classes of Feelings.—These principles of classification may be applied for the purpose of exhibiting the various phases of both affection and desire as springs of action in the human agent. There results the following

General Scheme of the Feelings.

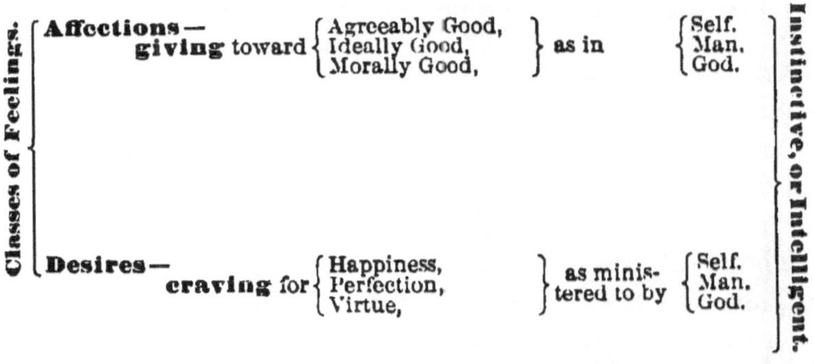

Positive Aspect only.—It is evident that this scheme expresses, strictly speaking, only the positive aspect of the feelings. Affection properly includes the giving of hate as well as love; while desire includes aversion as well as craving.

3d. Special Classes of Affections.—*Affections* are impulses of feeling arising upon the cognition of some form of good, positive or negative, in other beings, and disposing the agent to give out of his own being or resources, toward the object of affection, that which may influence it for good or ill.

Objects of Affection.—Strictly speaking, affection is cherished toward rational beings only; but the term is often used in a looser sense as applicable to irrational beings also. In such case some attribute of the rational being is attributed to the irrational. In the looser sense, a man may have an affection for his dog, or a child for its toys.

The affections may be still further subdivided so as to present more fully their exact sphere and their great importance in the origination of human action. There results the following

Special Scheme of the Affections.

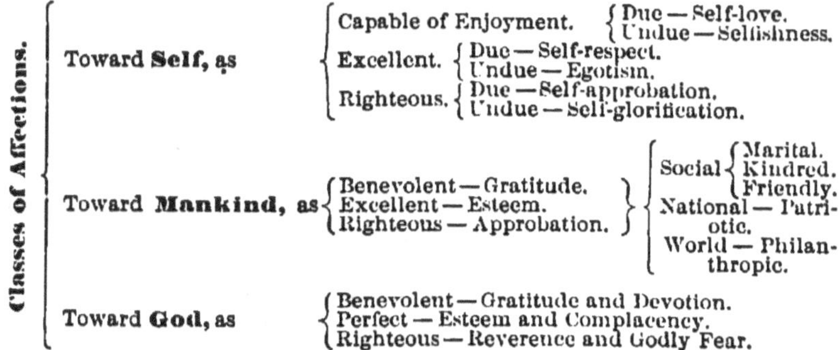

4th. Special Classes of Desires.— *Desires* are impulses of feeling, arising upon the cognition of some form of the good which is fitted to satisfy some need of the agent's being, involving a craving for that good, and impelling him to secure it for the satisfaction of the need.

The desires may be subdivided into the Primary, or Natural, and the Secondary, or Modified. These will be treated in order,— the *Secondary* requiring only a brief consideration.

A. Primary, or Natural Desires.— *The Primary*, or *Natural Desires* are the original, practical tendencies, or cravings, implanted in the nature of man. They are in such a sense a part of his nature that they spontaneously manifest themselves in some degree in all men, when the appropriate objects, or forms of the good, are in any way presented to the intelligence.

They may be divided into *Simple Desires* and *Complex Natural Tendencies*, which will be treated in this order.

(A.) The Simple Desires.—The Simple Desires, considered as motive forces, may be arranged in three *Classes:*

1st Class. Desires for Happiness.

2d Class. Desires for Perfection, or Ideal Completeness.

3d Class. Desires for Virtue, or Duty.

1st Class.— Desires for Happiness.

1.— In Man Individual.

(1.) Instinctive and Blind Movements.

Tendency to Preserve Life — by

Appetites for
{ Food and Drink.
{ Sleep, Air, and Warmth.
{ Pleasure.

(2.) Rational and Intelligent Movements.

Tendency to Preserve and make the most of Life — by providing for

{ Sustenance.
{ Pleasure.
{ Plenty.

2.— In Man Social.

(1.) Instinctive and Blind Movements.

Tendency to Preserve the Species — shown in

Appetites — in
{ Attraction of the Sexes.
{ Care for Young.
{ Humanity to the Wretched.

(2.) Rational and Intelligent Movements.

Tendency to Preserve and make men happy — shown by seeking

{ Association in Family, State, and other relations.
{ Freedom of those associated from Pain and Want.

Appetites.— At the basis are the appetites, or cravings of the animal nature, which have for their object the well-being of the body and the continuance of the race. Appetites and desires proper belong to the same class of *craving powers;* the difference between them being, that appetites are blind impulses, and do not imply intelligence. It is true that in the appetites generally there are two elements: an uneasy sensation and a tendency toward something to remove it, but these are not the fundamental distinctions. The appetites are either *individual,* as having reference to the preservation of the agent himself; or *social,* as having reference to the preservation of the race. The appetites usually enumerated are those of hunger, thirst, and sex; but it is hoped that the enumeration given above will commend itself as embracing more of the facts of man's nature.

Intelligent Desires for Happiness.— Corresponding in some measure to the blind impulses of appetite, there is a range of intelligent desires which have in view the happiness (including pleasure in its physical relations) of the agent and of society. These desires lead men to seek their gratification intelligently, by the thoughtful use of appropriate means in securing provision for their satisfaction.

2d Class.— Desires for Perfection, or Ideal Completeness.

1.— In Man Individual.

{ (1.) **Craving** *to Develop the Powers*— shown in
{   Desires for Activity, Knowledge. Power, Property.
{ (2.) **Craving** *to Perfect the Being*—shown in
{   Desires for Ideal Excellence and Complete Manhood.
{ (3.) **Craving** *to Accomplish a Manly Life Work*— shown in

    { Desire for Plan to Economize the Energies.
    { Desire to Direct the Powers to Execution of some Grand
        Purpose.

2. — In Man Social.

(1.) Craving *to Associate the Life and Development with others*—shown in

    { Desire for Esteem, or Good Reputation, as the basis.
    { Desire for Society in the Family, Community, State and Race.

(2.) Craving *for Mutual Helpfulness* in the Individual Mission — shown in

    { Desire to secure the Aid of others in his own Life Task.
    { Desire to Aid others in their Life Task.

(3.) Craving *for Co-operation with others* for grander than Individual Aims — shown in

    { Desire to fulfil Highest Mission of Family.
    { Desire   "   "   "   State.
    { Desire   "   "   "   Race.

Signification of Desires for Perfection. — In the normal condition of the agent these cravings direct him to that unfolding and use of his active powers which are essential to the attainment of a rationally complete manhood. Each natural craving points him to something essential to the accomplishment of his life work. Were the agent without sin, he would always be found in the line of his mission when living in accordance with the cravings of his nature.

Order of Desires in Man as an Individual Being. — Following the order of the *Scheme*, there arise the following *Cravings:*

1st Craving — for Developing the Powers. — The craving for the development of the active powers naturally lies at the foundation of this class of desires. Of the four forms of this craving there is placed first —

The Desire for Action. — The infant begins life with movement, action. The forces of life must work or death will ensue. The good which man craves is never reached except through the exercise of his bodily and mental powers. In this universal *restlessness* implanted in human nature is laid the foundation for the agent's development, and for all his work in life. There accompanies it —

The Desire for Knowledge. — With action comes the dawn of intelligence. The infant is active with eye and hand all through his waking hours. Restless curiosity impels him to observe, and with advancing years to think, classify, reason, to explain, to trace causes and consequences, to arrange thought in system. The direction in which the craving for knowledge impels the agent is determined by the order of his wants and necessities; being at first confined to those properties of material objects an acquaintance with which is essential to the preservation of his animal existence; advancing afterward to all the forms of thought involved in the various callings in life up to the very highest;

and appearing finally in the complete man as a thirst for science in all its forms. As the principle of curiosity it appears even in men lowest in the scale of human beings. This craving for knowledge, by revealing to the agent's mind the existence and value of the various forces physical and mental that are at work in the world, leads to —

The Desire for Power.—It is first a craving for *personal power*, beginning with physical power and advancing to soul power. With the infant, the child, the youth, the activities are largely used in developing physical power; with the man, if he be a complete man, chiefly in developing soul power. The craving for *power in general* immediately follows upon that for personal power. This leads the agent to seek to gain influence over men. It appears as a desire for superiority, and as ambition. In process of time man learns that there are certain forces and treasures in the world, furnished by nature, by means of which he can influence men more powerfully. There is thus called forth —

The Desire for Property.—Property confers influence, brings under control of the agent resources which he may use as the means for increasing and extending his power over nature and man. The craving for it for its legitimate ends leads to industry, frugality, and thrift, to enterprise and energy, in securing it. It gives birth to the perfected arts of agriculture and manufactures, to commerce, to all the varied industries of civilized society.

2d Craving — for Perfecting the Powers.—The craving for the perfecting of the being naturally follows upon that for the development of the active powers. It appears as —

The Desire for Excellence, or Complete Manhood.—The preceding desires never reach any large development without leading the agent to a higher craving to become the complete man. In seeking this manhood, there comes to light —

The Desire to form a High Ideal of Life.—It is natural for man to desire to be the *best man* in his own particular line of activity. The principle of emulation works powerfully in all men, from the child up to the sage. So man is made to form ideals of life and conduct which shall represent for him that best man, and serve as his pattern in attaining to the coveted manhood. This is a truly noble propensity of the human imagination, or reason, and, when the agent is guided in his constructions by the higher revelations of God's will as his moral governor, is of vast importance to him in perfecting his being; but without such guidance, and under the influence of sin, what are fashioned for high ideals are often the falsest and the basest, — leading the lawyer to aim to become the shrewd trickster; the merchant, the cunning cheat; and the gentleman, the polished hypocrite.

3d Craving — for Directing the Powers to Manly Life Work.—Advancing another step, there arises in the individual the craving to direct his developed and perfected powers to the accomplishment of such a life work as befits a man. This manifests itself in —

The Desire for some Plan, or Order of Work. — Power must be economized if it is to avail much in the work of life. So the agent naturally works by plan. Punctuality, order, timeliness, fitness, steadiness, and dispatch are in place in his activity; so that the least possible power may be lost or wasted. The craving for rational order in the work of the agent co-operates with —

The Desire to Direct the Powers to the Execution of some Grand Purpose. — In some such purpose is found the complete life task of the true man as an individual. What the one grand purpose of life should be can only be learned from God's revelation of his will as the moral governor; but that there is such a craving to direct the powers to some one end or aim may be readily learned from common observation.

Order of Desires in Man as a Social Being.—Man is by his constitution a social being. Following the order of the *Scheme,* there is in him a —

1st Craving — to Associate his Life and Development with Others. — To furnish the requisite basis for such association, there is placed within him —

The Desire for Esteem, or Good Reputation. — The esteem of his fellows is the true foundation for the regard and affection upon which society rests. Were man not made to crave the esteem of others, society would perish. The craving for esteem opens the way for —

The Desire for Society. — Man desires not more truly the continuance of his own being than he desires the society of man, in the family, the state, and the race. The child dreads solitude, craves the presence of familiar faces, seeks the company of children, and pines without it. His many years of dependence and comparative helplessness compel both the child and parents to be social beings. The human being finds many of his keenest and highest enjoyments, and many of his highest motives to exertion and elevation, in the social relations. In this association with men, there manifests itself in the human agent a —

2d Craving — for Mutual Helpfulness in the Individual Mission. — This appears in the agent as —

The Desire to Secure the Aid of Others in his own Work. — Man is dependent upon man, and the craving for his assistance rises up spontaneously. It is a legitimate desire. The humblest mission in the world could not be accomplished without that assistance; the grandest missions are only accomplished by securing it on the largest scale. If one man has broader and truer views, is a better and more complete man, and is carrying out a nobler and grander purpose than other men, it is best for the world that others should help him in his mission, and best for those who help him; and the provision made in our social nature and relations, by which willing and affectionate aid is rendered him, is one of the most beneficent arrangements of Providence. But in the true man there is also —

The Desire to Aid Others in their Life Task.—There is in man a craving for calling forth the activities of others, for communicating knowledge to them, for increasing their power, for elevating them to the true manhood, and for directing them to the accomplishment of the manly work in life, — as truly as there is in him a craving to do this work for himself. This desire to help and influence men is universal. It is seen in the child, it grows in the youth, it bears sway in the man. It prepares for the world its great *leaders* in all the departments of human effort. In still another and higher form man's desires as a social being appear as a —

3d Craving—for Co-operation for Grander than Individual Ends.—These grander ends are found in the mission of the family as the training-place of man; in the mission of the state, as furnishing a broader theatre for human activity, by the protection of life, freedom, industry, and property; and in the wider mission for the race, which to so large an extent needs to be delivered from ignorance and error and tyranny and want and misery.

3d Class.—Desires for Virtue, or Duty.

1. In Man Individual.

Tendency *to the Right* — shown in

Recognition of Obligation to the Moral Governor — in Duties to God, to Self, and to Mankind.
Recognition of Obligation to Accomplish a Supreme Mission of Duty.

2. In Man Social.

Tendency *to bind his Associates to the Right* — shown in

Desire to Instruct in Duty by Precept and Law.
Desire to Bind to Duty by Reward and Punishment.

Signification of the Desires for Duty.— In duty the agent views the action in its relation to the law of the moral governor. The question asked concerning the action is, *Is it right, or in accordance with the moral law?* If it be, then the agent feels bound to do it. The desire for duty is God's voice in man seeking to bring his conduct up to the divine standard of human action. It will be seen, subsequently, that man's moral nature has been somehow thrown into disorder; but while sin pleads for wrong and evil, there are still unequivocal voices in the soul commanding and urging to the right and the good.

5 *

Order of Desires in Man Individual.— The natural craving for duty shows itself in all men in —

The Desire to Recognize Duty.— That man does recognize his obligation to the moral governor appears clearly from the fact that among all nations and always he has recognized duties to God, to himself, and to his fellow-men. The Hindoo and the Chinese agree with the Greek, the Roman, and the Hebrew in this acknowledgment and distribution of human duty. But where man is at all adequately developed morally, his craving for duty exhibits itself in —

The Desire to Accomplish a Supreme Mission of Duty.— The best men always feel that the true height of their manhood is not reached until they have ascertained the full mission of duty appointed to them by God, and have turned all the energies of their being to the accomplishment of it. In such men this desire becomes the most powerful of all the springs of action, controls all the others, and prepares the way for the *moral hero*.

Order of Desires in Man Social.— In the accomplishment of this mission of duty the agent is linked with men in society. The craving to bring others, associated with him in the various relations of life, to right and duty is truly natural to man, and is shown in —

The Desire to Instruct in Duty.— Accordingly, in all ages and nations there has been found in man the tendency to propagate the ideas of duty by teaching men its precepts and by enacting laws to bind them to it. Men propagate their ideas of virtue and religion with a zeal as much greater than that with which they propagate their ideas of other subjects, as the ideas of virtue and religion seem to them to be more important than all these other ideas.

As the moral nature is in disorder, so that men often fail to do what they approve as right, and often do what they disapprove as wrong, there manifests itself in the agent —

The Desire to Bind to Duty by Reward and Punishment.— This desire has embodied itself in the whole system of human law, in which protection and safety follow obedience, and the infliction of penalty is the consequence of disobedience. It is the natural striving of man to hold mankind to the appointed mission of duty. It begins with simple approbation and disapprobation, but ends in the rewards and penalties.

(B.) The Complex Natural Tendencies.— Besides the simple natural desires there are certain general and complex tendencies in man as an agent which result from his special bodily organization and mental activities. They include Temperament and Temper.

These are natural and primary tendencies, since they arise from the original endowment of the body and spirit.

1st Class.—Temperaments.

Temperament includes the general tendencies of the agent resulting from his bodily constitution. The various forms of temperament, individual and national, result from the various disposition or arrangement of the parts of the physical system in the complete bodily organization.,

Doctrine of Temperament.— It is matter of common observation that, from its organization, the infant receives with its existence certain peculiar qualities. The ancient Greeks classified men by these peculiarities of organization, and accounted for the peculiarities by the *doctrine of temperaments.* With the progress of accurate and systematic knowledge, that doctrine has been placed by the moderns upon a solid scientific basis.

The three principal vital systems of which the body consists, —the respiratory and circulatory system, the nutritive system, and the nervous system,—give character to the several temperaments.

The predominance of the first system produces the sanguine or athletic temperament; the predominance of the second system, the bilious and melancholic temperament; the predominance of the third system, the nervous temperament; the comparative weakness of all three systems, the phlegmatic temperament; and the proper and tempered combination of all three systems, the tempered temperament.

The Various Temperaments.—As certain duties will be found — in *Practical Ethics* — to grow out of the different temperaments, it will be necessary to treat them somewhat more in detail, in order to prepare for a correct understanding of those duties.

The Sanguine Temperament results from the predominance of the circulatory system of which the heart and lungs are the centre. It manifests itself in a fulness of animal life and the highest degree of physical beauty; the capacious lungs and powerful heart produce the Apollo of the Vatican. Men possessed of this temperament are amiable, genial, impulsive, inconstant, excitable, given to the tender passion, the gayest of the gay, not wise in council but often dashing in execution, not over-firmly bound to moral principle, *peculiarly liable to excess.*

When in the fulness of life there is an excess of muscular force over the sensitive, the lightness, grace, and beauty, the activity of spirit, and the flow of sentiment disappear, the soul is overshadowed by the body, the man becomes a Hercules or a Samson, and the sanguine temperament becomes the *athletic*.

The Bilious Temperament results from the predominance of the nutritive system of which the stomach and liver are the centre. A powerfully working stomach and liver do not result in the grace, or impulsiveness, or sentiment, or liability to excess, seen in the man of sanguine organization; but in power, firmness, and perseverance in enterprise, ambition, and sovereignty over men. The bilious temperament has furnished the men to whom the destinies of the world have been generally committed,—men such as Hannibal, Julius Cæsar, Oliver Cromwell, Napoleon Bonaparte, Paul, Calvin, and John Knox.

With the disordered action of a powerful nutritive system the bilious temperament becomes the *melancholic*, which inclines the man to withdraw from the society of men, to brood over his own sorrows and trials, to take prevailingly gloomy views of things. This was the temperament of Milton in his old age, of Dante and of Tasso, of Demosthenes, of Columbus and Magellan.

The Nervous Temperament results from the predominance of the nervous system of which the brain is the centre. Its characteristic is the excessive action of the sensitive part of the system. It produces intense and varied activity in thought and feeling; but this is accompanied with fickleness and want of power, unless the body is otherwise powerfully organized in its circulatory or nutritive system. Socrates, Frederick the Great, and Voltaire were of this temperament in its better form.

The Phlegmatic Temperament results from the comparative weakness of the three vital systems. It is seen where the heart and lungs, the liver and stomach, the brain and nerves act slowly or feebly, and where the building forces are not in excess of the destructive forces of the body. The phlegmatic man is born to sluggishness, is a good sleeper and fond of eating and drinking, is generally doomed to mediocrity, and can never be a great leader among men; in poetry he may, at the best, make a Thomson, and in art, a Rembrandt.

The Tempered Temperament results from the proper combination of all the three vital systems. It is seen where a powerful brain is sustained by equally powerful circulatory and nutritive systems. The model of this temperament "may never have existed in perfection: many of the wise and good, who have been the benefactors of mankind, have approached near to it; our own Washington nearest of all."

Temperaments not Unmixed. — It will readily appear that in mankind generally the sanguine, the bilious, and the nervous temperaments appear combined in various proportions. It is the predominance of one element that gives name to the temperament in each case. The exclusive presence of any one element would show a diseased, rather than normal and natural, condition of the man. The tempered temperament is that of the perfect man, since in that the whole physical system is fitted to be the powerful, complete, and willing instrument of the self-active spirit.

2d Class. — Tempers, or Dispositions.

Temper or *Disposition* includes the general tendencies of the agent resulting from his mental constitution. The various forms of temper, individual and national, result from the various disposition or arrangement of the faculties and tendencies of the soul in the spiritual organization.

Doctrine of Temper or Mental Disposition. — It is matter of common observation that, with its spiritual constitution, the infant receives certain peculiar mental qualities, — just as truly as by its bodily organization it receives certain peculiar physical qualities. Dugald Stewart used the word *temper* to denote "the habitual state of a man's mind in point of irascibility; or, in other words, to mark the habitual predominance of the benevolent or malevolent affections in his intercourse with his fellow-creatures." This is the common use of the word. But it is here used as synonymous with *disposition*, and to denote the prevailing tone or turn of a man's mind, not so much in reference to his intercourse with his fellow-creatures, as in reference to *the spiritual make-up of the soul.*

The three principal spiritual faculties of which the soul consists, — the intellect, the feelings, and the will, — give character to the several varieties of human temper or disposition. The predominance of the first faculty produces the *intellectual man;* the predominance of the second, the *sentimental man;* the predominance of the third, the *active man;* the comparative weakness of all three faculties, the *imbecile* or *inefficient man;* and the proper and balanced combination of all three, the *well-balanced man.*

Modifications of Disposition. — These fundamental forms of temper or mental disposition are almost endlessly modified, by the predominance of any special element of intellect, of feelings, or of will.

The Well-balanced Man is the man of most perfect disposition. In him the intellect observes, thinks, and constructs its thought-systems of truth, beauty, and goodness, with power; the feelings respond quickly and fully; and the will is the ready and active servant to urge to the formation of the best and noblest purpose, and to execute it with ease and energy.

B. Secondary, or Modified Tendencies.—Man's nature is such that he can form certain secondary or adventitious tendencies, called *habits*, which may come in process of time to be prominent motive forces. There is some native tendency or power at the foundation of each habit.

Habit may be defined to be "a facility in doing a thing, and an inclination to do it, acquired by having done it more or less frequently."

Importance of Habits.—"To habits, as involving a facility in doing things which have been done frequently, may be traced all the arts of human life, and all the progress and improvement of which they are susceptible. But it is of habit, as implying tendency or inclination to do what has been done frequently, that the moral philosopher especially takes cognizance."

(Habit is the result of repetition, association of ideas, or custom, acting upon the original power or tendency. These may be set to their work of forming habits, by authority, education, example, fashion, from without; or by mental constitution, or bodily temperament, or mental or bodily condition, or experience, or opinion.

The modified tendencies or habits may be divided into *bodily* and *mental;* and these have been again divided *objectively* into generic and specific, and, *subjectively*, into active and passive.

Habits, whether Bodily or Mental, have been distinguished, "*objectively*, into specific and generic, — according as they are formed in reference to single, isolated acts or indulgences, or in reference to acts which constitute a course of conduct or a mode of living."

Habits are distinguished, "*subjectively*, into active and passive, — according as the agent is active or passive as to their formation and power. When habits manifest themselves by an increased facility of acting, as in the use of the organs of speech in speaking and of the hand in writing, they may be called *active;* and when they manifest themselves by the recurrence of thoughts and feelings and inclinations which come into the mind readily and of course, by reason of their having been there before, as in the readiness with which the meaning of words is understood by us when we hear them pronounced, they may be called *passive*."

These habits, or acquired active tendencies, become most powerful springs. They are as varied in their range and form as the native activities in which they have their origin.

SECTION III.

The Arbiter and Executor of Action.

Statement and Subdivision.

The third element to be considered is the arbiter and executor of action, the will.

The agent himself, as the efficient cause of his own action, determines upon that action in the exercise of his will.

General Function of Will.—Says Dr. McCosh (*Div. Gov.*, p. 269), "It is the will which determines what is to be preferred or rejected. Doubtless the other powers of the mind must furnish the objects. The physical or mental sensibility must announce what is painful or pleasurable; the conscience declares what is morally right, and what is morally wrong; the reason may proclaim what is true, and what is false; but it is not the province of one or all these to make the choice. By the sensibility the mind feels pleasure and pain; but it is another power which chooses the former and avoids the latter. So far as the true is preferred to the false, or the right to the wrong, or the pleasurable to the right, it is by the exercise, not of the reason, or the conscience, or the sensibility, but of the will."

Relation of Will to other Elements.—If the good and the agent's need for it did not exist, the soul would have no interest in the world and no objects of choice—no field of action. If the intellect, as the power to perceive the good and the need and their mutual adaptation, did not act, and thus bring forward objects of choice and awaken the interest of affection and desire, there could still be no action, since the field of action would be beyond the view of the agent, and there could be no starting-points, or springs of action. All these things are the necessary conditions to any exercise of the will.

By the exercise of the will, the agent, when in his normal condition, decides upon the act or course of conduct to be pursued, and bends all his other powers to the accomplishment of that act or course. The former of these functions of the will may be called choice; the latter, volition. Choice and volition are the essential elements of will.

Choice and Volition distinguished.— President Hopkins (*Law of Love and Love as a Law*) gives special prominence to this power of preference or choice in distinction from the power of volition. The former involves only the choosing of what we desire; the latter, the putting forth of energy for the attainment of that which we choose. "Of these the putting forth of energy is the more obtrusive, and has attracted more attention, but the elective is the leading power. A generic choice once made and continuing must be followed by executive volitions, if the means are possessed for attaining the end chosen. If not, the choice will stand alone, and bide its time."

Topic First. Power of Choice.—*Choice*, the first element of will, is very closely connected with the feelings, or immediate springs of action. It adds to the natural giving and craving of the affection and desire, the distinct and definite wish or preference for its satisfaction.

Feeling and Choice distinguished.— So close is the connection between the desires and the choices, that the desires have been placed by many of the psychologists under the general head of the will. But there is clearly a distinction between the two. Many things are desired that are not chosen. The desires may be manifold, and the choice may be to gratify some one of them only. A desire may be very strong, and yet the agent may not choose to gratify it. There may be a conflict of desires, and the agent may make choice between them. He may desire both wealth and knowledge, but may choose only one to the exclusion of the other. The distinction between the affections and choices is too obvious to require to be stated.

Subject 1st. The Elements of Choice.— The will, in its first aspect, may appear as spontaneous choice, or as rational preference.

In spontaneous choice the agent consents that some existing impulse or craving shall have way and seek its gratification. It is will going along with the feeling as *consent*, and inseparable from it.

In rational preference the agent refers the whole matter of choice to the reason, the authorized guide of action; and a deliberate conclusion regarding what is to be chosen is reached in this way.

Will as Spontaneity.—There has been marked variance or confusion in the views of moralists touching the question what action is voluntary and what not. Some have affirmed that the feelings are not voluntary at all, others that they are. A correct psychology will at once remove the difficulties and relieve the confusion, by making it clear that the faculties of the soul do not act apart from and independently of one another. Intelligence, as has been already seen, always precedes and furnishes the basis for rational affections and desires, and both intelligence and feeling always precede the acting of the will. It is in like manner true that a measure of the activity of the will always goes along with the moving of the feelings and the acting of the intellect. Where the feeling is an affection, the will appears acting spontaneously, as consent to the giving to which that affection moves; where the feeling is a desire, as consent to the craving to which that desire moves. All the rational feelings may therefore be truly voluntary in the sense of being *spontaneous*, since the will accompanies them as *consent*.

Spontaneous Choice.— A large part of human action is spontaneous. It is provided for in the giving and craving tendencies of the feelings. When there is nothing in the way, these affections and desires lead on to choice and action. The agent's will falls in with them and moves along with them, or rather acts in them, without need of special deliberation or of conscious reference to the ends of action.

Rational Preference.—The remaining part of human action is decided upon by a consideration of the various forms of the good and a weighing of their claims. It is voluntary and rational in a higher sense than the other. A rational preference may be reached where several things, which appear as good, invite the agent to different courses of action. An enjoyment of mind may be preferred to one of body; duty may be preferred to pleasure, or *vice versa*. Or where two or more of the different forms of the good invite to different courses of action, the decision may be reached by choosing between them, or by rejecting all. A course promising pleasure may be deliberately chosen before one leading to right conduct; or a course leading to the morally good, before both the perfect and the pleasurable.

Subject 2d. The Grounds of Choice.—In all rational action the agent determines his own act or course, as a rational being must: as seems to him on the whole best; or, in accordance with the greatest apparent good; or, in accordance with the strongest motive.

The Agent Determines.—The determining power is the agent himself acting by the will. Every intelligent agent is conscious that he himself determines his own course, whenever he is left free. He *determines*, and is therefore not simply *determined* by influences outside of himself or beyond his control. Out of this consciousness springs the sense of responsibility for his acts. He is free, and therefore responsible.

Determines in View of Rational Considerations.—The agent determines his course as a rational being ought to determine it,—in view of reasonable considerations. The three forms made use of to express this: *what seems best; the greatest apparent good;* and *the strongest motive,*—are substantially equivalent. He himself decides what seems best to him, and chooses it. If his character be low and base, his best may be base and low. It may be found in mere pleasure, and that of the lowest kind. What seems worst to the true man, seems best to the libertine and is chosen by him. "The will is as the greatest apparent good is," is Edwards's celebrated maxim. It is true that the agent always decides in accordance with that which *appears to him* to be on the whole the greatest good; and not in accordance with what is *really* the greatest good. That the agent decides *in accordance with the strongest motive,* is simply another form of stating the same thing. The motive must be regarded as covering the whole ground of motive object and motive spring.

Topic Second. Power of Volition.—*Volition proper,* the second element of will, is concerned with the execution or carrying out of the action or course of action decided upon by the agent. It directs his powers to the completion of the chosen action, whether that action be decided upon by spontaneous choice or by rational preference.

Relations of the Volition.—It is evident that before there can be a volition, there must be something to be done, some motive for doing it, and the choice or determination to do it. The executive volition follows upon these, and is the act of the agent which leads to the actual accomplishment of the thing to be done.

Subject 1st. The Elements of Volition.—In volitional action the agent directs his will, first, to a preliminary effort to design the plan, or the series of efforts, by which the end

may be reached; and, secondly, to the exertion of the powers in reaching that end.

Volition in Planning.— The intellect is the planning power. In any action, or course of action, determined upon, there must be a plan before there can be the execution of the plan. The agent therefore directs the intellect first to form the plan, or fix upon the series of efforts, by which he conceives that the desired end may be reached.

Volition in Execution.— It is universally admitted that every volition must have an object; that this object is always something that we conceive to be in our power; that it is always something future; that when the time for accomplishing the object comes, the volition is accompanied by a proportionate exertion of our active powers. Consciousness testifies that when we have formed a volition or purpose, we make an effort to execute it.

Powers used by Volition.— The powers which the agent may, in his exertions, direct to the end decided upon, include all the powers brought within his reach by his whole being, spiritual and material. He may exert all the powers of intellect and of feeling; he may bring into requisition all the forces which the embodiment of his soul subjects to his dominion, by opening communication and establishing connection with the material world and with mankind through the senses and bodily powers.

Subject 2d. The Will expressing the Person.—The will, as the arbiter and executor of action, is thus seen to be the highest and most complete expression of the *self*, or *personality*, of the agent. By the action of the will the agent commits *himself* to the course decided upon and pursued, so as to become fully responsible for it. This is true both where the action of the will begins with spontaneous choice and where it begins with rational preference.

Consequent Importance of Will.— Why the will has always occupied so important a place in ethical discussions is thus made clear. It is the natural self-expressing power of the intelligent, personal agent. It is the agent himself *acting* in the highest sense. The exertion of the will is *the central and decisive act* between the inner and preliminary movings of the soul and the outer accomplishment of purpose. It thus becomes a capital point in the consideration of moral action and moral responsibility, since it gives the man's endorsement to good or evil.

SECTION IV.

The Guides of Action.

Statement and Subdivision.

The fourth and last element to be considered is the guides of action.

For man as an agent there are certain arrangements for the guidance of action toward those ends which a rational being must will to reach.

Guides Needed.—A glance at the manifold forms which the motive principles assume makes it evident that man's being and conduct, without some controlling and directing principle or principles, would be an utter chaos. "Among the various springs of action there is no subordination and government; but each, in its turn, prompts to its own particular end or gratification, and is satisfied for a time when that has been gained; and not till it has been gained. A creature with no other principles of action but such as have been denominated *springs*, would be hurried impulsively from one thing to another, without any scheme of life or plan of conduct; and without being able to resist or control the impulse which was strongest at the time." Man needs not only active powers, springs of action and an executor of action, but also guides of action. Such guides have been given him.

In general, it may be said that reason, or the intelligence, is the appointed guide of human action. But reason, in performing this office, may have respect to any one of the three possible ends of action: happiness, perfection, or rightness. Hence the one guide of action takes three different forms:

1st. Reason, as directing action with a regard to what is pleasurable or advantageous, gives rise to what may be called a *sense of prudence.*

2d. Reason, as directing action with a regard to what is involved in perfection, or completeness of being, gives rise to a *sense of the ideal,* or *perfect.*

3d. Reason, as directing action with a regard to what is right and obligatory, gives rise to *conscience,* or a *sense of duty.*

Prominence of Different Guides.—In one man the conduct may be controlled with a constant reference to that which is agreeable or advantageous; in another the aim may be to control it so as to realize some ideal of perfection in the manhood or work; in a third the aim may be to conform the conduct to the law of right; in most men all these three principles have more or less directing influence.

Topic First. Prudence as a Guide.—Reason, directing the conduct with a regard to what is advantageous, or agreeable in experience, is an important guide of human action.

As prudence it involves foresight, and can therefore exist in a rational being only. As having regard to the advantageous, it can exist only in a being naturally having desires for happiness.

Found in Rational Beings.—"Appetite and desire, passion and affection, in themselves considered, are mere states of feeling, moving us to act in one way. But when we act from a regard to what is most for our advantage, we contemplate ourselves as ends, and other things as means subordinate to us, and select and employ them accordingly; that is, we act reasonably, or employ the faculties which belong to us as rational beings. Without the powers of understanding and reason we could not frame the conception of what is most for our advantage, nor make it the end or aim of our actions.

"It is common, indeed, to say that every living creature naturally seeks what is best for it; but brutes seek it blindly, under the impulse of sense and feeling, and without knowing that what they thus tend towards constitutes the perfection of their nature and the happiness of their condition. It is the prerogative of man, above the inferior animals, to know what is most for his advantage, and, knowing it, to seek it. This he does in virtue of those powers of intelligence and reflection which are generally comprehended under the name of reason." See Fleming, *Moral Phil.*, pp. 67–68.

Acts in All Men.—The natural and necessary result of placing rational beings in such a world as this, — where they are liable to feel pleasure and pain, and to experience good and evil,— is to lead them to seek the one and to shun the other. Inexperienced youth may be giddy and thoughtless for a season, unmindful of the past and careless of the future; but with larger experience, man learns sooner or later "to pause and to deliberate, to weigh actions and their consequences, and to adopt that course of conduct which promises on the whole to be productive of the greatest advantage to him."

When therefore, in the course of experience and on the ground of experience, man comes to frame intelligently some conclusion or conception as to what is best or most advantageous for him, then this conclusion or conception will exert a powerful influence in directing and regulating his conduct, and especially in subordinating the lower and blind appetites to the higher and intelligent desires.

An Intelligent Governing Principle. — Intelligence is of the very essence of this principle. " It is a principle different in nature from, and superior in kind to, the incitements of appetite and passion. It operates, not blindly nor impulsively, but calmly and with deliberation. It opposes itself to the violence of appetite and passion, and takes a careful survey of actions and their consequences; setting one thing over against another. When men act under the influence of this principle, guarding against the errors into which they see others fall, correcting such as they may have made themselves, and cautiously and prudently regulating their conduct, so as to avoid the pains and inconveniences to which they are here exposed, and to secure the greatest possible amount of advantage,— they are exercising their powers in the way and to the end for which they were intended, and are acting agreeably to their nature as rational beings."

Reason, acting only with a regard to the advantageous, is at once too low in its nature and too narrow in its range to be the supreme guide of human action. Directed by a regard to advantage alone, man becomes utterly selfish. This guide needs, therefore, to be supplemented and controlled by the other and higher principles furnished by the perfect and the right.

Discussion Deferred.—The defects of a sense of prudence as a supreme guide of human action will be considered under the supreme end of moral action.

Topic Second. The Ideal, or Perfect, as a Guide.— Reason, directing the conduct with a regard to the ideal manhood, or man's conception of the perfect man, is a higher guide of human action.

An ideal, as involving the imagination in its formation, can only be formed by a being possessed of a constructive imagination. As having in view the perfect, it can only be formed by an imaginative being naturally having desires for realizing the perfect in himself.

Such a Principle Exists.—That such a principle exists in man is evident from the fact, that men do actually make this distinction in referring their conduct to various ends,—regarding the completeness and perfection of their being, or manhood, as distinct from both enjoyment and right-doing. Hence perfection, in its various aspects, comes to occupy so prominent a place in some ethical systems, especially in the systems of men in whom intellect and taste predominate. Dr. Hickok makes "the highest good—the *summum bonum*—the worthiness of spiritual approbation."

In Man as having Imagination.— It is the office of the imagination to create standards of achievement or character. When the feelings or choices do not satisfy the taste or conscience, when the character or conduct falls below what the man conceives to be worthy of man, he then creates for himself an ideal standard of attainment. He perhaps selects the most satisfying example of the actual man which he can find, and, by putting away all defects and limitations and adding all conceivable excellences, forms his ideal conception of the true manhood.

Found in All Men.— The tendency to form ideals of life is among the natural and original tendencies of the soul. Every man forms his ideal of manhood. With one it may contemplate sheer brute enjoyment, with another rational pleasure; with one it may contemplate intellectual or æsthetic culture, with another high moral culture; with one, the extraordinary development of some one power, with another the balanced and complete development of all the powers.

It must not be forgotten, that, since man is fallen and under the dominion of sin, his ideal, or conceived perfect, is oftenest most imperfect. The example containing some perverted or wrongly developed tendency is oftener made the starting-point of imagination in forming that ideal than is the worthy example—the good fellow, the sharper, oftener than the really good man and the thoroughly honest and energetic man. The ideals of man thus become in themselves base and in their influence debasing. In the case of the intelligent and refined, human culture comes in to modify the ideal; in the case of the Christian, the precepts and examples of the Word of God, and especially of Jesus Christ himself, exert a like modifying influence. Men, from the lowest to the highest, have their ideals.

A Powerful Governing Principle. — It will be readily seen that a man's conception of the ideal manhood must have much to do with deciding the character of his real manhood. If his conception be low and selfish, the man will be low and selfish; if it be truly noble, if it contemplate self-sacrifice and suffering in the attainment of the true nobility, then the man will be in measure transformed; if it be the perfect man as seen in Jesus Christ, then he will reach the highest toward the true manhood. The facts correspond with the necessity; for in real life the ideal actually exerts this powerful directing influence.

Whenever there is any apparent conflict between the sense of the perfect and the sense of prudence, reason gives the supremacy to the former as having the worthier end in view.

A Higher Guide. — The appeal for the truth of this proposition is to human consciousness. Man is conscious that he was made to distinguish between the motives, which appeal to these two sides of his nature, as being higher or lower. The greatest feat in gymnastics is lightly esteemed by the side of such intellectual achievements as those of a Newton; and these again fall far below the greater achievements in blessing and elevating men by deeds of generosity and philanthropy. Man was made to distinguish thus between the various forms of action as higher and lower. In the same way he was made to distinguish between the pleasurable and the perfect, and to look upon the latter as worthier than the former, even when he neglects it to secure the former.

Reason, directing the conduct with a regard to the ideal, is too narrow in its range of control, too low in its character, and too short-sighted in its vision, to furnish the supreme guide of human action. This guide needs to be supplemented and controlled by a higher guiding principle furnished in a sense of duty or conscience.

The Truth of these Statements will appear in the discussion of the supreme end and rule of moral action.

Topic Third. Conscience as a Guide. — Reason, directing the conduct with a regard to what is right, or prescribed by God in the moral law, claims to be the supreme guide of human action in the fulfilment of the mission of duty.

This guide can exist only in a being having some revelation of the moral law, and made capable of distinguishing between right and wrong, and of desiring and choosing the right or wrong.

Discussion Deferred. — This is not the place for a complete discussion of the constitution and workings of man's moral nature. It is sufficient for the present to state clearly the place which the sense of duty holds as the supreme guide of human conduct, and to indicate some reasons for believing that such a principle exists.

A Sense of Duty exists as a Guiding Principle.—We are certain that this sense of duty exists in man, from being conscious of it in ourselves; and from observing it in others, and in human conduct, laws, and languages in general.

First, our own consciousness assures that a sense of duty exists. We know that we have ideas of right and wrong, and that we do some actions, and refrain from doing others, from a sense of duty. We approve of the right and condemn the wrong both in ourselves and in others.

Secondly, our observation of the conduct of others assures us of the same thing.

The difference between right and wrong is recognized from the earliest years, and children acknowledge the sense of duty as a guiding principle even in their sports and amusements by appealing to what is fair, honorable, and right.

The same acknowledgment is made by men in all the ordinary intercourse and business of life, in believing in testimony, in trusting in promises, and in entering into contracts with one another, on the understanding that the duties of faithfulness and truth, and the evil and baseness of perfidy and deceit, are universally acknowledged.

A like acknowledgment is involved in the uniformity with which, under all forms of law and government and in all ages, the great fundamental principles of right and justice have been recognized by men, and appeal been made to men for their acknowledgment.

The same acknowledgment of a sense of duty is seen in the uniformity and universality with which the principles of right and justice have been embodied in human laws and languages, written and unwritten. See Mackintosh, *Discourse on the Law of Nature and Nations;* and Bacon, *Dign. and Advant. of Learning.* Says Hume, "Had nature made no such distinction, founded on the original frame and constitution of the mind, the words *honorable* and *shameful, lovely* and *odious, noble* and *despicable,* never had had place in any language."

Place as Supreme Guide.— It will be shown at a subsequent stage of the discussion that while prudence and the ideal have a restricted sphere of operation, "it is the function of conscience to survey the whole constitution of our being, and assign limits to the gratification of all our various passions and desires. Differing not in degree but in kind from the other principles of our nature, we feel that a course of conduct which is opposed to it may be intelligibly described as unnatural, even when in accordance with our most natural appetites; for to conscience is assigned the prerogative of both judging and restraining them all. Its *power* may be insignificant, but its *title* is undisputed, and 'if it had might as it has right, it would govern the world.'" See Butler, *Sermons on Hum. Nat.;* and Lecky, *Hist. Europ. Morals.*

The Supreme Place Claimed.—It will appear that wherever there is a conflict between the three guides, the reason always asserts the supremacy of the sense of duty over the sense of prudence and the sense of the perfect. Conscience alone has authority to make use of an *ought* in giving its directions. "It is this faculty, distinct from and superior to all appetites, passions, and tastes, that makes virtue the supreme law of life, and adds an imperative character to the feeling of attraction it inspires. It is this which was described by Cicero as the *God ruling within us;* by the Stoics as *the sovereignty of reason;* by St. Paul as *the law of nature;* by Butler as *the supremacy of conscience."* *Hist. Europ. Morals,* Lecky.

SUMMARY.

This general view of the personal agent, who is to work out a moral mission in the world, is essential to a complete and consistent theory of morality. The following facts and truths have been made evident in the course of it:

This personal agent is a self-active spirit, possessed of an endless existence, capable of limitless development, and embodied in order to bring him into connection with the rest of the universe.

He is a creature of manifold wants, which take shape in the feelings, placed in a universe of good, endowed with an intelligence to perceive and appreciate that good, and with a will to choose and lay hold of it and direct his powers in view of it, so as to satisfy and enlarge his being.

He is a being of varied and ceaseless activities, capable of setting before himself, as objects for his achievement, ends which would embrace, in their ever-widening sweep, the universe of good in happiness, perfection, and righteousness.

He is a rational being, conscious that he must work out a moral mission and an immortal destiny under God the moral governor, and acknowledging conscience, or the moral faculty, to be his supreme guide in the fulfilment of his great task.

A careful investigation of conscience, or the moral nature of man, must therefore be the first step toward the construction of a philosophy of the life of human duty.

CHAPTER II.

SPECIAL VIEW OF THE MORAL AGENT.

IT has been shown that the sense of duty, or conscience, or the moral nature, fits man for a life of duty, and claims to be the authoritative guide of his conduct in the fulfilment of his duty. It is evident, therefore, that it is necessary, in order to understand man as a moral agent, to investigate the elements of his conscience, or moral nature.

The Moral Nature, called Conscience.— Ethical writers have used *conscience* in various senses. By mankind generally, however, it is clearly used as synonymous with man's entire moral nature, or all those endowments and arrangements of his soul by which he is capable of distinguishing between right and wrong, and of conforming his conduct to the law of duty. Any different use of the word must necessarily tend to confusion. *Conscience, moral faculty,* and *moral nature* will therefore be used interchangeably.

The question, *What is man's moral nature ?* may be answered either by an examination of the chief ethical systems, or by a direct inspection of the moral consciousness. The subject of the chapter will therefore furnish two *Sections:*

Section 1. The Elements of Man's Moral Nature from the Theories of Moralists.

Section 2. The Elements of Man's Moral Nature from the Moral Consciousness.

Reason for this Method.— It is always an aid in scientific investigations to know what men have thought and believed. Without the help of the past ages, made available in this way, each generation would be obliged to start where the first generation started, and there could never

71

be any completed science. The theories of moralists embody the results of all past attempts to read and explain the moral consciousness of man, and the essential elements of the moral nature will be found to hold a prominent place in them. The results of past investigation will therefore furnish the best preparation for making more intelligent and decisive that direct appeal to the moral consciousness of mankind, which alone can determine finally and conclusively what conscience is.

SECTION I.

The Elements of the Moral Nature from the Theories of Moralists.

The answers of moralists to the question, *What is man's moral nature?* are of value chiefly as giving the views of those who have attempted the reading of the moral consciousness. Psychologically viewed, there have always existed two distinct and opposing schools of moralists, which may for convenience be designated experientialists and intuitionalists.

The Experientialist affirms that conscience, or the moral faculty, is derived from sense and experience. Man is not born with it, nor even with the germ of it.

The Intuitionalist affirms that conscience is a special, inborn, or original capacity, which the workings of sense and experience can do nothing more than develop.

The Antagonism Perpetual.— Under the names of *idealist, intellectualist,* and many other related designations, on the one hand, and of *empiricist, materialist, externalist, sensationalist, experientialist,* and similar titles on the other, the thinkers of all ages, even from before the time of Socrates, have inevitably divided and massed themselves.

The Antagonism Radical.— The perpetuity of this antagonism shows that the difference between the two schools of moralists is a radical one, and one which needs to be understood before the investigation of the facts of the moral consciousness can be undertaken with any prospect of clear and satisfactory results.

A Truth in Each View.— It may be fairly assumed that each of these views must have in it an element of truth; for an out-and-out falsehood never holds continuous sway over even a small class of men. As it is true of all false religions (Mohammedanism, Judaism, etc.), that the modicum or mass of truth in them gives them all the power they have, and is needed to account for their continuous sway over the human mind ; so it is true that any ethical system, that has held continuous sway over even a class of minds, must have an element of truth in it to account for that sway.

Topic First. The View of the Experientialists.— The experientialists all agree in holding conscience to be a product of man's common experience, derived through the external senses; they disagree about the mode in which it is so derived. With them all alike the soul is to begin with morally a blank. There is in it no idea of right, obligation, duty, and not even the germ of any such idea. Man creates for himself the distinction between virtue and vice, and creates it by the aid of experience.

The varying views of the experientialists may be illustrated by the theories of eminent writers of this school.

Hobbes' Theory.— Man's soul is morally a blank at the outset. His pleasure is his only law. The mode in which man's moral ideas are originated is as follows : he finds in the course of his experience such a thing as civil government laying down civil law and claiming obedience, establishing religion, and demanding conformity. He obeys and conforms. He must give this obedience and conformity a name, and so he learns to call it *duty, virtue,* and learns to think it such. If government demanded just the opposite, then that opposite would be right, dutiful, virtuous. All the conscience man has is therefore originated through his connection with civil government.

Adam Smith's Theory.— Man's soul is morally a blank at the outset. There is nothing in it that can properly be called a germ of conscience. The moral ideas are all originated by experience, through the principle of sympathy. Man sees an agent performing some act. He considers all the circumstances in which that agent is placed. If he feels a complete sympathy with his feelings, he approves the action. He needs some term by which to characterize the act, and so he calls it *right.* If this principle of sympathy should lead him to approve just the opposite, then that would be right. Virtue is simple *fitness, propriety, decency,* as decided by each man from his own point of view. All the conscience man has is originated through his sympathy with his fellow-man.

Paley's Theory.— The soul is morally a blank at first, with no inborn germ of a moral nature. Looking abroad over the world of human experience, man concludes that happiness is the chief good and the grand end of life. If this be so, then it follows logically that virtue consists in a correct calculation of our own personal interests, either in this world only or also in the next. The calculating power with reference to self-interest needs a name, and it is called *conscience*. The impulse to action which man receives from his own selfishness requires a name, and it is called *obligation* or a *sense of duty*. The course of conduct in seeking happiness needs to be characterized, and it is called *virtuous*. All the conscience man has is therefore originated through his desire for happiness.

John Stuart Mill's Theory.— The soul is held to be morally a blank at the outset, as by the other empiricists, and also *intellectually* a blank. The entire mental and moral nature is a pure development. Man begins with bare *sensations*, and out of these, by certain processes of association, the intelligence is developed. These processes of association are known as the laws of similarity, of contiguity, of repetition, and of persistence. Having by these processes reached intelligence, or mind, which may be defined to be *a conscious string of sensations*, man proceeds, by the aid of the distinction — noticed as existing in sensations — of pleasurable and painful, to reach the idea of right and wrong in action. He decides actions to be right in proportion as they tend to promote happiness; wrong, as they tend to produce the reverse of happiness. But man, according to Mr. Mill, proceeds further to distinguish between pleasures as higher and lower. That pleasure which is of the highest quality, and calls into exercise the higher faculties, is decided to be the higher, and right in a higher sense. The mind at last rises from the mere selfishness, with which it starts, to *usefulness*. The usefulness of actions in securing happiness for ourselves and others determines their moral character. Here, in *utility*, is found the basis of right, duty, virtue. All the conscience man has is therefore originated out of nothing but the bare power of sensation.

Alexander Bain adopts the utilitarian theory of Mr. Mill, but he differs from him in reaching the development of the moral nature more nearly after the manner of Hobbes, as already described. All the conscience man has is originated by experience through our "education under government, or authority."

Dr. Herbert Spencer adopts the association theory of Mr. Mill, as but part of the still wider *theory of evolution* advocated by Darwin, and held to be applicable to all being and all activity whether material or spiritual. The evolution theory, in its application to ethics, is still in a very crude shape, if it may be said to have assumed definite shape at all.

Topic Second. The View of the Intuitionalists. — The intuitionalists all agree in holding that conscience is in some sense original or native to man ; they disagree about whether it is a simple faculty or a complex faculty, or both a faculty or combination of faculties and an inner intuitive law or rule.

Conscience Original in what Sense.—Conscience is original or native in the same sense, of course, in which reason is. It is in man as a capacity, or germ, at the first. It is developed in the course of human experience, as reason is developed.

Paley's Example not Relevant.— Paley, in putting his famous case of the *wild boy*, has shown either an utter ignorance of the structure of man's nature, or an utter regardlessness for truth. "Would a savage — without experience and without instruction, cut off in his infancy from all intercourse with his species, and consequently under no possible influence of example, authority, education, sympathy, or habit — feel any degree of that sentiment of disapprobation which we feel when the story of a son betraying his father is told to him?" Such a case proves nothing. Such a being would be little, if any, above an idiot—unable to follow the plainest steps of reasoning, or to discern, in the simplest cases, between right and wrong. By such an experience neither reason nor conscience would be brought into *exercise;* and it is as absurd to argue from such an example, whether invented or real, that man is not originally and by birth a moral being, as it is to argue that he is not a rational being. The non-exercise, or non-development, of a power is no sure proof of its non-existence. All our powers of body and soul—even such as are unquestionably original — require exercise and culture, or occasion and opportunity, for their full development.

Illustration of Differences.— The varying views of the intuitional moralists might be illustrated at large by the theories of eminent ethical writers ; but present purposes require only a brief statement of the principal views.

Subject 1st. First Class: Simple Faculty.—The intuitionalists, who affirm that conscience is a simple faculty, divide over the question, Is conscience an intuitive function connected with the intellect, or with the feelings, or with the will?

Conscience is an intuitive function of the intellect, say some. It is an intuitive moral sense or an intuitive moral judgment.

A Moral Sense.— There is a moral sense, say some of this class, by means of which man perceives things moral, just as there are in his constitution the bodily senses by means of which he perceives the objects of the external world. He has a power of perceiving directly and intuitively the moral quality in actions, just as he has a power of perceiving directly the color of objects. This was Hutcheson's view. It had been broached earlier by Shaftesbury.

A Moral Judgment.— Conscience is a moral judgment, say others of this class. Man has in his intellect not only a power of judging in general, but he has also a power of judging immediately and intuitively of moral subjects in particular. This is therefore a distinct and independent power. Moral reflection, moral approbation and disapprobation, are actings of this moral judgment. This was maintained by the Scottish school, of which Dugald Stewart was a leader.

Conscience is an intuitive function of the sensibilities, say others. It is an intuitive moral feeling, or tact.

A Moral Feeling.— Conscience is moral feeling, or moral tact, or the power of immediately and intuitively *feeling* (or, as it were, touching,) moral qualities or differences, just as one feels pleasure or pain, or feels the qualities of objects by the sense of touch, or feeling. This moral tact is found in every man, and is the whole of conscience, say the moralists of this class. This was Hume's view. He uses *moral sense*— differently from Hutcheson—to denote a mere capacity for unintelligent feeling of moral qualities, or feeling unaccompanied by judgment.

Conscience is an intuitive function of the will, say others. Conscience is a moral instinct, or intuitive moral impulse.

A Moral Instinct.—Conscience is a moral instinct which has an affirmative and negative manifestation. In its affirmative function it solicits to a given action as right; in its negative, if it does not deter from, it reacts against a given action as wrong. Or, taken in its relation to the moral life, it is that in the moral agent which in its positive form immediately and intuitively impels to the realization of the morally good, and which in its negative form immediately and intuitively restrains from the morally evil. Conscience is then simply an impulsive power connected with the will and pushing to the right or from the wrong.

Subject 2d. Second Class: Complex Faculty.— The intuitionalists, who hold that conscience is a complex faculty, divide over the question, With what combination of the simple faculties is the intuitive function of conscience connected?

Conscience is an intuitive function connected with the combined exercise of intellect, sensibilities, and will, say some.

A Threefold Faculty.— According to this view there is an intuitive action of all three of the fundamental faculties of the soul; in other words, conscience involves the complex working of intellect, feelings, and will,—the intellect immediately and intuitively discerning the right or wrong, and giving a judgment of approval or disapproval; the feelings moving in accordance with that judgment; and the will instinctively influencing or impelling toward the right or influencing against or deterring from the wrong.

Conscience is an intuitive function connected with the combined exercise of some two of the three fundamental faculties of the soul.

A Twofold Faculty.— In its statement, Butler's system recognizes the complex working of intellect and feelings, and so would belong to the class of views maintaining that conscience is a double faculty; but it implies, as essential to it, a moral action of the will corresponding to the moral action of the intellect and feelings, and therefore really belongs to the class of views maintaining that conscience is an intuitive function connected with a threefold working of the faculties.

Subject 3d. Third Class: Inner Law. The intuitionalists, who hold either of the preceding views in any of its modifications, divide over the question, Does this intuitive function of the soul, called conscience, furnish also an inner law, or standard of right?

The Inner Law.— All intuitionalists agree that conscience is in some sense a faculty, simple or complex. Does it also involve an inner law, or rule, which furnishes the standard to which the workings of that faculty should be conformed? It has been said that "if such a rule existed in the mind prior to the observation of particular acts of a moral nature, we should be conscious of it: nothing of the nature of a law, or rule, can have existence in the mind, without the knowledge of the mind itself." This argument is evidently based upon a misconception of the nature of such a rule, and of the relation of the intuitions of man to his experiences. Says Dr. Charles Hodge, "There is an imperfect revelation of the law made in the very constitution of our nature, by which those who have no other revelation are to be judged." This is in accordance with the ethical view of Paul, in the *Epistle to the Romans*, and is a fundamental principle in the ethical system of Bishop Butler.

7 *

Conclusion.

This brief view of the Moral Theories warrants the conclusion that both experience and intuition enter largely into the working of the moral nature, and that an inner law has also an important place in it.

SECTION II.

Elements of the Moral Nature from Consciousness.

The precise facts of man's moral nature may best be ascertained by a direct appeal to the individual moral consciousness, or by the introspective method.

The Facts All-important.— It is evident that the all-important thing is the ascertaining of the precise facts of man's moral nature. Every theory must be baseless and worthless, however ingenious, without the solid foundation of fact. The inquiry already made after the answers of the moralists to the question, What is conscience? has value only as it is an indirect method of reaching the fundamental facts of consciousness.

Facts to be Learned from Consciousness.—The facts must be directly ascertained by an appeal to consciousness, or by the introspective method, rather than by the logical method. Neither reasoning nor the constructive faculty—the chief instruments of the speculative thinker—is of any avail without this introspection, or scanning of consciousness.

The facts of the moral nature can be found in their completeness only in the fully developed and complete man.

The Facts in their Completeness.—The first law of the scientific method of inquiry requires that nothing be invented, and only that which actually exists be sought for. It leads us to seek for all the facts, to accept no more and to be content with no less.

Facts only from the Complete Man.— The consciousness in which these moral facts are to be sought for is the consciousness of civilized and fully developed man. "We absolutely deny," says Cousin (*The True, the Beautiful, and the Good*, p. 217), "that it is necessary to study human nature in the famous savage of Aveyron, or in the like of him of the isles of the ocean or of the American Continent. The savage state offers us humanity in swaddling-clothes, thus to speak, the germ of humanity, but not humanity entire. In that, without doubt, may be found signs or *souvenirs* of humanity; and, if this were the plea, we might, in our turn, examine the recitals of voyages, and find, even in that darkness of infancy or decrepitude, admirable flashes of light, noble instincts, which already appear, or still subsist, presaging or recalling humanity. But, for the sake of exactness of method and true analysis, we turn our eyes from infancy and the savage state, in order to direct them towards the being who is the sole object of our studies,—the actual man, the real and completed man." It were better to say the *wreck* of humanity, than the *germ* of humanity, for the savage is shown by history to be only that. As we gain a true idea of man as a rational being, not in the idiot, but in the man of mind, so we gain a true and adequate idea of man as a moral being only in the perfect or highest man.

It is admitted by the intuitionalist that the moral intuitions first appear in concrete form in the moral experiences. The two are essential to each other and to the moral life of man, the experience always implying the intuition, and the intuition always requiring the experience for its manifestation.

Intuitions First in Concrete Form.— This is a familiar and well-established principle of psychology. Rightness and obligation are first recognized in some right or obligatory act or state, and in this concrete form are familiar to all men. It is only the man of reflective thought or the philosopher that attempts, by a process of reflection and generalization, to reach a conception of the abstract rightness and obligation.

The order of the investigation of the moral consciousness is decided by the principle that the concrete must be understood before the abstract can be understood, the experiential before the intuitional. The two *Topics* for consideration, therefore, are —

Topic 1st. Experiential Facts of Moral Consciousness.
Topic 2d. Intuitional Facts of Moral Consciousness.

Topic First. Experiential Facts of Moral Consciousness.— The simplest and most obvious facts of the moral nature are to be found in the moral experience, or in the actual workings of the various powers of the soul in connection with moral action. They are to be examined as the moral facts of intellect, feelings, and will.

Sphere of Experience.— As it is in the experience that the intuitive notions and judgments are brought to light, the experience needs to be understood to prepare for the investigation of the intuitions. The experientialist justly claims for experience a large and prominent place in the practical workings of man's moral nature.

Subject 1st. Moral Facts of Intellect.— In moral action the intellect furnishes certain moral judgments involving certain moral conceptions.

Nature of Moral Judgments.— All acts of judgment are acts of the intellect judging; all acts of moral judgment are acts of the intellect judging upon moral subjects.

There are certain fundamental moral judgments which reveal themselves to careful observation.

First Moral Judgment.— When we witness any moral action, we judge it to be *right* or *wrong.* This is the simplest form of the moral judgment. It has its constant illustrations in the experiences of every-day life. A man who cannot swim falls overboard from a ship and is drowning. A strong sailor, skilled in swimming, plunges in after him and rescues him at the risk of his own life. We pronounce that a right action. Here is the familiar judgment of *moral approbation.* A strong man armed falls upon another man, feeble and unarmed, and maltreats and kills him in order to take from him his purse. We pronounce that act wrong. It is base and wicked,— a crime. Here is the familiar judgment of *moral disapprobation.*

Second Moral Judgment.— When we consider any such moral action, we judge that there is an *obligation* to perform it as right, or to refrain from it as wrong. If it is right to rescue the drowning man, then it ought to be done, and the sailor who is able to do it is under obligation to do it. If it is wrong to murder and rob a man, then the strong man armed is morally bound not to do it. Here is the familiar judgment of *moral obligation.*

Third Moral Judgment.— We judge that the action has *merit* or *demerit ;* it ought to be rewarded or punished; the agent is not guilty, or he is guilty, in performing it. We say of the action of the sailor, it is meritorious and ought to be rewarded ; and we say of the action of the murderer, it has demerit ; he is guilty and ought to be punished. Here is the familiar judgment of *moral merit* and *demerit* in its various forms.

Fourth Moral Judgment.— We judge that the agent is *free to choose or to reject* the morally good or evil. The sailor may or may not attempt the rescue of the drowning man, as he pleases; the murderer may or may not murder and rob a man, as he pleases. This freedom of choice in action is that by which the agent makes the action his own and becomes responsible for it. Here is the familiar judgment of *moral freedom*, which lies at the basis of responsibility.

Fifth Moral Judgment.—We go further and judge the agent to be *under and amenable to the moral law*, which law—as soon as we come to a belief in the Divine Being — is judged to be the law of God. Here is the familiar judgment of *responsibility* or *accountability to God*.

These constitute the fundamental moral judgments. They are similar, with changed circumstances, whether the action contemplated by the agent be his own or that of some other agent.

. **Subject 2d. Moral Facts of Feeling.**—In moral action the sensibilities furnish certain moral feelings which follow upon the moral judgments. These feelings correspond to the judgments, since they arise out of them. They may have reference to the agent's own action or to the action of another.

Arrangement of Moral Feelings, or Sentiments.—For convenience and brevity the moral sentiments may be arranged under two classes, as they have reference to right actions or to wrong actions.

1st. Moral Feelings with Right Action.—When the judgment pronounces action right, obligatory, or meritorious, it awakens in the agent, if it be his own act, a feeling of moral approval and satisfaction: if it be another's act, a feeling of moral approval and esteem.

2d. Moral Feelings with Wrong Action.—When the judgment decides that an action is wrong,—one that ought not to be done, or one deserving of punishment,—there arises, if the action be the agent's own, a feeling of moral disapproval and shame, or self-reproach, often deepening into remorse: if it be another's act, a feeling of moral disapproval and indignation, often deepening into moral aversion, or into moral vindictiveness, or a feeling which would lead to the avenging of the wrong.

Subject 3d. Moral Facts of Will.—In connection with the moral judgments and moral feelings the will furnishes certain phenomena of moral choice and moral purpose. In general, the normal tendency of the will is to impel the agent to adopt and attempt to realize the morally good in his own conduct and that of others, and to reject and prevent the morally evil.

1st. The Will in the Agent's Own Moral Action.—When the action contemplated by the intellect and appealing to the moral feelings is something that may be done by ourselves, there arises, as has been seen,

—when the will has free play,—first, the choice, or preference, to do it; then, the volition, or purpose, to do it; and finally, the effort, resulting in the completed action. In the case of failure of the will thus to move the powers to the performance of that which is right and obligatory, there arises a moral protest of the agent against his own course, which often leads to a perpetual moral strife in his soul, and, when suffered to continue, ends in despair of achieving the moral task of life and in utter moral wreck.

2d. The Will in the Moral Action of Another. —When the action contemplated and inciting to feeling pertains to some one else than the agent contemplating it, there arises the wish to see or not to see it accomplished, as it is right or wrong; and the purpose to aid or hinder its accomplishment. If it be already done, there arises the impulse to reward or punish the agent, as the case may require.

These facts of intellect, feeling, and will are what may be called the simple facts of the moral experience. For the correctness of the reading of these experiential facts, the appeal must be to man's *moral consciousness.* Every complete moral agent finds them all in his own experience.

These ascertained facts of experience prepare the way for the investigation of the facts of intuition which come to light only in connection with them.

Topic Second. Intuitional Facts of Moral Consciousness. —The examination of the moral consciousness reveals not only the moral workings of the faculties, already considered, but also certain facts of intuition which are essential to moral action. These facts may be considered under intuitive moral ideas, or conceptions, and intuitive moral judgments, or principles.

Subject 1st. Intuitive Moral Ideas. —Involved in experience and brought to light by its workings there are certain intuitive moral ideas which alone render a moral experience possible. Among these ideas are those expressed by *right, wrong, duty, desert, responsibility, obligation,* and the other kindred terms used as predicates in the various moral judgments enumerated under the previous *Topic.*

Moral Ideas Exist. — It is obvious that such ideas as *right, wrong,* etc., exist. They are not mere sounds, but sounds of the deepest significance.

"It would be as reasonable," says Sir James Mackintosh, "to deny that *space* and *greenness* are significant words, as to affirm that *ought, right, duty, virtue,* are sounds without meaning." Evidence of their existence has already been presented (p. 69). It all resolves itself, in the last analysis, into the testimony of consciousness.

Moral Ideas at the Basis of Moral Experience. — Moral judgment is the fundamental moral exercise. We judge an action to be *right* or *obligatory.* Such judgments would be impossible, if there were not in the soul the ideas of rightness and obligation, which we predicate of the action.

That these moral ideas are intuitive and not experiential is shown by their standing the test of intuitive ideas: they are universal, necessary, and logically independent and original.

Universally Received. — All men, whether they consciously recognize them or not, have everywhere and always shown their practical faith — by their action, thought, and speech — in these moral ideas. They are involved in all moral knowledge. While no mere animal has ever been found possessed of them, no race of men, not even the most degraded, has ever been found without them.

They are Necessary. — The human agent is constrained, by the constitution of his being and the spontaneous workings of his nature, to make use of these moral ideas. They are just as truly and inevitably presupposed by all men, in all moral judgments, feelings, and purposes, as are the ideas of substance and attribute and of resemblance, in all generalization, or the idea of reason and consequent, in all reasoning. Even theorists, such as Mill and Bain, in every effort which they make to explain away these ideas, or to derive them from experience, are compelled, by their own intellectual and moral nature, to assume and use them. They *compel* practical belief.

They are Logically Independent and Original. — These moral ideas cannot be resolved by any process of thought into any more ultimate ideas on which they depend, or into any simpler elements of which they are made up. The experientialist in morals, in all such attempts to resolve or account for them, always presupposes or assumes them. John Stuart Mill's logical passage from the *pleasurable* to the *right* (as seen in the statement of his theory, p. 74,) will illustrate the logical vice inherent in all empirical systems of ethics. He acquires the ability to leap the chasm which separates the two, by quietly ignoring the essential difference between the wish for the pleasure and the obligation to the right, and, from that point onward in his theory, *assuming the idea of right as accounted for.*

The truth concerning the moral ideas, therefore, is that, while they are brought to light by experience, they are not originated by it, but are a part of the original intuitive furnishing of the human soul.

Subject 2d. Intuitive Moral Judgments. — Involved in experience, and brought to light by its workings, there are also certain intuitive moral judgments, or principles, which furnish the agent with that inner copy of the moral law which has been given him for his guidance in his moral action.

Man under Law. — That man is an agent under law is implied, as has been seen, in the very idea of morality and moral conduct. There is need of a more explicit statement of his relation to that law. The term *law* is used in various senses:

1st. Law is an established order in the sequence of events. A law in this sense is a mere fact, or rather a general statement comprehending many similar facts, without any reference to an explanation of the fact or facts by some uniformly acting force.

2d. Law is a uniformly acting force which determines the sequence of events. In this sense the physical forces, which we see in operation around us, are called the laws of nature. This is an ambiguous use of the term *law* for the force which explains the law, or uniform sequence of events.

3d. Law is a rule of action which binds the conscience of an agent. It imposes the obligation of conformity to its demands upon all rational creatures. This is true of the moral law in its widest sense; and also of human law within its own proper sphere.

Law in the first sense, is the rule which controls the action of the physical forces; in the last sense, the rule which should control the action of an intelligent agent. Man, as considered in ethics, is under law in this latter sense.

Man under the Moral Law, or Law of Right. — Man is an agent under the law of right, a law which binds him to duty. He is conscious of obligation and responsibility. This consciousness is sufficient proof that he is subject to a prescribed law of right. Where this prescribed law is to be found will appear in its proper place. This law of right, when once ascertained, must decide all human duties, as well as all human rights.

The Inner Copy of the Moral Law, to which conscience subjects the agent, will be shown to be made up of the intuitive moral judgments.

It is therefore necessary, first, to ascertain what these moral judgments are; and, secondly, to consider them as furnishing an inner law, or rule, of moral conduct.

1st. The Intuitive Moral Judgments Ascertained. — The intuitive moral judgments, or principles, found in the moral consciousness of the agent, may respect either the three great relations in which he is to fulfil his mission of duty, or the three forms of the good which furnish the ends of his action.

Intuitive Moral Judgments respecting the Three Great Relations. — The three great relations in which the agent is to fulfil his mission of duty, are his relations to God, to himself, and to his fellow-man. Certain fundamental and germinal moral judgments respecting these relations have been admitted in all ages, and have been brought out with great clearness under the Christian system of morality.

In His Relation to God, the enlightened moral consciousness reveals the judgment, that the agent, as a religious being, is bound to render supreme devotion to God.

In His Relation to Himself, the enlightened moral consciousness reveals the judgment, that the agent, as an individual, responsible person, is bound to preserve his being, develop his powers to the utmost, and direct them to the accomplishment of the true mission of man.

In His Relation to His Fellow-Man, the enlightened moral consciousness reveals the judgment, that the agent, as a social being, is bound to love his fellow-men as himself, or — so far as in his power, and as connected with them in society — to seek to preserve the being of men, to develop their powers, and direct them to the accomplishment of man's true mission.

These judgments furnish the basis of all human duties, and are therefore the foundation of Practical Ethics.

The Obligation Admitted. — The three great relations of man, and the duties growing out of them, have been recognized and acknowledged in all ages. Paul declares that the grace of God teaches that we should "live soberly, righteously, and godly" in this present world; — sobriety comprising the duties we owe to ourselves; righteousness, those we owe to our fellow-men; and godliness, those due directly to God. Cicero, in his *Tusculan Disputations*, gives the same classification; as does also Marcus Antoninus in his works. The same is also found in the East. The *Tunkla Nameh,* one of their sacred books, declares that "a Sikh should set his heart on God, on charity, and on purity."

Intuitive Moral Judgment respecting the Three Forms of the Good. — The three forms of the good which furnish the ends of the agent's action, have been found to be happiness, perfection, and rightness. The fundamental and germinal moral judgment respecting man's relation to these ends of action has been admitted in all ages, and has been brought out with special clearness under the Christian system.

The enlightened moral consciousness furnishes the moral judgment, that, in striving after the different forms of the good for the satisfaction of the wants of his being, the agent should place the right highest, the perfect next, and the merely pleasurable last.

This judgment furnishes the basis of the supremacy of conscience, and decides the supreme obligation of virtue.

The Morally Good, or Right, holds the Place of Supremacy. — The enlightened moral consciousness invariably gives it this place. Such consciousness as invariably exalts the perfect above the merely pleasurable. This is especially manifest among those who have felt the influence of that most perfect ethical system embraced in the Christian religion, and who have been brought by it the nearest to the true moral manhood.

This subject will come up for more extended treatment in the discussion of the nature of virtue, or the dutiful in conduct.

These Moral Judgments Intuitive and Permanent. — These moral judgments are not mere uncertain generalizations from experience, but intuitive and self-evident principles. The moral agent, in his normal condition, immediately and intuitively discerns the rightness of them and their binding force on himself and all other like agents, now and always, in this world and in all worlds.

The Moral Principles Intuitive. — Man is so made that he intuitively perceives these principles and recognizes in them the rule of his conduct. Why does a man judge that course of conduct to be right and obligatory which preserves, develops, and perfects his being? Why that which advances the highest interests of his neighbor? Why that which honors God? He is so made that he cannot help judging thus, if in his normal condition; so made that he cannot help condemning himself if his conduct is at variance with these principles; so made that he cannot help holding himself accountable to God for a departure from them.

The Moral Principles Immutable and Universal.—Says Dr. McCosh, in *The Intuitions of the Mind:* "Moral good is moral good to all intelligences so high in the scale of being as to be able to discern it. I lay down this position in order to guard against the idea that moral excellence is something depending on the peculiar nature of man, and that it is allowable to suppose that there may be intelligent beings in other worlds to whom virtue does not appear as virtue. Such a view seems altogether inconsistent with our intuitive convictions, and would effectually undermine the foundations of morality." We are conscious that these moral judgments are necessary. This may be shown by subjecting any one of them to the test of the moral consciousness. For example, take the love of our neighbor. Is it right or wrong? If right, is it right necessarily, immutably, and universally; or only contingently, changeably, and in some cases only? Is it right for one man and wrong for another; right in America and wrong in Asia or the far distant parts of the universe; right two thousand years ago and wrong now? To all such questioning the response of consciousness is clear and emphatic.

These Moral Judgments made Clearer with Man's Elevation.—It is obvious from these considerations that these moral principles will be clear to the agent in proportion to his moral enlightenment. Accordingly, it is found that—

There are vestiges of these principles found in all men who are at all developed morally. The principles are recognized as existing and obligatory the world over,—even where men make the most perverse applications of them in their practice.

In proportion as the agent reaches a more complete moral development, these principles are always more clearly and fully recognized.

In the system of the most perfect moral agent and teacher, Jesus of Nazareth, all these moral principles are at once fully and consciously recognized and clearly and completely stated.

2d. The Intuitive Moral Judgments as an Inner Law.—
The examination of the moral consciousness reveals a moral
rule, or law of duty, impressed upon the soul of the human
agent himself when he has reached the mature moral manhood. This inner law is made up of the intuitive moral judgments already enumerated. In its completeness it constitutes
man's mission of duty, or appointed life task.

Three points are thus suggested : the fact of the inner law;
its composition ; and its nature as mission and rule of duty.

Fact of the Inner Law Established.—That there is found
in the agent, whose moral nature has been developed, an
inner standard by the aid of which he reaches his practical
conclusions concerning what is duty, and which binds him to
duty, may be established by various proofs, negative and
positive.

First Argument: Negative. —The fact that man's moral
conclusions are not always in accordance with absolute rectitude, and that his moral conduct is not always what it ought
to be, does not prove the absence of a standard of right.
Man is conscious that his nature is not now in its original
perfection. The moral law in his constitution has been in
some degree overlaid or defaced ; and the moral nature has
been warped and perverted, and needs to be corrected and
perfected before it can become a safe and sufficient standard
in all cases.

Extreme Views. — So marked is the disorganization and wreck of
our common human nature, that some are even disposed to deny that
there are any vestiges left in man of a nobler moral nature. On the
other hand, there are those who are ready to claim that in man's nature
as it now is, subject to all the manifold biases of corruption, reason
and conscience furnish a *certain* standard of truth and duty — an *infal-*
lible indication of the mind and will of Deity.

True View of Man's Condition. — Dr. McCosh (*Div. Gov.,* p. 54,)
presents the correct view of man's condition, and then confirms that
view by an apt quotation from Pascal's *Thoughts:* "There is a schism in
the very soul itself. Two facts here present themselves — the one, that
man, by the very constitution of his mind, approves of moral good
and disapproves of moral evil ; the other, that he neglects the good

and commits the evil. . . . . This double truth, which explains the double fact, has been grasped by Pascal, and developed with singular conciseness and beauty. 'The greatness and misery of man being alike conspicuous, religion, in order to be true, must necessarily teach us that he has in himself some noble principles of greatness, and at the same time some profound source of misery. For true religion cannot answer its character, otherwise than by such an entire knowledge of our nature as perfectly to understand all that is great and all that is miserable in it, together with the reasons of the one and of the other.' . . . . . 'Now, then, consider all the great and glorious aspirations which the sense of so many miseries is not able to extinguish, and inquire whether they can proceed from any other cause save a higher nature. Had man never fallen, he would have enjoyed eternal truth and happiness; and had man never been otherwise than corrupt, he would have retained no idea either of truth or happiness. . . . . So manifest is it that we were in a state of perfection, from which we are now unhappily fallen.'"

In Accordance with this View, while Paul teaches everywhere that man's nature is corrupt, he likewise teaches (*Rom.* i. 18–21) that the revelation of the law in the heathen, who have no written law, is sufficient to leave them without excuse before God.

Second Argument: from Authority. —The authority of most of the great men who have examined the consciousness most carefully, and thought most deeply on this subject, is in favor of the existence and binding force of a moral standard in man. Even the writers on morals, who deny the existence of any such standard, assume its existence in all their reasonings, just as inevitably as the experientialists assume the existence of the innate moral ideas in their reasonings.

The Authority of Great Thinkers.— Paul says that the heathen "show the work of the law written on their hearts." In the absence of a written law of God "they are a law unto themselves." They have in their own nature a rule of duty by which they judge themselves, and by which God will judge them. Says Dr. Charles Hodge, in commenting upon this passage: "The same works which the Jews have prescribed in their law, the Gentiles show to be written in their hearts." Says Bishop Butler: "Man, by his very make, or constitution, is a law to himself; and the law which results from regarding his nature as an economy, or system, is the law of him who is the Author of the nature in its right and normal state. The law of God is promulgated by the nature of man."

8*

Says Dr. McCosh in his *Divine Government*, in considering the schism in man's soul, "Certain it is, that when his conduct is brought under review, man is condemned by the very principles in his own bosom." In the same work, in inquiring into the nature of conscience, he says: "The conscience is the mind looking to a moral law, and pronouncing judgments giving rise to emotions."

The Appeal to the Unconscious Admission of the Opposers of this view may be justified by even a cursory examination of their writings on this subject.

Third Argument: from Moral Practice. — Examples will show that, when the moral intelligence is in some degree developed, the agent actually and consciously makes use of this inner standard in testing moral conduct. The moral conclusions are reached by the comparison of the particular case to be tested with some general principle involved in this standard.

Example 1st. — A moral agent sees a strong man take away the money of a weaker for no other reason than that he covets it. The act appeals to the agent's sense of justice. But what is *justice?* What decides it? There must be some principle or standard at the basis by which to decide what man's just rights are. The agent tries the conduct of the robber by the principle that *every man has a right to his own property.* By this fundamental law he judges the act, and when he decides that it actually comes under this law and violates it, he pronounces it wrong and unjust. There is evident reference to a moral standard, and the wrongness consists in the want of conformity to that standard.

Example 2d. — Chinese parents often murder their own female children. They do not immediately and intuitively decide this course to be right. There is reasoning somewhat on this wise: "Is it right to destroy our child? Parents are bound to consult the best interests of their offspring. The destruction of this child will save it from the incalculable evils of this present world, and will be for its best interests. Therefore it is right to destroy it." Dr. Alexander (*Mor. Sci.*, p. 33) teaches that the matter is referred to the general principle that "*parents should consult the best interests of their offspring.*" The moral standard is apparent again.

Example 3d. — In their religious services the heathen perform acts of extreme cruelty, and consider them right, obligatory, and meritorious. "They are performed," says Dr. Alexander, "on the principle that *what God requires, or what pleases him, or what will secure happiness for* *ourselves or friends, should be done."* That is, each case is referred to some principle or standard, by agreement or disagreement with which it is decided to be right or the opposite.

Composition of the Inner Law Shown.—The inner moral law is made up of the intuitive judgments already enumerated. It demands of the agent adherence to right, or duty, in all the three great relations in which man is placed for the fulfilment of his mission,—to God, to himself, and to mankind.

This needs only to be stated in order to become obvious. It will appear at once that the rules made use of in testing conduct are referable to these germinal moral judgments, and may all readily be traced to them.

Although in the mature moral agent these principles appear in their abstract form as rules for the government of conduct, they appear at the beginning of moral agency only in the concrete form, or as embodied in the agent's judgment of some special instance of moral conduct and in immediate connection with the experience.

It is true of these principles, as of the moral ideas, that while they are involved in all moral experience, and brought to light by its workings, they are yet not originated by experience, but are a part of the original *intuitive furnishing* of the human soul.

Genesis of the Rules.—A moral agent may make application of these principles in the concrete for a lifetime without ever coming to a conscious recognition of them as abstract principles or rules. A man may see intuitively that any particular act of violence against his neighbor is wrong, without ever having distinctly stated to himself the moral principle which requires a due regard to all his neighbor's interests. The moral decisions are made at the first intuitively; but in the course of observation and experience the intelligent man lays hold of the principle thus involved as an intuition, consciously states it to himself as a principle of conduct, and intelligently applies it in regulating his life.

The Inner Law as the Moral Mission.—The inner moral law is the expression of man's mission of duty.

Duty in the three great relations of the agent's present

sphere of action covers the whole of human duty.   In the treatment of *Practical Ethics*, it will appear that the whole life of duty is merely an unfolding of the three fundamental moral judgments having reference to these three great relations.

As having place in the intuitive part of the moral constitution, these three judgments, or principles, furnish the agent with a life rule: as indicating the moral end of his being and energies, they express for him the life task which he ought to accomplish, or the moral mission for which he was made by the Creator.

Distinction of Rule and Mission.—It is evident that the inner law may be regarded as a rule by which man is to govern his whole life in its separate moral acts.   But man's life is not simply a succession of single moral points; it may also be looked upon as one uninterrupted career, one great and complete act.   The accomplishment of this one act is the end of his being, his life task, or his mission.   The inner law in its completeness may be regarded as the expression of that mission, revealing to the agent the true measure of his being and work.

The Appointed Mission.— In the plan of the world every creature has its special place, and is fitted to accomplish some special end limited only by its capacities or endowments.   Man has his special place and end.   The mission which he is to fulfil is limited only by his capacities as a self-active spirit embodied, and by the sphere of action in which he has been placed.   The moral law is the expression of his mission, as well as his rule of duty; since in the full application of the whole law to the whole sphere of his life is found his whole duty.   The law of duty thus prescribes the highest life task possible to man in his appointed sphere.

By the inner law as a life rule, the agent is enabled to decide concerning the moral character and binding force of any act or course of action.   By the inner law as expressing his mission of duty, he is enabled to comprehend in some measure the grand end of his being in the moral task which his Maker has set him to accomplish, and in the complete moral manhood to which he has called him to attain.

DIVISION II.

NATURE OF VIRTUE, OR THE DUTIFUL IN CONDUCT.

Statement and Subdivision.

DIVISION II. treats of the nature of virtue, or the dutiful in conduct. It aims to investigate, arrange, and explain the principles involved in the essential nature of morality, or virtue.

In general terms, *virtue* may be defined to be that quality in human action (in the wide sense) which commends it to the approval of the moral nature, or conscience. Such action as it approves conscience pronounces virtuous.

Relation of Conscience and Virtue. — The relation of conscience, or the moral nature, to virtue, or morality, is easily understood. When we ask the question, What is conscience? the inquiry leads us to seek to ascertain *what is in man;* to learn what are those powers and capacities of his nature by which he is constituted a moral being, capable of making a distinction between right and wrong, and of fulfilling a moral mission; in short, to learn how his nature fits him for the life of duty, or virtue. When we ask the question, What is virtue? the inquiry leads us to seek to ascertain *what it is in action and disposition* that is presented to the conscience and appreciated and approved by it. The former inquiry is subjective; the latter, objective.

Use of Terms. — Various terms are used to designate the subject of this division of ethics: *virtue, the right, the dutiful, the moral, morality,* etc. The place for making a careful distinction between these various terms would be later in this discussion. It may be remarked that *the right* is too narrow, as it is only a single element in virtue. The other terms may be regarded as substantially equivalent, — with merely a variation in point of view; as *virtue* brings out the essential quality of the thing signified (originally its relation to the manhood); *the moral* and *morality*, the relation to the law of right; and *the dutiful*, the characteristic feature of obligation.

As there are three fundamental questions concerning the nature of virtue, which lead to the investigation of all the essential elements of virtue, this division will be treated in three *Chapters*:

Chapter I. The Supreme End of Virtuous Action.

Chapter II. The Supreme Rule of Rightness.

Chapter III. The Ultimate Ground of Rightness, or of Moral Obligation.

CHAPTER I.

SUPREME END OF VIRTUOUS ACTION.

THE fundamental question in deciding the nature of virtue is, What is the supreme end or aim which the agent must have in view in his action, in order that it may be virtuous? What is the end which makes an act moral and binds the agent to its performance?

An End Essential. — It has been seen that the conception of an end, toward which the agent voluntarily directs his action, is essential to moral action. There can be no such thing as rational intention without some end to which it is directed. "An end has been defined to be that for the sake of which an action is done. Hence it has been said to be, *principium in intentione et terminus in exccutione.*" Man sees and understands the connection between means and ends; he determines to attain the ends by the use of the proper means; he deliberately adopts and follows out the rules according to which the end may be attained. It is when he does this that his actions are regarded as rational actions.

Distinction of Ends. — An end may be subordinate or intermediate, ultimate or supreme. A *subordinate* or *intermediate end* is one chosen for the sake of something beyond itself. Such an end becomes simply a means to some further and higher end. An end which is aimed at for its own sake is the *ultimate end* of the actions which are done with a view to it. In case of conflict between two or more ultimate ends, that which ought to be chosen becomes the *supreme end.*

Supreme End Necessary. — "No man in this world," says Gœthe, "can safely live at random: the ship that sails at random will be wrecked even in a calm, and the man who lives at random will be ruined without the help of any positive vices." There must be a controlling, supreme end, if there is to be any unity in the life of the agent.

Moralists are agreed in finding the supreme end of virtuous action in some form of the good.

The Supreme Moral End in the Good. — Christian theologians agree in placing the supreme *religious end* of man in the glory of God. The religious problem then is, — "given, man himself, the world, and the sovereign Creator and Governor of all things, in which to find a supreme end of action." The Creator and Ruler is above everything, and the exhibition of his glory — that is, the exhibition of his glorious attributes of power, wisdom, justice, love, and grace — comprehends in itself the highest good of all the universe. The glory of God is therefore man's chief end as a religious being. But moralists agree that the supreme *moral end* of the agent must be found in some form of the good: in the pleasurable, in the perfect, or in the right. These have already been seen to furnish the possible ends of human action.

The Cardinal Question therefore is, Which form of the good is supreme?

SECTION I.

Theories of the Supreme End.

Out of the answers to the question, Which form of the good is supreme and controlling as the end of moral action? there have arisen three general theories concerning the end and consequent nature of virtuous action: the first makes happi- ness the supreme end of such action; the second, perfection; the third, rightness.

Topic First. First General Theory: Utilitarianism. — The first general theory makes happiness the supreme end of virtuous action. It accounts happiness the highest good of man. It argues that the course of conduct which aims at and secures it is therefore virtuous.

But the happiness idea takes on various forms, and thus gives rise to those various modifications of this general theory, which are included under euthumism and cudæmonism.

Subject 1st.   Euthumism, or the Moral Pleasure Theory. — *Euthumism* is the name given to the theory that the moral pleasure — the peace and cheerfulness of mind and the applause of conscience, enjoyed in virtue — is the proper motive to the practice of virtue; and that the moral pain — the moral shame, self-reproach, remorse, resulting from vice — is the proper dissuadent from vice.

Elements of the View. — Democritus, the Greek, first gave shape to this view. Its advocates hold that this moral pleasure is the highest good. That course of conduct which secures it is right and virtuous. Man is bound to do the right because it will secure him this moral pleasure, and to avoid the wrong because it will insure him this moral pain.

Subject 2d.   Eudæmonism, or the Happiness Theory Proper. — *Eudæmonism* is the name given to the theory that the happiness, or advantage in general, resulting from a virtuous course of conduct is the proper motive for the practice of virtue, and the misery and loss resulting from the opposite course are the proper dissuadents from vice.

Elements of the View. — The advocates of this view hold that happiness or advantage is the highest good of man. That course of conduct which aims at and secures it is virtuous. Man is bound to do right because it will secure this happiness or advantage, and to refrain from doing wrong because it will bring him misery and loss.

The pleasurable or painful experience contemplated by an agent may be that of himself alone, or that of others; and hence arise private and public eudæmonism.

Private Eudæmonism, or Pure Self-Interest. — Private eudæmonism, or self-interest — which regards the happiness or advantage of the individual agent himself as the supreme end to be aimed at in virtuous action — again gives rise to several subordinate views. These may be designated as follows:

Gross Self-Interest, or Hedonism. — In this view happiness is understood in the narrow Epicurean sense — as chiefly bodily, or of the lower appetites.

Refined Self-Interest, or the Old Eudæmonism. — In this view happiness is used in the higher sense of advantage as including enjoyments intellectual and affectional as well as sensual. *Mill.*

Gross Religious Self-Interest, or the Everlasting Happiness Scheme.— In this view happiness is used as including the pleasurable experience of the whole being for time and eternity, and is to be sought by obedience to God. *Paley.*

Refined Religious Self-Interest, or the Holy Blessedness Scheme.— This view makes the happiness aimed at equivalent to holy blessedness. It mingles with happiness — as a subordinate element, however — the idea of moral perfection, and does not consider the lower elements of pleasure worthy of any prominent place. *Pres. Hopkins.*

Public Eudæmonism, or Public Interest. — Public eudæmonism is the name applicable to that view which regards the happiness or advantage of more than the individual agent. This view has several subordinate forms:

Happiness of Mankind.—There are those who regard the happiness or advantage of mankind, or the happiness of the greatest number, as the end of virtuous action.

Happiness of Being.—There are others who make the happiness or advantage of being, or of the universe, the end of virtuous action.

Topic Second. Second General Theory: Perfectionism.— The second general theory makes perfection the supreme end of virtuous action. It regards perfection, or rational completeness of being, as the highest good of man. That course of conduct which seeks to secure it is virtuous, and virtuous because it seeks to secure it.

As there are various ideals of perfection, there arise various modifications of this general theory. Some of these have reference to the individual agent himself, and others to some public reaching beyond himself: hence there are private and public perfectionism.

Subject 1st. Private Perfectionism.—*Private Perfectionism* is that form of the general theory in which the perfection of the agent himself is regarded as the supreme end of virtuous action. It may be looked upon as including various subordinate views:

Perfection of Honor is the designation chosen for that idea of perfection which appeared so prominently in the darkness of the Middle Ages, as embodied in Chivalry. Its law was the law of honor, and it roused man to seek his supreme good in perfecting his active physical courage, his truth, generosity, and courtesy.

Perfection of Culture characterizes the view of those who style themselves the "advanced thinkers" of the present age. The culturists recommend culture — chiefly intellectual — "the one panacea for the ills of humanity" — as the supreme end of virtuous action. *Huxley, Matthew Arnold, Spencer.*

Perfection of the Spiritual Being designates the view which makes the perfection of the agent's own spiritual being the supreme end of virtuous action. Whatever action aims at this is virtuous, and virtuous because it aims at this. No action with any other aim can be virtuous. *Hickok.*

Subject 2d. Public Perfectionism.—*Public Perfectionism* is that form of the general theory which regards the perfection of more than the individual agent. There are various subordinate views:

Public Perfectionism may place the supreme end in the perfection of honor, of culture, or of spiritual being. Under the latter may be found that Christian form of the *disinterested benevolence scheme* which subordinates the happiness or advantage of mankind, and of being in general, to their perfection, and which also subordinates the perfection of the individual to the general perfection of mankind, or of the universe.

Topic Third. Third General Theory: The Rectitude Theory. — The third general theory finds the supreme end of virtuous action in its rightness rather than in its tendency to happiness or to perfection. Rectitude is the highest good of man. That course of conduct which aims to conform to the right is so far virtuous, and virtuous because it aims to do this.

This may be called the Disinterested, or Unselfish Theory of Virtue.— It regards the right as itself the supreme end, and therefore neither needing nor admitting any end beyond itself. If any course of conduct be right, then man's moral nature binds him to follow it, regardless of tendencies or consequences. *Virtue consists in doing the right for its own sake.*

SECTION II.

The True Theory Established.

That the third general theory of the supreme end of virtuous action, or the rectitude theory, is the true one, may be shown, from the general consciousness of mankind; from the nature, sphere, and tendency of virtuous action itself; and from the practical moral necessities of man.

Argument 1st: from General Consciousness.—The response from the general consciousness of men to the question, What is the supreme end in virtuous action? is, that it is rectitude, or rightness itself. Virtuous action, so far as its aim is concerned, consists in doing the right for its own sake, or because it is right. The moment a man is seen to be governed by a supreme regard for his own interests, or for his own ideal, the voice of mankind ceases to pronounce either himself or his conduct virtuous.

Consciousness Consulted.—Why do we judge that we *ought* to worship God? Because it will make us happy? Because it will tend to our perfection? Or, because it is right? Evidently because it is right. Why does the patriot volunteer to enter the war for the defence of his country? Because it will make him happier? True, he will win the approval of conscience in that way, but he risks untold suffering, and perils his life. Because it will advance the perfection of his being? He may come home wrecked in body and mind. Because it is *right*, and therefore obligatory, is the answer of consciousness.

Action not Done because Right is not Virtuous.—Says Dr. Alexander: "When we perceive an action to be virtuous, we are conscious that it is not from any view of the connection of the action with our happiness." And again: "And in many cases virtue requires us to deny ourselves personal gratification for the sake of others. A man supremely governed by a regard to his own interests is never esteemed a virtuous man by the impartial judgment of mankind." Consciousness responds that, so far forth, *virtue consists in doing the right for its own sake.* No action is virtuous which is not done for this supreme end and from this motive. This response of the moral consciousness is *absolutely conclusive* as against all mere theorists.

Argument 2d: from the Nature of Virtuous Actions.—

The first two general theories lose sight of that intrinsic difference between good and evil which is one of the clearest and best established facts of the universe. In the place of immutable rectitude, as the end of virtuous action, they put regard for the happiness, advantage, or culture of self.

Utilitarianism loses Sight of Moral Distinctions.—Utilitarianism merely repeats the empirical ethical philosophy of Aristotle, "putting the element of *eudaimonia* in the van, which he had wisely kept in the rear." "It degrades morality," says Dr. Blackie, "from a manifestation of true expression, pure emotion, and lofty purpose, into a low consideration and a slippery calculation of consequences."

A brief examination of one or two of the higher and more popular forms of utilitarianism will make it plain that they do thus degrade morality.

Gross Religious Self-Interest. — According to Paley, "virtue is the doing good to mankind, in obedience to the will of God, for the sake of everlasting happiness." The *good of mankind* is the object, the *will of God* the rule, and *everlasting happiness* the motive of virtue. Why should we seek the good of mankind? Why make the will of God our rule of conduct? The common answer is, "From a regard to our everlasting happiness." All virtue is thus at once resolved into a supreme regard for one's own happiness. The good man and the bad man alike seek happiness; the only difference is that the former takes a wiser course for securing happiness than the latter.

Says Dr. Blackie: "This definition of Paley characterizes the man, the book, the age, the country, and the profession to which he belonged, admirably. It is a definition that, taken as a matter of fact, in all likelihood expressed the feeling of nine hundred and ninety-nine out of every one thousand British Christians living in these islands in the generation immediately preceding the French Revolution; still, it is a definition which contains *as many errors as it contains clauses.*"

Dr. Blackie is perhaps a little too sweeping in his statement, for the *will of God* has an important relation to virtue; but two of the clauses are certainly erroneous. It can readily be seen that *the doing good to mankind* is not an essential element in the definition; for, however much prominence Christianity gives to works of charity and brotherly kindness, it is certain that "virtue of various kinds may be exercised where no men exist to be the objects of benevolence, as with Adam in Paradise, and Robinson Crusoe in his desert island, and the poet Campbell's

Last Man.'' Benevolence is at the best but one of the forms which virtue may possibly take. Equally false is the clause that teaches that *everlasting happiness is the proper motive to virtuous action.* " It may no doubt be very true, under the relations in which it was spoken, that if in this life only we have hope in Christ we are of all men most miserable; that was a sentence which applied with the most vivid pointedness to St. Paul, and to many others in similar circumstances; but it is very far from furnishing a warrant for the general proposition that the sure expectation of an everlasting reward is a motive necessary for the existence of virtue in this mortal life. For if this really were the case, either the virtue of Socrates was no virtue at all, or a virtue above the standard of any Christian virtue, according to Paley's definition; for Socrates died the death of a martyr, with a very doubtful faith of what might happen to him after death. But, in fact, the prospect of an external reward is *no part of any virtue,* either Christian or heathen,—rather in many cases *would annihilate the very idea of virtue.* To give away ten pounds to-day with a sure expectation of getting a thousand pounds for it to-morrow would be no act of generosity. Aristotle says that ' *a man is bound to be virtuous by the distinctive law of his nature, whether he lives seventy years or seven hundred years;* ' and *Christianity surely ought to say no less." Four Phases of Morals,* pp. 371–3.

Refined Religious Self-Interest.—According to this scheme, the happiness which comes from holy activity is the supreme end contemplated in moral action. The action which secures this happiness this theory teaches to be virtuous because it secures the happiness, while the true theory would teach that it secures the happiness because it is virtuous.

Says President Hopkins: "If we suppose enjoyment, satisfaction, blessedness, to be wholly withdrawn from the universe, we should feel, whatever form of activity there might be, that its value was gone. It would be a vast machine, producing nothing. But if we suppose the highest possible blessedness of God and his universe secured, we are satisfied. It must surely be difficult to satisfy those who cannot find an adequate end in their own highest blessedness, and in the highest blessedness of God and his universe." *Lects. on Mor. Sci.,* p. 54. "Here is the *supreme end :* in the 'enjoyment, satisfaction, blessedness,' of the subject himself, of God, and of the universe. Man and all moral beings are capable, as such, of a high and holy blessedness which can be compared with nothing else, ... but has, in itself, an infinite worth." In his later work (*The Law of Love and Love as a Law*), Pres. Hopkins says (p. 53), "Our supreme good is the joy from holy activity in the love and service of God." The doctrine is the same as that of the earlier volume.

The fundamental error of this view is that of utilitarianism in general. It exalts *happiness* to the place of the supreme good and the supreme end of moral action. It is true that it makes *blessedness*—a higher form of happiness than Paley's—prominent; but that does not exalt it above the *essential selfishness* of all utilitarian schemes. It even lays stress upon *holy* blessedness,—thus seeking to introduce the idea of holiness or perfection along with that of happiness; but even this, while lifting it *in some degree* above Paleyism, cannot change it *in kind*, and so cannot relieve it from the fatal objections which lie against the other forms of the utilitarian philosophy (*Law of Love*, p. 54), for the plain reason that it makes the blessedness the *supreme end*, and persistently gives to perfection only the dignity of a *subordinate end*. In all such theories the intrinsic difference between moral good and moral evil is lost sight of.

Perfectionism loses Sight of Moral Distinctions.—It is equally true that perfectionism loses sight of the ultimate moral distinction of right and wrong. It has already been seen that as an ultimate end of human action perfection is vastly higher than happiness, and that as a guide of human action a sense of the perfect is superior to a mere sense of prudence; but in none of its forms can this idea give the character of *virtue* to the action which flows from it. Man's ideal has no claim to the place of supreme law.

A brief examination of a single form of ethical perfectionism will make it plain that it loses sight of the intrinsic difference between moral good and moral evil. Let it be the highest form of private perfectionism.

Perfection of Spiritual Being.—Says Dr. Hickok (*System of Moral Science*): "Every man has consciously the bond upon him *to do that, and that only, which is due to his spiritual excellency*. . . . . To be worthy of spiritual approbation is the attainment of the highest dignity, and may be called the *subjective* end of ethics, and is a *moral good*. . . . . The *good* is the *being worthy*, not that he is to get something for it. The highest good — the *summum bonum* — is *worthiness of spiritual approbation*" (pp. 42–3). And again (p. 59): "In personal worthiness, as end of all action, every claim centres; and in the attainment and preservation of this all imperatives are satisfied. In this is the ultimate right, inclusive of all rights; and submission to its constraint is that great duty which involves all other duties." And again (p. 54): "Every virtue finds here its end. Why I should be benevolent to man, and why reverent toward God, have each the same end—namely, then, and then only, am I acting according to that which is due to my spirit, and thus worthy of spiritual approbation. God is worthy in himself of my reverent worship and service, but the only way in which that truth can make itself an imperative to me is through my conscience; I must know that I, a finite spirit, debase myself if I do not reverently adore the Absolute Spirit."

It is obvious that the *spiritual worthiness*, which Dr. Hickok makes the supreme end of moral action, is vastly higher than even the highest form of selfishness the ordinary utilitarian can present; but it is only by a self-deification, by making man a god to himself, that it can be made a supreme end. Says a writer, in noticing Dr. Hickok's system (*Princeton Review*, 1854): "This, as we understand the matter, *destroys the very nature of morals.* What I do out of regard to my own dignity can never rise into a sphere of moral excellence. There is on this ground no specific difference between the undignified and the immoral; between folly and wickedness. The very idea of morality is lost, just as effectually (though not in the same disgusting place) as on the utility system. Morality, moreover, involves of necessity obligation or responsibility. This responsibility is not to society, not to reason, not to ourselves, but to God; and it is that which raises it to a higher sphere, and identifies it with piety in its ultimate principle. Without that principle it ceases even to be virtue, or to have in it the nature of moral excellence. In the Scriptures, therefore, — which are not a more perfect revelation of God than they are of our own nature and constitution, — all moral obligations are made to terminate on God, and are enforced by considerations drawn from his being, perfections, will, and work. A perfectly virtuous atheist is an association of ideas which could not exist in Scripture. To do a thing because it is *right* is to do it for an ultimate end infinitely higher than to do it because it ministers to self-approbation; and into the idea of right and responsibility that of a personal God enters as the soul or the life-blood. According to Dr. Hickok, even our reverence to God is obligatory only out of regard to our own spirit. In morality and piety, then, the sole motive comes to be, that we may stand well in our own sight as worthy of spiritual approbation. This cannot be, unless men are God, which Dr. Hickok of course denies as clearly and as strenuously as we do."

The same essential defect is inherent in all the forms of the second general theory, or that which attempts to make perfection the supreme end of moral action. They all lose sight of the true nature of morality.

Argument 3d: from the Sphere of Duty.—Neither of the

ends proposed in the first and second general theories is broad enough to cover the whole ground of human duty. Benevolence, or the tendency to promote happiness, can in no way be made to comprehend all virtue, and the want of it can in no way be made to comprehend all vice. The aim at perfection covers only a portion of the range of duty ; since in its private forms it withdraws attention from God and men to self, and in its public forms usually omits self and God.

Says Bishop Butler: "Benevolence and the want of it, singly considered, are in no sort the whole of virtue and vice. For, if this were the case, in the review of one's own character, or that of others, our moral understanding and moral sense would be indifferent to everything but the degrees in which benevolence prevails, and the degrees in which it was wanting. That is, we should neither approve of benevolence to some persons rather than others, nor disapprove injustice and falsehood, upon any other account, than merely as an overbalance of happiness was foreseen likely to be produced by the first, and misery by the second." But so far is this from being true, that "the fact appears to be, that we are constituted so as to condemn falsehood, unprovoked violence, and injustice, and to approve of benevolence to some rather than others, abstracted from all consideration of which conduct is likely to produce an overbalance of happiness or misery." Much of benevolence, therefore, may not be virtue, and much of virtue is not benevolence.

In like manner, even if it should be admitted that all that which the agent does to secure his *ideal of perfection* is virtuous, it may readily be seen that there is a great part of virtuous action which is done without any reference to this end.

Neither happiness nor perfection, as a supreme end of moral action, is therefore broad enough to take in the whole of man's duty.

Argument 4th: from Confounding Tendency with End. —

The first and second general theories confound the tendencies, or results, or consequences, of moral action, with the end or aim of it. Virtue doubtless tends to produce both happiness and perfection, but its end or aim is the right and not the happiness nor the completeness of being.

Virtue tends to Produce Happiness and Perfection. — There is a divinely imparted tendency in virtue to produce happiness and perfection, and a like tendency in vice to produce misery and ruin. Or, in other words, God has made his world and carries on his government of it in favor of righteousness and right, and therefore all the forces of the universe are pledged against and directed against the wrong and unrighteous. While, therefore, virtuous action may not be done *for* happiness or perfection, in any of their forms, it is true that such action uniformly results, in the long run, in both happiness and perfection.

But neither Happiness nor Perfection is the Supreme End in Virtuous Action. — When ethical writers attempt to put happiness or perfection in the place of right as the *end* or *motive* of moral action, they confound *tendencies* or *results* with the moral *end*. Says Dr. Alexander (*Mor. Sci.*, p. 161): "That true happiness is the natural effect of virtue falls entirely short of proof that the *essence* of virtue consists in the *tendency* of certain actions to the person's true interests." The same is true as against the *perfection theory.* Moreover, it is a well established moral principle, that the man who exalts what is really a subordinate end into a supreme end *utterly fails of attaining that subordinate end.* Says Dr. Newman: "In the gospel kingdom is evinced a remarkable law of ethics, which is well known to all who have given their minds to the subject. All virtue and goodness tend to make men powerful in this world; but they who aim at the power have not the virtue. Again, virtue is its own reward, and brings with it the truest and highest pleasures; but they who cultivate it for the pleasure's sake are selfish, not religious, and will never gain the pleasure, because they never can have the virtue."

Argument 5th: from the Practical Necessities of Man. — To adopt either the first or second general theory of the supreme end of moral action is to throw away the only plain and practical rule of life — the rule furnished by the right. The question asked concerning any act, Is this act right? may ordinarily be answered without difficulty by the simplest person; because right and wrong are intuitive ideas, and a standard of right and wrong has been put in man's constitution; but the question, What will be the tendency of this act, or its results? will often require Omniscience to answer it.

Expediency and Perfection give Incomprehensible Rules of Life. — When happiness is considered the supreme end, the rule is, "Do what is expedient." But it is what is expedient, upon the whole, in the long run; not for one, but for all, and forever. Such a rule cannot be comprehended, nor acted on, by a being like man. In the language of Dr. Samuel Johnson, "It presupposes more knowledge of the universal system than man has attained," or ever can attain. "In instances the most level to our capacities," says another writer, "we perceive no more than a part of the effects which may result from our conduct; a part, perhaps, which, in point either of extent or importance, bears no assignable proportion to that which remains unseen." "As well might a man determine," says Dr. Dwight, "that a path, whose direction he can discover only for a furlong, will conduct him in a straight course to a city, distant from him a thousand miles, as to determine that an action, whose immediate tendency he perceives to be useful, will, therefore, be useful through a thousand years, or even through ten. How much less able must he be to perceive what will be its real tendency in the remote ages of endless duration." Says Fleming: "God may consult for the happiness of the universe, or of the world, for he knows in what that happiness consists, and how to promote it. But, to a feeble and short-sighted being like a man, some more comprehensible rule than that of universal expediency is necessary."

The same considerations apply in the main to the *perfect* as to the *expedient*. It could offer only an incomprehensible rule.

The Right, in Contrast with Happiness and Perfection, gives a Simple Rule of Life.—The question, Is any act right? may ordinarily be answered without difficulty by the simplest person, because the moral ideas are intuitive. The question, What will be the tendency of any act, or the results? will often require Omniscience to answer it. God has, therefore, dealt beneficently with man in making the right the supreme end of moral action. It has been shown that were happiness made the supreme end, there would be required in the moral agent intellectual capabilities for the calculation of consequences, such as would make man equal to God in this respect; so that happiness would be an impossible end to be aimed at by man.

Following perfection as the supreme end would involve capabilities of forming a high and complete ideal, such as the mass of mankind could not possibly possess. In short, it would involve such knowledge of the nature of man, of the nature of God, and of the laws of the universe, as would only be within the reach of a God. In making the right the supreme end, Omniscience has provided for the plain and ignorant man,—so that even without the all-embracing reach of intellect he need not miss of attaining to virtue, to perfection, and to happiness.

The conclusion from this discussion of the supreme end of moral action is, therefore, that the end is found in rightness alone. No action can be formally right, or right in its form, that has not the right as its end or aim.

CHAPTER II.

THE SUPREME RULE OF RIGHTNESS.

HAVING ascertained that rightness is the supreme end of moral action, or that at which the agent is morally bound to aim in his conduct, the question arises, What is rightness?

In general, rightness in action implies conformity to some law or standard, which furnishes the supreme rule of human conduct.

Nature of Rightness. — The right (*rectus*) is that which is *ruled*, or *straight*, according to some rule or standard. *Ethics* and *morals* both imply in their very origin and etymology a *way*, or *law*, guiding and governing human conduct, and therefore, of course, controlling moral conclusions. In all the workings of the moral nature there is recognized or implied a moral law under which the agent is placed, and which he is bound to obey. Rightness is found in *obligatory conformity to this law.*

If rightness consists in obligatory conformity of the conduct to some supreme rule of right, the question next arises, What is the supreme rule of rightness? What is the rule by which actions are to be decided to be right or wrong, to be morally binding or the opposite?

The answer to this question will be considered in two *Sections:*

Section 1.   Unsatisfactory Theories of the Supreme Rule.
Section 2.   The True Theory of the Supreme Rule.

Distinction of Rules. — Rules of action may be subordinate or supreme. The supreme rule is the one which has the right of control, as against all subordinate rules, in all cases of conflict. The will of God,

e. g., is a supreme rule of conduct: the will of parents, the will of church authorities, the will of national governments, furnish subordinate rules to this one supreme rule.

Importance of the Question. — The importance of the question, What is the supreme rule? is apparent from the fact that the height of a moral theory, and of the conduct resulting from its application, must depend upon the elevation of the supreme rule adopted by the agent. Both the theory and the conduct of the culturist are vastly higher than those of the Epicurean because the supreme rule of the former is almost inconceivably higher than that of the latter.

SECTION I.

Unsatisfactory Theories of the Supreme Rule.

Moralists have advanced various theories concerning what constitutes the supreme rule of right. A brief view of some of the false or defective theories will prepare the way for a better understanding of the true theory. Some of these find the rule without man, others within him.

Topic First. First General Theory: the Authority of the State the Supreme Rule. — Some hold that the supreme standard of moral obligation is found in the authority of the state. Man must live in civil society. The state, in conserving the public welfare, necessarily makes its laws, which every citizen is bound to obey. The law as found in the statute-books is thus the supreme rule of right and ground of moral obligation.

This is the Theory of Hobbes, already noticed as one of the forms of experientialism. According to this view, "no one has a right to go back of the law and judge it by some imaginary standard; the civil authority is ultimate, and the citizen has nothing to do but to obey. The whole duty, where the state has legislated, is to read the law and act accordingly." That is right which is in accordance with the law; that is wrong which is not in accordance with it. In different communities or states, things precisely opposite may at the same time be right. This evidently destroys all essential moral distinctions. If a state legalizes murder, that is right; and so of every other crime. In a Mormon state polygamy is right; in an antimormon state it is wrong.

The doctrine of Hobbes was but a revival of ancient sophistries which had been exploded ages before by Plato and Cicero. Prof. Bowen (*Metaphysics and Ethics*, p. 14) justly says, that his "philosophy is now a by-word from its degrading principles, and its tendencies to selfishness in morals, to materialism in philosophy, and to despotism in politics."

Topic Second. Second General Theory: The Nature of Things the Supreme Rule.

The supreme standard of right and of moral obligation is found in the nature of things, say some. But moralists differ very greatly respecting what it is in the nature of things that furnishes the standard by which moral obligation is to be decided.

The Fitness in Things Themselves: — e. g., in love and honor toward parents. Dr. Clarke taught, "that, from the eternal and necessary differences of things, there naturally and necessarily arise certain moral obligations, which are of themselves incumbent on all rational creatures, antecedent to all positive institution and to all expectation of reward and punishment." Having thus taught that actions have a nature or character antecedent to all will or law, he maintained that this nature or character arises from the congruity between certain actions and certain relations; which relations are founded on the eternal and necessary differences of things. *This congruity as perceived by reason* furnishes the supreme rule of human conduct. That course of conduct which is decided by this rule to be fit and reasonable is right, that which is not fit and reasonable is wrong.

The Truth of Things. — There is a truth in everything, which obligates men to regard and treat everything according to its nature: e. g., man is a rational being, and therefore ought to be treated as such. Wollaston taught that those propositions are true which express things as they are. A true proposition may be denied, or things may be denied to be what they are, by deeds as well as by words. When a man lives as if he had an amount of income which he has not, or as if he were in other respects what he is not, he does wrong. He lives a lie. The supreme rule of human conduct is therefore *truth*. Whatever action denies the truth is wrong; whatever action conforms to it is right.

The Relations of Things. — There exist certain relations between things, and in these existing relations is to be found the supreme standard of right and ground of obligation. The instant man knows the relations he sees the duties involved in them. "It is manifest to every one," says Dr. Wayland, "that we all stand in various and dissimilar relations to all the sentient beings, created and uncreated, with which we are acquainted. Among our relations to created beings are those of man to man, or that of substantial equality, of parent and child, of benefactor and recipient, of husband and wife, of brother and sister, citizen and citizen, citizen and magistrate, and a thousand others." The Infinite Being stands to us in the relation of Creator, Preserver, Benefactor, Lawgiver, and Judge; and we stand to him in the relation of dependent, helpless, ignorant, and sinful creatures. As soon as a human being comprehends any of these relations, "there arises in his mind a consciousness of moral obligation, connected, by our Creator, with the very conception of this relation." These relations are thus the rule and measure of obligation. Conformity to them is right; want of conformity to them is wrong.

The Completeness of All Being. — There is a fitness in the union and agreement of each being with the great whole of being, in which the essence of virtue consists. Edwards taught that "true virtue most essentially consists in benevolence to being in general. Or, perhaps, to speak more accurately, it is that consent, propensity, and union of heart, to being in general, that is immediately exercised in a general good will." Benevolence becomes thus the supreme rule of human conduct. That action which is benevolent is right; that action which is without benevolence is wrong.

Topic Third. Third General Theory: The Nature of Man gives the Supreme Rule.

— The supreme standard of moral obligation is found in something in the nature of man, say some. Moralists hold different views respecting what that something in man's nature is which binds him to the right.

An Immediate Intellectual Intuition. — According to Kant, the conscience is simply the power of perceiving by intellectual intuition the great moral principles which constitute man's supreme law. It is absolutely infallible. "An erring conscience is a chimera." Says Calderwood, following Kant, "Conscience is a faculty which, from its very nature, cannot be educated. Education, either in the sense of instruction or of training, is impossible. As well propose to teach the eye, how and what to see: and the ear, how and what to hear: as to teach reason how to perceive the self-evident, and what truths are of this nature. All these have been provided for in the human constitution." This provision in the conscience furnishes the supreme rule of right.

An Inner Sense, or Feeling, which gives Moral Distinctions. — Shaftesbury taught that there is a peculiar faculty of the mind whose office it is to perceive moral distinctions, and to this faculty he gave the name of the *moral sense.* Hutcheson seized upon this idea and made it the basis of his moral system. Hume carried this view to its extreme results, making virtue and vice purely matters of taste or sentiment. As "tastes and colors, and all other sensible qualities, lie not in the bodies, but merely in the senses ;" so right and wrong do not denote any independent quality in any object thus designated, but only an effect or sensation produced in our own minds. The agent's moral sense, or power of perceiving moral distinctions, is the supreme rule of moral conduct. That is right which conforms to this moral sense; that is wrong which does not.

The Moral Emotions. — Dr. Thomas Brown derives our notions of right and wrong from our moral emotions. "We have a susceptibility of moral emotions; and the emotions spring directly from the contemplation of actions, without any exercise of judgment or comparison, by which the actions are referred to any previous notions of right or wrong." These moral emotions furnish the supreme rule of right.

- **The Inherent Spiritual Worthiness, or Excellency of Man,** furnishes the supreme rule of right, according to Dr. Hickok.

SECTION II.

True Theory of the Supreme Rule.

The will of God is the supreme standard that decides moral obligation. That is right and obligatory which conforms to the will of God ; and that is wrong, and ought not to be done, which does not conform to his will.

The subject will be considered under two *Topics :*
Topic 1st.   The True Theory Confirmed.
Topic 2d.   The Three Revelations Considered.

Topic First. The True Theory Confirmed. — That the theory, that the will of God is the supreme rule of moral obligation, is the true theory, may be shown from the mutual relations of God and man ; from man's moral consciousness ;

from man's moral conduct; and from contrast with the unsatisfactory views.

Argument 1st: from Mutual Relations of God and Man.— God, as the infinitely wise, beneficent, and holy Creator and Upholder of the world and everything in it, is of right the Moral Governor of the world and of man as in the world. The supreme rule by which man's conduct is to be regulated must therefore be the will of God, the Supreme Governor.

Theism at the Basis.— It has already been seen that the theistic theory of the world is involved in a system of Christian ethics. Man believes in God, is dependent on him, is consciously subject to God as his Governor and accountable to him as his Judge, and finds in God the true end of his being. Holding such relations to God, it is evident that he can find the supreme rule of his conduct only in the will of God.

Argument 2d: from the Moral Consciousness.— The argument includes two cases: where there is no direct and conscious reference of the moral conduct to the will of God; and where there is such reference.

Where there is no conscious reference of the moral conduct to the will of God as the standard of moral obligation, and even where there is no clear and definite knowledge of God, the sense of responsibility — which has been observed as one of the facts of man's moral nature, necessarily involved in the idea of moral obligation — is itself the recognition of the rule of the Supreme Governor.

When, in the course of experience and development, the idea of God springs up into full consciousness, so that there may be a direct and conscious reference of the moral conduct to him, man cannot but feel that it is the duty of all intelligent creatures to be conformed to the divine will.

First Case.— Says Dr. Alexander: "As soon as we get the idea of God, we cannot but feel that it is the duty of all creatures to be conformed to his will. But if the question be whether, in judging an action to be virtuous, it is necessary to consider distinctly of its conformity to the will of God, we are of opinion that this conception is not necessary to enable us to perceive that certain actions are morally good and others morally evil. In order to this judgment nothing is required but a knowledge of the circumstances and motives of the action. Even the atheist cannot avoid the conviction that particular actions are praiseworthy, and others deserving blame." The conduct of mankind therefore implies the recognition of this supreme place of the will of God, even where there is not a clear and positive recognition of God himself.

Second Case. — Belief in God, however, adds great force to the dictates of conscience. As soon as the moral agent gets the idea of God, he cannot but feel that it is the duty of all rational creatures to be conformed to his will; and as the idea of God grows in clearness, this conviction of rightful subjection to his will as the supreme rule of conduct increases in fulness and power.

Argument 3d: from Man's Moral Conduct.

— In the conduct — individual, social, and religious — of the good and the bad, in all conditions of society, and in all ages of the world, there is evidence that man was made to refer his conduct to the will of God as the supreme rule of right and obligation.

Belief in God and Responsibility. — Historically, the conviction that God exists has shown itself beyond all others indestructible and cumulative. Equally indestructible has the conviction of responsibility to God shown itself. No condition of society in any age of the world has ever been able to destroy it from the souls of men. The good have always rejoiced to proclaim it, and those most given to vice have borne witness to virtue and the supreme rule by condemning themselves.

Argument 4th: from Contrast with Unsatisfactory Theories.

— The theory that the will of God is the supreme rule of right has the advantage over the other theories, inasmuch as the will of God furnishes a definite, decisive, comprehensible, and practical standard of rectitude.

The Other Theories Fail. — It will be seen that the other general theories of the supreme rule of right fail in some or all of these respects. The *first theory* — that the authority of the state furnishes the supreme rule — takes away the very nature of right, by making it a changeable thing, dependent upon human laws, which may be modified or reversed at any time. The *second theory* — that something in the nature of things furnishes the supreme rule — gives an indefinite, incomprehensible, and impracticable standard. Man is a finite being, and not capable of grasping and understanding in any adequate degree the eternal reason and fitness of things, the truth of things, or the completeness of being. The *third theory*, in its extreme form, makes rightness depend upon mere human opinion or sentiment, and so removes everything like a decisive standard. It makes right and wrong vary with man's education or with his moods.

The True Theory does not Fail. — The will of the unchangeable God furnishes a definite, decisive standard of right. It will be seen from the revelations made of that will that it also furnishes a comprehensible and thoroughly practical standard for man's guidance.

Topic Second. The Three Revelations Considered. — The will of God as the supreme rule of right is found expressed in the moral constitution of the world; in the moral constitution of the agent himself; and in the moral system of the Holy Scriptures.

Three Forms Admitted. — Christians generally admit the existence of these three forms of revelation of the divine will. Some, however, are disposed to undervalue the *light of nature,* or the moral teaching derived from the first two sources. The deist, on the other hand, overestimates the light of nature, and denies all value to the revelation of God's will in the Scriptures.

It could be readily shown that these three copies of the will of God are from the same divine Mind. The same fundamental moral principles and tendencies are embodied in all of them.

Subject 1st. Revelation in External Nature. — Man discerns but dimly, and interprets with difficulty, the revelation of the will of God in the constitution of the world. He needs both the light of conscience and of revelation to aid him in reading it.

God's Will as Moral Law Revealed in Nature. — It is true that the moralist may know something of the will of God from the constitution of external nature. The government of God is so carried on that there is clearly a fixed connection between virtue and happiness, and between vice and misery. God thus testifies to his approval of virtue and to his disapproval of vice. These moral tendencies are *universal,*— being observed everywhere in creation and providence, and in individual and social experience. They are *inevitable,*— vice in the long run producing misery, and virtue happiness, by a law as unchangeable as the law of gravitation. Plato puts in the mouth of the Sophist Hippias, in his discussion with Socrates, this remarkable language: "Now, by Jove, I must confess that I here do see plain traces of a Divine law; for that laws should bring along with them their own penalty when broken, is a most rare device, to which no mere human legislator has ever yet been able to attain." No profound and right-thinking man can fail to recognize in God's universe a vast and wondrous *system of moral compensation* and *moral retribution*, embracing all the subjects of the Divine government.

This Revelation not Easily Interpreted. — But it is evident that the will of God as expressed in this form is vastly more difficult of interpretation than when expressed in the two other forms. While it is abundantly true that the invisible things of God — his *eternal power* and *Deity* — are in some degree made known by the things that are seen; it is true, on the other hand, that man with his present faculties, in his present condition, and without any light from other sources, can find only a dim record of God's *moral attributes* and of his *moral law* in the tendencies of the outer world. Even the most incomplete view of the rule of right could be gained from this source, only by a philosophy too high and a reasoning too complicated to be within the reach of the majority of mankind.

The Revelation Comparatively Unimportant Considered Alone. — At the best, and considered alone, the law as expressed in the world can do but a very little toward making clearer the inner law of conscience. It needs both the light of conscience and of revelation for its own interpretation. The pretensions of the modern deists to be able to deduce a perfect law of conduct from the light of nature — exclusive of the light of conscience — are as baseless as possible. What of value has found its way into their moral codes has been chiefly taken, consciously or unconsciously, from the higher revelations of God.

Subject 2d. Revelation in Man's Nature.

Subject 2d. Revelation in Man's Nature.— The revelation of the will of God in man's moral constitution was originally perfect and clear, but is now defective and dim, except as corrected by the Christian system. Nevertheless, it must still be the immediate and practical rule of right for the guidance of man.

This Revelation was once Perfect, but is now Defective. — That there is such an inner law in man's constitution has already been shown. That it was originally perfect may be inferred from the nature of its Creator, and from the necessity of such moral perfection to the completeness of man's nature. That it is now defective and dim is made equally clear both by the observation and experience of every man, and by the teachings of revelation.

This the Immediate and Practical Rule. — A rule of right, in order to be in the highest sense *practical*, must be *always at hand* and in *readable form*. For a being essentially and always active, the emergencies of moral action must be constant, and often sudden and unexpected, so that time is not always given for consulting some outward rule to be comprehended by the processes of reasoning. The Author of man's being has, therefore, placed a revelation of the rule of right in the soul, to be read intuitively, and so to furnish a practical guide suited to his circumstances.

Observation and experience show this inner rule to be still the chief practical guide of moral conduct for mankind in general. "Within certain limits," says Prof. Haven, "the moral nature of man decides without hesitation as to the character of given actions, and approves and condemns accordingly. It is seldom at a loss as to the great dividing lines which separate the kingdom of right and wrong. It is the voice of nature, essentially the same in all climes and ages of the world, approving the right, condemning the wrong. It is the voice of God speaking through the moral nature and constitution which he has bestowed upon his creatures. Thus it is, that they which have not the law (written) 'are a law unto themselves.' "

Other revelations of the will of God become of practical value as they aid in reconstructing or correcting and completing this inner and immediate practical rule of right.

Subject 3d. The Revelation in Scriptures.—The third form of the revelation of God's will as the supreme rule for the guidance of man's moral conduct is that made in the moral system embodied in the Sacred Scriptures. This appeals to the moral consciousness of mankind — especially of enlightened and good men — as the most perfect expression of the law of human duty.

In bringing to light new relations, as arising out of man's sin, the ethical system of the Bible has vastly widened the sphere of duty; and in the Christian nations has cleared and greatly modified the revelation of the supreme rule in the human soul.

Originally no Written Rule Needed.—Unfallen man may have needed no written rule of right; but in his present condition there arises a necessity for a written revelation, to make clear the pathway of duty and of life, and to bring to bear upon him the most powerful motives to obedience and right life.

The Law in the Scriptures. — In the Scriptures is accordingly found the grandest revelation of the rule of right, and the strongest possible motives, drawn from the present and the future life, to conform to that rule. The revelation makes duty clear. The doctrines of immortality and of accountability, of retribution and reward, furnish most powerful incentives to obedience. The infinite condescension and grace of God in redemption add new obligations, far surpassing in their constraining force all those arising out of creation and providence.

This Written Revelation is the Perfect Form of the Supreme Rule. — It is this because it is the clearest expression of the divine will. Moreover, both observation and experience teach us that every life fashioned by any other rule is morally incomplete and imperfect. The advocates of the natural code of morals — or that drawn from nature in the constitution of the external world and the soul — habitually ignore or neglect the highest aspects of duty, and can therefore reach only an essentially incomplete manhood. Ignoring the higher relations of spirit, they confine man's conduct to the sphere of earthly vocations, and in so doing they take out all the higher elements of even the merely earthly morality.

Conclusion.

The conclusion from the discussion of the supreme rule of rightness is, then, that this rule is found in the will of God, the Supreme Governor. No action can be materially right, or right in its matter, that does not conform to this supreme rule.

CHAPTER III.

THE ULTIMATE GROUND OF MORAL OBLIGATION.

THE question next arises, What is the ultimate ground on which the supreme rule rests? Why is the right, as revealed in the supreme rule, morally binding upon man?

It is obvious that this question requires that the *rule*, and the *reason* for the rule, be carefully distinguished. The supreme rule in its perfect form declares what is absolutely right and obligatory; the reason why its requirements are right and obligatory is to be found in something back of the rule itself.

The Rule and the Reason Distinguished. — There is a difference between a *rule* and the *reason* of a rule; between a *law* and the *principle* of a law, which must be understood in this connection. "Law," says Fleming, "is an *exposition*, not an *origination*, of duty. The law *declares* what is right, but does not *constitute* anything right." The supreme *rule* in its perfect form declares what is absolutely right; the *reason* why its requirements are right must be sought in something else. Much of confusion and controversy has arisen from the failure to make this distinction.

Various views have been held concerning the ultimate ground of the obligation of the supreme rule. There is need of a brief presentation of some of the more important of the incorrect views, and also of the correct theory. These will be given in the following *Sections:*

Section 1. Incorrect Theories of the Ground of Moral Obligation.

Section 2. Correct Theories of the Ground of Moral Obligation.

SECTION I.

Incorrect Theories of the Ground of Moral Obligation.

Various incorrect views have been held on this subject. The chief among these are the two following: that which bases moral obligation in the nature of things; and that which bases it in the arbitrary will of God.

Topic First. First General Theory: the Nature of Things. — It is affirmed by some moralists that the supreme rule is morally binding on man, because it is in accordance with the eternal and immutable nature of things. This nature of things is beyond all control of the Moral Governor, and, indeed, controls him. The supreme rule of right as resting on this basis is therefore alike binding upon God, man, and all other moral beings in the universe.

View Stated. — Says Prof. Haven: "Right and wrong are distinctions immutable and inherent in the nature of things. They are not the creations of expediency, nor of law; nor yet do they originate in the divine character. They have no origin; they are as eternal as the throne of Deity; they are immutable as God himself. Nay, were God himself to change, these distinctions would change not. Omnipotence has no power over them, but they make law. They are the source and spring of all obligation. Reason points out these distinctions; the moral nature recognizes and approves them. God's law, and will, and nature, are in conformity to these distinctions; else that law were not just and right, nor that nature holy."

The View Denied. — This view is at once contrary to the true conception of God and of the constitution of things. It originates in the attempt to "understand the Almighty unto perfection," and to measure completely his universal system with the yardstick of man's reason. According to this hypothesis, there is something back of God which shapes all his course in spite of himself — a modern *fate*. The Deity becomes a mere figure-head in his universe. On the contrary, it is obvious that according to the Christian system God is himself at the foundation of all things, — the Creator, Orderer, and Controller of all things material and moral. Man is neither competent to think him out of his universe, nor to think him different from what he is, nor to reconstruct the universe with God left out.   God is at least *as eternal and immutable as morality.   There is no nature of things except that which God has constituted.*   Right and wrong are doubtless inherent in this the only existing nature of things.

Topic Second. Second General Theory: the Arbitrary Will of God. — It is affirmed by some moralists that the supreme rule is morally binding on man simply because it is the expression of the arbitrary will of God.   The simple fact that it is an expression of God's will makes the supreme rule obligatory, whatever its requirements.

The View Inconsistent. — From the very nature of God as an infinitely wise and perfect being there can be no arbitrary will of God. To attribute arbitrary purposes to a Being of infinite wisdom and love is to bring him down to the level of fallen humanity, and to give him an attribute which belongs even to man only as he is a fallen being. The will of God is the expression of his infinite being and perfect character.   The reasons may not always be known to us why God wills that man should do some particular act, but so far as he has seen fit to reveal the grounds of his requirements they uniformly commend themselves to right reason.   God never has done, and never can do, an unreasonable and arbitrary deed, and he never has made, and never can make, an unreasonable and arbitrary requirement.

SECTION II.

Correct Theory of the Ground of Obligation.

The will of God as the expression of his perfect character is the ultimate ground, or reason, why the requirements of the supreme rule are right and binding.   The true statement is, therefore, that the supreme rule is right and obligatory because it is the expression of God's will, and this again the expression of God's character.   The true relation is, that God's character or nature, as wise, benevolent, and holy, requires this rule, and therefore his will enacts it.

The Objection. — It is objected: " If right or wrong depend ultimately on the character of God, then we have only to suppose God to change,

11

or to have been originally other than he is, and our duties and obligations change at once; — that which was a virtue, becomes a crime; that which was a crime, is transformed into a virtue. Had he been precisely the reverse of which he is, he had still been, as now, the source of right, and his own character would have been as truly good, and just, and right as it is now."

The Answer. — In reply, it need only be reiterated that the supposition of such a change in God is an *impossible,* not to say *blasphemous, supposition;* and that the human intellect is not competent to decide what *must* be, or even *would* be, if such a supposition were to be admitted. Says Dr. Hodge: "The common doctrine of Christians on this subject is, that the will of God is the ultimate ground of moral obligation to all rational creatures. No higher reason can be assigned why anything is right than that God commands it. This means, (1) That the divine will is the only rule for deciding what is right and what is wrong; (2) That his will is that which binds us, or that to which we are bound to be conformed. By the word 'will' is not meant any arbitrary purpose, so that it were conceivable that God should will right to be wrong, or wrong right. The will of God is the expression or revelation of his nature, or is determined by it; so that his will, as revealed, makes known to us what infinite wisdom and goodness demand. Sometimes things are right simply because God has commanded them; as circumcision and other ritual institutions were to the Jews. Other things are right because of the present constitution of things which God has ordained: such as the duties relating to property, and the permanent relations of society. Others, again, are right because they are demanded by the immutable excellence of God. In all cases, however, so far as we are concerned, it is his will that binds us, and constitutes the difference between right and wrong; his will, that is, as the expression of his infinite perfection. *So that the ultimate foundation of moral obligation is the nature of God."* Dr. Hodge, *Systematic Theology,* Vol. I., p. 406.

DIVISION III.

PHILOSOPHY OF THE LIFE OF DUTY.

Statement and Subdivision.

THE facts of man's moral constitution, and the essential nature of virtue, having been investigated in the two preceding Divisions of Theoretical Ethics, it remains to present the philosophy of the life of duty, as ascertained or determined by the preceding investigations.

Division III. will therefore properly unfold the philosophy of that complete moral manhood to which the Moral Governor has called the human agent, and of that complete moral task which he has assigned him.

The vital questions with man as a moral agent are: What is the full mission of duty? What are the natural requisites to its fulfilment? What is rendered necessary by the moral disorder of human nature? The answers to these questions will be considered in three *Chapters*:

Chapter I.   The True Conception of Human Duty.

Chapter II.   The Natural Requisites for the Life of Duty.

Chapter III.   The Requisite Moral Reconstruction.

CHAPTER I.

THE TRUE CONCEPTION OF HUMAN DUTY.

Statement and Subdivision.

IT has been seen that there are two aspects in which the action of the moral agent may be regarded: as single, isolated dutiful, or virtuous acts; and as one entire life of duty, or virtue. A true theory of human duty must present a consistent view of moral agency in both these aspects. They will therefore furnish the subjects of the following *Sections*:

Section 1. The True Idea of a Virtuous or Dutiful Action.
Section 2. The True Idea of the Life of Virtue, or of Duty.

SECTION I.

The True Idea of a Virtuous Action.

The decision whether any particular action is virtuous or not must depend upon the answers to the two questions: Was the action materially right, or in accordance with the supreme rule? Was it formally right, or did the agent intend the right?

The answers to these questions, as determined by the investigations of the two preceding Divisions, will be given in the following *Topics*.

The Two Vital Questions. — One question always asked in judging an agent's conduct is, What end had he in view? This is put in various forms: What was his *aim, purpose, motive, intention?* There are those who teach that the end, or intention, solely and wholly decides the character of any action. The end had in view by the agent is certainly a very important element in deciding the moral character of his action; but no amount of honesty of purpose on the part of Paul could have made his persecution of the early Christians virtuous. In their practical judgments, men go still further, and ask not only, What was the agent's intention? but also, Was his action right? They recognize thus an *essential rectitude,* which presupposes a reference of the conduct to the supreme rule.

Topic First.   A Virtuous Action must be Materially Right.—It has been made evident that action, in order to be virtuous, must be in accordance with the requirements of the supreme rule, wherever that rule prescribes a course of action.

There is a wide range of action *in which the right course is definitely prescribed* by some revelation of the will of God. This moralists call *essentially moral action.* Action agreeing with this prescribed rule is *materially right.*

There is another wide range of action *in which no course has been prescribed* by the Moral Governor. This moralists call *morally indeterminate,* or *indifferent, action,* i. e., action which, in itself considered, is neither right nor wrong.

The first of these kinds of action is properly to be considered under the present *Topic;* the second, under the next *Topic.*

There are three classes of essentially moral requirements, determined by the permanence of the human relations for which they are prescribed, and giving rise to three classes of materially right actions.

First Class of Materially Right Actions.—There are permanent and eternal relations of the moral agent, which arise out of the very natures of God and man, and for which God has prescribed immutable laws.

Everlasting Relations.—The very nature of God as man's Creator and Lord makes it eternally obligatory on man, that he should love God supremely; that he should be just, merciful, and kind to God's creatures; and that he should preserve and make the most of his own being and powers. It is impossible for man to conceive of any such change

11 *

in his relation to God the Moral Governor as would release him from subjection to these principles of the supreme rule. Ingratitude to God, or blasphemy, can never become right in any circumstances nor in any moral being. The opposites must eternally be materially right.

Second Class of Materially Right Actions.—There are relations of the moral agent, which arise out of the constitution of this world, which God has seen fit to ordain shall last during man's present state of existence, and for which he has prescribed laws which must be binding upon the agent during his continuance in this present life.

Life Relations. — To this class of relations belong those arising out of property, the family, the state, and the race. The infinitely wise, beneficent, and holy character of God, as expressed in the present constitution of things, makes it obligatory upon man that, so long as these present relations remain, he should obey the moral principles prescribed for the regulation of his conduct in these relations. In some other state of existence this constitution of things may be changed, and these relations and the laws prescribed for them may cease to exist; but until that time obedience to them is and must be materially right.

Third Class of Materially Right Actions.— There are temporary relations of the moral agent, which may arise out of altogether peculiar circumstances and positions, into which the Moral Governor may see fit to bring individuals, or society, or the nation, and for which that Governor has prescribed laws which are binding only so long as these circumstances continue the same.

Temporary Relations.—To this class belong many of the regulations prescribed in the Old Testament Scriptures for the guidance of the Israelites in the fulfilment of their peculiar mission. The laws, e. g., which prohibited them from intimate connection and intercourse with foreign nations, were intended to preserve them from the false religions of those nations until the world-religion which God had committed to them should be fully developed and established. When this had been accomplished, the special laws ceased to be binding. While they remained in those peculiar circumstances, it could not but continue to be wrong for the Jews to eat swine's flesh, etc.; since this would bring them into intercourse with the idolatrous races, would lead to their moral ruin, and, above all, would imperil the true religion which had been committed to their charge. The character of God, as entering into all such temporary moral enactments, and furnishing their basis, makes it binding upon man that he should regard them so long as the peculiar relations in which they have their origin continue. So long it is and must be materially right to obey them.

Topic Second. Virtuous Action must be Intentionally, or Formally, Right.— It has been shown that moral action must be right in its motive, or aim, or intention. Virtue has therefore been defined to be intentional conformity to the rule of right because of its rightness. Moralists call that action, which is intentionally conformed to the right, *formally right*, or right in its form.

The various relations of human action to moral law and moral ends give rise to several classes of actions which need to be distinguished.

Subject 1st. Prescribed Moral Action and Intention.— Where the course to be pursued by the moral agent is prescribed by some revelation of the will of God, the action in order to be virtuous must be right in itself, or conformable to the prescribed rule, and must be done with the intention of doing right.

Legally, but not Intentionally, Right.— Strictly legal, or materially right, action is not virtuous, unless it is also formally right. The Pharisees gave much alms to the poor: that conduct was in accordance with the prescribed rule of right; but there was no virtue in it, since they gave with the intention of winning the applause of man, and not with the aim of doing right. A rich man gives a large sum of money for the founding of some charitable or benevolent institution: the act is materially right; but if it be done to perpetuate his own name, there is no virtue in it. Mere *legality*, without reference to the moral intention, is not enough to make action virtuous.

Intentionally, but not Legally, Right.— Action, even if done with the right intention, is not virtuous if it be materially wrong. No action which is materially wrong, and known to be so, can become virtuous. To give away what is not our own does not become right by our intention to show kindness. The intention, or motive, of an agent is only part of an action, where the action is prescribed by the moral law. The intention has its own character of rightness or wrongness, but the rightness of the intention cannot be transfused into the *matter* of an action which is of a different character. No amount of *good intention* can make atheism, or blasphemy, or murder, right and virtuous.

Subject 2d. Morally Indifferent Action and Intention.— In accordance with the foregoing principles, the agent may make his action, in itself morally indifferent, right and virtuous by performing it with the view of attaining some right moral end; and he may make it wrong and vicious by directing it to some wrong moral end. The agent may make all the action of his entire life virtuous by strictly subordinating it to right moral ends.

The Whole Work of Life may become Virtuous.—The Apostle Paul exhorted the early Christians to lift up all the common activity of life and make it religious. "Whether therefore ye eat or drink, or whatsoever ye do, do all to the glory of God." In like manner the true man may make even the common work of life virtuous by doing it for the advancement of right moral ends. The least important acts of the every-day life may be done with a constant reference to an increased fitness for the moral mission, or efficiency in it, and things vastly less important than eating and drinking may then acquire an elevated moral character.

Subject 3d. Perplexed Moral Action.— It is evident that, in connection with this twofold reference of virtuous action to rule and intention, there is a sphere of what may be called perplexed moral action.

Forms of this Action.—Of prescribed moral action, that which is done exactly as the supreme rule requires, but with a wrong intention, is at the same time materially right and formally wrong. This is illustrated in the alms-giving, prayer, and fasting of the Pharisee. Or, such action may not be done as the rule requires, and may therefore be materially wrong; but may at the same time be done with a right intention. This is illustrated in Paul's persecution of Jesus of Nazareth, which was done in all good conscience.

Subject 4th. Distinction of Rightness and Virtuousness. —If *rightness* and *virtuousness* are to be distinguished, the former should, strictly speaking, be referred more especially to the conformity of conduct to the moral law; the latter, to the intention of conformity to that law.

Ordinary Usage.—Ordinarily *right* and *virtue*, and the corresponding derivative terms of both, are used in a loose sense as synonymous. A little reflection will however justify the statement that there is a tendency with the more thoughtful to use *rightness* to express the relation of conduct to the supreme rule, and to apply *virtuousness* rather to a quality of the soul or of some exercise of its activity, as involving the disposition to do what is right. In this sense it is said of actions that they are right or wrong, and of men that they are virtuous or vicious.

SECTION II.

The True Idea of the Life of Duty.

The true idea of man's moral agency is reached in rising above the single and isolated act, or line, of duty, and regarding him as bound to fulfil the highest mission of which he is capable in every line. The agent is bound to complete the full moral task of life, and, in order to do this, to rise to the full moral manhood. Hence the proper *Topics* for consideration.

Topic First. The Moral Task, or Life of Duty. — The views of conscience and duty already given have made it evident that the moral agent can fulfil the end of his being, in the highest sense, only as he gives to the sense of duty the supreme place as his guide, and sets himself to the completion of that perfect life of duty prescribed for him by the moral law.

Says Dr. Thomas Reid: "It is evidently the intention of our Maker, that man should be an active, and not merely a speculative being. For this purpose, certain active powers have been given him, limited indeed in many respects, but suited to his rank and place in the creation. Our business is to manage these powers, by proposing to ourselves the best ends, planning the most proper system of conduct that is in our power, and executing it with industry and zeal. This is true wisdom; this is the very intention of our being." In working out this end of his being, the powers for moral action claim a first and controlling place.

The life task, which the moral agent is appointed to accomplish, may be summed up as a life-long obedience to the entire law of his being as prescribed by his Moral Governor.

I

This moral task is summarily comprehended in the inner moral law, investigated in a preceding *Division*. This inner law as a whole expresses man's moral mission; and in its separate intuitive moral principles furnishes the rules which the agent needs for his guidance in the life of virtue.

Topic Second. The Complete Moral Manhood. — The working out of the complete life of duty is impossible except by the complete moral man. In order to the life of duty, the agent must therefore secure the true moral manhood.

The requisites to the complete moral manhood are treated in the following *Chapters,* — to which this *Topic* affords the proper transition.

CHAPTER II.

THE NATURAL REQUISITES FOR THE LIFE OF DUTY.

Statement and Subdivision.

THE natural requisites for the mission of duty indicated by the supreme rule are the elements of the complete moral manhood. These are: an intelligence broad enough to understand the moral task; a conscience sufficiently cultivated to direct and impel toward the accomplishment of that task; and a will disposed to execute that task under the direction of intelligence and conscience.

These requisites, treated in relation to the moral task, furnish the subjects of the following *Sections :*

Section 1. The Broad Intelligence and Moral Task.
Section 2. The Cultivated Conscience and Moral Task.
Section 3. The Free and Holy Will and Moral Task.

Each of these requisites will be considered, first, with reference to the separate acts of duty; and, secondly, with reference to the complete life of duty.

SECTION I.

The Broad Intelligence and Moral Task.

It is obvious from the investigations already made that intelligence is essential to even a single responsible act; and that only the broadest intelligence can prepare the moral agent for the most complete life of duty.

Topic First.   Intelligence before Responsibility. — In order to be obligated to duty at all, the agent must possess the intellectual faculties, or intelligence, in sound condition and somewhat developed.   This arises from the fact that the intelligence is the power by which man discerns the good and its adaptation to his needs; so that (as has been seen) there can be no rational action without intelligence.

Moral Action Intelligent. — The agent must have his mental faculties. In the strict sense, an *action* has been seen to be an intelligent exercise of power so as to produce a given result.   A moral act must always be *intelligent*.   The agent must be capable of some understanding of himself and his own activities.   He must know what he is about; must understand the bearing of what he does.

Responsibility According to Intelligence, or Opportunity. — The agent is obviously held responsible according to the nature and amount of his knowledge of the action and its consequences.   The knowledge of a moral agent may be *erroneous*, or *defective*.

Knowledge Erroneous. — "Mistake as to the nature and consequences of action is *error*.   Error is said to be *avoidable* or *unavoidable*, according as the mistake is such as could or could not have been avoided, by due diligence as to the means of obtaining knowledge."

Knowledge Defective. — "Want of knowledge as to actions is *ignorance*. In respect of the *action*, ignorance is called *efficacious* or *concomitant*, according as the removal of it would, or would not, prevent the action from being done.   In respect to the *agent*, ignorance is said to be *vincible* or *invincible*, according as it could, or could not, be removed by the use of accessible means of knowledge.   Vincible ignorance is distinguished into *affected* or *wilful*, and *supine* or *crass*, by which the means of knowing are indolently or stupidly neglected.

"Ignorance is said to be invincible in two ways: *in itself* and also *in its cause*, as when a man knows not what he does through disease of body or mind; and *in itself* but *not in its cause*, as when a man knows not what he does through intoxication or passion."   *Fleming.*

Intellect must be Developed. — The mental faculties must be somewhat developed.   The *idiot* is not capable of moral action.   If he has the mental faculties, they are not sufficiently developed to be capable of the requisite service.   As he rises into intelligence he rises into moral accountability. The *infant* is not capable of moral action, for its powers are yet undeveloped. In proportion as they are developed it rises to accountability.

Intellect must be Sound. — The mental faculties must be in sound condition. The man must have his reason. The *insane* man is not capable of moral action. He is *not of a sound mind*, and is therefore not held responsible for his acts.

Topic Second. Broad Intelligence before the Complete Life Task. — In order to the perfect fulfilment of the highest possible life task by any agent, there are obviously three things that must be understood and appreciated: the agent's own capabilities, or personal power; his relations and position in his present sphere of action; and his prescribed life task. Only the broadest and most fully developed intelligence can lift the moral agent up to the high point of view from which the highest mission becomes possible.

Subject 1st. Knowledge of the Agent's Capabilities Requisite. — In order to the highest duty, there is requisite in the moral agent an intelligence so broad and so fully developed as to enable him to appreciate the capabilities of his own complex being. In these capabilities is found his *personal power*, which decides the *possibilities of action*. So far as he fails of this, or is ignorant, his whole life must therefore be essentially incomplete.

Subject 2d. Knowledge of the Agent's Position and Relations Requisite. — In order to the highest duty, there is requisite in the moral agent an intelligence which shall enable him to understand and appreciate his position and his various relations in his present sphere of action. His position and relations indicate to the agent *the line of present action*. So far as he fails to comprehend them, or is ignorant, his present conduct must fall below what his opportunities demand of him.

Subject 3d. Knowledge of the Prescribed Task Requisite. — In order to the highest duty, there is requisite in the moral agent an intelligence that shall enable him fully to understand and appreciate his prescribed life task in his various

12

relations. It has been seen that knowledge of the moral task furnishes at once the rule and goal of moral action. So far as he fails to attain to a knowledge of this, or is ignorant, his entire life must fall below what the Moral Governor requires of him.

SECTION II.

The Cultivated Conscience and Moral Task.

It is obvious that a moral nature, or conscience, is essential to even a single responsible action; and that only a most highly cultivated moral nature can prepare the agent for the highest life of duty.

Topic First. Conscience before Responsibility.—In order to be bound to duty at all, the agent must possess a moral nature complete in its elements and somewhat developed. This is apparent from the fact that it is the moral nature alone that fits man to know, to appreciate, and to do the right, — so that (as has been seen) there can be no moral action without such a nature.

Moral Nature Essential. — Morality and responsibility begin with the existence and action of the moral nature. No agent can be bound to do what he has no *natural* capacity for discerning or appreciating.

Moral Development Essential. — It is not enough in order to responsibility that man's moral nature should exist in germ,— it must be somewhat developed. With the beginning of this development comes the beginning of responsibility; and responsibility advances toward completeness as the development advances. The *infant* is not responsible, because its moral nature is not developed, and so long as it is not in any degree developed. The *idiot* is, for a like reason, not responsible. The *insane* man, when he loses the power of recognizing and feeling moral distinctions, ceases to be capable of moral action.

Defects of Conscience. — Conscience may be defective in respect to its *law* or *rule*, or in respect to its own *certainty* or *clearness*.

'*First*, in respect to its *rule*, conscience may be *true*,— that is, it may be plainly and clearly in accordance with the will of God, or the ultimate and absolute rule of rectitude. It may be *erroneous*,— that is, its decisions, instead of being in accordance with right reason and the revealed will of God, may be not in conformity with the one or the other. And this error may be vincible or invincible, according as it might and ought to have been removed, or as it could not have been removed, by the diligent use of means to enlighten and correct the conscience.

'Conscience as *erroneous* has been denominated *lax*, when on slight grounds it judges an action not to be vicious which is truly vicious, or slightly vicious when it is greatly so; *scrupulous*, when on slight grounds it judges an action to be vicious, when it is not truly vicious, or greatly vicious when it is not so; *perplexed*, when it judges that there will be sin, whether the action is done or not done.

'*Secondly*, in respect to its *certainty*, conscience is said to be *certain* or *clear*, when there is no fear of error as to our judgment of an action as right or wrong; *probable*, when in reference to two actions, or courses of action, it determines that the probability is that the one is right rather than the other; *doubtful*, when it cannot clearly determine whether an action is or is not in accordance with the law of absolute rectitude.' *Fleming.*

Topic Second. Cultivated Conscience before Complete Life Task. — In order to the perfect fulfilment of the highest possible moral task by any agent, the moral nature, or conscience, must be cultivated to such a degree that it will direct the agent toward that task *with unerring certainty* and bind him to its accomplishment *with unhesitating firmness.*

Subject 1st. Moral Nature Improved by Culture. — The moral nature is subject to the general law of exercise which applies to the other faculties. It is strengthened by use and weakened by disuse. This is true of it, as judgment, as sentiment, as impulse, and as furnishing the moral rule and moral mission.

The Discriminating Power of the Moral Judgment is Increased by Exercise. — The appropriate exercise may be secured:

By the careful study of the most perfect moral systems, and especially by the study of the Christian moral system;

By meditation upon the most perfect moral characters, especially upon that most perfect character of Jesus of Nazareth;

By the practical application of the intuitive principles of morals to the vast range of voluntary action in all its relations;

By maintaining a rational purpose of " exercising ourselves to have a conscience void of offence toward God and toward man."

The discriminating power of moral judgment may be weakened by failure to exercise it thus; and, still more effectively, by giving the being over to the contemplation, purpose, and pursuit of vice.

The Moral Sentiments Increase in Accuracy and Power by Use. — By sincerely and earnestly contemplating, purposing, and doing the right, the sentiments of moral approval and disapproval, of moral satisfaction and shame and self-reproach, of moral esteem and indignation, of moral affection and aversion, of moral benevolence and retribution, — all increase in the spontaneousness, power, and pleasurableness of their action.

By neglecting to do the right, still more by refraining from doing it, and most of all by doing the wrong, the moral sentiments are weakened and the conscience becomes seared.

The Impulsive Power of Conscience is Strengthened by Exercise. — The same exercise that improves its discriminating and sensitive power improves its impulsive power also, — since it leads to the clear discernment and feeling of the morally good as an object of desire and ground of obligation, and thus calls into action the most powerful motives, and tends to make them the ruling motives. The law of habit also comes in to aid in the work of culture, — since the exercise of the impulsive power of the moral nature begets both ease and increasing energy in its use.

The moral impulses are weakened by neglect to exercise them.

Greater Clearness of the Inner Law, in both its aspects, is also secured by the diligent exercise of the moral powers, and lost by want of such exercise. That *the faithful use of present light leads to greater light, and neglect of it to its loss,* is a law of the moral no less than of the spiritual world.

The View of Kant. — Kant and the moralists who follow him deny the possibility of educating conscience, as has already appeared (p. 111). By conscience they mean only the *intuitional element* of the moral nature. All the truth in their view is, that by no process of education can any new intuitive idea or moral principle be added to the general stock of mankind. But all intuitions, though not derived from experience, are educed by experience, and are never brought out fully without the educating process. The error is in the denial of this.

Subject 2d. Perfect Moral Culture Essential. — To the highest mission of duty, there is requisite in the moral agent a moral nature cultivated to such a degree, that, as *moral judgment*, it shall discriminate with delicacy, accuracy, and promptness between the morally good and evil: that, as *moral sentiment*, it shall respond quickly and appropriately to every form of the morally good and evil: that, as *moral impulse*, it

shall impel persistently and powerfully to all right living:
and that, as *moral rule*, it shall always hold up before the
agent the most perfect standard of life and the highest possible mission of duty.

SECTION III.

The Free and Holy Will and Moral Task.

It is obvious that a free will is essential to even a single
responsible act; and that only a will powerfully inclined to
the right can prepare the agent for his complete moral task.

Topic First.   Free Will before Responsibility. — It is
generally admitted that no action can be moral and responsible that is not under the direction of the agent's own free
will.   This is apparent from the fact (already noted) that the
will is the power by which the agent makes any act his own, in
consenting to it or deciding upon it, and in committing himself to it.

At the same time it is true (as has been shown), that moral
action receives its moral character, not from its relation to
will *merely*, but from the relation to moral end and moral rule,
into which the will brings it.

The following questions arise in connection with this subject:

In what sense must moral action be voluntary?

In what sense must it be free?

How does voluntary and free action become moral?

**Subject 1st.   Sense in which Moral Action must be Vol-
untary.** — From the true doctrine of the will — as a faculty
whose action is involved, as consent or spontaneous choice, in
all the ordinary workings of the feelings — it becomes evident
that spontaneous action of the feelings is as truly the agent's
own voluntary action, as is the action from rational preference
or from direct volition.

12*

Doctrine of Will and its Bearing. — It has been seen that the will includes two elements : choice and volition ; and that all action is therefore voluntary, into which the will enters as spontaneous choice, as rational preference, or as volition. The agent in exerting the will in any of these forms makes the action his own.

Distinction of Actions as Related to Will. — Actions may be voluntary, involuntary, or mixed. A *voluntary action* is one done in accordance with the will of the agent. An *involuntary action* is one done without the exercise of the agent's will, and may not imply knowledge or design. There are also *mixed actions*, which are done volitionally, yet without full consent of will and judgment, but with reluctance and hesitation as to the action in its nature and consequences. They are neither simply and absolutely voluntary nor involuntary. The throwing overboard of his goods by the mariner, to avoid shipwreck ; the delivering up of his purse to a robber, by the traveller, from the fear of being murdered ; and, in general, the choosing of a lesser ill in order to escape from a greater, — may be given as examples of what have been called mixed actions.

Voluntary Wider than Volitional. — The maxim that " no action is of a moral nature that is not voluntary " is not true, if voluntary is to be understood in the strict sense of *volitional* or *intentional*. The maxim is only true of *external action*, which covers only a small part of the sphere of moral action. If the element of choice is involved in the will, then the action of the will enters into all internal acts of spontaneous choice and of rational preference in such a sense as to make those acts truly voluntary.

Necessary Qualification. — It is necessary to keep in view the fact that a true psychology assures us that intellect, feelings, and will are not separate and isolated in their actings. The normal activity of the soul (see Porter, *Human Intellect*, p. 44,) "includes all these elements." "If we conceive of it as knowing without feeling, and as feeling without choosing, we conceive of it as either undeveloped or abnormal in its actings, and as incomplete or mutilated in their results." One of the three elements may be predominant in any particular act or state of the soul, but both the others are always present in some degree. Along with the action of the affections and desires the will appears as spontaneity ; and they are voluntary in so far as the will suffers them to act, or consents to their action, or goes along with them in their action.

View of Dr. Alexander. — "The word *voluntary*, as employed in the maxim under consideration, includes more than volition ; it comprehends all the spontaneous exercises of the mind ; that is, all its affections and emotions. Formerly all these were included under the word *will*, and we still use language that requires this latitude in the construction of the term. Thus it would be consonant to the best usage to say that man is perfectly voluntary in loving his friend or hating his enemy; but by this is not meant that these affections are the effect of volition, but only that they are the free, spontaneous exercise of the mind. That all virtue consists in volition, is not true—as we have seen; but that all virtuous exercises are spontaneous, is undoubtedly correct."

That the moral agent is responsible for all action that is voluntary in this wide sense, is attested by his own consciousness. In particular and especially does the consciousness, as enlightened and elevated by the Christian system, declare that the agent is responsible for the springs and motives of action — the affections, desires, habits, and tendencies of the soul — so far as he encourages or discourages them, consents to them or refuses compliance.

Spontaneous Action Responsible. — That volitional action is responsible action is generally admitted, so that the testimony of consciousness needs only to be sought with reference to action that is not properly volitional. Observation assures us that "certain affections and desires which are neither produced by volitions nor terminate in volitions are, in the judgment of all reflecting men, of a moral nature. For example, *envy* at the prosperity of a neighbor is not the result of any volition, and it may be cherished inwardly without leading to any volition, the will being controlled by other feelings which prevent action; yet all must admit it to be a morally evil disposition." The same may be shown of the desires. It is true that men always and everywhere approve or condemn themselves for the affections and desires which they cherish.

The Relation of the Springs of Action to Responsibility. — Not only is it true that spontaneous action is responsible action, but it is still further true that men judge of any action *by the character of the spring from which it proceeds*, rather than from any *volition* connected with it. Dr. Alexander has in mind this element, along with intention, when he says: "Men are more accountable for their motives than for anything else; and, primarily, morality consists in the motives." In any investigation into the character of a particular act of which some one is accused, the court and jury wish to ascertain by witnesses from what motives the accused acted, and they determine his innocence or guilt by these.

Will, in the Wide Sense, carries Responsibility with it.— It is not the will in the narrow sense of *volition*, therefore, that is the chief thing in deciding the responsibility of action, but the will as entering into the affections and desires, into the habits and dispositions of the soul. Men in general, when not biased by some philosophical or moral theory, admit that the agent is accountable for the principles or springs from which the more conspicuous forms of action flow. These springs are themselves truly *voluntary actions* of the soul. Men trace habitual right-doing and wrong-doing back to a good or evil disposition or habit; and wicked and malignant passions to a wicked and malignant temper; and they look upon the dispositions, habits, and temper as being the truest expression of the character of the agent, for which he is fully responsible.

View of Jesus of Nazareth.— It cannot be doubted that this was the view of the most perfect moral Teacher the world has ever had. Says Henry Rogers (*Superhuman Origin of the Bible*), after showing how Christianity "canonizes, and takes under its special patronage" those virtues of humility, patient endurance, and unlimited forgiveness of injuries, which the world has never either admired or practised: "As little can the world in general sympathize with the sternness with which the Gospel so absolutely gauges and determines moral turpitude by thought and feeling. It pronounces unresisted evil inclinations to be equally guilty with evil actions;—not so pernicious in their influence on moral habit, it may be; not so pernicious to others, certainly; nor so deplorable in their effects on society; but as equally constituting moral *guilt;* consequently, that covetousness indulged is 'theft;' lascivious looks, with no attempt to repress them, 'adultery;' malignant hatred, which would fain go forth in act, 'murder.' "

Subject 2d.   Sense in which Moral Action must be Free.

— Human consciousness testifies that action in order to be moral and responsible must not only be voluntary as opposed to involuntary, but *free* as opposed to *necessary.* The same consciousness, as exhibited both in the individual and in bodies of men, embraces a sense of freedom along with a sense of responsibility, and so testifies that man is a free agent.

Distinction of Action.— A *free action* proceeds from a principle intrinsic to the agent, or is determined by the agent himself, and is in accordance with his wishes. A *necessary action* proceeds from a principle which is extrinsic to the agent, and is compulsory or contrary to the will of the agent.

Distinction between Voluntary and Free.— There are those who admit that man is a *voluntary* agent, but who nevertheless deny that he is a *free* agent. They affirm that the *will acts necessarily*, the human soul being operated upon by *causes*, which we call motives, which decide the will as inevitably as physical causes decide the growth and changes of the body, or of a tree. According to this view freedom and voluntariness may be distinguished, and while man is a voluntary agent he is not a free agent.

Man consciously Possessed of a Free Will.— The above distinction between *voluntariness* and *freedom* is contrary to the consciousness of mankind. The will is free. *To have and exercise a will is to be free.* Says Dr. McCosh: "This truth is revealed to us by immediate consciousness, and is not to be set aside by any other truth whatever. It is a first truth equal to the highest, to no one of which will it ever yield. It cannot be set aside by any other truth, not even by any other first truth, and certainly by no derived truth. Whatever other proposition is true, this is true also, that man's will is free. If there be any other truth apparently inconsistent with it, care must be taken so to express it that it may not be truly contradictory."

Freedom of the Will the Great Postulate.— In short, the freedom of the will, so far from being a doubtful question in philosophy, is the fundamental postulate upon which all man's thinking proceeds; upon which all his work in the world, in business, law, and government, depends; and without which his nature as a moral and accountable being would be utterly inexplicable.

The objections which are urged by necessarians against the freedom of the will are purely speculative, and have therefore no force as against the intuitive conviction of freedom implanted in the soul of every man.

Speculative Objection from Foreknowledge.— The doctrine of the divine foreknowledge and sovereignty is generally admitted to be in accordance with right reason. One class of objections arises from the attempt to reconcile this doctrine with the doctrine of freedom. The great question has been, *How can God foreknow and as Sovereign decide what is to come to pass and yet man be free?* That man cannot answer the question is simply proof of his own ignorance and littleness, or of his false, narrow, and inadequate view of God and of his vast plan of the universe, and does not weigh a feather against the clear intuition and plain fact of human freedom.

Objection from Causation.— "There is the *appearance of causation* in the workings of the mind and even in its voluntary workings." The objection based upon this *appearance* is speciously urged in the form of a question: *How can the principle of cause and effect rule in the workings of the will, as it rules in the material world, and yet man be free?*

This Objection Assumes a False Principle.—As ordinarily put, it is an illustration of the common fallacy of a false assertion or implication, by means of a question so put as to convey the impression that the thing asserted or implied is beyond dispute. In the present instance the principle so confidently assumed is absolutely false, being contrary to consciousness and to all we know of the nature of mind and matter. The principle of cause and effect *does not rule* in the workings of the will as it rules in the material world.) There is not the slightest proof of any such thing, but all the proof possible in the case to the contrary.

It leaves out of View the Essential Distinction between Mind and Matter.—Consciousness and observation assure us that there are two distinct kinds of being in the universe: that which is self-active and that which is only acted upon, mind and matter. This objection ignores this essential and conscious self-activity of mind, and the no less essential inertness of matter. The law of causation, of which it makes so much, is founded on the acknowledged inertness of matter. "The true maxim is that every physical event, every *material* phenomenon, must have a cause, *because it cannot act itself; but it does not follow that this cause must also have a cause, for it is itself a source of power;* it is *mind,* or *person,* which, unlike matter, *can act of itself,* and therefore does not need a cause. It is an unauthorized extension of the law of causality, to say that every *action* of a conscious agent must have a cause, just as much as a material phenomenon. This would be begging the question in the present case, and it is refuted by the direct evidence of consciousness, which teaches us that the will is a true source of power in itself." Bowen, *Metaphysics and Ethics,* pp. 125-6.

The Objection accordingly Ignores the True Relations of the Motives to the Volitions.—In all the rational actions of man consciousness assures us that there are three elements found together: first, the consideration of the motives; second, the subsequent putting forth of a volition; and, third, the act following upon the volition.) The relation between the second and third, the volition and the act, as in the case of forced attention, is truly causative, the consciousness of effort or exertion of power being perfectly distinct. The man knows himself as *determining upon* and *causing* an effect. But the relation between the first and second elements, the consideration of motives and the volition, is entirely different. These are two successive states of the same person. Their relation is that of mere *sequence in time,* of mere antecedent and consequent, but not of cause and effect. There is no consciousness of a causal relation between the two, as in the other case; but rather the consciousness of the opposite. "If there were a causal or necessary union between them, the latter would *immediately* succeed the former; for when the cause is present, the effect cannot be delayed. But we often and involuntarily pause and dwell upon various motives, holding them up in various lights, and balancing them against each other, the will remaining quiescent during this process, the understanding and reason alone being active. Now, if the strongest motive is necessarily followed by the volition, why is it not *immediately* so followed, the motives being certainly before the mind?" Given, in any case, a present and efficient cause and the effect of necessity immediately follows. But there is nothing of this sort in the working of mind in view of motives. The man is always conscious of his own freedom, self-activity, and sovereignty in the presence of all the motives that can possibly be brought before him.

It Mistakes entirely the Nature of Motives.+ "Whatever may be the operation of motives, they operate on the man, or on *self;* whatever may be the nature of the action, it is not the motives which act, but the man acts. We must not lose sight of the absolute indivisibility of person, and the consequent fact, that what are called the separate faculties of mind are but different and successive states, or conditions of being, of the same individual. There is no *will*, but only the *man willing*,— no *motive*, only the man contemplating various objects of desire." The necessarian, in seeking for a cause of the phenomena of volition, "is obliged to look to an *antecedent state of the man himself*, —that is, to a motive, a pre-existent or concomitant longing or desire. He thinks to make out his theory, then, by saying, that *the strongest motive* causes the change, or, in other words, determines the will. But as the mind or person is *absolutely single*, and only exhibits itself under different phases, or as variously employed, *the motive* means nothing but *the man himself wishing for some object;* and the determination of the will means nothing but the same person acting. The assertion that the motive determines the will, therefore, is only an abstract statement of the fact that the *man wishing* determines the *man acting*, or that the will determines itself, —which is precisely the theory of the advocate for human freedom. The necessarian theory is absurd, for it assigns an abstraction as the cause of a reality." See Bowen, *Metaphysics and Ethics*, pp. 121-2.

Truths of Freedom.— Accepting the fundamental fact of free will, the main truths concerning the real nature of human freedom may be embodied in a series of simple *Propositions*.

Proposition 1st. — True freedom is not inconsistent with human dependence and limitation.

Man Dependent. — God only is absolutely independent and unlimited in his agency. Every other being is finite and dependent. It is true, as Dr. Thomas Reid has shown:

That free agency is not fully developed nor enjoyed till a man's powers of body and mind have attained to full maturity and exercise;

That it is liable to be impaired or lost by disease of body or derangement of mind;

That it may be abridged or overborne by the force of circumstances;

That in man it is limited in its nature, and may be overruled in its exercise by the will and power of God. In short, man is only *free under law.*

All these limitations actually coexist with human freedom, and it therefore cannot be inconsistent with them.

Proposition 2d. — True freedom in action, while not consistent with necessity, is nevertheless not inconsistent with certainty.

Free Action may be Certain. — An event may be absolutely certain without being necessary. If a man have good principles, and all temptation to do wrong be removed, it is morally certain that, in any given case, he will do right. But there is no compulsion in the case, and therefore no necessity. It is absolutely certain that God will always do right, but he is nevertheless infinitely free in doing right. It may be absolutely certain that in a manufactory, in any given week, a definite amount of the fabric there manufactured will be produced, and yet both the proprietor and the operatives are perfectly free in their planning and working. So all the results of the ongoing of the universe may be perfectly certain, and yet all the intelligent agents employed in it may be truly free.

Improper Use of the Term Necessity. — The difficulty which has perplexed the minds of men in this connection has arisen from an improper use of the term *necessity* for *certainty.* Says Dr. Alexander: "The word *necessary* should never have been applied to any exercises which are spontaneous or voluntary, because all such are free in their very nature. When we apply this term to them, although we may qualify it by calling it a *moral* or *philosophical* necessity, still the idea naturally and insensibly arises, that if necessary they cannot be free. It is highly important not to use a term out of its proper signification; especially when such consequences may arise from an ambiguous use." A free act is one produced with will, or voluntarily; a necessary act is one produced against will, or without will. There is nothing therefore to prevent an action from being at the same time both free and certain.

Proposition 3d. — In general, man's action is free, when, within his own proper sphere of action, he can will just what he pleases.

Nature of the Liberty. — The greatest conceivable liberty of an agent is the *liberty to act as he pleases.* If we suppose that in addition to this a power be given to man to act independently of all reasons and motives, this power would evidently destroy his very nature as a rational being. It would unfit him for all reasonable work in life, and disqualify him for accountability and moral government; in short, it would make him a creature of caprice.

Limits of the Sphere. — Freedom, as has already been shown, is not inconsistent with limitation and dependence. The exact sphere of human freedom is determined by the nature of man as a self-active spirit embodied. He is free to do what he pleases in this sphere. It is no abridgment of his true freedom that he is not able to create or destroy a world, or to fly to the sun or the moon if he wishes to do so.

Proposition 4th. — In order to free action, therefore, the agent must possess the liberty of indifference in the sense that it must be in his power, if he be disposed, to do or not to do, to do this or that; but not in the sense that it must be in his power to choose against all reason and motive. Liberty in the latter sense, if possible, would make him an irrational being.

Latitude of Indifference. — In all voluntary action there must be at least two things that may be done. The ancients accordingly distinguished two kinds of liberty: the liberty of *contradiction* and the liberty of *contrariety.* A choice is permitted between doing and not doing some particular proposed act. This is the liberty of *contradiction.* A choice is offered between one object and some other or several others. This is the liberty of *contrariety.* Herein is the indifference.

Choice Implies that Indifference has Ceased. — The agent in such case may choose one act or another; but whatever choice may be made, that very choice implies that indifference toward the chosen course or act has ceased, and some reason or motive has come into play. With other and different motives, the choice might have been different; but so long as man remains a reasonable being, there must be some reason or motive before there can be a choice. We choose because we desire. The *power* *of contrary choice,* as the power to choose irrespective of all motives, is an absurdity. See *Power of Contrary Choice, Princeton Theological Essays. First Series.*

Proposition 5th.—The preceding statement decides in what sense an agent can and must be possessed of a self-determining power, in order to be free and accountable. He must be able to make his choices for himself, spontaneously or volitionally, in accordance with reasons or motives.

Self-Determining Power.—It has been shown that external objects are in themselves inert, passive; man is the efficient cause in human agency. External objects have influence only as the active principles of man's nature go out after them and lay hold of them. *The agent himself wills.* The law governing the action of his will is, that it shall be in view of reasons and motives. This law is morally *the rule of action* of the will; but it lays no more restraint upon it than the laws which govern the reason in the search for truth lay upon the action of the reasoning faculty. *Freedom under law is the only freedom possible to an intelligent finite being.*

Subject 3d. Voluntary and Free Action as Moral and Responsible.—Free volitional or spontaneous action is not moral and responsible simply because of its relation to the will; in other words, it is not will merely that gives to action its moral character. This is evident from the fact that innumerable acts volitional and spontaneous are not moral in their nature, *i. e.,* are neither right nor wrong in themselves considered.

Moral action has been shown to be action with moral intention and in agreement with the requirements of the moral law. Some moral object, or end of action, as embraced or thought to be embraced in the moral law, and toward which by his will the agent directs his action, always decides the moral character of such action, so far as the agent's relation to it is concerned.

Topic Second. Holy Free Will before the Complete Life Task.—To the full life of duty there is requisite in the moral agent a will at once freely and powerfully inclined toward the right. This follows as well from the nature of the moral task itself as from the condition of struggle in which it must be wrought out.

1st. The Nature of the Moral Task requires a Holy Will. — If the complete work of life is the fulfilment of all God's will, during the entire period of the agent's existence on earth as a moral and responsible being, then, in order to its accomplishment, the agent's will must be in perfect accord with God's will.

The Holy Will. — It is evident that in order to the complete life of virtue man's will must not only be right, but always right; since a single departure from the right would leave the whole of duty incomplete. It is only as the agent's whole being is in accordance with the law of the Moral Governor, that he can fulfil the true end of that being. The true manhood is completed in the perfectly holy character only, and the perfect moral life is therefore possible to the true man only.

2d. The Condition of Struggle with Evil requires a Holy Will. — As this present world is a scene of struggle with evil in all its forms, open and insidious, the moral agent can only hope to accomplish the perfect moral task, if his character be strong and holy, *i. e.*, if his will be right and permanently and powerfully right.

A Holy and Strong Will. — It is manifest that, in order to the working out of the perfect life in such a condition of evil, the entire human nature, with all its tendencies and dispositions, as expressing itself in the will, must be powerfully, as well as permanently, inclined in the right direction. Without both the elements of strength and holiness, the agent must inevitably be borne down in the unequal conflict and make failure in his task.

CHAPTER III.

THE REQUISITE MORAL RECONSTRUCTION.

Statement and Subdivision.

THE preceding investigations have repeatedly brought to light evidence that man's nature is in a condition of moral disorder, and that the prescribed life of duty has therefore become impossible to him without a moral reconstruction of that nature. To complete a true theory of ethics, it therefore becomes necessary to consider the subjects presented in the following *Sections:*

Section 1.   The Moral Disorder of Man's Nature.
Section 2.   The True Reconstruction Scheme.

The Propriety of Treating this Subject may easily be made to appear. If man's moral nature is in such a state of disorder as to prevent him from accomplishing his prescribed mission of duty, then it becomes essential to a helpful philosophy of morals to point out the method of restoring that nature to its normal condition, so that the true and full moral mission may be accomplished.

SECTION I.

The Moral Disorder of Man's Nature.

The moral disorder of man's nature becomes manifest in three ways:

First, in that general evil condition from which, as from the fountain, all evil in action flows;

Second, in the actual working of all the powers essential to the fulfilment of the moral task;

Third, in that general wreck and misery of the being which results as the penalty of a broken law.

Topic First. Condition of the Moral Nature. — The most cursory examination makes it manifest:

First, that man's moral judgment is both weakened and darkened;

Secondly, that his moral feelings are both deadened and perverted;

Thirdly, that his strongest moral impulses are persistently inclined toward the evil;

So that, while his whole being shows that he was undoubtedly made for virtue, he is now just as evidently very strongly biased toward the morally evil.

Disorder in the Moral Judgment. — That man's moral judgment is weakened and darkened appears, from the want of clearness in his apprehension of the fundamental principles of the moral law given for his guidance; from the great diversity of conduct that results from the application of these same principles, even when clearly apprehended; and from his failure to grasp the moral law in its unity and totality as setting forth the law of complete manhood and the appointed work of life.

Disorder in the Moral Feelings. — That man's moral feelings are deadened and perverted appears, from the insubordination of the lower and irrational feelings, as in the opposition of natural appetites to the guidance of conscience; from the action of feelings which are in their nature immoral, as having a wrong and evil object, or end; from the experience of the peculiar moral sentiments of self-disapprobation, shame, and remorse, whose special office is to check the increase of moral disorder; and from the absence of that enthusiastic interest in his appointed moral mission which its grandeur and nobleness warrant.

Disorder in the Moral Impulses. — That man's moral impulses are powerfully and persistently inclined toward the evil, appears from the fact that he needs only to abstain from struggle toward the good to insure a constant progress toward the evil.

Topic Second. Workings of the Moral Nature. — Man's

13 *

moral nature does not work harmoniously under the moral law, either as moral rule or moral mission.

In the three great relations in which the moral agent is to fulfil his mission of duty, his conduct does not accord with the requirements of the moral law.

It is True of the Majority of Mankind : —That, while acknowledging their obligation to supreme devotion to God, they yet practically neglect or even reject God ;

That while acknowledging their obligation to a proper regard for their own being, they yet in the worst sense neglect or abuse that being ;

That while acknowledging their obligation to do to others as they would that others should do to them, they yet selfishly disregard all the interests of others, or even do their utmost to injure them.

This is True of Men Universally, except so far as some extraneous influence comes in to prevent. Positive law, and government, using force to restrain evil and to inflict penalty, are necessary for the preservation of the individual and society from destruction ; and even these have never been able to preserve the man and the state without the added power of Christianity.

In respect to the three forms of the good which furnish the ends of human action, man's conduct as a rational being does not accord with the requirements of the moral law.

The Majority of Men, while acknowledging their obligation to set the perfect above the pleasurable, and the right above everything else, yet persistently make pleasure and even the lowest forms of pleasure the chief end of their pursuit, or exalt culture and even the lowest forms of culture above virtue. The existence of the *pleasure theory* of morals in its manifold forms, and the powerful sway it has held and still holds over such numbers, even in Christian lands, is proof that most men actually put pleasure first, in spite of the intuitive moral judgment to the contrary.

Topic Third. Consequences of the Moral Disorder.—The consequences of this abnormal condition and working of man's moral nature appear in the inevitable penalty of wreck and wretchedness which follow all breaking of law. The nature of this penalty ; its inevitable attendance upon the transgression of law ; and its actual visitation upon man as a transgressor of the moral law,—furnish *Subjects* that need to be considered in this connection.

Subject 1st. Nature of the Penalty.

—The penalty attached to man's transgression of all law has in it two elements: *the wreck of the being*, and *pain*. It will be seen that the first of these, though ordinarily to a great extent overlooked in the consideration of this subject, is yet the chief element in the penalty of law-breaking.

1st. The Penalty of Wrecked Being.

— Human consciousness and observation testify to the substantial truth of the Scriptural sentence upon the transgressor: "The soul that sinneth it shall die." It is a sentence written in man's nature and embodied in all the constitution of the universe. In breaking the moral law the agent wrecks his own moral being, renders the complete life of duty impossible, and puts himself in the way to ultimate and complete moral ruin.

The Divine Government, Physical and Moral. — There are two acknowledged phases of the divine government: the physical, which controls the order of nature in general, and which manifests to us the wisdom and power of the Lawgiver; and the moral, which controls beings possessed of an intellectual and moral nature, and which evinces the justice, benevolence, and holiness of the Lawgiver. The scientific observation of the facts of God's moral government of the world, and especially of the world of mankind, concurs with the common experience of men, to indicate that the Creator and Governor of the universe "has established a harmony between the requisitions of that law which he has imprinted on the conscience, and the external fortunes of men, or the current of this world's affairs." "It is not more certain," says Prof. Bowen, "that the forms and changes of aggregations of matter are determined according to the principles of gravitation, affinity, definite proportions, and the like, than it is that the consequences of human action and the annals of human life accord with the fixed principles of morals and the stern demands of distributive justice."

It will readily be observed that these two phases of the divine government are everywhere intertwined as parts of one complete system, and can, in fact, be separated only in thought. Man, as both a material and spiritual being, finds himself a subject of God's government in both its forms,—his material nature bringing him in large degree under the system of physical law, reward, and penalty; and his spiritual nature bringing him to a still larger degree under the system of moral law, reward, and penalty.

It will moreover appear that although, as has been shown, neither happiness nor completeness of being is the proper end of virtuous action, the divine government is yet so arranged that the keeper of the law of right may uniformly expect both happiness and perfection to result from his obedience, and the breaker of the law of right may no less uniformly expect misery, degradation, and destruction to result from his disobedience.

Transgression Begins the Wreck of the Moral Nature. — "The first departure from obedience in man creates a tendency to continued departing. Any derangement, either in the physical or moral system, is self-aggravating and self-perpetuating, without aid from other parts. A single act of sin is a departure from rectitude, and the departure strengthens the depraved tendency. Sin thus enfeebles man's moral nature. The conservative or recuperative power of his moral constitution grows less by every act of transgression. Conscience becomes less potential, and the will more inclined to err; in other words, the strength of moral emotion is abated, and evil inclination strengthened, by every act of transgression." See Walker, *God Revealed in Creation and in Christ*, p. 177.

Transgression Binds to Moral Evil with Increasing Power. — As the exercise of any bodily member increases its strength, so the exercise of our moral faculties, whether in a good or bad direction, increases the inclination of the will to good or evil. Thus, as transgression begets transgression, the power of sin over the soul increases. This is human experience, and it agrees with human observation in relation to the effect of transgression in all other cases. The first transgression puts the soul in the road to ruin as certainly as the first impulse of a weight down an inclined plane tends to accelerate the movement and to prevent return;)continued transgression increases the tendency, velocity, and momentum in the downward way.

Transgression Tends to the Extreme of Moral Evil. — By the law of habit, it tends to reduce man to the stupidity of the brute or the moral recklessness of the fiend. One of the elements involved in habit is *unconsciousness* in the performance of the accustomed action. Repeated transgression of any law results in a tendency to the easy, continued, and *unconscious* transgression of it. The first utterance of profanity makes the man shudder at the thought of the offence against God; by repeated utterances he ceases to have any more apparent sense of sin than the brute. From the first exhibition of a malicious temper the man may shrink with horror; but through the long-continued exercise of such a disposition he may come to manifest, in the most horrible crimes, the moral recklessness of the demon. In short, that very principle of habit, which, when acting along the line of virtue, is so powerful an aid in exalting man to the position of a saint, shows itself no less powerful, when working along the line of vice, in degrading him to the place of a fiend.

Transgression Ends in Utter Moral Wreck. — So far as the attainment of the true end of man's being is concerned, therefore, the transgression of the moral law results in the utter wreck of that being. By transgression both the true moral manhood and the full moral task must become unattainable, and the agent's condition must ultimately become one of complete moral degradation and helplessness.

2d. The Penalty of Pain. — Human consciousness and observation also alike testify that by his transgression of the law the agent brings pain upon himself. This pain is the warning of the Moral Governor against the wreck of the being, and is only a small part of the penalty.

First Design. — It may easily be seen that pain has its mission in man's nature as penalty, or punishment for transgression.

The derivation of the word *penalty* from *pain* is a fact in etymology familiar to every student. *Penalty* was doubtless so derived and so named because it was considered to be *pain inflicted for transgression.* While this origin of the word *penalty* shows a very narrow view of its nature, — by leaving out of view the greater penalty of wreck of being, which may be to a great extent painless, — it is nevertheless proof from human consciousness that pain has a mission in human nature as punishment for transgression.

Second Design. — It may also be seen that pain, as an attendant upon transgression, has a mission in warning the agent against impending ruin, as it is a result from ruin already begun.

The Result of Wreck. — Some work of destruction or dislocation always precedes pain, which may be considered as man's waking up to the consciousness of the destruction or dislocation. This is equally true in both man's physical and moral being.

The Warning against Ruin. — Pain has well been declared to be "the deepest thing in man's nature." It is a provision of the Moral Governor for hedging up the way to destruction. It is his perpetual warning against ruin. Taking *fear* in its bald sense, of *fear of God's wrath*, it is therefore one of the profoundest truths ever embodied in language that "*The fear of the Lord is the beginning of wisdom.*"

Subject 2d. Inevitable Infliction of Penalty. — In the moral government of the world, arrangement is made for the revelation of all transgression, and for the ultimate infliction of the penalty affixed.

1st. Transgression Self-Recording. — Every transgression is self-recording, so that there is no possibility of its being ultimately, or even for an instant, concealed from the Moral Governor.

The Record of the Memory. — There are facts in the experience of almost every one which indicate that man never really forgets anything that has once found a place in his soul. Such cases as that recorded by Coleridge, in his *Biographia Literaria*, — of the young woman who could neither read nor write, but who, in the delirium of fever, recalled sentences in Latin, Greek, and Hebrew (languages to her wholly unknown and unintelligible) which she had overheard a clergyman repeating in his study when she was but a girl, — furnish a still clearer indication that the memory of every man contains an indelible record of all his conscious experience.

The Record of the Universe. — Every movement of man, whether of body or soul, makes a complete record of itself on the universe of matter and mind. President Hitchcock has ably presented this idea, from the point of view of the Christian scientist, in *The Religion of Geology*, in the chapter entitled, *The Telegraphic System of the Universe.*

"Men fancy that the wave of oblivion passes over the greater part of their actions;" but the discoveries of modern science show us, that there is a literal sense in which the *material creation* receives from all our words and actions an impression that can never be effaced. These actions are transfused into the very texture of the universe, so that no waters can wash them, and no erosions or metamorphoses can obliterate them. "Thrown into poetic form, this principle converts creation

Into a vast sounding gallery;
Into a vast picture gallery;
And into a universal telegraph."

The principle is proved by the doctrine of the correlation and conservation of forces.

By the grosser mechanical forces man writes out his being and life on the world, — not by the ordinary outward works which men observe, and name, and record in their books, but by influences and in forms to men invisible. Every impression on the air, the waters, and the solid earth, produces an endless series of changes. Man utters his *word*. It causes pulsations, or waves of the air. These go out in ceaseless circles and alter the whole atmosphere of the earth forever. So it is true, as Prof. Babbage remarks, that "the air is one vast library, on whose pages are forever written all that man has ever said, or woman whispered." "Not a word has ever escaped from mortal lips, whether for the defence of virtue or the perversion of truth, not a cry of agony has ever been uttered by the oppressed, not a mandate of cruelty by the oppressor, not a false and flattering word by the deceiver, — but it is registered indelibly upon the atmosphere we breathe. And could man command the mathematics of superior minds, every particle of air thus set in motion could be traced through all its changes, with as much precision as the astronomer can point out the path of the heavenly bodies. No matter how many storms have raised the atmosphere into wild commotion, and whirled it into countless forms; no matter how many conflicting waves have mixed and crossed one another; the path of each pulsation is definite, and subject to the laws of mathematics. To follow it requires, indeed, a power of analysis superior to human; but we can conceive it to be far inferior to the divine." The same is true of every impulse given to the waters and to the solid earth itself, — it will sweep round and round the globe forever, and make every atom of that globe a perpetual witness to it. So the whispered curse uttered to-day in solitude will be recorded on all the world against him who utters it, — nay, shall sweep out on the ether to other worlds and through the universe, so that he can never place himself beyond its reach.

Or *by the action of the light* every man's life is in part photographed for all time and for all the universe. Let him but stand forth in the light of heaven. He need not utter a word. The light reflected from him flashes away into space with its picture of the man — in whatever act engaged. In eight minutes it will reach the Sun; in one hour, Jupiter; in four hours, Neptune; some star of the twelfth magnitude in four thousand years. So every act in the light of heaven makes a perpetual picture of itself. All human history as transacted in the light has thus its everlasting record.

Or, if the man refuse to utter his word upon the air, or to stand forth for his deed of good and evil in the light, he cannot, in the deepest solitude and the densest darkness, escape the recording of himself by *electrical* or *chemical action*. He cannot move, cannot even think, without setting in motion the electrical and chemical forces; and these make their indelible record of his movements and his thoughts everywhere — sweeping out through the universe, or affixed to every atom of his body and of all nature.

So man stands at the centre of this awful telegraphic system, unconsciously sending out the story of his thoughts and words and deeds to be forever a witness for or against him. No breath is so faint that it can escape recording itself, — no whisper so low, no pulsation so weak, no thought so secret, no deed of evil so dark and silent. An indelible record the Moral Governor has, therefore, against every transgressor, written on all the world. The man may not be able to read any of it now, but his eyes may one day be opened to read and understand it all. How can he say, "God hath forgotten. He hideth his face; he will never see it?" The story of every human life is perpetually before the Judge of all.

All transgression of law must therefore be self-recording, so that not one deed of guilt can ever for one instant be concealed from the Moral Governor. There is no secrecy for sin in the government of God.

2d. Transgression Self-Punishing. — Every transgression of law is self-punishing, or is made to draw after it its own punishment, — so that there is no possibility that the transgressor will ultimately escape the death penalty prescribed by the Moral Governor.

Penalty a Necessity of Law. — Says Dr. Walker: "As law is a necessity of things," — a necessity to process, harmony, and stability, in any system, — "so penalty is a necessity of law." "Natural penalty, or rather the penalty natural to law, is progressive derangement tending to ultimate destruction." If law is simply *the established order in accordance with which the Moral Governor works with his forces* in the universe, or in any of its parts, then it at once becomes evident that every transgression of that law must bring man sooner or later into conflict with those forces. Every law must therefore have its *natural penalty*, as just stated.

Penalty is therefore not Malevolently Inflicted by the Moral Governor, but Guiltily Incurred by the Moral Agent. — The transgressor deranges, turns aside, and perverts the very forces upon which the support of his life depends, and which are therefore in the intention of the Creator . most beneficent forces. Upon gravitation depend the stability, order, and enjoyment of the universe; but the man who casts himself down from a precipice turns this most beneficent force to his own destruction. The appetite of thirst was given to secure the requisite supply of fluids

In the system; but the man who gives himself up to strong drink wrests the good gift of the Creator to his own destruction. The principle of habit was placed in man that he might make more easy, rapid, and powerful the progress toward moral perfection; but he perverts the helpful principle into an agency for his swifter and more complete moral degradation. Conscience was given to be a guide to the true moral manhood and mission; but the transgressor changes it into an accuser and judge, and makes it the source of the torture of remorse. So it might be shown that, through the whole range of the divine government, the punishment of transgression is guiltily incurred by the transgressor, rather than malevolently inflicted by the Lawgiver.

Law Inexorable to the Disobedient. — It is evident from the nature of law that obedience is the one condition of safety and life, and that therefore "pardon without restoration to obedience is absurd and impossible in a system governed by law." Law permits no transgression and provides for no pardon. If it did, it would annul itself. Even ignorance does not exempt man from the penalty natural to law transgressed. In whatever way one passes from under law he passes to penalty. This is no less true of moral than of physical law, — it can neither license, pardon, nor pass over transgression; else would the Lawgiver be unholy.

The Moral Penalty not always Immediate. — Every observer knows that all transgression is not immediately followed by its full penalty. Some physical forces work their results rapidly, or even instantaneously; others slowly and through long periods. This is true of moral forces, except that in the case of these the penalty is oftener deferred. We are not to look, "in the current of human fortunes, *for that immediate and invariable enforcement of the moral law, which would either deprive man of his free agency, or reduce his virtues to a mere selfish regard for his own happiness.* If, for instance, honesty were the best policy, not merely as a general principle, and in the long run, but always, instantly, and plainly, there would be great danger that men would altogether cease to be honest, in the proper sense of the term, and would be only politic. So weak are human purposes, that we cannot often be certain of ourselves, until an emergency arises in which we are required to be virtuous at some apparent cost, or by some sacrifice." (Bowen, *Metaphysics and Ethics*, p. 328.) By this method man's life under the moral law may be made a constant process of training to virtue.

The Extreme Penalty of Moral Death Inevitable. — It has been seen that pain is not all the penalty of transgressing either physical or moral law. "It is a part of the penalty only as progress is part of the result —as derangement is linked with disaster." Pain indicates disease or derangement, and warns against it. A cancer is a different thing from

14

the pain which it produces. Often the pain abates, although there be no remedy for the disease. Suffering, physical or moral, indicates the beginning of a derangement of the being, which tends to its complete derangement or death. The penalty attached to all sin is *moral death,* and no man who continues to sin can escape it. It includes the darkening and deadening of the moral nature in all its elements, until all that belongs to the true moral manhood and life becomes impossible and hateful, and the man gives himself over to the willing service of evil, and becomes as truly dead to all the high moral ends for which he was made as the dead body is dead to all the activities of human life. "*Thou shalt surely die*" was the penalty attached to the first transgression, and it is the penalty which must inevitably follow the moral disorder so manifest and so wide-spreading in man's nature. The only escape from the penalty is to be found in the removal of the disorder. There is neither secrecy nor impunity for sin in God's moral government. As the righteous man will suffer all pain rather than commit sin, so the righteous Moral Governor will inflict the extreme penalty rather than suffer sin.

Subject 3d. Actual Infliction of the Penalty. — Both consciousness and observation give assurance that the moral agent has made guilty failure in his appointed moral task. They give evidence, likewise, that he is actually suffering the penalty of transgression, both as pain and as moral wreck.

The Penalty as Pain appears in the general misery of man, and especially in the constant condemnation of conscience for his guilty failure in duty.

The Penalty as Wreck appears in the moral degradation and helplessness of man. He has actually fallen from the true moral manhood, and his moral achievements cannot rise above his knowledge and desires and aims, so that the prescribed life of duty has become impossible to him. "Sin when it is finished bringeth forth death."

Man's moral condition, as one of disorder tending to utter ruin, gives inconceivable emphasis, therefore, to the great practical moral question, — *Is there any way of escape or of moral restoration?*

SECTION II.

The True Scheme of Moral Reconstruction.

The grand problem of all ages has been, How may man be brought up to the true moral manhood and to the accomplishment of the true moral task? The best results of the attempts to solve this problem have been embodied in the great religions and philosophies of the world. A complete philosophy of morals must take into account these attempted solutions of the problem, and must seek to find the true solution.

1st. Conditions of a True Solution. — Any scheme of reconstruction that can promise satisfactory results must evidently take into account all the main facts of man's moral nature, condition, and destiny.

First, it must <u>neither</u> leave out of consideration, body nor soul, the mental nor moral, the individual nor social, freedom nor responsibility, progressiveness nor immortality.

Secondly, it must neither overlook the wreck of the moral manhood nor the failure in the moral task, but must furnish a power for reconstructing the one and a universal motive and mission for lifting up the other to the normal standard.

Thirdly, it must make provision for rolling back the tide of forces which are set to work by transgression, and which must else bear perpetual pain and ruin to the agent.

It is obvious, from the nature of the case, that any scheme that fails to do all this is not the true reconstruction scheme of the moral world: while any scheme that does it furnishes the completion of the science of the moral manhood and the moral work.

The application of these conditions of a true solution of the great moral problem, to the various schemes, inadequate and adequate, which have been proposed, will, therefore, complete the theory of the moral life, and bring to a close the discussions of theoretical ethics.

2d. Application of the Test. — The principal schemes

which have been proposed, and are still on trial, are: Self-Reconstruction; the False Religions; the New Philosophies; and Christianity.

Condemned Schemes. — It is evident that in examining the schemes of reconstruction it will only be necessary to turn attention to those of the present day. The fact that so many of the favorite schemes of the earlier times have passed away is sufficient proof of their inadequacy to the work proposed.

Topic First. Inadequate Solutions. — It may be shown that all these proposed solutions, save that of Christianity, are inadequate. Philosophically and historically they have failed to meet the conditions of a true solution.

Subject 1st. Self-Reconstruction Impracticable. — The moral reconstruction of the agent by his own effort would be the simplest method, if practicable. That it is impracticable may readily be shown.

1st. Philosophically. — There are certain laws of mind in accordance with which all successful conflict with the wrong and evil must be carried on:

First, the agent must understand and give heed to the moral law as the rule of life;

Secondly, he must bring all his powers and dispositions, and especially all the springs of action, under the control of the will and into accord with this moral law;

Thirdly, he must repeat the act of voluntarily subjecting his powers to this law until the ascendency of the right becomes complete and habitual.

The method of self-reconstruction in accordance with these principles must inevitably fail. The darkening and deadening of the agent's moral nature, and its powerful bias to evil tending to moral helplessness, make such struggle toward the good always irksome, and often impossible, without some aid from without, and put the true moral manhood and the complete moral task above his reach.

That this must be so is evident from considerations already presented.

Like all other derangements, it has been seen that the tendency to sin augments itself by its own action; and all things "are so constituted that any aberration from the line of law decreases the power which holds subjects of law in their place, and gives strength to the influence which draws them from obedience. As a stream passing over a rock wears for itself a channel from which it cannot escape, so the will, moving in obedience to a selfish inclination, is alienated from the standard of rectitude, and confirms itself by its natural action, in opposition to the divine law. Affectionate obedience to God, and affectionate effort for human good, is holiness; but the transgressor has not only lost his holiness, but his disposition to be holy. As inclination is to a falling body, so disposition is to the mind. Restoration, therefore, without light and aid from without the soul itself, is morally impossible. On the other hand, the natural tendency is to depart, not to return." *Walker.*

2d. Historically. — In accordance with the deduction from these principles is the fact that, historically viewed, the scheme of self-reconstruction has always failed to produce the highest man and the highest life.

Subject 2d. The False Religions Insufficient. — Confucianism, Brahmanism, Buddhism, and Mohammedanism present the chief theories, proposed by the world beyond the bounds of Christendom, concerning man's true life and manhood. They may be shown to be insufficient for the end proposed.

1st. Philosophically. — They do not meet the requisite conditions of the solution of the great moral problem. They are all utterly imperfect, — holding only a modicum of the truth concerning man's nature, relations, condition, and destiny, and furnishing no power to lift him up to his true place in the moral world.

Confucianism is the system which has had chiefly to do with making China what it has been for many centuries. Its central idea is reverence for the past; and its great end is, by means of a set of mechanical utilitarian rules, working only on the outward life, to secure the permanent stability of the social and governmental order. The sum of its maxims is: "Follow the fathers; in them is to be found all wisdom." Its spirit is therefore the spirit of conservatism, of stagnation. Confucianism has not the power needed to lift mankind up to the true moral manhood and life. It ignores all the noblest elements, and especially all the powerful elevating motives, peculiar to man's nature, and from which all progress and high attainment must proceed. Ignoring at the same time the moral wreck of his nature, and furnishing no regenerating and reconstructing agency from without and above, it must utterly fail to accomplish what man needs, and must result in mental, moral, social, and political stagnation.

Brahmanism has for ages moulded the Hindoo race. It is a form of Pantheism. All forms of life and activity are only manifestations of the one, all-pervasive, pantheistic Brahm. Brahm himself is not consciously existent, except as he wakes up into the various forms of transitory, personal being; but is eternally absorbed in a sort of day-dream of slumberous self-contemplation. Conscious, individual existence is to the Brahman the only real evil. He has by some fate become entangled in a series of births and deaths — in the bodies of men, or fishes, or reptiles, or birds, or some other beings — from which the only worthy aim is to escape. Such a system is essentially deadening to all man's nature. It leaves out all that is of any value in it, — freedom, progress, immortality, union with God. It takes away the sense of responsibility, and leads him to look upon virtue and vice as names only. It takes a radically false view of man's entire condition and destiny, and does not even dream of furnishing any power that shall lift him up to his true place. As a scheme of moral reconstruction, it must inevitably prove an utter failure.

Buddhism is an attempted reformation of Brahmanism, and an attempted advance upon it. It adds to Brahmanism a proposed method of escape, from this perpetual round of life and death, into Nirvana, or the Buddhist perfect life or heaven. Its central idea is, "the selfish salvation of the individual soul from the rounds and changes of continued earthly existence, by contemplation of truth, and good works." *Death* is its salvation; personal *annihilation*, its heaven. There is nothing in it to make a true man. Added to the defects it has in common with its parent system, it is a scheme of self-reconstruction, with all the motives to struggle for a noble life and a high manhood left out. Its own principles doom the system to failure.

Mohammedanism, for more than a thousand years, has held sway over many millions of the human race. Deism, fate, the divine mission of a cruel and sensual impostor, inhumanity, and an immortal sensuality, are its essential elements. Along with supreme loyalty to its one God, it fosters ignorance, treachery, cruelty, and sensuality; it furnishes no watchword of elevation and progression, individual or social; and it proposes no regenerating agency from without. Islamism can never produce the true moral man, nor the complete moral life, since it every-where fails to meet the conditions requisite to moral reconstruction.

2d. Historically. — These great false religions, viewed historically, have always failed to lift man up to the best manhood and the highest life. The verdict of history agrees with that of a true philosophy in pronouncing them all failures. The more perfectly men have conformed their lives to these various systems, the more incomplete, or ignoble, or enslaved, or fossilized has been the manhood.

Subject 3d. The New Philosophies Insufficient. — Modern Pantheism, Positivism, and Culturism are the chief theories, proposed by recent philosophers, concerning man's life and manhood. They may be shown to be inadequate to accomplish the end proposed.

1st. Philosophically. — They ignore the essential conditions of a true moral reconstruction. They are partial and shallow in their view of the universe, and of man's nature, relations, condition, and destiny; and offer no adequate aid in lifting him to the normal life and manhood.

Modern Pantheism — as originated and advocated by German thinkers — begins with denying all dualism in the universe. It therefore denies the essential distinction between mind and matter, between soul and body, between God and the world, between the infinite and the finite; and affirms that there is but one substance, one real being. This infinite and absolute being (the universe) has in itself neither consciousness, intelligence, nor will, save only as it comes into existence in the finite — in animals and men; and therefore is not a personal being. Man, who is only a mode of God's existence, a moment in his life, is not an individual subsistence. His personality perishes with that body upon which it depends. His acts are God's acts, the results of necessary forces, so that there can be no freedom, no responsibility, no sin. There is no essential distinction of good and evil, since both are elements of the All, or of God. It is obvious that such a system must go far toward extinguishing that *individuality* along the line of which all true development must be reached. It offers no rational progress and no conscious personal immortality, and therefore takes away the motives to growth, both in this life and in the future life. It takes away freedom and consigns man to a hopeless bondage to the forces of material

nature. Denying a personal God, it destroys responsibility in man, and
blots out the essential distinction between virtue and vice. In place of
moral reconstruction, it offers only moral extinction. There is not a
single element in it fitted to meet the wants of a moral agent and lift
him toward the true life and manhood.

Positivism originated with M. Auguste Comte, a French philosopher of the present century, and has been further developed by his
principal disciples, Mill and Spencer, aided by Lewes, Buckle, Bain,
and Huxley. Man has come to his present advanced position by a
social progress consisting of three stages. The infancy or childhood of
the race began with the *theological stage,* in which all things are referred
to divine causes and agents. The race advances toward maturity through
the *metaphysical stage,* in which it deals with transcendental ideas and
relations, and attempts to ascertain the nature and causes of things.
The race reaches its mature manhood in the *third stage,* which is that of
the *positive philosophy,* in which it learns that man can know nothing of
the nature and causes of things, in short, that he can know nothing
beyond observed material facts and changes. The individual man is of
no importance; he is only an element in the great solidarity of humanity.
If he has a spirit, if he has an immortality, it cannot be known. If
there be a God, he must forever be an unknown God. Psychology is
at once an impossibility and an absurdity. Finding that man would
have some religion, in spite of the positive philosophy, Comte hits
upon an object of worship in *collective humanity,* the *grand Being.* This
god was especially to be worshipped in the great and illustrious of the
past, and, above all, in woman, who, as embodying the highest form of
love, represents the best attribute of humanity, and that which ought to
regulate all human life. This system begins with a baseless misrepre-
sentation of all history. It leaves everything that is highest in man
unprovided for. It ignores the soul, immortality, and God. It would
destroy every powerful motive to progress and virtue. It takes no
notice of the wreck of man's nature. It makes provision for debasing
rather than elevating humanity. It is logically linked with atheism
and sensuality. There is no promise in it of a true moral life and
manhood. It is but a blind leader of the blind.

Culturism is the latest and most pretentious solution offered of the
great moral problem. Along the line of positivism, Mr. Huxley has
reached a theory of *scientific culture* which he proposes for the adoption
of mankind. The goal of humanity is to be found in a truly liberal
education. Says Mr. Huxley: "That man, I think, has had a liberal
education who has been so trained in youth that his body is the ready
servant of his will, and does with ease and pleasure all the work that,

as a mechanism, it is capable of; whose intellect is a clear, cold, logic engine, with all its parts of equal strength, and in smooth working order; ready, like a steam-engine, to be turned to any kind of work, and spin the gossamers as well as forge the anchors of the mind; whose mind is stored with a knowledge of the great and fundamental truths of nature, and of the laws of her operations; one who, no stunted ascetic, is full of life and fire, but whose passions are trained to come to heel by a vigorous will, the servant of a tender conscience; who has learned to love all beauty, whether of nature or art, to hate all vileness, and to respect others as himself." This theory has all the philosophic defects of *Positivism.* It acknowledges no human and immortal spirit, and not even an unknown God. It does not tell whence is to be brought into a wrecked human nature this "vigorous will, the servant of a tender conscience." It has not a whisper of a reconstruction, much less of a reconstructing agency. It does not even furnish a single moral motive to elevation, since in fact it has no morality. "We, as intelligent, thinking beings, find ourselves in a universe which meets us at all points with fixed laws, which encompass us about externally, and rule us also within; fixed laws in the region of matter, fixed laws in the region of mind; that, therefore, knowledge for us is knowledge of laws, and can be nothing more; and that wisdom in us is simply the skill to turn the knowledge of these laws to the best account, conforming ourselves to them, and availing ourselves of them to appropriate to ourselves all the good they bring within our reach." The theory may lead to moral despair and tend to moral degradation and annihilation, but never to the true moral life and manhood. It would annihilate virtue.

Along the line of classical and literary study, Matthew Arnold has reached a theory of *literary* and *æsthetic culture* which he proposes to mankind. Greece, rather than Judea, had the true idea of the perfected humanity. Religion must become secondary to *culture.* The age of the world, in which "sweetness and light"—"an inward and spiritual activity, having for its characters increased sweetness, increased light, increased life, increased sympathy"—were pre-eminently combined, was the best age of Athens, that which is represented in the poetry of Sophocles, in whom "the idea of beauty and a full-developed humanity" took to itself a religion and devout energy, in the strength of which it worked. This Neo-pagan theory proposes *culture,* then, as something higher and better for the perfection of humanity than religion can be. Its aim is to develop *self;* its ideal is the *best self;* its agency is *self-reliance,* "built on the criticism of inward experience and the experimental sanction of our moral instincts and intuitions." Such a theory can do little for man. It does not meet the conditions of a true solution of the great moral problem. It concentrates the attention on self; puts literary culture in the place of God and duty and immortality; evinces a low conception of character; proves the inadequacy of its author's view of man's moral wants, and, in short, of all the wants of man's being; and fails to furnish any sufficient motive or suitable reconstructing agency whereby the moral agent may be elevated to the true life and manhood.

2d. Historically. — Examined historically, these new philosophies are proved to have failed to produce the complete manhood and the highest life. The verdict of history agrees with that of philosophy. They need no better refutation than the disregard of the highest obligations, social, moral, and religious, to which they have led some of their originators and ablest advocates.

Topic Second. The Only Adequate Solution. — Of all the theories proposed, Christianity alone meets the demands legitimately made of any scheme of moral reconstruction that claims the attention of mankind.

Subject 1st. The Solution which Christianity Offers. — Christianity takes into account and provides for all the essential elements of human nature. It proposes to make the most and the best of body and soul, of intellect and moral nature, of the individual and of society. It gives the grandest scope and solemnity to freedom and responsibility, to progressiveness and immortality. It exalts God to his true kingdom of power and wisdom and love over the life and destiny of man.

It takes full cognizance of the all-important facts of the wreck of the moral manhood and the failure in the moral task. It provides for the restoration of the former by an almighty reconstructing power; and for the lifting up of the latter by the new and universal motive power of divine faith and love, and by the mighty and everlasting mission for the glory of God.

It embodies its perfect system of morality and its marvellous scheme of grace in a person, Jesus Christ, who is at once the perfect example of human right doing and the complete exhibition of divine love for man, and the almighty helper of man in his struggle up toward the right life and manhood.

Subject 2d. The Solution Adequate. — That the solution which Christianity proposes meets and fully satisfies all the demands of the case may be made to appear as it is viewed both philosophically and historically.

1st. Philosophically. — It points man always to the noblest and the best, and proposes to lead him toward perfect conformity to that moral law, which requires of him supreme devotion to God, a wise regard for his own being, and an unselfish love and helpfulness to his fellow-man.

The Proposed Aim. — That Christianity proposes this moral perfection, as the aim for those who accept it, will not be denied by any intelligent and candid man. That this is an aim perfectly adapted to man's nature and wants, and that it is morally the grandest possible, is equally obvious.

That it presents a reasonable method, and furnishes the requisite means and agencies for the attainment of its high moral end, is apparent from the mere statement of its proposed solution of the moral problem. The perfect moral rule, the perfect example of moral manhood and life, the perfect moral mission, the divine regenerating power, the mediatorial sovereignty of Christ, are but a few of the elements which it embraces, that have no part in any other scheme of moral reconstruction that has ever been proposed.

It is acknowledged by even the worst enemies of Christianity, that when those who claim to adhere to it fail to reach a noble life and manhood, it is not the fault of the system, in its aim, in its method, or in its agencies, but the fault of themselves.

2d. Historically. — In general, history places the influence of Christianity upon the world for good in marked contrast with all other schemes, whether of philosophy or religion.

The Contrast. — The elements of new moral aim, moral motive, and moral power, centering in the person of Christ, have everywhere manifested their transforming influence. Says Dr. Fraser (*Blending Lights*): "In the multifarious religions of the world, this motive to action and this aim were absent. There was an abiding and ever deeply felt want, which they utterly failed to remove or lessen. The sublime moral maxims of Oriental nations, — the early learning of Egypt, — the philosophic and æsthetic culture of Greece, — and the jurisprudence of Rome, rising from the midst of an all-embracing idolatry, — never produced any results approaching those which the preaching of the gospel has diffused through every generation. For at least six thousand years, the world has done its best to repress evil and lessen sorrow, but has failed. Untaught by experience, the world continues its vain struggle. Philosophy has long striven to solve the problem of human life, and has failed. Poetry has long sung its most ennobling strains, and has failed. Political wisdom has run its course of secular expedients, and has failed. Unaided humanity has had no spirit with power enough to rise above its own dark and troubled waters, and evolve from its chaos light, beauty, and stability. But in the doctrines of the cross, in the Gospel revealing the love of God in Christ Jesus, there is the supernatural introduction of a new motive power, there is that which is changing the intellectual and moral aspects of the whole world. Although heathen philosophers understood not the gospel, the olden prophets proclaimed its power; although earliest poets could assign it no place in their strains, it gave a tenderer thrill to David's lyre, and with it Solomon enriched his song; although to the Greek it was foolishness, and to the Jew a stumbling-block, it became mighty to the pulling down of the strongholds of Satan ; and although Saul of Tarsus constrained men to attempt to swear it down, it subdued his own heart, and led him, in the face alike of friend and foe, henceforth with unfaltering tongue to proclaim his one great resolve, — 'God forbid that I should glory, save in the Cross of our Lord Jesus Christ.'"

In particular, history demonstrates that, wherever Christianity has been allowed to do its appropriate work, it has actually reconstructed the moral life, individual, social, and national.

Reconstruction of Individual Life. — The faith in Christ combines in itself the absolute self-surrender and self-abnegation of Orientalism, and an intense enthusiasm for a lofty ideal, and has thus shown itself able with equal ease to transform the cultivated Paul and the savage

Africaner. It has shown men, up to the highest and down to the lowest, their true moral condition; it has awakened in them intense longings for the true and noble manhood and mission; it has made them "new creatures." It summons every man to know, to act, and to be for himself alone as accountable to God; and offers to every man a place among the sons of God. Its universal product is a nobler life and man. The world owes to it its best men and its grandest and most beneficent lives in all ages.

Reconstruction of Social Life. — Christianity has shown itself able with equal ease to transform society. It has broken down the old wall of separation between the Jew and the Gentile, between the high and the low, between the learned and the unlearned, and made the world one on the nobler basis of character and common humanity. It has brought in care for the once despised poor, given freedom to the slave, lifted woman to her rightful place, filled all Christendom with its infirmaries and hospitals and asylums, and introduced an intense love and an enthusiastic self-sacrifice for universal humanity. It alone, of all the systems that plead for man's adoption, has introduced this practical recognition of the universal brotherhood.

Reconstruction of National Life. — No less complete has been the power of Christianity over nations than over individuals and society. Its transforming power was exhibited in the early ages in the Roman Empire. Guizot declares that it was in studying for the annotation of Gibbon, he became impressed, "not only with the moral and social grandeur of Christianity, but with the difficulty of explaining it by purely human forces and causes." All the great nations of the present day are monuments of the elevating and ennobling power of Christianity. More convincing still are the records of the Missionary movement of the present age. "The most ferocious and debased cannibal tribes have been subdued by the influence of the gospel, — the most sunken tribes in the world, — men of all races, of all grades in society, and of all stages in culture," have been lifted up to a truly noble manhood. Greenlanders and Fuegians, South Sea Islanders and Bechuanas, Turks, and inhabitants of Madagascar, are living witnesses of the reconstructing power of Christianity. Among all the systems of the ages, it stands alone in its power to produce the true moral life and man.

Christianity is thus shown to be the only true scheme of moral reconstruction. It furnishes the only adequate solution to the problem upon which all ages have wrought, *How may*

15

man be brought up to the true moral manhood and to the accomplishment of the true moral task?

If man's nature be in a condition of moral disorder, as was made evident in the preceding *Section*, then Christianity presents the only way by which moral philosophy can point the agent to the complete life of virtue, and is the only hope of the world.

SUMMARY.

The line of thought which has thus been pursued in constructing — from the facts of conscience and the principles of virtue — a *Philosophy of Human Duty*, has shown especially:

First, that virtue consists in the intentional conformity of the action to the right, or to the will of the Moral Governor; and that the principles of a true morality call every man to the noblest possible manhood and an unswerving life of duty;

Secondly, that the natural requisites for the accomplishment of this task of duty have been given to every man, in intelligence, conscience, and free will; but that so grand a task can only be accomplished by aid of powers disciplined to the perfect: an intellect the keenest and broadest; a conscience the quickest, clearest, and most decisive; and a will the strongest and holiest;

Thirdly, that, by reason of the wreck of man's moral nature, the moral manhood is lost and the mission has become impossible; but that Christianity offers a moral reconstruction which fully meets the demands of the case, and opens to mankind the way back from moral death and shame to the noblest moral achievements and the truest moral glory.

The Philosophy of the Life of Duty therefore reaches its completion only in Christianity, — the true **Moral System** culminating in the true **Religious System**, and founding on this the strongest claim to the title of *Christian Ethics.*

PART II.

PRACTICAL ETHICS.

Definition and Division.

Practical Ethics is that part of Christian Ethics which applies the theory of duty, as determined by Theoretical Ethics, to the regulation of man's conduct in working out the complete mission of duty in the position and relations in which the Moral Governor has placed him.

It has already been shown that the duties which constitute man's moral task appear in germinal form in the intuitive moral judgments, or principles, investigated in Theoretical Ethics. All duties are therefore simply unfoldings and applications of the three great moral requirements: of due regard toward self, toward mankind, and toward God.

Germs of the Law. — These germs of the law, as canons of duty, have been variously stated. As drawn from the Scriptures, they may be stated as follows:

Thou shalt love thyself as bearing the image of God.

Thou shalt love thy neighbor as thyself.

Thou shalt love God with all thy heart, and with all thy soul, and with all thy mind, and with all thy strength.

A convenient form for the purposes of Practical Ethics, drawn more directly from the intuitive moral judgments, and stated in the form of requirements, is as follows:

Thou shalt conserve and perfect thy being, and direct it to the attainment of the true end of life.

Thou shalt seek to do like work for thy neighbor's being.

Thou shalt render supreme devotion to God.

Advantages of System.—A system unfolded from germinal principles will necessarily have certain advantages over one constructed by the ordinary method of gathering together empirical moral principles from all quarters and arranging them in a mechanical order. *First*, it will furnish a *real system*, each part of which will aid in understanding, remembering, and applying the other parts. *Secondly*, if the view be at all what it should be, it will furnish a *complete system*, which shall be an adequate guide to the agent in the accomplishment of his full moral mission. *Thirdly*, it will furnish a *certain and valid system*, since, if it is properly unfolded from the intuitive germs of the moral law, there can be no reasonable doubt that its principles are exact and trustworthy.

Strictly considered, *all duty is owed originally to God only;* but in consequence of the three great relations of the moral agent, in which he is to accomplish his mission, duties *to* God may be distributed, according to the three directions which they may take, into duties *toward* self, *toward* mankind, and *toward* God.

All Duty to God.—Strictly speaking, all obligation must be to God the Moral Governor and Author of the moral law, and all duties must therefore be *duties to God.* It is only in a loose and improper sense that they can be spoken of as duties to self, to mankind, and to God. To make the proper distinction, the word *toward* should be used instead of *to*, when these separate spheres of duty are to be indicated.

As the three great relations of man decide the spheres of duty, Practical Ethics will therefore be treated under three *Divisions:*

Division I. Individual Ethics, treating of Duties toward Self.

Division II. Social Ethics, treating of Duties toward Mankind.

Division III. Theistic Ethics, treating of Duties toward God.

Order of Treatment. — As God is at the foundation of all moral obligation, Theistic Ethics would logically come first in order; but, as man's ideas of duty are developed in connection with his moral experience, he naturally acquaints himself with those duties having reference to himself, first; with those having reference to mankind, next in order; and with those having reference to God, last. The order of experience furnishes the more convenient order of study.

DIVISION I.

INDIVIDUAL ETHICS.

Statement and Subdivision.

Individual Ethics is that division of Practical Ethics which treats of the application of the moral law to the regulation of man's conduct, so far as it has reference to himself as an individual moral agent.

As man's duty toward himself is summed up in a due regard to the continuance, improvement, and proper direction of his being, the natural unfolding of this intuitive moral principle furnishes the subjects of the following *Chapters:*

Chapter I.   Duty of Self-Conservation.
Chapter II.   Duty of Self-Culture.
Chapter III.   Duty of Self-Conduct.

The Usual Subdivision. — Kant proposes two topics of Individual Ethics: the first, "*the formal duties,* which are limitary or negative duties; the second, *the material duties,* which are positive duties owed by man to himself." "The former forbid mankind to act contrary to the ends and purposes of his being, and so concern simply his ethical self-preservation; the latter ordain him to make a given object of choice his end, and command the perfecting of his own nature. Both these, as moral duties, are elements of virtue; the one as duties of omission (*sustine et abstine*), the other as duties of commission (*viribus concessis utere*); the first go to constitute man's ethic health (*ad esse*), and to the preservation of the entireness of his system . . . . ; the second constitute his ethic opulence (*ad melius esse*), a wealth consisting in the possession of functions adapted for the realization of all ends, in so far as these powers and functions are matter of acquisition, and belong to self-culture as an active and attained perfection. The first principle of duty is couched in the adage, '*naturæ convenienter vive,*' *i. e.,* '*Maintain thyself in the original perfection of thy nature;*' the second in the position, '*perfice te ut finem, perfice te ut medium,*' '*Study to perfect and advance thy being.*'" Others, as Wuttke, present substantially the same phases of duty toward self by the expressions *moral sparing* and *moral forming.*

Grounds of the Present Subdivision. — If it be true that man was made for the accomplishment of a grand moral task, then it becomes evident that his highest duty toward himself must be the direction of his powers to this great end. Duty toward himself must therefore require of him : first, that he conserve the being and powers given him for the work of life; secondly, that he develop and perfect them, that they may become fully equal to that work; and, thirdly, that he direct them to the accomplishment of that work of life and end of his being.

CHAPTER I.

DUTY OF SELF-CONSERVATION.

AS the continuance of man's existence as a living being, with all his powers in their integrity, is indispensable to the fulfilment of his moral mission, it is his *first duty toward himself* to conserve his being and powers in their integrity.

Binding Force of the Duty.—This duty is evidently immediately connected with the fundamental moral judgment on which Individual Ethics rests; so that, as soon as the idea of his moral mission is made known to man, even in its most imperfect form, the duty of self-conservation becomes self-evident, as an element of that intuitive judgment. It is at once seen to be of immediate and universal obligation.

Man is to conserve his being from the three great enemies which would prevent the fulfilment of his mission: death; sickness and disease; and, poverty and want. His duty may therefore have reference to his life, his health, or his well-being. These distinctions furnish the divisions of self-conservation, and indicate the subjects of the following *Sections:*

Section 1.   Duty of Self-Preservation.
Section 2.   Duty of Self-Care.
Section 3.   Duty of Self-Support.

As man is constituted of body and spirit, and self-conservation may have reference to both, each of these three forms of duty may be regarded in its twofold relation to body and spirit.

SECTION I.

Duty of Self-Preservation.

Man is exposed to the forces of death which threaten to destroy his being, and thus to prevent his mission. It therefore becomes his duty to preserve his life and to avoid or resist everything tending toward death. He is equally bound to protect himself against death from his own agency and from that of others, — from death of body and soul.

Preserve thy Being — is a first and universal law of all nature. It is fixed in the constitution of all organized being. The functions of vegetable life have the preservation and continuance of that life as one great end. The inferior animals are impelled by instinct to take their natural food and reject that which is noxious; to flee from danger and from their natural enemies. They never spontaneously do anything to shorten or terminate their existence. Even the case of the viper, which, when surrounded by flames, gradually retires to the centre of the circle, and dies by its own sting, and which has often been cited as an exception to this otherwise universal law of self-preservation, is better explained as a case of unconscious muscular contraction.

Unlike other beings, man is capable of consciously making the preservation of his being an end, and of seeking that end in an intelligent and rational manner.

Topic First. Preservation of Bodily Life.

1st. From Self. — As the body is the home and working-place of the spirit, and its medium of communication and instrument for work, man's duty toward himself requires a sacred regard for his bodily life. It forbids, in general, all that is destructive to it; and, especially, *self-mutilation* and *self-murder.*

A Sacred Regard for the Body is Required. — It has been seen, in Theoretical Ethics, that the complete man is the man who has a whole body and a whole soul. In man's present condition the body is as truly essential to his mission as the soul. Hence a sacred regard for the body in its relations to the mission becomes a high and holy duty, which is intuitively recognized as soon as the agent comes to understand the true relations of body and soul. He who neglects his bodily life puts his mission in peril; he who destroys that life brings his mission to a premature end.

Self-Mutilation is Forbidden.—This prohibition includes any bodily injury or dismemberment which lames or disfigures the person or removes any part that is essential to the complete physical man. It includes the practice, among savages, of painting, scarring, or disfiguring the face or person, and the like practices in so-called civilized races; the practice of forcing a more fashionable shape, as of feet, as among the Chinese; or of body, as by fashionable dress; or of head, as among the Flathead Indians, and in so-called civilized society.

It is further included, that no one may voluntarily part with what is essential to his bodily frame with a view to procure gain to himself, or from any such low motive. It is plain, however, that the parting with a diseased limb or member of the body may become a duty, as essential to preserving the life; and that one, in the performance of a greater duty, may risk any maiming of the body.

Self-Murder is Forbidden. — Wherever the moral consciousness of mankind has been enlightened, they have agreed in the intuitive judgment that *suicide* is contrary to the end for which and the condition under which life is given. It prevents the fulfilment of the mission of life. The work is great, the time is short, and man has no right to shorten it. In the warfare of life every one has his post, and he is not at liberty to desert it. He is bound by more than military oath to keep it. This view of human life was distinctly taken and strongly exhibited by many of the ancient moralists. Pythagoras is represented as saying (*Cic. de Senec.*): "that no one should depart from his station without the command of his general, that is, God." Plato has said: "that in this life we are placed in a garrison, from which we must not retire nor withdraw ourselves." It is true that both the Cynic and Cyrenaic Schools of philosophy furnished their disciples with reasons for the justification of suicide, and that some of the ancient heathen sages escaped public execution by suicide: but the perversion of the moral judgment in these instances may be accounted for by their incomplete views of man's being, position, and destiny.

It is, moreover, true that suicide has been discouraged and punished by the laws of all nations as a sin against the state.

In all ages, the conscience of men enlightened by the Christian system of morals has agreed in condemning self-murder. Among the early Christians, those who exposed themselves to death in their attempts to deface or demolish the idols of the heathen were forbidden to be enrolled among the number of the martyrs. Throughout all modern

M

Christendom the obligation of the maxim, *Do thyself no harm*, is acknowledged and maintained.

2d. From Others. — Self-preservation against death from others renders self-defence a duty, and may even justify the infliction of death on an attacking party.

Defend thy Being. — This maxim is but a special application of the fundamental and universal principle of self-conservation. In defending himself, man may do harm to others, but he is justifiable in doing so when the harm to himself cannot otherwise be prevented. In defending his own life he may be free from blame, even in taking away the life of another. This is universally recognized by human law.

Self-Defense not Unchristian. — The question is sometimes asked, Does not Christianity prohibit self-defense? It says: "Forgive your enemies." "Resist not evil." The answer is that the prohibition in these cases is not of self-defense, but of *revenge*. When the injury has been inflicted, let God avenge, not yourself. Rather let the injury be repeated than retaliate. Even in strict self-defense, *the least blending of retaliatory vengeance would be an immorality,*—as violating the law requiring man to love his neighbor as himself. But self-defense without malice and revenge is proper and right. The disabling of the assailant must always be done by the agent *solely to save himself*, and not to take vengeance.

3d. Bodily Life not Supreme. — But, while the preservation of the bodily life is so sacred a duty, it is not the supreme duty. There are higher interests of the spirit, of society, and of the world, the preservation of which may require the sacrifice of the bodily life of the individual.

Says Dr. Haven: "Rather than betray the cause of truth and right, rather than desert the principles of justice and honor, and prove recreant to duty and to faith, a man may well die. In defence of the innocent and helpless, in defence of the right, in defence of his family and his country, in defence of his religious belief, he may well lay down his life, if need be. As a martyr, as a patriot, as a lover of truth and justice, there may be occasion to die. Life is not the highest duty, nor the most sacred treasure of man."

The most Heroic Virtue may be reached through such perilling of life. Prompted by a desire to alleviate the moral and physical degradation of the prisoners and criminals of the world, John Howard plunged into the unwholesomeness of the dungeon and the infection of the prison-house, and met, himself, with the death from which he sought to save others. Florence Nightingale nearly lost her own life in her devotion to the wounded and dying soldiers. They exhibited a moral heroism worthy of all admiration.

Topic Second. Preservation of the Spirit's Life. — There are forces of spiritual death to which man is exposed, and which may destroy the fitness of his spirit both for its earthly mission and for its mission of immortality. It therefore becomes man's duty to preserve himself from such death, both from his own agency and from the agency of others.

Moral Death-Forces to be Resisted. — It has been shown that transgression of the moral law benumbs and wrecks, and so renders worthless, the higher powers of the soul. The moral agent may thus become blind to duty and to God, and incapable of fulfilling his true mission. It therefore becomes a very solemn duty for man to guard himself against death in this higher and profounder sense. He must hold out as for life against the evil tendencies of his own nature, which will else make his being a fountain of corruption and death; and, for the same end and with the same ceaseless vigilance, he must guard against all corrupting influences from those around and associated with him.

SECTION II.

Duty of Self-Care.

Man is exposed to the forces of sickness and disease, which threaten to impair the vigor and efficiency of his powers, and thus to prevent the accomplishment of his full mission. It therefore becomes his duty to care for his health of body and of spirit, and to avoid or resist everything that would tend to weaken or impair it.

Topic First. Care of the Body. — Proper care of the body requires, in general, due attention to the laws of man's physical system. It forbids all transgression of these laws, as putting in peril his moral work.

The General Duty of man to keep the law of his physical being is commonly admitted in the present age. Disease results from transgressing this law; and while the dreams of those who expect the race ultimately to reach absolution from death through the perfect observance of this law will doubtless never be realized, it is still true that man has already risen in civilized lands to a comparative exemption from some of those diseases that are the worst scourges of the savage, and that in the progress of knowledge he may hope for still larger exemption from disease in many other forms.

Violation by Asceticism. — Neglect and mortification of the body have, however, often been taught as duties of the first importance, so that it has been too true, as Pascal says, that "in trying to make themselves angels, men have made themselves brutes." *Asceticism*, in both its theological and philosophical forms, has weakened and impaired the bodily health, and so unfitted man for his moral mission, — in the one form, by conceiving the body to be the source and seat of evil, and so seeking to expiate the sin and to appease the offended Deity by voluntarily inflicting bodily pain, even to the extent of torture; and in the other form, by regarding the spirit as enslaved by the body, and so making light of and despising man's physical nature, and seeking to free the spirit wholly from it. In both forms it has forgotten the all-important truth, that the complete manhood is realized only in the sound mind in the sound body.

Health to be Sought. — The health of the body is viewed in its true light, when it is regarded as essential to the soundness and vigor of the spirit, and as thus necessary to the fulfilment of man's appointed mission. Ill health may prevent the exercise and discipline which are necessary for the first development of the mental faculties; disease may impair or impede their use after they have been developed, and so may make the life a failure, and the man a burden to himself and all about him. It is therefore of the utmost importance that one who would do the true work of life should take all reasonable care of his bodily health, as necessary to that strength and serenity of mind, and to that activity and energy of the whole being, which are the elements of power essential to the accomplishment of the noblest mission.

Abuse of Powers to be Avoided. — It is obvious that the moral principle, which governs man in his duty toward his body, forbids, not only the penances, mortifications, fastings, and rigid austerities of asceticism, but also all over-taxing and straining of the powers, all enervating habits and careless neglect, all excessive indulgence and all engrossing attention to business, whereby the physical powers become weakened or disordered. The fasts and self-denials of a true Christianity tend rather to invigorate than to enfeeble the human system. The law requiring them is never to be pushed to man's physical injury: where the danger of this comes in, mercy becomes better than sacrifice.

Proper care of the bodily health requires, in particular, special attention to diet, air, cleanliness, exercise, rest, and sleep; since these are most closely connected with the sources of vigor and the inlets of disease.

Eating and Drinking. — Modern chemical analysis confirms the statement of Scripture, that "the Lord God formed man out of the dust of the ground;" since the soil, the world over, is shown to contain the elements found in the human body. It is true, likewise, that the nutriment which is to support the body must be drawn from the earth; and as man has not himself the power of taking up directly and assimilating the requisite chemical elements, the vegetable and animal kingdoms have been ordained to prepare his food for him. This food may be divided into three classes: the *carbonates*, in which carbon predominates, and which supply the lungs with fuel and thus furnish heat to the system, and which also contribute the fat, or adipose substance; the *nitrates*, in which nitrogen predominates, and which supply the waste of the muscles; and the *phosphates*, in which phosphorus predominates, and which supply the bones, brain, and nerves and give vital power. A deficiency in any of these requisite kinds of food must necessarily tend to disease, and hence to impaired activity of the man. It is clearly his duty to understand the wants of the human system, and the fitness or unfitness of the various articles of diet proposed to supply these wants.

But while health depends so largely upon the *matter* of eating, it depends no less upon the *manner*. Dr. Abernethy used to say that the two great killing powers in the world are *stuff* and *fret*. It is the tendency of this fast age to ignore the necessity for mastication and to save time by "bolting" the food. The natural result is excess in quantity, derangement of the system, dyspepsia, and general unfitness for the full work of body and brain, — in short, a species of suicide.

Drinking is of like great importance to health. More than three-fourths of the human system is composed of water. Without water no vital process could be carried on for a single moment. The circulation, secretion, downtaking, and upbuilding of the system, and the preservation of the body at an almost absolutely uniform temperature, in all men and all climates, depend upon it. *Thirst is the demand of the system for water.* If the drink contains anything besides water, the system proceeds at once to distil and purify it of this, before appropriating it. Pure water is the drink provided by nature and intended by God for

16

man. Says Dr. Blackie (*Self-Culture*): "'Honest water certainly has this merit, that it never made any man a sinner;' and of whiskey it may be said that, however beneficial it may be on a wet moor, or on the top of a frosty Ben in the Highlands, when indulged in habitually, it never made any man either fair or fat. He who abstains from it altogether will never die in a ditch, and will always find a penny in his pocket to help himself and his friend in an emergency."

It is the province of ethics to make clear and enforce man's duty in eating and drinking: Dietetics must furnish and unfold the scientific view of diet.

Air. — Food, even if perfect in quality and quantity, does not fulfil its office of building up the human system, unless there be added the agency of the air acting through the lungs. The office of the air in the human lungs is to burn up the waste and poisonous particles which are constantly being taken down and removed from the various parts of the system, and to furnish heat and oxygen to the currents which build up the body. An imperfect supply of oxygen, or the presence of any noxious elements in the air breathed, must generate feebleness and disease. Pure air and full breathing — that both quality and quantity may be right — are thus equally essential to health; and it becomes man's duty to make sure of them both.

The changes of the last fifty years, in science and civilization, have made this subject one of special and even vital importance. The closely-built house, the introduction of stoves and furnaces, and the vastly increased necessity for economy in fuel, have entirely changed the conditions of modern family life and made the subject of *ventilation*, or the furnishing of a constant supply of pure air, one of prime importance. At the same time, science has shown so clearly the dependence of bodily health and vigor upon perfectly oxygenated blood, and the connection of consumption and a large class of the most terrible diseases with the absence of this, as to convince all intelligent men of the duty of securing a full and constant supply of pure air in order to health.

Cleanliness is another of the requirements of self-care. A most important function is performed by the skin of the body, in carrying off the impurities from the blood by the insensible perspiration, and in regulating the temperature of the system. Twenty-eight miles of perspiratory glands and ducts open the way through the skin to the outside world by some seven million mouths. It is estimated that on the average about two pounds of liquid are carried off by the insensible perspiration every twenty-four hours. In times of great exertion, in high temperature, several pounds are sometimes thrown off in an hour. These myriad canals are the chief safety-valves of the human system;

and hence on their being kept open by a proper regard to cleanliness depend, in large measure, the vigor and health of the body. Many diseases originate in want of cleanliness, and may be cured by attention to it. So simple a thing as the failure to keep the teeth properly cleansed may result in their loss; may impair the speech and leave the orator shorn of his power; may destroy the digestion and the vigor of the entire system and cut off half of the allotted period of life. So great is the indirect influence of regard for cleanliness on the strength and life of man.

It has been remarked, also, that they who are careless about the clean and wholesome state of the body are not often distinguished by the purity or spirituality of their thoughts. Hence it is that attention to cleanliness has so often been conjoined with the observances of religion.

It is obviously the duty of man to attend intelligently and carefully to so important a matter as this, upon which health, and even life, must depend. It belongs to ethics to make clear and enforce the duty of attending to pure air and cleanliness: the requisite knowledge of the laws of health, as connected with them, must be furnished by Hygienics.

Exercise, in its simpler forms as essential to the conservation of the being, belongs among the duties of *self-care:* as an agency in the development of the powers, it belongs under *self-culture.* Exercise is requisite in order to keep up the vigor and tone of the human system. As any unused power of mind is soon weakened or lost, so the body without exercise soon becomes weak and diseased, and alike unable to assimilate the food and to cast off the impurities from the blood. Says Dr. Blackie: "All life is an energizing or working; absolute rest is found only in the grave; and the measure of a man's vitality is the measure of his working power. To possess every faculty and function of the body in harmonious working order is to be healthy; to be healthy, with a high degree of vital force, is to be strong. A man may be healthy without being strong; but all health tends, more or less, towards strength, and all disease is weakness."

It belongs to ethics to emphasize the duty of exercise: its forms and principles are treated in Gymnastics and Callisthenics.

Rest and Sleep are required in due proportion under self-care. There are limits to human exertion and endurance. Labor exhausts; so that it must be followed by rest. It wears out the frame also. Every movement — even to the slightest — of any part of the body burns up or breaks down some portion of the cells or tissues; and these can only be properly replaced in the hours of perfect rest furnished by sleep.

Without proper attention to rest and sleep — both of which should be adapted to the temperament of the individual and the nature of his employment — man's mission must be at least a partial failure. Ethics must therefore emphasize the duty of rest and sleep: Hygienics must furnish the directions for the proper performance of the duty.

Topic Second. Care of the Spirit. — Self-care requires, in general, due attention to the laws of man's spiritual being, and forbids all transgression of them as putting in peril his life of duty.

This Duty is now Generally Admitted. — There are laws of the spirit, as of the body, which must be obeyed. There are wrong conditions of spirit which need to be guarded against. Insanity, mental imbecility, and moral worthlessness are but results of these abnormal conditions. The maxim, *Care for thy being*, forbids everything that would tend to such wreck, as fatal to the true mission of man.

Proper care for the spirit's health requires, in particular, special attention to the preservation of the spirit in its normal condition of self-activity, freedom, truth, and subjection to reason; since these are most closely connected with the integrity of the soul, as the sources of vigor and the inlets of disease.

Self-Activity to be Preserved in its Integrity. — If the soul is essentially self-active, then whatever impairs this activity, so far impairs the very life and health of the soul itself, and saps the foundations of progress. It becomes man's duty therefore to guard against all enervating influences which may be brought to bear upon it. Narcotics and stimulants, which stupefy and ultimately destroy the tone of the mind; fear and anxiety, which overstrain and ultimately paralyze it; ceaseless and unresting exertions, which wear out and wreck its powers; all agencies and influences whatsoever, which tend to mental weakness and sluggishness, — are to be guarded against with the utmost moral vigilance as enemies to man's true mission.

Freedom to be Preserved in its Integrity. — It has been seen that, along with self-activity, freedom helps to form the basis of the true moral manhood, and is therefore essential to the moral wholeness or health. It includes the right of a man to the disposal of his powers of body and soul according to his own will, subject only to the law of his moral agency. Next to life, it is man's choicest possession. The loss of it puts the full mission beyond his reach. In the course of a free and right development, it is therefore a most sacred duty of man to preserve his liberty, from the encroachment of his own perverted appetites and habits, and from every influence, agency, or being, that would tend to enslave him.

Truth to be Preserved in its Integrity. — *Truthfulness* will be exhibited under *Social Ethics* as a duty toward mankind; but duty toward self requires that man be *true* — even if there be no human being besides himself. The integrity of his being requires, that in his development he should be true to his nature; in his acts, true to his law; in his words, true to his character and being; in his whole life, true to his mission; in short, that he be *in every way true.* Development contrary to nature, action not in accord with the law, speech not the expression of the man, and life neglectful of the mission, are all indications of an abnormal and unhealthy condition of the spirit, and are therefore to be conscientiously avoided as fatal to the moral mission.

Subjection to Reason to be Preserved in its Integrity. — As reason, in its three aspects, is the authorized guide of human action, it is necessary, in order that man's self-activity may be kept free and true, that he should give to reason its rightful place as guide. Appetite, passion, prejudice, fashion, evil habit, enthroned in the place of reason, weaken, stupefy, enslave, and destroy the moral integrity of man, and prevent the fulfilment of his mission. It is his duty, therefore, to keep himself, as a rational being, from the power of these and all kindred false influences; and, while giving due heed to the happiness and perfection of his being, to keep always before him righteousness as the supreme end of his activities.

<hr>

SECTION III.

Duty of Self-Support.

Man is liable to certain wants, for which the means of supply is provided by the beneficence of the Moral Governor in nature, or furnished by the skill of man himself in art. These wants unsupplied hamper his action and prevent the accomplishment of his mission. It therefore becomes his duty to guard against want and poverty, and to provide for his

16 *

well-being by laying hold of and using the means of satisfaction and wealth furnished for this end.

"Resolve not to be Poor," wrote Dr. Johnson to Boswell. "Whatever
you have, spend less. Poverty is a great enemy to human happiness:
it certainly destroys liberty; it makes some virtues impracticable, and
others extremely difficult." It is evident that neither poverty nor
riches is to be sought for its own sake.

In Nature and Art is found the storehouse of treasures and forces to
relieve man from poverty and want.

Topic First.   Support of the Body.—It is obvious that the
means by which the body is kept in being and health are at
the same time means by which the well-being of man is conserved.   But proper regard for the well-being requires especially, that man should secure and use, in every right way, that
which is furnished in nature and art for sustaining the body
in its full vigor and freedom in effort.

Nature was made for Man. —It furnishes him with the means of sustenance and enjoyment; with forces which may be made to assist him
in all his work in life; and, in short, with the basis for those varied
possessions known as *wealth*. In art, man has applied his own intelligence and skill in modifying and increasing the value of all these gifts
of nature; and has thus added permanently to the value and extent of
his means of support. It is evidently his duty to make the most of
these aids. By so doing he may vastly multiply the power and range
of his activities, while releasing his body from servile drudgery and
guarding it against weakness, disease, and death.

Out of self-support, therefore, arises man's duty to improve
nature and to perfect art, — that they may yield more abundantly that which he needs for his well-being, and that they
may furnish a better theatre on which he may work out his
moral task.

Duty to Improve Nature. —Properly speaking, man can have no
duties toward nature, since nature has no endowment of rationality and
no likeness of God. Nature is simply a means to be used by man in
attaining a certain end. It can have no rights of its own; is not under
control of moral law; and has therefore no place in any moral system
for its own sake. It will appear, however, in Theistic Ethics, that a

certain regard and reverence for nature, as a work, possession, and revelation of the Moral Governor, may be due for the sake of the Moral Governor, though not for its own sake.

Duty through Nature.—But, from the point of view of Individual Ethics, man has duties that centre in himself and that have reference to nature. It is his duty (to God and toward himself) to make nature an aid in his mission to the fullest extent possible,—to make the best use of its truth, its treasures, and its forces. It thus becomes his duty to understand nature as one of the chief lessons of God; not wantonly to mar, but to beautify and perfect, nature, as once his paradise, and now his dwelling-place, which he is appointed to "dress and keep;" and, above all, to make nature his willing and mighty servant in the accomplishment of his moral task.

Duty to Improve the Arts.—Man's duties having reference to art have like origin and end with those having reference to nature. Art is a means to the great end of life, and is to be cherished and perfected for that. It is the combination and application of the treasures and forces of nature to the purposes of man's mission. The appreciation and use of nature and art for man's ends constitute one of the chief differences between the power and helpfulness of the civilization of the great nations of the present time and the weakness and helplessness of the savage state.

It is generally admitted that the Moral Governor has given man dominion over the brute creation that he may use it in furthering the accomplishment of his mission. Man is therefore bound to use the animals as God's creatures for this end.

The Use of Animals.—Man may use the animals for his necessities. They furnish a part of his appointed food, and it is therefore proper for him to slay them for this purpose. They furnish one of the forms of the forces of nature, and he may therefore use them for the performance of labor, by which his own time and energies may be saved for the higher work of life.

The Abuse of Animals.—He must use them only for the ends for which he was given dominion over them. Wanton cruelty to animals indicates a degraded and ferocious temper, which fits a human being for the worst of crimes. Hunting merely for sport or as a trial of skill too often involves this element of cruelty. Man has no right to take animal life simply for the sake of showing his skill as a marksman or a sportsman. Such amusements as horse-racing involve something of this same wanton cruelty to animals, in addition to many other attendant vices and immoralities. Such so-called sports break the law of the Moral Governor, since they do not use the animals for the ends for which they were given. "Hence," says Dr. Wayland, "all amusements which consist in inflicting pain upon animals — such as bull-baiting, cock-fighting, etc.— are purely wicked. God never gave us power over animals for such purposes. I can scarcely conceive of a more revolting exhibition of human nature than that which is seen when men assemble to witness the misery which brutes inflict upon each other. Surely, nothing can tend more directly to harden men in worse than brutal ferocity."

The proper use of the treasures of nature and art for man's well-being renders necessary, therefore, the duties of industry, economy, and frugality, and forbids idleness, extravagance, and luxuriousness.

Industry is Essential to the rightful acquisition of the wealth to be used for the great ends of the moral agent. It is man's duty to devote himself, "with activity and zeal, to some fair and honorable calling," and thus "provide things honest in the sight of all men." No amount of wealth in man's possession can for a moment justify a life of idleness, since wealth is given only as an aid in the life of duty. "Idleness is the rust of the mind, and the occasion of vice; and they who wisely consult for their own happiness will find that it is most likely to be promoted and secured by fixing on some fair and honorable pursuit, and prosecuting it with activity and diligence." It was a wise and beneficent custom among the ancient Jews to train every child in some useful trade, so that Paul was a tent-maker and Jesus of Nazareth a carpenter: it is a foolish and destructive modern tendency that would lead all children to despise labor and hate industry, and to seek to "live by their wits."

Economy and Frugality are Essential to the right use of wealth once acquired or possessed. As industry is opposed to indolence or idleness, *economy* is opposed to prodigality or extravagance, and *frugality* to luxuriousness. Failure in these duties weakens man's powers and wastes that wealth which is one of his most powerful agencies for accomplishing the ends of life.

Topic Second.   Support of the Spirit. — Proper regard for the support of man's spiritual well-being requires, that he should secure and use in every right way those treasures of truth, beauty, and goodness, which have been provided by the

Moral Governor for sustaining the spirit in its full freedom and vigor in effort.

The True, the Beautiful, and the Good have been recognized, from the days of Plato, as the three aspects in which the Moral Governor reveals himself to the agent made in his own image, and therefore fitted to appreciate these three aspects of his revelation. These three things constitute the food and sustenance of the human spirit: the *true*, enlarging its vision and extending its grasp and power in action; the *beautiful*, especially in its spiritual phase, lending it true grace and glory in its action; and the *good*, in its three forms, impelling to the use of its powers in action, and in its highest form, the morally good, lifting it up to the true godlikeness in its character and mission. The true conservation of man's nobler self, the soul, makes it therefore his most solemn duty to lay hold of these spiritual treasures thus furnished by the Moral Governor, that his life may prove a complete moral success.

CHAPTER II.

DUTY OF SELF-CULTURE.

AS the full development of man's powers of body and soul is indispensable to the fulfilment of his moral mission, it is his *second duty toward himself* to develop and improve these powers to the utmost.

It will be seen that self-culture is a duty of universal obligation, and that it should aim to develop the powers in their completeness and harmony.

1st. The Universal Obligation. — If man has the capacity for an immortal progression in development of being and power, and if the accomplishment of his divinely appointed mission depends upon his development, — then self-culture becomes the duty of every human being, since it is thus brought under the fundamental moral principle which decides all duty toward self and which applies to every man. No fancied want of talent to cultivate, or of opportunity to cultivate it when possessed, can excuse from the duty. Every man has all the talent and opportunity necessary to bind him to fulfil the mission, which the Moral Governor has assigned him, and, therefore, to bind him to prepare himself by self-culture to fulfil it in the best manner.

No Want of Talent Excuses. — Duty is not for men of genius only, but for all men. It does not consist in doing great work, but *right* work, which, whether great or not, is always noble. The humblest man has powers sufficient, if properly developed and directed, to make of himself a noble man and prepare him for a noble mission. John

Ruskin has well said: "It is no man's business whether he has genius or not; work he must, whatever he is, but quietly and steadily, and the natural and unforced results of such work will be always the things that God meant him to do, and will be his best."

Great Talents not Essential to Success. — It is moreover an error, as great as it is common, to suppose that extraordinary talents are necessary to one who would achieve more than ordinary success. Says Wm. Penn: "Industry supplies the want of parts; patience and diligence, like faith, remove mountains." Says Sir Joshua Reynolds of man's adaptation to a special task: "If he has great talents, industry will improve them; if he has but moderate abilities, industry will supply their deficiency." Besides, the *right application* of the power one has is even more important to the achievement of worthy ends, than the extent of that power. He who knows his own abilities, chooses his work accordingly, and with singleness of aim under the guidance of the Moral Governor devotes himself to it, may demonstrate to himself — what all observation shows to be true — that, in order to the best and most useful work done in the world, good sense, when combined with industry and good principles, is a better talent than even genius.

New Powers Reveal Themselves. — It is still further a most important principle, that a man can never find out what his real powers are, until he places himself along this line of industrious exertion of the powers he seems to have. Such exertion often brings to light unsuspected powers; and sometimes even seems to call into being a nobler range of capabilities, on the divine principle, everywhere illustrated, that to him that hath shall be given and he shall have more abundantly. It is man's duty therefore to cultivate assiduously what powers he has, while hoping for enlarged powers.

No Fancied Want of Opportunity Excuses. — In the strict sense, it is not true that any man is entirely the victim of circumstances. The maxim is true as familiar: *Where there is a will, there is a way.* The strong will may become stronger and all the powers unfold more rapidly in the struggle with adverse circumstances, so that the true man may create a better opportunity for improvement out of what seems his worst want of opportunity. In all ages of the world men like Demosthenes and John Bunyan have become such by conquering disabilities and enemies; and men like Daniel Webster, Francis Wayland, and Michael Faraday have become such without any opportunities save such as they have won for themselves in spite of poverty and obscurity. No fancied want of opportunity or mission can, therefore, excuse any man from the duty of improving himself to the utmost. Each man has his place to fill in the great moral system of things, and even the humblest is bound to show himself in his own place indispensable to the successful ongoing of the world.

2d. The Completeness and Harmony. — The right culture of self must obviously seek to develop and improve all the elements of man's being in their completeness and harmony. As the complete man is neither a body nor a soul, but both these united into one complex being, his culture must have proper reference to both these essential elements. As in the complete mission the body is subordinate to the soul and for the soul, the two must be developed in harmony with this law of man's mission.

These considerations must be borne in mind in presenting the subject of self-culture in the two following *Sections :*

Section 1.   The Duty of Physical Self-Culture.
Section 2.   The Duty of Spiritual Self-Culture.

SECTION I.

The Duty of Physical Self-Culture.

Physical culture may be considered with reference either to that general improvement of the physical system, which is essential to the accomplishment of the mission of man, and which is equally the duty of every human being; or with reference to that special training, which may be rendered necessary by those peculiarities which modify the duty of individuals.

Topic First.   General Physical Culture. — As the body is the physical basis of the soul's activity, the medium of the soul's communication with the world, and the instrument on which the perfection of the soul's work in the world depends (p. 32), it is, therefore, man's duty to improve it to the utmost in seeking to make it the perfect basis, medium, and instrument of the soul.

Subject 1st. Culture of the Physical System. — It is man's duty to develop a strong physical system, as the proper basis for a strong mental life. This is to be secured mainly by suitable and persistent exercise of the physical powers.

The Physical Basis. — The connection of the physical system with the vigor of the spiritual life is now very generally acknowledged. Says Dr. Blackie: "It is a patent fact, as certain as anything in mathematics, that whatever exists must have a basis on which to stand, a root from which to grow, a hinge on which to turn, a something which, however subordinate in itself with reference to the complete whole, is the indispensable point of attachment from which the existence of the whole depends. No house can be raised except on a foundation, a substructure which has no independent virtue, and which, when it exists in the greatest perfection, is generally not visible, but rather loves to hide itself in darkness. Now this is exactly the sort of relation which subsists between a man's thinking faculty and his body, between his mental activity and his bodily health." This strong physical basis of man's spiritual life, Dr. Matthews (*Getting on in the World*) calls "constitutional talent," which he defines to be "the warmth and vigor imparted to a man's ideas by superior bodily stamina, by a stout physical constitution."

A Powerful Element of Success. — That a strong physical constitution becomes thus, other things being equal, a powerful element of success, is a matter of common experience and observation. The Greek race owed its intellectual supremacy largely to its perfect physical training. The Englishman is indebted for his Waterloos and Trafalgars, for his world-encircling sway and his matchless literature, largely to his powerful and fully developed bodily frame. "The orators, philosophers, poets, warriors, and statesmen of Greece and Rome gained strength of mind as well as of muscle by the systematic drill of the palæstra. The brain was filled thereby with a quick-pulsing and finely-oxygenated blood, the nerves made healthy and strong, the digestion sharp and powerful, and the whole physical man, as the statues of antiquity show, developed into the fullest health and vigor." When Cicero became dyspeptic, "he hastened, not to the physicians, which might have hastened his death, but to Greece; flung himself into the gymnasium; submitted to its regimen for two entire years; and returned to the struggles of the forum as vigorous as the peasants that tilled his farm." "Peel, Brougham, Lyndhurst, Campbell, Bright, Gladstone, — nearly all the great political and legal leaders, the prodigious workers at the bar and in the senate, — have been full-chested men, who have been as sedulous to train their bodies as to train their intellects." See *Matthews*.

The Consequent Duty.—Hence the duty of caring diligently for the culture of the physical system becomes one of very great importance and binding force. For the sake of his spirit, man is bound to be the very best animal possible, with the circulatory, respiratory, nutritive and nervous systems all fully and powerfully developed and in perfect balance and equipoise. Gymnastics, callisthenics, vocal culture, in their various forms, all appeal to the man who is desirous of faithfully performing his duty toward his body; and out of the various possible forms of physical training, each one should intelligently choose that one best adapted to his own condition and wants, and make the most of it for the higher ends of his being. All systematic exercise which is devoted to this end, keeping in view the proper relation of body and spirit, adds to the springs of spiritual vigor and endurance, and greatly aids man in his mission.

Subject 2d. Culture of the Senses.—It is man's duty to cultivate the senses as the means to be used in perfecting the communication of the soul through the body with nature and mankind. (They should be trained to acute, accurate, and rapid action, that they may be the agents of easy and wide intercourse with the universe of which man forms a part, and free communication with which is essential to his mission.)

Subject 3d. Culture of the Powers of Action and Expression.— Especially is it man's duty to make the body in every way possible the perfect instrument of the soul in its mission in the world. It should be trained to be the facile servant, under the guidance of the will, in the expression of every worthy thought and feeling, and in the execution of every noble purpose.

Topic Second. Special Physical Culture.— As the peculiarities of temperament, sex, and vocation modify the requirements of the individual mission, it becomes man's duty to give special attention to these peculiarities, in his physical self-culture.

Subject 1st. Physical Culture and Temperament.—The

various temperaments (p. 55) require as various treatment and training. The training which may increase power if applied to one temperament, may destroy both vigor and life if applied to a different temperament. It is man's duty therefore to understand his own peculiar temperament and to order his physical culture in harmony with it.

The Sanguine or Athletic Temperament betokens a predominance of the purely animal life and forces over the spiritual forces. Its great danger is excess in that direction ; it is peculiarly liable to the sudden and often early giving way and decay of the powers, and, what is worse, to the sinking of the rational being in the animal. If a man's temperament is *sanguine* simply, his duty is to "avoid excess. He should take much active, but not violent exercise; and must be careful to diminish his tendency to plethora. Nature has made him prone to indulgence, but has made indulgence doubly dangerous for his constitution and his morals." If the sanguine man becomes the *athletic*, still more depends upon the treatment of the physical system. While it might seem to be the best of temperaments, it is in reality the most dangerous. When the constitution once begins to fail, it breaks up suddenly and rapidly, and there is really less of the true vital principle in this temperament than in any other. Hippocrates pronounces the usual condition of the athletic man to be a state of malady. He is not made for long life. *His one aim* in his self-culture should be to bring the body to its true place as the servant and instrument of the spirit, and thus to become the reasonable being rather than the animal, the repository of brute strength.

The Bilious or Melancholic Temperament betokens a predominance of the nutritive or building forces of the system, — building firmly and truly in the first form, but abnormally in the second form. With the *bilious* form of this temperament, the body furnishes the best physical basis for the strong, determined, ambitious, and intensely active spirit. Excess lies in the direction of the will forces, — of inflexibility as transformed into obstinacy, of ambition cut loose from principle, in short, of a self-will regardless of man and God. When the building forces become disordered and the man becomes *melancholic*, he loses the spring of the strong will, and his besetting danger is despondency, which destroys not only ambition, but emulation also. By the gloom with which it invests life it takes away all motive to activity, and often dooms to insanity or premature death. If the temperament be *bilious* simply, it is the man's duty to guard against its exclusive control, and to seek to modify it by a treatment calculated to bring it under the control of moral principle. "The bilious man has no excess of humors that require to be dissipated by violent exercise. He may use almost any kind of motion in a moderated degree. In summer, he must avoid fatiguing labors during the heat of the day. Autumn is the best season for him, especially when the air is at once cool and moist." The building forces do not need to be driven; the brain forces should rather be cherished and their complete and harmonious development sought. If the bilious man becomes the *melancholic*, his duty increases with his dangers. The melancholic man, if he values health of body, or mental peace, should never yield to indolence, should shun solitude when he begins to brood over his cares and disappointments. Judicious exercise, generous diet, cheerful companionship, and a high moral purpose in life, indicate the line of duty and of safety for the melancholic man. His chief aim in his self-culture should be to make the most of his powerful working forces by intelligently, firmly, and persistently subordinating them to the attainment of the complete moral manhood and the achievement of the true moral task.

The Nervous Temperament betokens a predominance of purely spiritual life and forces. Its great danger lies in excess in that direction; so that the man is liable to have no adequate and enduring physical basis for his spiritual activity, and is therefore likely to be deficient in the animal and will forces. In consequence of this weakness and inconstancy, such a man often drags out life as a physical and mental wreck, and comes to its end having accomplished nothing worthy of the varied and versatile powers implied in such a temperament. The duty of the man of nervous temperament is therefore very urgent. "Where this temperament exists in an intense degree, it becomes a malady. Its remedy is exercise. The balance must be restored between the sensitive and the muscular forces; and this can be effected only by diminishing the action of the intellect and cultivating that of the animal nature. Nothing else can give rest. Friendship, letters, business, action, all will not avail, or, rather, will but increase the evil. The labors of agriculture, or any labor abroad, which will gently occupy the thoughts, and at the same time strengthen the body, are of most service. Children of this class suffer from too early attempts to cultivate their minds. Such attempts are immediately followed by great apparent results, but do in fact confirm the natural weakness and misfortune of the individual." *The one aim* of the man of this temperament should be to develop a body fitted to be the willing and adequate servant of the spirit in its mission.

The Phlegmatic Temperament betokens a weakness of the three vital systems, and its great danger is therefore that of universal sluggishness of being and life. In a man of this temperament there is no strong intellectual life and no strong will, and no proper physical basis for these. *The one aim* of the man of this temperament should be to turn all the power he has to the work of self-emancipation. "No exercise is too violent for the man of this temperament. His sleeping energies must be awakened; his imagination roused from its lethargy by powerful excitement. In summer, to guard against his natural lassitude, let him rise in time to help Hyperion to his horse; and quicken his system by a cold bath; then, careless of the heat, he may plunge into the forest and pursue the chase, till real fatigue gives him a claim to repose. In winter he may run at full speed till his heavy frame pants for breath, or wrestle violently with an equal antagonist till his chill blood flows warmly to his cheek."

The Tempered Temperament betokens the proper and harmonious action of all the forces of the being. The duty of the man who has it is to seek to preserve the happy balance and equipoise, while aiming to develop himself into the most powerful manhood. See Bancroft, *Miscellaneous Essays.*

Subject 2d. Physical Culture and Sex. — The different sexes require different treatment and training. The physiological motto, "Educate a man for manhood, a woman for womanhood, both for humanity," holds especially in physical culture. The aim of physical self-culture should be to bring out, and develop into completeness and power, those elements which prepare the different sexes for their different missions.

The Sexes have different Missions. — This is made evident by the essential difference in the sexes. Says Dr. Rauch: "The *whole* organization in *all*, and not in *some* only, of its parts is different in man and woman." Bone and muscle, the respiratory and nutritive systems, the circulatory and nervous systems, differ in structure and function in the two. Woman is *woman* in her whole structure and in every fibre of her being; and with equal distinctness and entireness man is *man*. This radical difference is proof that the Moral Governor designed them for different missions, requiring a training adapted in each case to prepare the individual for it.

The Organization must Decide the Training. — The organization of man and woman not only decides the different spheres and points out the different missions of the two, but also limits the power of both. In the development of the organization is to be found the way of power and virtue for both sexes. Limitation or abortion of development leads not only to weakness and failure, but to vice and misery.

17 *

The Man should Train Himself for the Mission of a Man.— His nature decides that he is to be the leader in the business and conflict of the world, and the protector and supporter of woman. He was made for the rough and strong work of life. It is his duty therefore to train his physical system for this, that he may have the proper basis for power in seeking to become the best possible in his mission of leadership, of labor, of protection, and of support.

The Woman should Train Herself for the Mission of a Woman.— Her nature decides that she is to be the central figure in the family life, where her love and faith and patience and delicacy and purity are to mould the race, and furnish the world its best inspiration to noble deeds. It is her duty to prepare herself for so grand a place by such a physical culture as will best fit her for this most important of missions. See Dr. Clark, on *Sex in Education.*

Subject 3d.   Physical Culture and Vocation.— It is obvious that different vocations in life require different treatment and training. The aim of self-culture should be to develop the physical system in that way which shall best fit the individual for success in his proper vocation.

⸱⸱⸱⸺⸱⸱⸱

SECTION II.

The Duty of Spiritual Self-Culture.

As the spirit is the self-active element in the moral agent, it becomes his duty to seek with the greatest diligence the most perfect development of his spiritual being.

The requisites to such best development are: accurate knowledge of the individual spirit to be developed; a correct theory of education; and the patient application of the theory to the improvement of the spirit. These give the *Topics* for consideration.

Necessity for Self-Education.— The education which is given by parents and teachers may prepare for self-culture, but cannot take the place of it. As a rational and responsible being, man must educate himself. Nor is his education to stop with his early years; the development of childhood and youth is but the beginning of a work which is to end only with life. He is bound to seek both increased power and increased acquaintance with its uses, and so to grow in efficiency in duty to the end.

Topic First. Knowledge of the Individual Spirit.—Intelligent spiritual culture requires an exact and profound knowledge of the human spirit in all its essential elements and relations. It requires both a general and a special psychology.

Subject 1st. A General Psychology.—All intelligent self-culture must proceed upon a correct knowledge of the essential elements of the human spirit itself. It therefore becomes the duty of every moral agent to aim to secure this requisite knowledge of himself, as it is embraced in a correct system of general psychology.

This Knowledge Essential.—The highest excellence is not reached by a rational being by stumbling into it. A vast amount of precious time, and still more precious energy, is wasted in unintelligent effort at improvement. Man as a rational being should aim to secure culture of spirit in the one reasonable way. In order to know what he is about, he must first secure an accurate knowledge of the essential elements of the soul which is to be improved.

Subject 2d. A Special Psychology.—All intelligent self-culture must proceed upon a correct knowledge of the individual peculiarities of the agent's own spirit. It therefore becomes the duty of every moral agent to study to acquire the requisite knowledge of his spirit, as it is embraced in a correct special psychology.

This is no less Essential than a General Psychology.—No two men are precisely alike in their spirits. The same training will not produce precisely the same results in any two men. Each one should find precisely what is in him, in order that he may wisely set to work to make the most of himself. Says Dean Swift: "It is an uncontroverted truth, that no man ever made an ill figure who understood his own talents, nor a good one who mistook them."

The Individual Mission. — Every man has his place of duty to fill in the world, and to decide what that place is he must understand the peculiar bias of his nature which fits him for, and providentially appoints him to, it. His true success will be won in cultivating his powers with special reference to that appointed place. It is of the first importance that he should know *himself* as distinguished from and unlike all other men, and thus prepare for his own intelligent culture.

Topic Second. Knowledge of Correct Theory of Education. — Intelligent spiritual culture requires a knowledge of the correct theory of educating in the best manner those powers of soul of which the agent may find himself possessed. There are certain general principles involved in such a theory, which may be stated in order.

First Principle. — All true education must aim to unfold or develop the powers of the soul. Both truth and the power to make the right use of it will be best acquired in this way.

The Two Theories. — There are two things which man is to seek to acquire in the work of self-improvement: mental power, and truth. Two diverse theories of education are based upon these two necessities. The first is the *theory of tuition.* It proceeds upon the supposition, that the one great aim of a man in cultivating himself is to secure the greatest possible number of truths. Hence the work of self-culture must be a pouring in or cramming process, in which the chief power to be exercised is the mechanical memory. By this process a man invariably makes of himself a drudge and a weakling, and destroys the value of the truth he may secure, by failing to elevate himself to the place of power in which he can use it to the best advantage. The second is the *theory of education.* It proceeds upon the supposition, that the first great thing in self-culture is to develop the powers of the soul by which truth is apprehended and applied. Hence the work of self-culture must be a *drawing out,* or *educing,* or *educating* process, by means of which the soul is constantly being better fitted in insight and grasp to seek, find, appreciate, retain, and apply truth. By this process a man invariably secures an ever-increasing power of soul, and an ever-increasing treasure of truth held in firm grasp for ready use by a philosophical memory. The profoundest thinkers of modern times have held this view of the theory of self-culture. "If," says Mallebranche, "I held truth captive in my hand, I should open my hand and let it fly, in order that I might again pursue and capture it." "Did the Almighty," says Lessing, "holding in his right hand *truth*, and in his left *search after truth*, deign to tender me the one I might prefer, — in all humility, but without hesitation, I should request *search after truth*."

Second Principle. — All true education must aim to develop the powers of the soul by exercise, bearing in mind that no power can be educated except by exercising it along its own peculiar line of action.

Definite Exercise of Faculties. — It is a principle which is coming to be seen more and more clearly, that the only way to educate any power is to exercise that particular power in the best way in its own proper definite direction. Memory can only be trained by remembering, imagination by imagining, judgment by judging, generalization by generalizing, reason by reasoning. Education which fails to take this into account is not the true education. To the man who undertakes the culture of his own spirit, blundering into power is a slow, discouraging, and costly, not to say impossible, way. It is no better when he submits himself to the same process under the misdirection of others. Says John Ruskin, in entering his strong protest against such false method and the plea by which it is sustained: "I know well the common censure by which objections to such futilities of so-called education are met by the men who have been ruined by them, — the common plea that anything does to 'exercise the mind upon.' It is an utterly false one. The human soul, in youth, is *not* a machine of which you can polish the cogs with any kelp or brick-dust near at hand; and, having got it into working order, and good, empty, oiled serviceableness, start your immortal locomotive, at twenty-five years old or thirty, express from the Strait Gate, on the Narrow Road. The whole period of youth is one essentially of formation, edification, instruction. I use the words with their weight in them; intaking of stores, establishment in vital habits, hopes, and faiths. There is not an hour of it but is trembling with destinies, — not a moment of which, once past, the appointed work can ever be done again, or the neglected blow struck on the cold iron. Take your vase of Venice glass out of the furnace, and strew chaff over it in its transparent heat, and recover *that* to its clearness and rubied glory when the north wind has blown upon it; but do not think to strew chaff over the child fresh from God's presence, and to bring the heavenly colors back to him — at least in this world." *Modern Painters*, Vol. IV., *Appendix*.

Third Principle. — All true education must aim to develop the powers of the soul, in their true relations of co-ordination and subordination to one another, and in their true relations to the mission of the soul.

The Relative Importance of the Powers Regarded. — All the powers of soul are not of equal importance in culture. Some are subordinate to others, and must be so treated in all right culture. The intellect is not for itself alone; the sensibilities and the will depend upon it, as do all the higher and nobler activities of man. It is therefore to be cultivated as a means to a higher end, rather than as an end in itself. The purely intellectual man has only a small and comparatively mean element of the best manhood: without the due development of the affectional, moral, and religious powers, he is not at all fitted for the true mission of a man. Equally futile must be all attempts at culture which aim to develop these higher elements of man's nature, without giving them a solid basis in a fully developed intellect.

Or considering the powers of intellect by themselves: the cognitive faculty is subordinate to the conservative; both these to the comparative; all three of these to the constructive. A true culture must begin therefore with the cognitive faculty, and train first to the power of observation, external and internal, analytic and synthetic. The conservative faculty, or memory, will thus be stored with the facts of knowledge, and the way be prepared for the use of the comparative, or thought faculty, to do its work of generalizing, judging, and reasoning, with this gathered and conserved material. The constructive faculty is the last and highest in the work of education, and is to be trained to group all this cognized, conserved, and compared material, by the threefold law of the true, the beautiful, and the good, into scientific, artistic, and practical systems, which shall be of avail to man in helping to the highest truth, beauty, and goodness in his life.

The End of Life Regarded. — The aim of all self-culture should be the best furnishing for the true work of life. This is evident. Any theory of education which leaves it out must be false and pernicious. The cultivation of the powers of intellect to the neglect of the moral nature, and without reference to the moral mission, may make shrewd men in the little things of life, but it will make narrow, unscrupulous, and unprincipled men at the best, while at the worst it is just the training to produce vice and crime.

Fourth Principle. — All true education must aim to take advantage of that law of habit by which each of the various powers may be trained to a tendency to act easily, powerfully, and constantly in its own proper direction, and the whole tide of being thus be strongly set toward the true end of human action.

The Law of Habit is one of the most powerful principles connected with man's culture.

First, it requires that the act, or exercise, of the power be repeated at regular and moderate intervals.

Secondly, this repetition results in inclination or tendency to the act repeated, although at the outset it may be disagreeable and even repulsive.

Thirdly, this tendency increases in power with the repetition of the act, and gives increasing pleasure to him who complies with it, and growing pain to him who resists it.

Fourthly, when the tendency is fully confirmed, the agent comes at last to perform the accustomed act with no conscious effort. His being has acquired a *set* in that accustomed direction of action, which renders it certain that he will continue to perform the act with ease and power, without even thinking of it.

The Building Power of Habit.— While the law of habit is a powerful instrument for the destruction of the being, it is obvious that it may be made no less powerful for its building up, and especially for building up the moral being. It builds up the higher being by the same law by which, when perverted, it destroys it. Says Prof. Bowen: "The process is a simple one, being merely *a transference of the affections from the end to the means.* By the association of ideas, that which was at first loved or practised only as an *instrument* becomes the leading idea and the *chief object* of pursuit. Thus, in the downward course, *money*, at first desired only as a means of gratifying the appetites, or of answering some higher ends, becomes itself 'an appetite and a passion,' and the vicious habit of avarice is formed. And so, in our upward progress, the *honesty* which was first practised only because it was the best policy, the *worship of God* which was first paid only as the price of heaven, become at last the unbought and unselfish homage of the soul to uprightness, holiness, and truth." *Metaphysics and Ethics*, p. 308.

This beneficent arrangement furnishes one of the greatest encouragements to parents and instructors of the young. By firmly and prudently holding the young to prescribed tasks and courses of conduct, which may at first be irksome, but which are necessary and right, the proper habits are formed; and what is done at first unwillingly and only from the pressure of a superior will, comes to be done gladly and for its own sake.

Fifth Principle.—All true education must aim to take advantage of human interest and enthusiasm in the training of man's powers for his mission.

The Springs of Power must be Reached, or the results will be comparatively worthless. It is a law of man's being that what is done with painful effort or aversion will yield comparatively worthless results. A living interest must be awakened in the improvement to be made, and the enthusiasm becoming to a human soul must be aroused, in order that what is done may be done with vigor and energy and result in increased power in the doer.

Topic Third. Application of the Theory to Self-Culture.

— Intelligent spiritual culture requires the careful application of the accurate knowledge of the human soul and the correct theory of education to the practical training of the various powers.

Subject 1st. Culture of the Intellect.—Self-culture requires the improvement of the intellectual powers. It is a man's duty to cultivate exact and wide observation, vigorous and profound thought, and a power of understanding things in their system and completeness.

This Duty at the Basis.—In order to his mission, man needs knowledge of the facts of the world and the truths of science, and to the largest extent attainable. It therefore becomes his duty to cultivate to the highest degree possible his power to see, to remember, to think, and to construct. This may be done by observation, thought, study, reading, and intercourse with men of power, and by the exercise of his powers in productive thought.

It is therefore man's duty to avoid ignorance, stupidity, heedlessness, rashness, credulity, and scepticism, as fatal to the true mission. These vices all have their root in a _vincible ignorance_ (p. 132), and the agent is therefore bound to avoid them.

Ignorance may appear as want of knowledge as to the nature and consequences of any action, or want of knowledge of the mission of duty or of any of its parts. In whatever form, it is a reproach to the agent and a hindrance to his mission.

Stupidity is often not so much a defect of nature as of moral energy; and when it has this last origin it becomes immoral. The man refuses to awake to observation, reflection, and judgment; and his native powers therefore become weak, and he who might become a wise man makes of himself a blockhead. One has truly said, that "the brute is often less stupid than such a man, and would both avoid evils which come upon him, and gain benefits which he never attains." Such stupidity is immoral and vicious in proportion to the neglected endowments and the lost opportunities.

Heedlessness is rather occasional disregard of the nature and consequences of actions than perpetual forgetfulness. When the man allows himself to become engrossed with a few things, and these perhaps unimportant, and loses sight of the many and more important things which should properly be kept in view in deciding his action, the consequences of evil overtake him unexpectedly, and he fails in his undertakings. Such heedlessness is evidently immoral and guilty.

Rashness is the "hardy daring of consequences seen or unseen. The man is so intent on a particular end, that though he may have abundant occasion to anticipate evil consequences, he determines to risk them, and recklessly persist in his course until the blow falls." Passion is usually the leader in this vice. It is a worse vice than stupidity or heedlessness, for the depravity it manifests is in the fullest sense *wilful*, and shows the reckless determination to override the moral judgment and gratify passion at whatever cost or hazard.

Credulity and Scepticism are opposite forms of the same vice. Want of the proper intellectual culture leaves the agent weak in judgment, and, having little grasp of principles and less power of making safe deductions from facts, he gives or withholds his faith according to his own wishes or the opinions of any one who may have influence over him. If he be of an ardent temperament, he will be ready to believe anything,— or, will be credulous; if he be of an opposite temperament, or have an ambition to be thought brilliant and original, he will be equally ready to doubt everything, — or, will be sceptical.

It is obvious that there is a state of *philosophic doubt*, in which a man may properly hold himself, while engaged in a process of investigation; but this has nothing in common with that vicious *rationalistic doubt*, the bane of unbalanced minds, which doubts for the sake of doubting, and against all sound reason, and arrogantly claims for itself the right to be esteemed the chief of virtues. It is man's duty to doubt what he has reason for doubting, and to believe what he has reason for believing.

Subject 2d.)**Culture of the Feelings.**—Self-culture requires
18

the improvement of the affections and desires. It is a man's
duty to cultivate his feelings to the deepest, broadest, and
highest extent, that the springs which move to action may be
the most powerful possible. It is man's duty to love everything that is worthy of love and to the extent of its worthiness;
and to desire everything worthy to be desired to the extent
of that worthiness; keeping always in accord with the law of
his being and mission.

The Springs of Power. — Power of action depends upon power of
motive, and therefore upon power of feeling. The feelings are as important and worthy a part of man as the intellect or will. From the very
nature of the human soul, there can be no powerful and persistent will
in executing the mission of life unless there be powerful and sustained
feeling. It is therefore man's duty to aim to develop all the natural
affections and desires, in their proper proportion and harmony, in order
that he may become a man with the full dignity of manhood, and may
have a powerful motive-basis for his life.

It is therefore man's duty to avoid all repression, perversion,
or disproportionate development of the feelings. Insensibility
and passion are alike immoral and vicious.

Insensibility holds the same relation to the feelings which *stupidity*
holds to the intellect. It arises in a similar way, from the repression
of feeling; so that the genesis already given of stupidity will apply to it.
When it becomes general, it is one of the most deadening of vices.
When it is confirmed and wilful, it becomes *obduracy*, and must appear
both repulsive and guilty to every right-thinking being, and that
whether it takes the form of insensibility to man's own highest interests
and destiny, or to the claims of his fellows for affection and sympathy,
or to God's claims.

Passion arises from the inordinate and ungoverned action of the
affections and desires, as developed out of harmony and proportion, and
made the *end* of action rather than its spring. When passion has completed its development, reason and will become its slaves, and the man
loses his truest manhood.

Sphere of Passion. — It is obvious that under a wrong and evil culture
each of the springs of action furnishes the germ of some passion.

First, from Lower Feelings. — In the undue development of the
appetites and animal sensibilities arises the milder vice of *sentimental-
ity,* which leads its victim to weep with equal ease over the agonies of

a pet canary and of a victim of the Inquisition; together with all those base and brutal vices of *gluttony, intemperance, sensuality,* which are usually designated by *passion* in its basest sense.

Secondly, from Higher Feelings. — In the improper development of the higher feelings there arise, *from the side of the affections,*— *pride,* or that inordinate self-esteem which shows itself in the disposition to over-rate what one possesses, and in *haughtiness* and *loftiness* of manners; *egotism,* which leads one to make himself prominent; *vanity,* which is allied to pride, egotism, and conceit, self-praise and self-commendation, and which is manifested in a desire to attract notice and gain admiration in a small way, and which would therefore be ridiculed as weak if it were not condemned as immoral; and all the other forms of *selfishness:* —*from the side of the desires,* — aimless *restlessness,* irrational *curiosity,* unbridled *ambition,* and base *covetousness,* which are all easily understood, and which are all condemned by mankind as vicious.

Subject 3d. Culture of the Will.—Self-culture requires the improvement of the power of will. It is man's duty to cultivate his will to the greatest degree, that he may be able to direct all his being steadily and powerfully to the accomplishment of his mission.

It is therefore his duty to avoid all repression, perversion, or improper development of the will, as seen in servility and independence, fickleness and obstinacy.

Servility "includes not only the assent to be a slave and obey a master who regards only his own ends, but all mean and cringing submission or fawning sycophancy." It includes the blind surrender of the will to any finite and fallible leader whatever, whether in fashion, business, politics, morals, or religion; and the equally blind and irrational surrender of the will to perverse public sentiment in any of its aspects. It may manifest itself in *hypocrisy,* when the man does not dare openly to assert his freedom of opinion or action. It cringes to escape harm, flatters to win favor, makes a show of humility to procure praise, and indulges in false self-disparagement to gain compliments. It shows itself in general in *trimming* and *time-serving,* in which the man sacrifices his manhood and becomes the mere plaything of circumstances. In all its forms and manifestations, *servility* must be acknowledged at once base and immoral.

Independence, in its immoral form, is the opposite of servility. It is obvious that there is an independence, which consists in the proper self-assertion, and which is praiseworthy and virtuous. The improper and vicious independence consists in unnecessary and improper self-assertion, — as against rightful authority or just law, or where it involves a culpable disregard for the opinions or feelings of others. A weakness, no less immoral than that exhibited in servility, may be shown in "speaking one's mind" on all occasions, without reference to the timeliness of the utterance.

Fickleness and Obstinacy are vices of opposite characters. In the former, the will changes constantly, without reference to any proper reasons or motives; in the latter, the will remains fixedly the same, without any regard to any proper reasons or motives. Both are irrational. Both are likewise immoral, as it is man's duty to give due heed to all considerations fitted to influence a rational being. Both prevent the accomplishment of man's mission; the one by keeping him from turning his energies in any one direction long enough to accomplish anything, and the other by turning them persistently in some wrong direction.

Subject 4th. Culture of the Taste. — Self-culture requires

the improvement of the æsthetic faculty. It is man's duty to cultivate a taste which shall be acute, correct, and catholic.

It is therefore man's duty to avoid all repression, perversion, or improper development of the æsthetic faculty, — as seen in insensibility to the beautiful, in false views of it, or in extravagant regard for it.

Importance of the Beautiful.— The world has not only the side which we call the true, but also one which we call the beautiful. God reveals himself in the latter as well as in the former. Man's soul has not only an intellect by which to perceive the true, but also a faculty of taste by which to recognize and appreciate the beautiful. The beautiful and the sublime in the works of nature and of art are therefore fitted to elevate and ennoble the human soul.

The Prohibitions.— Insensibility to the beautiful shows an incomplete manhood, which cannot therefore accomplish the full mission of man. Incorrect views of the beautiful warp man's views of the world and of life in it. The worship of the beautiful, as by some of the culturists, weakens and degrades by putting beauty in the place of God. A taste *acute*, or quick to discern beauty; *correct*, or infallible in its judgment of it; and *catholic*, or recognizing and appreciating all beauty, — is the best for man's mission, and should therefore be sought.

Subject 5th. Culture of the Moral and Religious Nature.

—Self-culture requires the improvement of the moral and religious nature. It is man's highest duty to exalt himself toward the noblest manhood, by cultivating conscience till it becomes invariably true and certain in its response to duty, and by cultivating his religious nature until it shall bring him into complete and perpetual sympathy with the Moral Governor.

This is Obviously Necessary.—If these are the highest elements in man's nature, and if they furnish the guiding principles of his life, then to fail in the proper improvement of these is to fail in the highest sense, and to fail fatally.

It is therefore man's duty to avoid all repression, perversion, or improper development of the moral and religious nature. In *morality*, he must avoid the insensible, erroneous, and uncertain conscience. In *religion*, he must avoid cherishing indifference, scepticism, superstition, atheism, and godlessness, in his views; and must guard against evincing hypocrisy, cant, bigotry, and fanaticism, in his life.

The Defects of Conscience have already been presented in Theoretical Ethics (p. 134). It is the agent's duty to guard against all these.

The Defects of the Religious Nature still more seriously endanger the manhood and mission. The religious duties, as directed toward God, will be treated under Theistic Ethics; but the proper development of the religious nature is a duty directed toward man himself, and essential to the completeness of his being and work. The departures from that duty, as here given, must therefore be violations of the fundamental maxim of Individual Ethics: *Improve thy being.*

Religious Indifference expresses a state of mind in which the man is not moved by any affection or desire toward God. It is at once unreasonable and immoral, as exhibiting a want of attention to all the highest motives addressed to man and the grandest interests of man, and a want of regard for them.

Religious Scepticism comes to no conclusion for or against the existence and requirements of a Moral Governor. When it originates.in, or is accompanied with, a desire to escape the demands of the religious nature and of God, it becomes *infidelity*, debases the man by stifling his highest being, and is therefore in high degree immoral and vicious.

Superstition, says Whately, "is not an *excess of religion*,—at least in the ordinary sense of the word excess,—as if any one *could* have *too* *much* of true religion, but any *misdirection* of religious feeling, manifested either in showing religious veneration or regard to objects which deserve *none;* that is, properly speaking, the worship of false gods; or, in the assignment of such a degree, or such a kind of religious veneration to any object, as that object, though worthy of some reverence, does not deserve; or in the worship of the true God through the medium of improper rites and ceremonies. . . . . . It may arise from a sense of guilt, from bodily indisposition, or from erroneous reasoning." Its degrading, deadening effect upon the higher nature is proof of its immorality.

Atheism, in the ordinary acceptation, is the denial or disbelief of a Moral Governor. By some, *atheism* has been distinguished from *antitheism.* The former has been supposed to imply merely the non-recognition of God, while the latter asserts his non-existence. "This distinction is founded on the difference between *unbelief* and *disbelief,* and its validity is admitted in so far as it discriminates merely between *sceptical* and *dogmatic* atheism. In the ordinary usage, however, *atheism* includes both. Its denial of God rests on the slender basis of man's littleness and ignorance" (p. 38). Plato, in his *Laws,* observes that "atheism is a disease of the soul, before it becomes an error of the understanding." Bacon says: "A little philosophy inclineth a man's mind to atheism; but depth of philosophy bringeth men's minds to religion." The Bible gives it a like genesis, when it declares that "The fool" (*i. e.,* the *unreasonable* and *perverse* man) "hath said in his heart" (not in his *reason* or *understanding,* since the conclusion of atheism is not a dictate of man's reason,) "there is no God." Atheism is in high degree immoral and vicious, as rendering man's truest and best development and mission impossible.

Godlessness is practical atheism, or living as if there were no God. When it accompanies a knowledge and acknowledgment of God's existence and claims, *it is the last and worst of all vices,* as wilfully aiming the death-blow at man's highest being and mission.

The perversion of religious culture, as manifested *in the conduct,* is perhaps more offensive than that in the views. *Hypocrisy* would cover the absence of true reverence for God by playing a part and putting on all the outward show of piety. Rochefoucauld calls it "a sort of homage that vice pays to virtue." *Cant* is hypocrisy as exhibited in language and air. *Bigotry* is the manifestation of an irrational or blind partiality for a particular party or creed. *Fanaticism* adds to the blind partiality of bigotry an equally blind hatred of all opposers, and a pretension to inspiration. These are all religious vices of the most insidious and dangerous character: *hypocrisy* and *cant* dethrone truth and make man a living lie; *bigotry* and *fanaticism* dethrone reason and moral principle and give the man over to prejudice and passion.

CHAPTER III.

DUTY OF SELF-CONDUCT.

AS man's powers of body and soul are given, conserved, and developed to fit him for his true moral mission, it is his *third duty toward himself* to control and direct them to the accomplishment of that mission.

Binding Force and Importance of the Duty. — If man was made for such a life of duty, which requires his full powers with the best possible management, then the duty of self-conduct is self-evident. Moreover, it is as clearly at the summit of all duty of man toward himself, since the duties of self-conservation and self-culture but prepare the way for it.

Twofold Aspect of the Duty. — *Self-control* is the negative aspect of self-conduct or self-government: *self-direction*, the positive. Much of what may be said of self-government in its negative aspect belongs to the cardinal duty of *temperance*. This term has sometimes been employed, in a large sense, to denote "that moderation in which, according to some ancient philosophers, all virtue consists." In the New Testament Scriptures, the word which is translated *temperance* means *power over one's self*, and perhaps comprehends the whole of self-government.

The Twofold Aim. — The end or aim of these duties, *on the negative side*, is not to eradicate or extirpate, but to check or prune; not to destroy any of the powers and propensities of our nature, but to regulate and govern them, — to keep each and all of them in due subordination and order; and, *on the positive side*, to make the most of them as powerful stimulants to activity and improvement.

Self-conduct, as here considered, includes the government of the entire being, and involves self-control, or the getting and keeping of all the powers in hand; and self-direction, or

211

bending them all to the accomplishment of the true end of life. It will therefore be treated in two *Sections:*

Section 1.   The Duty of Self-Control.
Section 2.   The Duty of Self-Direction.

SECTION I.

Duty of Self-Control.

As man is ready for his work only when every element of his being is found in its proper place and ready to do its proper work, self-control, or the negative aspect of self-conduct, includes the restraint and government of the active propensities, and the maintenance of the balance of all the powers of man's being, in accordance with the requirements of the moral law. These furnish the *Topics* for consideration.

Topic First.   Government of the Active Propensities.— It has been seen that there is no necessary subordination or government among the various springs of action, but that each is an appetency or propensity to act toward its own particular end, and to cease acting only when that end is attained (p. 64). It therefore becomes man's duty to control these appetites, affections, and desires in accordance with the law of his being for their special ends.

Subject 1st.   Restraint of Appetites.— The duty of self-control requires of man the proper restraint of the natural appetites of hunger, thirst, and sex. These appetites were given for the ends of preserving the human body and the human race; and they should be held in strict subordination to these ends.

Hunger, or the appetite for food, has been given for the purpose of warning us to take, in due season and in due measure, the aliment which is necessary to sustain our bodily frame in health and vigor. Over-indulgence ultimately destroys all the pleasure otherwise connected with the partaking of food, and so proves that the appetite was only intended to be subservient to the building up of the body. The vices which may arise from the want of self-control are gluttony and luxuriousness. *Gluttony* is intemperance with respect to the quantity of food. It destroys bodily health, impairs the vigor and clearness of the mind, and makes man a slave to his lower nature. *Luxuriousness*, in the old sense, as applicable to the partaking of food, is excessive delicacy with respect to the kind or quality of our food.

Thirst is the appetite which has been given man to secure the requisite amount of fluids in the system. But in almost all countries the means used for quenching thirst lead to *intoxication*. Hence the special necessity for self-control.

Intemperance, in the narrow sense, or *drunkenness*, is the vice resulting from the failure to restrain this appetite. In connection with the abounding intemperance of this day and nation, it has become a vital practical question, *Is total abstinence from the use of all intoxicating liquors a duty?*

The Total Abstinence Question. — It may be answered:

First, it is certainly man's duty to abstain wholly from all drugged and adulterated liquors; and, so far as the use of any kinds whatsoever tend to the injury of body or soul, to abstain from them altogether,— since the opposite course is a direct violation of the law which requires him to conserve his being.

Secondly, that, — although a moderate use, as a beverage, of the comparatively pure and harmless wines and liquors should be granted to be not only not positively injurious, but absolutely beneficial, to the individual who can secure them, so that there is no *essential* breach of the moral law in such use, — it must yet be held logically that the probability of not securing them in their purity is so great, that the danger of becoming enslaved by the appetite is so imminent (especially to the American people, with their excitable temperament); that the evils of intemperance at the present day are so gigantic; and that the intimate relations of each man to society render the influence of his example so potent always and so perilous when on the side of evil,—that the question of *total abstinence from all liquors as a beverage* has a claim to the conscientious consideration and careful decision of every one.

Thirdly, that the decision of the enlightened moral consciousness, as expressed in the action of great Christian bodies, and in the conduct of the noblest Christian men, is very strongly in favor of such abstinence.

Subject 2d. Restraint of Affections and Desires.— The

duty of self-control requires of man the proper restraint of
the purely mental affections and desires, especially in their
lower forms. They were given to be the springs of human
action, to be held subordinate to the ends determined by the
proper guides of action, and they should therefore be strictly
subjected to those guides.

Reason — as the sense of prudence, of the perfect, and of the right
— has been seen to be the proper guide to which all action ought to be
subjected (p. 64). In the possession and use of this faculty is man's chief
distinction from the brute, and in its right use is his chief glory.

It is therefore man's duty to restrain his affections and
desires from fastening upon unworthy or wrong objects, and
to prevent that inordinate action already recognized (p. 206)
as passion.

The Imminent Danger. — Out of the very necessities of his being arise
the vices to which man is peculiarly exposed in this connection. Desire
for his well-being necessarily leads him to seek enjoyment, wealth, and
influence, as among the important objects of human pursuit. These
objects are improperly made the great ends of life, and, growing "by
what they feed on," assume the entire control of the man. By improperly and inordinately seeking power, he falls a victim to ambition;
by so pursuing wealth, he becomes covetous; and by so giving himself
to pleasure, he becomes the slave of dissipation and makes his life a
play, a revel, or a debauch. The duty of self-control demands that the
agent exert all his powers to save himself from these and all kindred
vices.

Topic Second.   The Balance of the Powers.

It has been
seen that man's mission is one which requires for its accomplishment the whole being with each element in its
proper place and proportion. It is therefore obviously man's
duty to hold all the powers thus in balanced and ready proportion for the accomplishment of the mission of life.

Unbalanced Powers. — Any single element of man's being, if out of
place, destroys the harmony and prevents the efficient action of the
whole, no less certainly than does the single misplaced cog or wheel in
a complicated piece of machinery. If the springs of action are not in
their true place and proper development, or if the will fails to do its

work or does it badly, or if the reason is wanting in capacity or in direction toward the right end or in control, there must be failure in the mission as the inevitable result.

As the prosperity and progress and the trials and hardships of life furnish the chief outward influences which tend to destroy this proper balance of the powers, it is man's duty to seek that magnanimity of disposition which will lift him above these influences and give him the control of them, and that equanimity of temper which will give him equal control of himself in all circumstances.

Subject 1st. Magnanimity. — Magnanimity is a certain greatness of soul which raises a man above the influence of the good or evil things of this world, so that he does not think the one necessary to make him happy, nor leave it in the power of the other to make him miserable. It manifests itself especially in *fortitude*, the office of which is to sustain and confirm the mind in adhering to what is right in opposition to pain and difficulty.

Temperance, in the wide sense, regulates desires and indulgences in the presence of temptations; fortitude girds him for work and conflict, and restrains his fears and weakness in the face of difficulties and hardships. It has therefore both an active and passive form.

Active Fortitude is demanded where evils are to be encountered and overcome. It comprehends *resolution* or *constancy*, and *intrepidity* or *courage*. *Resolution* is that steadiness with which a good man regards his duty as important and binding, and the firmness with which he adheres to it, although he well knows the calamities which the performance of it may bring upon him. The vice opposed to it is *irresolution* or *inconstancy*. *Intrepidity* is firmness and presence of mind in the midst of danger and difficulty. The vice opposed is *cowardice* or *fearfulness*.

Passive Fortitude is demanded where evils are to be met and endured. As *patience*, it is the calm endurance of the evils to which we are liable. As *humility*, it is a temper of mind which makes man slow in taking offence at any slight or disrespect which may be shown him. As *meekness*, it enables him to bear with composure wrong and injury. The vices opposed are *impatience*, *pride*, and *arrogance*.

Subject 2d. Equanimity. — Equanimity denotes that quality of spirit which enables man to preserve an even, uniform temper of mind amidst all the changes of life. The man of this temper " is not fawning and servile when poor and dependent, nor haughty and overbearing when rich and powerful; but kind and respectful in both conditions." It involves *contentment* and *cheerfulness* in the appointed lot; *submissiveness* and *confidence* toward the Moral Governor; and *considerateness* and *courtesy* toward others.

Man's Equanimity may evidently be tested equally by prosperity or adversity, by sickness or health. The opposing vices are *discontentment* and *melancholy, murmuring* and *despair, inconsiderateness* and *fretfulness.* Mankind generally regards these as little defects, but they are in reality great vices, which have a vast deal to do with filling the world with discomfort and misery, and preventing the accomplishment of man's mission. (They wear out more lives than war, famine, and pestilence, all combined, destroy.

SECTION II.

Duty of Self-Direction.

Self-direction, or the active form of self-conduct, requires that man should bend all his being, as conserved, improved, and controlled, to the accomplishment of the one appointed task of duty.

The duty obviously requires the true and noblest purpose, including a wise and complete plan for the attainment of it; and the steady and powerful adherence to the plan in using all the powers in the execution of the purpose. Hence the *Topics* for discussion.

Topic First. The True and Noblest Purpose. — It has been seen that the one great appointed task of man is to be found in the life of duty. As man is a rational being, it therefore becomes his duty to acquire an intelligent and complete view of this one grandest possible aim of life. In order to success, he must have one purpose, and that the true one and the noblest possible.

Subject 1st. The Single Aim. — As man is finite and life is short, it is essential to success in his mission that he should concentrate his energies upon a single purpose. To secure oneness of aim in life becomes therefore a most important duty.

Concentration is the first law of success in this day when there are so many possibilities. "The one prudence in life," says an American essayist, "is concentration, the one evil is dissipation; and it makes no difference whether our dissipations are coarse or fine,— property and its cares, friends and a social habit, or politics, or music, or feasting. Everything is good which takes away one plaything and delusion more, and drives us home to add one stroke of faithful work." The ordinary man who is to accomplish anything worth the while must be a *whole* man at it. If many things are to be learned and retained, it can best be done by gathering them up into one systematic view. If many things are to be accomplished, that may best be by making them all parts of some one greater thing. "The double-minded man is unstable in all his ways." Two aims in life distract and make the career a failure.

Subject 2d. The True Aim. — As man's mission is to be fulfilled under the Moral Governor, and in a world where only the true and right can ultimately succeed, it is essential to enduring success that his one purpose should be the true and right purpose. It becomes his duty therefore to fix upon that purpose which is in accordance with the will of the Moral Governor.

The Doom of Wrong Purpose. — That the doom of failure is fore-ordained for every purpose not in accordance with the law of the Governor, has been already shown (p. 156). No amount of human energy can push any purpose to ultimate success in the face of Omnipotence. For any real and abiding success, even in this present life, the first requisite is that a man have God on his side, and work in obedience to God and in sympathy with him.

Subject 3d. The Highest Aim. — As man can only reach the full dignity of his moral manhood by the accomplishment of the highest possible mission, it is essential to the greatest

19

success, that at the very outset of his work he set before himself that highest mission for accomplishment.   It is man's duty therefore, with the aid of the moral law in its various revelations, and by a broad intelligence and cultivated conscience, to form for himself the very noblest moral ideal, or, in other words, to get the noblest possible view of his mission.

The Moral Ideal of a man fixes the point above which his moral attainments cannot rise.   His power to construct such ideals is therefore one of the grandest and most important powers given him.   It has been seen that every man has his ideal of life (p. 67).   This is especially true of the moral life.   President Porter has shown that the law of duty as an ideal law " must precede the act which reaches or falls short of itself.   Every ethical rule must be a mental creation, an ideal formed by the creative power, and held before the soul as a guide and law. . . . . If these are conformed to a just ideal of life and character, they are most elevating in their influence.   If they are consistent with the conditions of our human nature and our human life, if they are conformed to the physical and moral laws of our nature, and the government and will of God, they are healthful and ennobling.   Such ideals can scarcely be too high, or too ardently and steadfastly adhered to.   But if they are false in their theory of life and happiness, if they are untrue to the conditions of our actual existence, if they involve the disappointment of our hopes, and discontent with real life, they are the bane of all enjoyment, and fatal to true happiness.   The brief excitement which these unreal dreams occasion, however highly wrought this excitement may be, is a poor offset to the painful contrasts which they necessarily involve."   *Human Intellect*, p. 371.

No more Important Duty, therefore, falls to the lot of man than the formation of his moral ideal of life.   It should be done with the utmost care, by the investigation of the law of duty as variously revealed, aided by the study of pure and noble human characters, and especially of that purest and noblest character of Jesus of Nazareth,— so that his ideal shall correspond with the idea of the Moral Governor or with the moral law.

As the power of man's ideals of life is so controlling, it becomes essential to the fulfilment of the noblest mission that he should avoid everything that would lead him to the adoption or formation of a false ideal.   It becomes his duty, therefore, to withhold his imagination from dwelling upon evil in any of its forms; and especially to guard against the two over-shadowing evil influences of the present age : that inordinate indulgence in reading base or unworthy so-called works of imagination, which so often leads to the formation of false ideals ; and that intimate intercourse with unprincipled men of genius, which so often leads to the adoption of their false ideals.

The Power of Evil Imagination. — Says Dr. McCosh: "According to the cherished imagination, so will be the prevailing sentiment. Low images will incite mean motives, and sooner or later land the person who indulges them in the mire. Lustful pictures will foment licentious purposes, which will hurry the individual, when occasion presents itself and permits, into the commission of the deed — to be remembered ever after, as Adam must have looked back upon the plucking of the forbidden fruit." By the power of the imagination, thus indulged in dwelling upon that which is evil, the evil comes to be looked upon as good, and darkness to appear as light, and the whole life is transformed and perverted.

False Works of Imagination. — The power of base works of imagination is one of the chief influences, of the present age, leading to the formation of false ideals of life.

Debasing Ideals of Poetry. — All *works of poetic genius* which present evil for its own sake, and affectionately array it in brilliant colors, are potent in inducing the formation of false ideals. Ostensibly the same being figures in *Paradise Lost*, in *Faust*, in *Cain*, in *A Drama of Exile*, and in the *Bible*. The Miltonic *Satan* has exalted virtues which attract, but he has vices which repel more, so that only the proud and scornful man of ambition, who "would rather reign in hell than serve in heaven," would be drawn to him ; the *Mephistopheles* of Goethe appeals to all the baser instincts, so that every basest man longs to be just such a devil; the Byronic *Lucifer* attracts more than the Byronic God, so that he who accepts the poet's delineation must, in his worship, put him in the place of God; the *Lucifer* of Mrs. Browning is one,

> "To whom the highest and the lowest alike
> Say, 'Go from us — we have no need of thee;'"

the *Satan* of the Bible is a terror to every human being, whether base or otherwise. The character by the man of moderate Christian instincts, if not drawn in truest lines, would yet lead the generality of men upward; the portraitures by the infidel and the God-hater are only and intensely evil, and can but hurry men downward; that by the woman, who represents Christianity in its more earnest form, is, in its power to repel men from evil, second only to that by the divine pen, which is made one of the mightiest motives to urge the lost heavenward. All sympathizing intercourse with the brilliant portraiture of the evil one, for the love of him, leads man to fashion his ideal in the image of the devil, and so debases and drags him down with it.

Debasing Ideals of Fiction. — No less evil in its influence is much of the portraiture of evil which abounds in the *novels* of the day. It inevitably lowers man's ideal. The vulgarity which is tainted by pretension and arrogance in the so-called higher classes, and by slang in the lower; the vulgarity that produces snappish wives, coarse husbands, and rude children; that shows itself in the envy, in the ill-temper, the vanity and the affectation, which good breeding corrects or at least conceals,— only disgusts and, when disgust is over, debases by actual contact in real life, and can do no better in the novel. Still worse is that deep probing of the moral ulcers of society which is so common with the novelists. Besides that class of pamphlets issued in the interests of vice and sold everywhere by the ton in defiance of law, there is a more pretentious class of works, of which the French school is the representative, whose aim it is to array deadly vices in gilded vesture and to paint the worst crimes in gorgeous colors to captivate the uninitiated. They have no better right in the world than have the vices and crimes which they portray and gild. Familiarity with vice lessens its repulsiveness to all. Human nature, shattered and defiled as it is, cannot gaze upon such scenes without peril of more complete wreck and deeper defilement.

Moral Influence of Novel Reading. — It has been shown by those princes among reasoners, Bishop Butler and Henry Rogers, — the former furnishing the principle, the latter its application, — that the *inordinate* reading of works of fiction, of even the highest character, must weaken the intellect and deaden true feeling. It is an admitted fact that such reading destroys all taste for the other and more solid reading, which is essential for every intelligent man or woman, and so, in the end, all taste for real, right life; and it is a still more momentous fact that when such immoderate reading of fiction becomes likewise *indiscriminate*, the reader is led by it away from the facts of history and the truths of science, away from the laws of ethics and the doctrines of religion, away from the realities of this life and the transcendent glories of the life to come; his precious time for mental improvement is wasted, and he is made to move in a fictitious world, until all his notions of society are warped, all his views of life perverted, all his ideas of religion distorted, in short, until his ideal of life is wholly transformed and base.

Base Men of Genius. — The evil influence of brilliant, but unprincipled, men is very marked, especially upon youth. Depraved human nature worships brilliancy rather than goodness, and brilliancy without goodness, rather than with it. One such man as Byron or Aaron Burr leads legions of young men to ruin. There is no more solemn duty, therefore, than that of guarding against the danger of being brought under the influence of such men, whether through personal intercourse or history or biography, and against the moral ruin that results from adopting their ideals of life.

As Christianity has been shown to be the only reconstructing agency that is able to lift man up from his condition of moral disorder to this noblest moral mission, it obviously becomes man's duty to avail himself of its provisions, in order that he may place himself in a condition to accomplish his true moral task.

The True Ideal. — With an ideal so formed, with such a perfect example, and with the plain law of duty brought out in clear characters on the soul by an almighty reconstructing power, the man is prepared to move toward the true and highest manhood.

Topic Second. The Execution of the Purpose. — As the true end of man's being is to be found in the highest purpose possible to his powers, it becomes his duty steadily and strongly to direct all the powers placed at his disposal to the execution of that purpose. This requires the best possible disposal and direction of all his personal powers, and of all the means at his command, under the lead of a decided and unbending will, to the one great object of life.

Subject 1st. Personal Powers and the Purpose of Life. — It has been seen (p. 133) that the capabilities, or personal powers, of the agent decide the possibilities of action, and that each one has his place to fill. It is therefore his duty to give the best disposition and direction to all his powers for the fulfilment of the mission for which he is specially fitted.

In order that he may make the most of his capabilities, it is therefore the duty of every man to make choice of the exact work or profession to which he is suited, and to bend his

19 *

personal powers to the achievement of the noblest success in it.

Choice of a Work in Life. — One of the most difficult and delicate things to be done by any man who would succeed in life is to make choice of his peculiar work. In making that choice, duty requires him to avoid certain errors and to be guided by certain principles.

Errors to be Avoided. — *A first and common error* is that it may be allowable for a man to live a life of idleness, having no work and no aim. Such lives are destructive to those who attempt to lead them, since "man's play-day is always the devil's working-day;" and in the highest degree immoral, as casting off allegiance to the law of the Moral Governor. For a being of such wonderful capacities as man, living in a state of preparation for a future immortal existence, and having such great things set before him to be accomplished in so short a time, to be idle and without a mission is to subject himself to inevitable moral condemnation and misery.

A second error is that of allowing mere trifles or fancies to decide his course for him. Multitudes accomplish nothing in life, because they allow themselves to drift thus irrationally into professions for which they have no fitness, or into a life-work the result of which is only evil. David Hume, who in his youth was a believer in Christianity, "was appointed in a debating society to advocate the cause of infidelity, and thus familiarizing himself with the subtle sophism of scepticism, became a life-long deist." Some romantic fancy often turns the youth to some pursuit for which he is utterly unfitted, and thus makes his life both a curse and a wreck.

A third error, especially prevalent at the present day, is that *money-getting* is the chief end of man. Such worship of mammon is an immorality, and its moral doom is seen in the *miser*.

A fourth, and perhaps most prevalent and pernicious, error of the times, is that respectability and honor are to be found only in the three so-called learned professions, — law, medicine, and divinity. It is robbing the other honest employments of life of noble workmen to add to the legions of dishonest lawyers, blundering doctors, and stupid and inefficient ministers; and it is one of the most portentous of the immoral tendencies of the age.

Principles to be Observed. — There are certain principles which should guide man in the choice of his work in life.

A first principle is that no work which the Moral Governor has appointed to be done can be disgraceful or degrading. There may be disgrace in man's not doing his work well, and degradation in doing it from base motives, but none in the work itself. Man should never shrink from any task that is clearly set before him, from that of the boot-black or the porter to that of the emperor or the evangelist.

A second principle is that a man should carefully study his aptitudes, learning just what powers he has, and just what they fit him for accomplishing. It may require time and effort to ascertain this; sometimes the peculiar talent does not show itself early in life; but ordinarily the mission may be discerned by careful, anxious investigation, and then the result is worth all the patience and the labor.

A third principle is that the man of correct moral tone may find in his wishes a true presentiment of his capabilities. Vanity may lead the immoral astray, but, in the case of a right-thinking man, a fondness for any pursuit creates a very strong probability that he was made for it, and ensures his devotion to it and success in it.

Devotion to the Work of Life.— The wise disposition and devotion of the powers to the work, when once it is found, is in the line of duty. What is required? How shall an intelligent, progressive, and immortal being, by the use of the powers given him, work out his best mission of duty along the line chosen, — on the farm, in the shop, at the desk, behind the counter, in the office, or in the pulpit? Such questions man must perpetually ask himself in the varied work of life, and, asking and answering in the right spirit, he will exalt his occupation and advance toward the true manhood and the real success.

Subject 2d. The Means Possessed and the Purpose of Life.— It has been seen that the Moral Governor has placed certain means at the disposal of man (p. 186), by the use of which he may greatly increase the grandeur and elevation of his moral mission. The chief of these are the forces and treasures of the world, and time. It is therefore the duty of every man to make the most of these, in supplementing his personal powers, for the exaltation of his work in life.

1st. Forces of Nature.— By the wise use of the forces of nature, man may vastly increase his power and sphere of action as a moral being. It is therefore his duty to give proper employment to these forces in furthering his high moral aims.

Use of Forces of Nature. — The subjection of the forces of nature to man has reached the grandest scale in the present age. By the use of steam, electricity, and other natural agencies, the United States does the

work of twice the adult working population of the globe, and Great
Britain a still larger work. The forces of nature are everywhere
waiting to be employed to do man's work and release him from the mere
physical drudgery of life for the higher work of a rational, moral, and
immortal being. The obligation to take advantage of this perpetual
offer of aid is of the very strongest kind. The intelligent and observant
man may accomplish vastly more in his mission by availing himself of
the generous offer of the Moral Governor.

2d. Wealth.

By the proper use of wealth man may
greatly elevate and extend his moral work. It is therefore
his duty to seek to secure wealth for this high end, and to
make diligent use of what the Moral Governor may bestow
upon him for the same end.

Wealth a Power. — The acquisition of wealth for its proper uses has
been shown (p. 185) to be one of the duties essential to man's well-being.
The Moral Governor has placed the power of *acquisitiveness* in man for
a good and noble purpose. Under the control of intelligence, wealth is
a most important and powerful means of extending human influence in
every direction.

Wealth a Curse. — The improper seeking and use of wealth make it
a power fruitful of evil.

The seeking of riches *for their own sake* is one of the prevalent vices
of all ages, and a vice of most degrading character, since it lifts a mere
inanimate thing above man and God, and begets selfishness and godlessness along with covetousness. Out of this irrational worship of gold
arises the so baneful tendency to estimate manhood, not by attainments
and character, but by the extent of the bank account.

Equally great is the error of seeking wealth *solely for the pleasure and
independence it will give.* The wisdom and experience of mankind, from
Solomon to Bacon, and from the Rothschilds to Stephen Girard, prove
that "he that getteth silver is not satisfied with silver," and that there
are no men more wretched and dependent than those who seek riches
and use them for selfish ends.

Peculiarly fatal to the young men of the day is the error that *economy
is meanness, and extravagance nobility,* and that money is therefore to be
sought and used for a mere show of generosity and nobleness. Such
miscalled generosity, which labors to earn in order to waste on pleasant
drinks and cigars, and in sight-seeing and dissipation, is no less immoral
than the covetousness of the miser; and it demonstrates its viciousness
by leaving its victims moral wrecks, and by robbing them of one of the

chief means given by the Moral Governor for reaching success in life, in the accomplishment of higher moral ends.

Wealth a Blessing. — *The true aim in seeking and using wealth* is to be found in connection with man's moral mission. It is to be sought and used in subordination to this mission. It is this that redeems it from the curse and makes it a blessing. He who seeks and uses it for this end will be saved from all the dangers which otherwise accompany its acquirement and possession. Such seeking and use of wealth will lead to the formation of true habits of economy and charity, by redeeming the former from meanness and the latter from impulse. It will secure the valuable discipline of self-denial, industry, and skill, which comes from its pursuit, and which fits man better for his higher moral work. The possibilities of duty will continually enlarge before him with the increasing means of power and usefulness. Every act, both of acquisition and use for the sake of his mission, will advance him toward a nobler and more complete manhood.

3d. Time. — It is only by making the most of time, in the use of his personal powers and the various means placed at his disposal, that man can work out the complete life of duty in his chosen pursuit. It is therefore his duty to practise a true and rigid economy of his time for the sake of his mission.

The Right Use of Time. — Time, like wealth, is to be used for the moral mission. This is evident, alike from the supreme importance of that mission and from the bearing of man's present work upon his future immortality. No one who has any large and correct conception of man's true nature and destiny will for a moment think of denying it. John Foster has shown, in his celebrated *Essay on the Improvement of Time*, that, "on the hypothesis that the existence of man terminates at death, there is no object of sufficient magnitude to call forth the combined and severe exertions which have been represented as essential to the noblest improvement of time;" and that man should choose his profession or business, and use the whole period of life "with a regard to the greatest moral advantage." Foster's *Essay* is one which a thoughtful man cannot afford to leave unread.

Time a Powerful Element in Success. — Time is clearly a most important element in the accomplishment of the moral mission. Its importance may be shown by a consideration of its *capacity* and its *fleetness*.

The Capacity of Time for holding a vast train of successive acts needs to be understood by every moral agent. It makes possible, for one who truly and constantly improves his time, the accomplishment in threescore and ten years of a task almost inconceivably great. The examples of such men as King Alfred, Richard Baxter, Sir William Jones, and Humboldt indicate that men differ more in the manner of improving the time allotted to them than in genius, and show how much might be accomplished even by inferior powers well-directed and constantly employed.

The Fleetness and Uncertainty of Time furnish an additional evidence of its importance and another motive for its improvement. It hastens its flight, whether man employs it or not. It is liable to end with any man at any hour. A great moral work may therefore have but the briefest period for its proper accomplishment; so that there is not a moment that man can afford either to waste or lose.

Principles governing Improvement of Time. — The improvement of time consists in its diligent and economical use for the accomplishment of the life of duty. It requires *method*, as opposed to the lack of it; *economy*, as opposed to waste and loss.

Method is indispensable to the best use of time, " since the application of its principles alone can produce that arrangement and combination which cause the diversified activity to be *a system*, instead of a confused multiplicity of efforts, without mutual dependence or connection, and perhaps counteracting one another." It is true of vast numbers that their situation, or plan, or duty, includes various forms of effort, which, with the proper consideration, they can dispose "into an order which will best combine the effect and advantage of them all," and make the whole work a unit. A carefully arranged order, appointing the several parts of the day or the week to their respective employments, will at the end of each effort bring to hand the next in succession, as regularly as the hours of the day follow one another; and will thus prevent the waste and loss of time which unavoidably result from hesitation in the change of occupation where the order is not prearranged.

It must be borne in mind, however, that "this method ought to be the implement of utility, and not the chain of slavery;" in other words, that a *rational method*, admitting of changes to meet emergencies which may arise, and in which the profit is in departure from method, rather than in rigidly adhering to it, is the only kind suited to a *rational being*. Tenfold more can be accomplished by any ordinary man, under the controlling influence of such method, than by capricious and desultory effort.

A Rigid Economy in the use of time is as essential as a rational method. A true economy must make provision, first, for the true *work of life;* and, secondly, for the *rest* and *recreation* needed to keep man in condition for that work. Such economy must guard against waste and loss of time, arising from want of broad view and of rational aim, from making a play of life, and from the neglect of its moments. It follows that —·

A first error, to be guarded against in the use of time, arises from forgetting that man is a weak and finite being, and must therefore wisely divide his life into periods of work and periods of rest and recreation. This is the failing of a few only of the nobler and more earnest spirits of the race. The sad result of overtasked powers is early wreck.

A second error springs from forgetting or ignoring the fact that life is given for an earnest moral mission, and that its rest and recreation are subordinate to this. This is the failing of the vast majority of the race, and appears in various forms: in the man who is too base to care to have any purpose in life; in the one who is too indolent to try to accomplish any purpose; and in the one who is so vicious and perverse as to seek to transform life from a work into a play. The *first* is the vice of the stupid and heedless man, who gives himself up to be swept hither and thither by the tide of circumstances, and whose life is little less irrational than that of the brute. The *second* is the vice of the indolent and sluggish man, who gives himself up to bodily ease and mental vacancy or stagnation, to excess of sleep, until every noble and elevating aspiration dies out of his nature. The *third* is the vice of the reckless reveller and play-goer, who exalts those recreations of life, which were designed to *create anew* man's exhausted energies for the prosecution of the work of life, to the place of the chief end of life, and then degrades human life itself into a round of senseless amusements.

A third error has its origin in the neglect of the scattered moments of time, or the intervals of work, as of no value. This is a wellnigh universal vice. The proper employment of the time so wasted by most men, might make them wise and powerful. Almost any young man could save an hour from time wasted in sleep, and another from the time lost here and there through the hours, and yet leave ample time for the ordinary work, rest, and recreation. Two hours a day thus saved from sheer waste and loss would in a single year carry him through fifty volumes of the standard works of literature; and in ten years make him a marvel of intelligence and culture.

A fourth error comes from letting time slip while dreaming over many and perhaps great things, instead of using the passing moments to good purpose in doing the right thing at the right time and with the one true and highest purpose. This has been the failing of many of those endowed with the greatest genius. " Distraction of pursuit is the rock on which most unsuccessful persons split in early life. Nine men out of ten lay out their plans on too vast a scale; and they who are competent to do almost anything do nothing, because they never make up their minds distinctly as to what they want, or what they intend to be. Hence, the mournful failures we see all around us in every walk of life. Behold a De Quincey, with all his wondrous and weird-like powers, — his enormous learning and wealth of thought, — producing nothing worthy of his rare gifts! See a Coleridge, a man of Shakesperian mould, possessing a creative power of Titanic grasp, and yet, for want of concentration, fathoming among all his vagrancies no foundation, filling no chasms, and of all his dazzling and colossal literary schemes not completing one! The heir of eternity, scorning to be the slave of time! Feeling that he has all the ages to work in, he squanders the precious present; so he lets his dreams go by ungrasped, his magnificent promises unrealized; and his life may be summed up in the words of Charles Lamb, who writes to a friend: 'Coleridge is dead, and is said to have left behind him above forty thousand treatises on metaphysic and divinity—not one of them complete!'" Dr. Matthews: *Getting on in the World.*

Subject 3d. The Decisive Will and the Purpose of Life.—

It is by the decisive and unbending will that the life purpose must be pushed to its completion. Man's last and highest duty toward himself culminates therefore in requiring him to bring the strong and holy will (p. 146) to the fulfilment of the task of life.

Importance of Decision of Character. — This is the substance of the duty just presented, and is one of the capital requisites to true and high success. It is the great distinguishing element between men of otherwise equal powers. Says John Foster, in his *Essay* on *Decision of Character:* " Without it, a human being, with powers at best but feeble and surrounded by innumerable things tending to perplex, to divert, and to frustrate, their operations, is indeed a pitiable atom, the sport of divers and casual impulses. It is a poor and disgraceful thing, not to be able to reply, with some degree of certainty, to the simple questions, What will you be? What will you do?"

It makes a Man's Powers and Life his Own. — As the will has been seen to be the self-assertive power, and the power by which man makes his actions in the highest sense *his own,* a man without decision can never be said to belong to himself, and his conduct, always the sport of surrounding influences, can never reach the dignity of a truly manly life.

This duty requires of every man that the decisive purpose

of his life, when once formed, shall be ceaselessly pushed to its execution, by decisive action with all the powers, through whatever of emergency and opposition, and under the influence of the highest moral enthusiasm.

Energy in Action. — Decisive action must follow the decisive purpose, if that purpose is to be of any value. The Moral Governor has placed high honor upon industry by his own ceaseless work. He has so made the world that it is universally true that there is no excellence to be expected without great labor to attain it. It will be true always. He who would achieve a noble purpose must bring to the work an activity of corresponding energy. Hard, honest, earnest work is the only safe road to true success. It must be work every stroke of which is in the right place. It must be work into every stroke of which all a man's power enters. It must be work in which the strokes are constant and ceaseless.

Obstacles to be Met. — Difficulties must be overcome and, if possible, made to help on the one purpose of life. Unforeseen emergencies will meet man continually. The same power of decision is requisite here as in the straight forward work, only in a higher degree. "The regulation of every man's plan must greatly depend on the course of events, which come in an order not to be foreseen or prevented. But in accommodating the plans of conduct to the train of events, the difference between two men may be no less than that, in the one instance, the man is subservient to the events, and in the other, the events are made subservient to the man. Some men seem to have been taken along by a succession of events, and, as it were, handed forward in helpless passiveness from one to another; having no determined principle in their own characters, by which they could constrain those events to serve a design formed antecedently to them, or apparently in defiance of them. The events seized them as a neutral material, not they the events. Others, advancing through life with an internal invincible determination, have seemed to make the train of circumstances, whatever they were, conduce as much to their chief design as if they had, by some directing interposition, been brought about on purpose. It is wonderful how even the casualties of life seem to bow to a spirit that will not bow to them, and yield to subserve a design which they may, in their first apparent tendency, threaten to frustrate." *Foster.* Opposition, desertion, success, may thus be made subservient to the decisive will in pushing on the work of life.

Enthusiasm to be Cherished. — An intense moral enthusiasm must underlie and furnish the most powerful spring of every truly noble life.

20

A soul without such motive must fail. Half-hearted work can never succeed where man has all the forces of nature, and all the adverse forces of his own being and of society, to contend with, master, and turn to account. (One who saw Michael Angelo engaged at his work tells us that he wrought with fearful energy and earnestness. He would accomplish many times as much as other men. Every stroke was so with all the soul, that, as he saw the huge fragments fly from the rapid blows, the observer trembled lest the statue should be ruined. But the enthusiastic workman held ceaselessly on, cutting and filing, dashing off as incumbrances every particle which hindered the completion of the likeness, until the once shapeless block took shape and polish and beauty, and stood forth the finished work of his hand, his brain, his soul, his life, and the perfect embodiment of his ideal. Any man who would accomplish the true work of life may see in the great sculptor his model. With the grandest possible mission of duty taking hold on God and immortality, his may well be the grandest possible moral enthusiasm; and with the whole being directed ceaselessly to the fulfilment of such a mission under the influence of such a motive, his may well be the grandest possible moral success. /

Such success in his mission of duty toward himself will prepare for and bear along with it a like success in his mission of duty toward mankind, which is next to be considered.

DIVISION II.

SOCIAL ETHICS.

Statement and Subdivision.

Social Ethics is that division of Practical Ethics which treats of the application of the moral law to the regulation of man's conduct toward his fellow-man in the several relations of life.

As man's duty toward his fellow-man is summed up in the Scriptural requirement to love his neighbor as himself, or in the intuitive moral requirement of a due regard to the continuance, improvement, and proper direction of mankind,—the natural unfolding of this principle would furnish subjects corresponding to those of Individual Ethics.

The Unselfish Theory.—The true theory of man's relation to mankind is the unselfish one. In the working out of that great mission of duty which is common to all, men are mutually dependent, and mutual helpfulness is therefore necessary. It was Cain who asked, "*Am I my brother's keeper?*" denying responsibility for anything beyond himself; and it is the spirit of Cain that echoes the question in all ages. But each man is bound to all men. The more intimate relations of human life may modify, but can never confine the duties of practical goodness.

The Selfish Theory.—The selfish theory of life has no foundation in moral principle on which to rest. *What am I to do in life?* The common immoral answer is, "I am to enter this or that profession, and, in antagonism with all the world, am to make my way to success in it." When *ambition* reigns, or *covetousness*, success is won at the expense to other men of woe and loss. The theory is, "Up for me means down for some one else. Wealth for me means poverty for some one else." In the light of Christian ethical principles, this is inhuman, and may become diabolical.

Perfect and Imperfect Rights. — To escape the curse of seeming to hold such a theory, men have devised many expedients. The most plausible of these is the division of obligations and rights into *perfect* and *imperfect.* "In the dispensation of justice there are only some duties which can be enforced under sanction of positive law; whereas others must be left to individual choice for their performance. The former are perfect obligations, with equivalent perfect rights; the latter are imperfect obligations, with imperfect rights." It is apparent at once that this distinction is made from the point of view of *civil* law, rather than of *moral.* *What is man's duty to his fellow-men?* is a very different question from, *How much of duty can be enforced by civil authority?* It is universally admitted that the obligations which belong to the internal sphere of action, as well as many of those agreed upon by men generally, and belonging to the outward and visible sphere of action, cannot be enforced by any form of human authority. The duty, however, is just as binding as if it could be enforced by the civil law. All obligations and all rights are perfect.

In the duties of man toward mankind originate the rights of man. What a man is morally bound to render to his neighbor, his neighbor has a moral right to claim from him. As the moral system is therefore one of mutual dependence, Social Ethics, in treating of duties to mankind, treats also of human rights.

Doctrine of Human Rights. — To the duties of man under the moral law correspond his rights. Says Prof. Calderwood: "Duties and rights are moral equivalents, resting equally upon the unchangeable warrant of moral law as the universal rule of human action. The ground on which any man can claim a right entitled to acknowledgment by others is exactly the ground on which, by necessity, he must own moral obligation." The *duties*, which, on the one side, a man owes to men, furnish the ground for the *rights*, which, on the other side, men may claim from him. The *rights* of man have accordingly been said to include "all that a man may lawfully do, all that he may lawfully possess and use, and all that he may lawfully claim of any person."

Mutual Helpfulness. — There is therefore no moral basis for the selfish theory of life. Mutual dependence is the great fact; mutual helpfulness the great duty as between mankind. Says a late writer: "That man is not perfect who is so in and for himself alone. An essential part of true manhood is in the relationships he sustains to other beings, in the midst of whom and with reference to whom his life is lived. . . . . Man is not great, nor rich, nor strong for himself alone. He is not, then, to make these the occasions for lording it over his fellows. The poor, the ignorant, the low, are not stepping-stones, nor lawful plunder; they are brothers to be respected and helped. He must use the advantage of his high position as a means of lifting up those beneath him. He is bound to help the weak by as much as he is stronger than they. His debt to all men is limited only by his superiority to them. Paul saw the law, when he wrote, 'I am debtor both to the Greeks and to the Barbarians, both to the wise and to the unwise.' " *Christianity the Science of Manhood:* Savage.

It is only with the help of all other men and helping all others that any one man can reach the highest possible life.

As man's power to perform different offices toward his fellow-men varies with the intimacy of the relations he holds to them in the race, family, and state, his social duties may best be treated in connection with these relations, in the following *Chapters:*

Chapter I.   General Ethics, or Duties toward Man as Man.

Chapter II.   Economical Ethics, or Duties in the House-hold.

Chapter III.   Civil Ethics, or Duties in the State.

The Ground of the Subdivision. — The moral agent is related to other men as men simply, or as members of the one human race; hence, *General Ethics,* which treats of the general duties which he owes as a man to mankind, presents the first phase of social duty. But the agent is brought into more intimate relations to a portion of the race, by two divine institutions, — the family and the state, — which relations involve special duties; hence, *Economical Ethics* and *Civil Ethics* present these two phases of social duty. There are thus three natural subdivisions of *Social Ethics,* the first of which presents duty toward mankind in society as unorganized, and the last two, toward mankind in society as organized.

20*

CHAPTER I.

GENERAL ETHICS.

General Ethics is that branch of Social Ethics which treats of the general duties of man toward his fellow-men as men, or as members with himself of the same general society of the human race.

As all the phases of social duty are but the simple unfolding of the intuitive moral judgment, which requires that man should to the utmost of opportunity and ability labor to conserve and improve the being of his fellow-man and direct it to the noblest moral ends, — the subject of General Ethics may most naturally be treated under the following *Sections*, corresponding to the subdivisions of Individual Ethics:

Section 1.   The Duty of Social Conservation.
Section 2.   The Duty of Social Improvement.
Section 3.   The Duty of Social Direction.

SECTION I.

The Duty of Social Conservation.

As the continued existence of men in the full exercise of their rights is indispensable to the fulfilment of their moral mission, *it is man's first duty toward his fellow-men* to seek, so far as ability and opportunity allow, to conserve their being and rights. His fellow-men may claim the right to the preservation of life, to the free exercise of their powers, to the control of their own property, to truthfulness in the intercourse and business of life, and to all that treatment required by a true brotherly regard.

The duty of Social Conservation therefore furnishes the following *Topics*:

Topic 1.   Duties pertaining to Life.
Topic 2.   Duties pertaining to Liberty.
Topic 3.   Duties pertaining to Property.
Topic 4.   Duties pertaining to Truthfulness.
Topic 5.   Duties pertaining to Human Brotherhood.

Grounds for the Division. — The duty of social conservation might naturally be distributed in the same manner as that of self-conservation (p. 175), since it is of course true that man is bound to seek to conserve the life, health, and well-being of his fellow-men as well as of himself. But, taking it for granted that the general principles there presented apply also here, the present division is adopted for the sake of greater simplicity, and to bring out more distinctly the *peculiar features* of social conservation.

Order of Topics. — The continuance of the life and being of men is at the foundation of all exertion of the powers: hence the duties pertaining to *life* come first. Freedom to develop and exert the powers of the being in accordance with their law is the next requisite to the life of duty: hence the duties pertaining to *liberty* come next in order. Property, which involves the exclusive possession and use of accumulated power for the purposes of life, is the indispensable means in the accomplishment of the work of life: hence the duties pertaining to *property* come third in order. The life, the free activity, and the accumulation of property all depend upon the maintenance of truthfulness between men in the social system: hence the duties pertaining to *truthfulness* come fourth in order. But men do not constitute merely an association of workers and traders, each intent on securing the most for himself; they form a great brotherhood, in which brotherly offices are mutually needed: hence the system of duties of social conservation is crowned by the duties pertaining to *human brotherhood.*

The Old Distinction. — The first four classes of duties just enumerated have usually been treated under the more general head of *social justice,* and the last under that of *benevolence;* but there is no good moral ground for any such distinction.

First, the duties of justice and benevolence, so-called, are of equal moral obligation. Acts of *benevolence* are truly acts of *justice*, — they are due to our fellow-creatures in the circumstances in which they are placed; they are due to our own social and rational nature; and they are in accordance with the arrangements of Providence and the will of God. Both have their foundation in our moral nature and in our social condition, and, in the eye of the moralist, both are equally binding.

Secondly, the reason for the distinction is extra-moral. "It is that many of the duties of strict justice are enforced by positive or civil law, while those of benevolence are not. A man can be compelled to pay his debts, but not to give alms. And this is one of the points of difference between *morality* and *jurisprudence*. Both rest upon the great law of right and wrong, as made known by the light of nature. Morality enjoins us to do what is *right*, because it is right. *Jurisprudence* enjoins us to give to others their *rights*, with ultimate reference, no doubt, to the truth made known to us by the light of nature, that we are morally bound to do so; but appealing more directly to the fact that our doing so can be demanded by our neighbor, and that his demand will be enforced by the authority of positive law." *Fleming.*

Topic First. Duties pertaining to Life. — As life is a sacred treasure and indispensable to the fulfilment of the mission, it is the duty of the moral agent to seek to preserve the life of his fellow-men, so far as it is placed in his power. He is equally bound to refrain from taking his neighbor's life, and to resist others who would take it.

Subject 1st. Preservation of the Life of Men. — The law of duty, in binding the moral agent to preserve the life of his fellow-man, so far as lies in his power, prohibits as immoral everything tending toward his death, from the inward malice to the outward death-blow.

1st. Duty of Avoiding Malice. — The worst of murderous deeds spring from the malice of the heart. It is therefore man's duty to avoid cherishing any such feeling toward mankind; and, on the other hand, actively to cherish a true brotherly love.

The Moral System of Christ first brought into prominence and power this higher and positive form of the *law of love*. The old Jew thought that only the death-blow was murder; but the great Teacher taught him and the world that the thought of evil in the heart is of the essence of murder. In a state of things where sin and evil abound, and where injuries and wrongs are constantly being inflicted, there is no more difficult duty than that of avoiding malice and keeping in exercise the feeling of brotherly regard for men. When it is remembered that the law of love requires such regard, not for the good alone, but for the bad, not for benefactors merely, but for enemies as well, the difficulty and importance of the duty become still more apparent.

2d. Duty of Defending Men. — As the moral agent is responsible for the evil which by due diligence he can prevent, the guilt of murder rests on him in large degree, if he neglects, as opportunity offers, to defend men from the causes which tend to produce death. It is therefore his duty to warn them against any course of conduct which he sees will result in the destruction of life; to rescue them, if possible, in peril, and to defend them to the extent of his ability against all improper assaults made upon them.

3d. Duty of Refraining from taking Human Life. — The greatest violation of the duty of the conservation of man is found in the unlawful taking of human life. *Homicide,* or the taking of human life, may be either intentional or unintentional, either moral or immoral. *Murder* (including killing in duel) and *manslaughter* are the principal forms of immoral homicide, and have been recognized as crimes by the enlightened moral consciousness in all ages and nations.

Intentional Homicide as Morally Wrong includes murder in the ordinary way, and killing in duelling.

Murder is the unlawful taking of human life, with premeditated malice, by a person of sound mind. When the murder is not only intentional and premeditated, but secret in its execution, the murderer becomes an *assassin.* The assassin, in not exposing his own life in giving his victim opportunity for self-defence, adds the meanness of cowardice to the guilt of murder.

A Duel is a premeditated combat between two persons, for the purpose of deciding some private difference or quarrel. It differs from ordinary assault with intent to kill, in being made with the knowledge and co-operation of the party assailed. It is a mutual attempt, on the part of two men, to murder each other. It may take the character of a *formal duel*, in which a challenge is previously given and accepted, and the combat is conducted according to certain prescribed rules; or it may differ from any other hostile encounter only in being an assault with intent to kill, with more or less of mutual premeditation and consent.

That Death inflicted in a Duel is Murder, cannot reasonably be denied. If it be said by its advocates that duelling is an appeal to the Supreme Ruler of men and events to decide the question of difference between the parties, it is a sufficient reply that the Moral Governor has never prescribed any such method of settlement, and that human law gives it no sanction. The duellist has not the slightest ground for supposing that the question of right or wrong, or of guilt or innocence, will be decided correctly in this way. If it be considered as an attempt to avenge any real or supposed personal insult or injury, then it is no less than taking vengeance, which is the prerogative of law, human or divine, into the man's own hands; and this is murder. Accordingly, the laws of almost all civilized nations treat the taking of life by the duellist as murder; and this has always been in accordance with the judgment of the enlightened Christian conscience.

Intentional Homicide as Morally Right. — Not all *intentional* taking of life is unlawful. As has been seen (p. 178), there are higher interests than the life of the individual. The right of a man to his life may be forfeited: *first*, by attempting the life of another; *secondly*, by attempting acts of violence, such as house-breaking or robbery especially at night, which endanger the lives of others; *thirdly*, by resisting the officers of the law; *fourthly*, by murder accomplished.

In proper *self-defence*, the agent in taking the life of another does not thereby become morally guilty (p. 178). The *executioner*, in taking the life of the murderer, does not thereby become a murderer, but performs a high and solemn duty, as the agent of the law, in punishing the greatest of crimes and as thereby preserving the lives of others from the hands of the murderer. The *officer* in taking the life of the prisoner who attempts to escape — if that taking is a necessity — is not guilty of unlawful taking of life.

Unintentional Homicide as Morally Wrong includes, besides what is known in the civil law as *manslaughter*, or inexcusable homicide, the *various other forms* of taking life excusable in civil law but contrary to the moral law. It differs from *murder* in not involving premeditation and cherished malice. It may be the result of sudden impulse of anger, or of criminal carelessness. It is an offence against the law of conservation, since man is bound to control such passion and to avoid such carelessness. An unlawful assault which results in death, even when death is not intended, as in a drunken mania, is manslaughter. The man who sacrifices human life by driving furiously through the crowded streets of a city; the engineer who does the same thing by recklessly urging the train along the broken rails, or the steamer upon the rocky shores; the proprietor who reaches like results by running a condemned or unsafe engine in his manufactory, — all alike are guilty of inexcusable homicide.

If the taking of life be in the heat of passion, in a sudden quarrel, arising from provocation, and without previous intention to take life, it is in law termed *manslaughter;* but if the passions have had time to cool and the killing is then done, it is *murder.* Homicide in any sudden affray, though not strictly in self-defence, is considered *excusable* in civil law, but not *justifiable* in moral law. Some states have made killing in games of boxing, sword-playing, etc., excusable, but it is not in morals justifiable. Death resulting from any dangerous or unlawful act — as shooting or casting stones in a town — may or may not be excusable in law, but it is unjustifiable in morals.

Unintentional Homicide as not Morally Wrong, as illustrated in the taking of life in self-defence and in the way of duty, has been seen to be justifiable. When the taking of life is purely accidental, so that it cannot be avoided by the use of any means within the reach of the man, it is justifiable.

Subject 2d. Preservation of Life in its Vigor. — As a

vigorous life is essential to success in the human mission, it is the duty of the moral agent to care for the healthful condition of his fellow-men, so far as lies in his power. He is bound actively to promote the health of men, according to his opportunity and ability, by example, influence, and instruction; and equally bound to refrain from everything tending to impair its vigor.

Violations of the Duty.— This duty is manifestly violated by improperly placing any cause of disease in the way of men. He who wittingly and wantonly exposes his neighbor to a noxious disease, which will tend to destroy his health and prevent his mission, is guilty, not of an immorality only, but of a crime.

This duty is oftenest violated in seeking gain in business pursuits, by requiring men to violate the laws of their physical being; and in particular those special laws (p. 181) upon which vigorous health depends. Much of oppression of the poor by the rich, and especially of workmen by their employers, is of this nature. The man who brings to physical degradation and disease those whom the Moral Governor makes dependent upon him, whether he does it by grinding down their wages until they are insufficient to procure food, in requisite quantity and quality, to sustain a vigorous life; or by imposing such conditions as prevent proper attention to cleanliness and exercise; or by demanding such constant and unremitting toil as to leave insufficient time for rest and sleep, — is guilty of a very grave immorality. This becomes self-evident the moment the duty of social conservation is understood. The enlightened conscience everywhere endorses the severe reprobation, so frequent in the Scriptures, of this selfish vice.

Topic Second. Duties pertaining to Liberty. — As personal liberty is as truly a right of men as personal existence, and as it is as truly essential to the fulfilment of the moral mission, it is the clear duty of the agent, so far as in his power, to preserve to his fellow-men their liberty for the great ends of their mission.

Liberty Defined. — Liberty has been defined to be the natural "right which a man has to himself." It includes the right to the unrestricted use of his powers and possessions for the ends for which they are given.

Natural Right to Liberty. — That the right to personal liberty is a natural right is self-evident to one who acknowledges the personal responsibility of man. Man naturally desires liberty, seeks for it, risks everything to secure it, is *conscious* of his right to it. If he is not allowed the right to himself, then there can be no responsibility for his being and powers, and no mission of duty possible to him.

The Limitation of Liberty by the Moral Law must evidently be taken into the account. The right to liberty is not to be made a plea for *licentiousness* or *lawlessness*. It has been seen that the only freedom possible to man *is freedom under law* (p. 146). No man can have a natural right to do wrong. This is especially plain where the wrong interferes with the just rights of others.

Subject 1st. Just Abridgments of Liberty. — Men justly forfeit their right to liberty when they use their powers in violation of the moral law and to the injury of others. Society may therefore justly deprive of their personal liberty the criminal, the insane, and those made captives in war.

The Imprisonment of the Criminal is a duty which the state owes to its citizens in carrying out its mission of protection. The criminal, by the use of his powers in direct violation of the moral law and to the injury of others, forfeits all right to continued freedom. Society has a right to confine him for trial, and after trial and sentence to punish him by imprisonment, and compel him to perform sufficient labor for his support. Even the criminal has, however, the moral right to claim that trial be not needlessly delayed; that the punishment be according to law and not an arbitrary infliction; and that in degree, duration, and mode that punishment shall bear some due proportion to the crime. Any violation of these principles constitutes an immorality on the part of society.

The Confinement of the Insane is likewise a duty which the state, in the fulfilment of its mission, owes to its citizens, whenever the safety of the insane person himself, or of his family, or of the community, demands it. As modern philanthropic efforts have demonstrated the restorative power of proper modes of treatment, it has become the duty of society to the insane, not only to secure them against any unnecessary severity or unkindness, but also to make application of the right method of treatment with a view to their restoration.

Captives in War — if war be justifiable — may justly be confined by their captors. As the object of such confinement is only to prevent them from engaging again in the conflict on the other side until properly exchanged, all cruelty and inhumanity in the treatment of such captives becomes a gross immorality.

There are abridgments of liberty by the individual that are justifiable. The parent is responsible for the conduct of the child, and has therefore the right to control it. He has a right also to the services of the youth, and therefore may use them. The man may transfer his right over his own services for a limited time for an equivalent. A man may temporarily deprive any one of his liberty to prevent the commission of crime. Any of these limitations of liberty becomes immoral, however, when it loses sight of the moral end for which alone it is permitted.

Subject 2d.   Unjust Deprivation of Liberty.—The law of conservation forbids the agent to enslave his fellow-men. Chattel slavery is always contrary to this fundamental principle of morality; since it deprives man of his natural right to liberty; reduces him from a man to a thing; subjects him to the lawless will of another; breaks the most sacred social ties, and prevents the attainment of that intellectual, moral, and religious culture which is his right as a being called to a high mission and responsible to God.

Immoral Slavery.—If slavery be involuntary servitude under the ownership of a master,—involving ownership, property, absolute control, as its elements,—then it is clearly contrary to the requirements of the moral law. Slaveholding in such circumstances becomes a gross immorality. Says Dr. Wayland: "It can only be justified upon one of two assumptions: either, 1st, that slavery is authorized by a general law, under which human beings are constituted; or, 2d, that in some manner it has been signified to us by the Creator that one portion of the human race is made to be the slaves of another portion." Both these suppositions are contrary to fact.

The so-called Scriptural Argument for Slavery has, as its foundation, the fact, that the divine system of the Scriptures found slavery existing in the world, and did not directly prohibit it by positive command. It, however, set at work the principle of brotherly love, and prescribed regulations which, when permitted to work, must always speedily destroy slavery.

The law of conservation also forbids all other immoralities against liberty: such as manstealing; all forms of unjust control and personal oppression exercised by the strong over the weak; and especially those forms of tyranny exercised over servants and children.

Topic Third. Duties pertaining to Property.— As property in its various forms is an important means given to men by God, to aid them in the accomplishment of their work in life, the duty of social conservation requires that the moral agent shall respect the rights of his fellow-men to their property.

Subject 1st. Nature and Right of Property. — *Property* is any object of value which a man may have honestly acquired or may lawfully hold. *The right of property* in an object is the right to its exclusive possession, use, and disposal.

The Origin of the Rights of Property. — The original rights of property follow directly from the exercise of personal power. Man has a right to what he produces in the exercise of that personal power, whether the production be by labor of body or of soul. By this principle, in a higher form, the Creator and Moral Governor has an *absolute right* to everything created; as in the lower sense man has a *relative right* to whatever he has in any way produced. This is the principle at the basis. By it the workman has a right to the product of his handicraft, the inventor to his invention, and the author to his book. A right to property may also be acquired·by the gift of God or man, and by exchange.

The Design of Property. — It has already been seen (p. 224) that property has been given to man as a means of support, and to enable him to fulfil his higher moral mission.

Exclusive Right a Necessity. — Every man has his own duties to perform; duties which belong to him alone, not to others, not to society; duties which arise out of his personal vocation and standing, especially such as belong to his own family. Therefore he must have what is exclusively his own. Property therefore is not intended for mere self-gratification or support; nor is it a mere objectless mastery over things external; it is the necessary means to enable a man to fulfil his divinely appointed destiny. Hence its great importance to man.

A Divine Right. — That the rights of property are sanctioned by the Moral Governor is evident from the following considerations:

He has so constituted man that he desires and needs this right of the exclusive use and possession of certain things.

Having made man a social being, he has made the right of property essential to the healthful development of human society.

He has implanted a sense of justice in the nature of man, which condemns as morally wrong everything inconsistent with the right in question.

He has declared in his Word that any and every violation of this right is immoral, in forbidding both *theft* and *covetousness*.

Subject 2d.   Violations of the Right of Property. — The duty of social conservation forbids all unjust and unfair appropriation of the property of others to our own use or advantage. Under this prohibition is included theft, highway robbery, monopoly, and cheating. These all involve violations of the requirements of the moral law: "Thou shalt not steal;" and, "Thou shalt not covet."

Theft is the taking of the property of another without his knowledge or consent. The enlightened moral consciousness of man agrees with the laws of all civilized nations in condemning it.

Highway Robbery is the taking of the property of another with his consent violently obtained. It adds the crime of putting in peril the life of its victim to the crime of taking his property, and has always and everywhere been condemned by the enlightened conscience.

Monopoly includes all attempts to take advantage of the necessities of others for personal interest. In its *simplest form*, it leads the covetous man promptly and greedily to seize upon the opportunity, which providentially occurs, for forcing his fellow-men to pay exorbitant prices for goods or services which they must have and which he alone can furnish. In its *worst form*, the man artfully arranges and laboriously executes his plan to bring men into such a condition of necessity, and then selfishly takes advantage of that necessity. All such monopoly is immoral, as being contrary to the law which requires of man the conservation of his fellow-men. It is unkind, unjust, and dishonest. Man may make the most of his skill and foresight, and honestly obtain a fair remuneration for them; but the instant he does this selfishly, at the expense of his fellows, he violates the law which binds him to them in society.

Cheating is taking the property of another with consent unjustly or fraudulently obtained. Cheating may occur where *no equivalent* is offered, as by a beggar who obtains money under false pretences; or where the *equivalent is different from what it purports to be*. Various forms of this immorality need to be signalized. All *gambling* is immoral, since it implies a desire to profit at the expense of others. There is like immorality in the gambling of the club-room, of the stock-room, and of the private circle. Modern *speculation* is condemned by the same principle, as it adds the vice of gambling to the crime of monopoly. *In business*, cheating is involved in representing an article as other and better than it is; in the adulteration of articles of food, of medicine, and of the materials of clothing; in selling an article, knowing it to be of less value than he to whom it is sold takes it to be; in depriving men of property, on the ground of any mere technical flaw or legal defect in their title. All these transactions involve the taking of what belongs to another, without rendering him any equivalent in return; and they therefore all break the command which says, "'Thou shalt not steal;' *i. e.*, thou shalt not take what in the sight of God does not belong to you." See Dr. Hodge, *Theology*, Vol. III., for a full discussion of this subject.

In view of the business immorality of the day, there is need to emphasize the truth that the Moral Governor requires of man, not simply that he should respect the property of his fellow-men *as the civil law requires*, but *as the law of right requires*.   He demands of him not only *legal justice*, but *absolute equity*.

Strict or Legal Justice consists in according to others all that is due by law and usage.   The man who fulfils this duty is the *upright* man, or the man of *integrity*, in the sight of the civil law.

But what is Fair and Equitable is required of man in cases which are not provided for by civil law.   *Equity*, or *fairness*, comes in to correct and supplement legal justice.   The law may fail by being erroneous, so that its strict application would lead to the grossest injustice.   Hence, in the most advanced systems of government, *courts of chancery*, for securing *equity*, have been added to *courts of justice*.   Beyond the reach of both these courts there is a vast domain of moral requirement to be enforced by the great Judge alone.

Legality therefore Fails. — There are thus multitudes, who adhere to the letter of the civil law, who are yet *thieves* in the sight of the Moral Governor and of all right-thinking men.   Says Dr. Hodge: "The code of morals held by many business and professional men is very far below the moral law as revealed in the Bible.   This is especially true in reference to the eighth commandment in the decalogue.   Many who have stood well in society, and even in the church, will be astonished at the last day to find the word 'Thieves' written after their names in the great book of judgment."

The principle of social conservation, as necessarily involved in a Christian morality, forbids not only the unlawful taking of the property of men, but also that unlawful desire for it involved in covetousness, which is the inward cause of the outward acts of theft.   It thus strikes at the root of all the evil.

"All Lawgivers Forbid us to Steal our Neighbor's Goods; but it is only the Divine Lawgiver, who looks not merely on the outward appearance, but looks upon the heart, that can effectually forbid us to *covet* them." *Whately*.

Topic Fourth.   Duties pertaining to Truthfulness. — As truthfulness is at the foundation of all safe and beneficial intercourse among men, the law of social conservation requires of the agent strict adherence to truth in his treatment of the character and reputation of men, and in conversation and business with them.

Truth at the Foundation. — Truth in God is at the foundation of the stability and order of the divine government. All knowledge and hope in man are based on the truth of God. Truth is therefore, in a sense, at the foundation of the universe. It is at the foundation of all safe intercourse with men, — the element of stability and trustworthiness in human intercourse. Man is made with a moral impulse to tell the truth, and to believe what is told him, and these are both essential to well-being. The man who violates the truth sins against the very foundations of his moral being, and against the very foundation of all things.

Subject 1st. Truthfulness as it respects Reputation. —

As the reputation of men is one of their chief possessions, social conservation binds the agent to the same regard for the. reputation of other men as for his own. So far as their good name is based upon their real character, they have an absolute right to it.

Character is the essential moral worth of a man ; *reputation* is the estimation in which he is held by men. It is evident that character is the true basis for a good name ; and that, so far as a man has not the good character, he has no absolute right to the good reputation.

A good Reputation is evidently one of the most important conditions to man's well-being. Desire for the esteem of his fellows has been seen to be inborn in him (p. 52). That esteem has been shown to be the basis of the regard and affection upon which society rests. Detraction may thus become a greater evil than the unlawful taking of a man's property ; it may destroy both happiness and influence at once.

The duty of social conservation therefore forbids false testimony in a court of justice ; slander, so-called ; the more common forms of detraction ; and the disposition of envy in which all these immoralities originate.

False Testimony, as given in a court of justice, with the sanction of an oath, is regarded as the most flagrant violation of duty pertaining to reputation. It includes the guilt of malice, falsehood, and mockery of God ; and the giving of it justly renders a man infamous, and subjects him to punishment by law, — as it strikes at the security of character, property, and even life.

Slander, in the narrow sense, is bearing false witness against one's neighbor. It includes the elements of malice and falsehood, and is universally condemned by the enlightened moral consciousness.

Detraction, in its most common forms, falls under the same condemnation with slander, as indicative of the same state of mind. It may appear in the circulation of false reports; in the expression of satisfaction in the disgrace of others; and in holding up others to ridicule. It may destroy the influence of men as completely as false testimony or slander. Its immorality is in proportion to its falsity and injustice.

Gossip is one of the most common, as it is one of the most pernicious, forms in which detraction manifests itself. The "one who runs from house to house, tattling and telling news," is always a liar, and may justly be regarded as one of the worst pests of society.

The Envious Disposition, which is the source of all such immoral conduct, comes under the full condemnation of a Christian morality. It appears, in its more common forms, in the suspicious temper; in a disposition to impute bad motives; in an unwillingness to believe that men are sincere and honest in the avowal of their principles and aims; and in cherishing satisfaction in the disgrace of others, even if our competitors or enemies. It originates in the better fortune or greater success of others associated with us, or in their higher honor or esteem. The Christian system of morals — unlike all other systems — aims its prohibition first at this evil disposition, as the spring and cause of all the slanderous words and deeds.

When the reputation of men has no proper basis in character, it may become the agent's highest duty, when the good of men requires it, to bring mankind to see the truth, and to destroy the false reputation, whether good or bad. This duty becomes the more imperative in an age which glories in sham and quackery and justifies success by whatever means attained.

A Good Man may be prevented from fulfilling his true moral mission by a bad reputation, which has become unjustly fastened upon him. In such case, regard, both for the well-being of the man and of mankind, demands that the moral agent should exert himself to bring to light his true character, and thus to free him from the undeserved evil reputation.

A Bad Man may unjustly acquire a good reputation, and may thus be placed in a position to do great harm to his fellow-men. The good of mankind may imperatively require the exposure of the faults and the follies, the vices and the crimes, of such a man. It may thus become the most solemn and important duty toward mankind to strip the guise from hypocrisy, and to expose shams and pretenders of every kind, that the world may be saved from their baleful influence. This has been a chief work with the great reformers in all ages, and it holds an important place in the work of the greatest of moral teachers, Jesus of Nazareth; and only so far as this work is done can man's estimate of character rest upon a true basis.

Subject 2d.   Veracity, or Truthfulness, in Ordinary Intercourse.

— The duty of social conservation requires strict adherence to truth in the common intercourse with men. So far as the well-being of men depends upon their receiving the truth from the moral agent, they have an absolute right to that truth, both as logical and moral.

Truth is Logical or Physical and Moral. — *Logical* or *physical truth* is adhered to when a thing is told exactly as it is: *moral truth* is adhered to when a thing is told sincerely and precisely as it appears to be. If a man declares that he sees another walking across the street, he tells the logical or physical truth if he does actually see him; but if he thinks so, and is mistaken, he tells the moral truth. Duty demands both when possible.

A falsehood involves three elements: the enunciation of what is false; the intention to deceive; and a violation of some obligation to give to others the truth. Veracity, or truthfulness, in common conversation, requires the avoidance of falsehood in all its forms. This includes equivocation, mental reservation, and the lie proper. Duty prohibits all departure from truth in look or gesture, no less than in word, as immoral.

Where the agent is under obligation to give the truth to men, his maxim should be, " Let the truth be told, though the heavens fall."

Equivocation consists in the intentional use of obscure or ambiguous words. Equivocation, whether in *sound* or *sense*, is a violation of truthfulness.

Reservation. — The same may be said of *reservation* or *restriction*, whether *real* or *mental*. *Real restriction* is when, if the words uttered be literally interpreted, they are not true; yet, if regard be had to the circumstances in which they are uttered, they are not false. In mental restriction, or reservation, the words uttered are untrue; but the speaker has some addition or explanation in his mind, by which they become to him true, but not to the party to whom they are addressed. In equivocation and mental reservation there is, first, the saying of something the contrary of which, or something different from which, is true, — that is, there is a lie; and, secondly, there is the intention or desire to mislead, — whereas the use of language is to inform and direct. So that, both in form and substance, equivocation and mental reservation amount to falsehood.

Simplicity and Sincerity of speech are opposed to *equivocation* and *mental reservation.* As a general rule, we ought not only to be plain and honest, but frank and full, in all our communications with our fellow-men. There are few things which contribute more to the comfort of social life than frankness. The opposite of this is *reserve,* or *closeness,* which is unamiable, and sometimes leads to mistake and mischief. See *Fleming.*

A Lie never Right. — The lie proper, as it is ordinarily understood, is the plainest form of falsehood. A true morality must teach that *it is never right to lie.* The only open question is, what constitutes a lie in any particular case. In discussing this question, it has been said, that " a man may depart from the truth, *first,* with the design of injuring some one; *secondly,* with the design of benefiting some one; or, *thirdly,* with no fixed intention of good or ill, but for the purpose of amusement. These have been technically designated *mendacium perniciosum, mendacium officiosum,* and *mendacium jocosum.*"

The First Form of Falsehood is condemned by all. It is clearly contrary to the will of God, inconsistent with the love of our neighbor, and injurious to society at large.

The Second Form of Falsehood some have thought admissible; but it may be " doubted whether, in any circumstances, true, general, and permanent good can be gained by falsehood; or whether men, in their individual and social capacity, ought not inviolably to adhere to the truth, and take the consequences, rather than, by avoiding some near and striking inconvenience, to run the risk of remote and permanent evils far more embarrassing. The obligations under which we lie to speak the truth are prior, both in order and authority, to any obligation which can be drawn from a calculation of consequences. Of these, in their full extent, we are not competent judges; and to set up our short-sighted views in opposition to the sacred majesty of truth is as impious as it is unwise."

Pious Frauds, etc. — " As to *pious frauds,* or falsehoods told to benefit the cause of religion, the thing is in itself absurd, and cannot be expressed but by a phrase which is self-contradictory. Religion is emphatically *the truth,* and seeks no aid but from sincere believers, and fears more harm from false friends than from open enemies."

"The saying of what is not true, to soothe children or to calm the fears of the nervous, should be avoided. Paley has said that we are not criminal in telling a falsehood to a madman for his own advantage, to a robber to conceal our property, or to an assassin to divert him from his purpose. These are extreme cases. But, if any allowance can be made for them, it should be so made as not to give countenance to the maxim: 'We may do evil that what we think good may come of it.'"

The Third Form of Falsehood has many modifications. Paley has said (*Mor. and Pol. Phil.*, book iii., ch. 15), in speaking of these: "There are falsehoods which are not lies; that is, are not criminal, as, for example, where no one is deceived, which is the case in parables, fables, novels, jests, tales to create mirth, ludicrous embellishments of a story, where the declared design of the speaker is not to inform, but to divert; compliments in the subscriptions of a letter, a servant's *denying* his master, a prisoner's pleading not guilty, an advocate asserting the justice, or his belief of the justice, of his client's case." See *Fleming*.

Parables, Fables, etc. — It is evident that parables, fables, and works of fiction do not involve any intentional deception, and that they are not therefore properly falsehoods.

Compliments, etc. — The compliments that pass in conversation, and those commonly added in the subscription of a letter, are liable to deceive, and should therefore be strictly in accordance with truth. The custom of having the servants declare to callers that the master or mistress of the house is not in, when he or she is in, is a clear violation of truthfulness. If one is not able to see visitors, or does not wish to see them, it is better to instruct his servants to say so.

The Plea Not Guilty. — So far as the plea of *not guilty* amounts to this, — "that the accused party is willing to abide the issue of the trial, and to take the condemnation or acquittal which the evidence will warrant," — it is proper. The advocate who advises the plea with this understanding does not violate any obligation to truthfulness. But it is far different with many of the present usages and principles of professional men. Lord Brougham is reported to have said in the House of Lords, "that an advocate knows no one but his client. He is bound *per fas et nefas*, if possible, to clear him. If necessary for the accomplishment of that object, he is at liberty to accuse and defame the innocent, and even (as the report stated) to ruin his country." Such morality is simply diabolical. Even Cicero taught a better doctrine; for, while he "maintained that, with a view to the protection of the innocent, it was necessary to plead the cause of those suspected to be guilty," he likewise maintained that the notoriously impious and wicked were not to be so defended.

The Habit of Exaggeration, so common with many in their ordinary conversation; and the habit of embellishing the truth and of changing or omitting its most important features, so common with public speakers and with certain classes of writers,—clearly come under the general condemnation of falsehood.

Flattery, or venal and insincere praise, has in it always the very essence of falsehood.

It is evident from the definition of falsehood that man is not always under obligation to make known to men all the truth. They may have no claims upon him for the truth or the whole truth ; or the whole truth on any subject may need to be withheld for the best interests of all parties concerned. In such cases the obligation is to silence rather than to speech.

Numerous Cases come under this Principle.— For example, a military commander is not bound to reveal his stratagems to the enemy ; a man is not bound to tell the robber where he may find his purse.

A Higher Obligation. — There may also be cases, as stated by Dr. Hodge, and others, in which the obligation to speak the truth may be merged in some higher obligation ; as when a mother sees a murderer in pursuit of her child, "she has an undoubted right to mislead him by any means in her power." But this principle requires to be used with great caution, as it has been perverted so as to furnish the foundation of Jesuitism. It is more than doubtful if it is not better to adhere strictly to the principles already laid down (p. 249) as applicable to the second form of falsehood.

Subject 3d. Fidelity, or Truthfulness as pertaining to more Formal Intercourse. — Fidelity or faithfulness is the preservation of truth with regard to the future. It is required in promises, contracts, oaths, and vows. The duty of social conservation makes fidelity obligatory in all these forms of the promise, since they furnish the immediate foundation for man's well-being as involved in the business of life.

1st. The Promise. — The well-being of man demands the fulfilment of promises when given, and in the same sense in which given and accepted. The law of truthfulness in our ordinary intercourse applies with greater force in promises. In the full promise there should be : first, the deliberate intention of the promiser ; secondly, the expressing or signifying of that intention; thirdly, the acceptance of it by the promisee. When any of these conditions fail, the obligation to fulfil may be relaxed or dissolved.

Forms of the Promise. — *Pollicitation* is a spontaneous expression of our intention to do something in favor of another. A *promise proper* is made in consequence of a request made. It implies two parties, — a promiser and a promisee. A *pact* implies two or more parties. A *contract* adds to this a bargain, or a *quid pro quo.* An agreement between two parties without a *consideration* is a *bare pact,* and cannot be legally enforced, but is of equal moral force with any other promise.

Promises that are not binding include the following cases :

A *conditional promise* is not binding if the condition fail; but the failure of the condition must be equally contingent to both parties.

An *impossible promise* is not binding, where the impossibility is not known at the time to the promiser, nor created by him afterward.

An *unlawful promise* is not binding. If the unlawfulness is known when it is made, then the guilt is in *making,* not in *breaking.*

An *erroneous promise* is not binding. It may take two forms : where the promisee is misled by the promiser; and where both parties mistake as to the ground on which the promise proceeds. The discovery of the mistake makes void the promise.

An *extorted promise* is not binding. Where the consent is not voluntary, of course there is no obligation to fulfil the promise.

2d. The Contract. — "In a promise only one party comes under obligation; in a contract each party comes under obligation to the other, and each reciprocally acquires a right to what is promised by the other."

The same moral principles apply to contracts as to promises, and they may cease to be binding in the same ways.

Contracts Originate in the fact that man is insufficient for his own comfort and happiness. Something is to be done which he cannot do; something to be had which he cannot procure. He therefore makes known his wants to those who can do or furnish what he cannot, and, on their agreement to fulfil his wishes, he engages to remunerate them, or render them some equivalent service. The consideration of the kinds of contracts would lead into the field of jurisprudence.

3d. The Oath. — An oath is "a religious asseveration by which we renounce the mercy and imprecate the vengeance of Heaven, if we speak not the truth." It has been customary to administer the oath in confirmation of promises and contracts. It is intended to add to the sense of obligation.

The moral principles governing oaths are similar to those of the promise. The violation of the oath gives rise to the crime of perjury.

The Oath with Promises and Contracts. — The *assertory oath*, or *oath of evidence*, is to confirm a promise of giving true evidence, in the present; the *promissory oath*, or *oath of office*, is to confirm a promise of discharging its duties in the future.

An Oath Creates no New Obligation. — It is merely the bringing in of a greater presence than human and greater issues than temporal to quicken our sense of obligation.

The Violation of the Oath is Perjury. — Its guilt is greater than simple falsehood, as —

It is a sin of greater deliberation.

It violates a higher confidence.

God has given to the oath a peculiar sacredness.

The Morality of Oaths has been Questioned, on the ground of the language used by Jesus of Nazareth to the Jews: "Swear not at all. . . . . But let your communication be, Yea, yea; Nay, nay; for whatsoever is more than these cometh of evil." (*Matt.* x. 34–37.) The questioning has arisen from a misconception.

It may readily be shown that Christ does not here prohibit the judicial, but the profane, oath; since in his trial he allowed the judicial oath to be administered to himself by the High Priest; and since he is here dealing with private and personal sins of the Scribes and Pharisees, of which profanity was prominent.

It may at the same time be admitted that the need of oaths indicates either want of truthfulness or want of confidence, or both, and therefore is the result of evil; but the necessity of their use has been felt in all lands and ages, and will doubtless be felt so long as the present evil condition of things remains.

It is still further apparent that the too frequent use of the oath may increase the evil and give rise to falsehood and profanity, by diminishing the sense of its solemnity and sacredness.

4th. The Vow, in the strict sense, is a promise, or rather an oath, made to God. It may therefore be defined to be "a firm promise solemnly made, as in the sight of God, and with imprecation of punishment from him should we fail through neglect."

The general law of the promise applies to the vow.

Topic Fifth. Duties pertaining to Human Brotherhood.— As the general offices of brotherly love are of the first importance to the welfare of men, the duty of social conservation binds the agent to these offices.

A brotherly regard for men prompts: first, to increase happiness; secondly, to alleviate misery; thirdly, to forgive injury; fourthly, to requite favor.

Subject 1st. Brotherly Regard prompting to Increase Happiness. — A brotherly regard for the comfort or happiness of men may be exhibited by the conversation and manner; by the duties of active kindness; and by liberality.

1st. In Conversation and Manner. — A proper regard for men will give rise to civility and politeness in conversation and manner. Civility avoids giving offence; politeness seeks to please.

Civility implies the desire to avoid giving offence, and the intelligence requisite to discern what is likely to be offensive. "The knowledge of what is likely to be offensive may be very much cultivated by intercourse with society. But if there be the disposition to avoid giving offence, the duty of civility will be easily practised. It lies not in any set form of words, or any studied peculiarity of manner. It is confined to no rank nor condition, but belongs to the peasant as well as to the finished gentleman. It springs from benevolence, and is a branch of that charity of which an Apostle hath said, that 'it vaunteth not itself, and doth not behave itself unseemly.'" He points to its true source when he connects it with brotherly love, and says (1 *Peter* iii. 8), "Love as brethren, be pitiful, be courteous." The fault opposed to civility is *rudeness*. It implies a want of attention to the rights and feelings of others. It springs from a want of benevolence, and is aggravated by want of discernment as to what is likely to prove offensive. See *Fleming*.

Politeness implies a stronger benevolence than mere civility. It seeks to say and do what may be agreeable to the feelings of others. It is the growth neither of town nor country, but of the heart. It adds to good manners and good breeding, *good disposition*. "Separate from a disposition to oblige and to please, mere politeness is an empty form; when grafted upon it, or springing from it, a high and valuable accomplishment."

2d. In Active Kindness. — A proper regard for men will lead beyond civility and politeness to the higher duties of active kindness. These duties are as various as are the relations of human society, and bind the agent to show an active interest in the welfare of men as often as opportunity offers.

Forms of Active Kindness. — "Sometimes we may benefit our neighbor by advice, and sometimes by reproof. He may need encouragement and support, or admonition and warning. Perhaps we may be called on to undergo labor and exertion, or to encounter difficulty and danger, for his sake. Some great evil may be averted, or some great good may be obtained, through our intervention and activity. His reputation may be assailed, and we may have to defend it. His confidence may be abused, and we may have the delicate task of undeceiving him. He may have roused the resentment of others, and we must try to soothe and to allay it. He may have engaged in undertakings which are beyond his means and strength, and we must endeavor to relieve him. He may be thrown out of employment, and we must help him to procure it. He may be aiming at distinction and honor, and we must aid him in attaining them. In short, the duties to which a spirit of *active kindness* may prompt are as varied as the circumstances and relations of human life." See *Fleming*.

3d. In Liberality. — A proper regard for men will lead to liberality. This involves the "free communication of our means and substance to promote the happiness of others;" the according to them, for the same reason, of the largest possible liberty of opinion and action; and the exercise of a generous hospitality.

Active Kindness not Complete without Liberality. — Active kindness may be combined with want of liberality. Some men will give their advice, and time, and exertions, for the good of their fellow-men, when they will not give of their means for that end. So, on the other hand, an *indolent liberality* is often exhibited by those who will give freely of their money for the good of others, but who have not enough of real interest in their good to see that the gifts are properly distributed and applied. Active kindness and liberality should, if possible, always go together.

Liberality in Conceding Rights. — Liberality is exhibited in a most important aspect, in according to others the fullest exercise of their right to freedom in action and opinion. " 'A liberal man deviseth liberal things, and by liberal things shall he stand.' A fair and open demeanor; a candid consideration of the rights and feelings of others; a relaxation or a waiving of our own rights when the pursuing of them is likely to be injurious; an avoidance of all captiousness and contention; a scorning to take advantage, and a willingness that others should be benefited as well as ourselves, — these are some of the ways in which true liberality will manifest itself." *Dr. Ferguson.*

Liberality as Hospitality. — The same good-will to others naturally leads to hospitality. This is a virtue whose exercise is rendered necessary in thinly-settled regions by the difficulty with which strangers and sojourners find accommodation; and in the city in counteracting the tendency to selfishness and exclusiveness. The Scriptures make this an important virtue, requiring of those who bear rule in the church, that they should be *lovers of hospitality,* and enjoining upon all Christians to *use hospitality without grudging.* This virtue was one of the few which maintained a vigorous existence all through the Dark Ages. Its exercise was enjoined and maintained by the vows of the clergy and oaths of the knights. *Churlishness* is the opposite of hospitality. Instead of sharing the bounties of Providence with others, and rejoicing in their well-being, it would devote everything to self alone. It is characteristic of an unbrotherly and selfish spirit, as hospitality is of a liberal and generous one.

Subject 2d. Brotherly Regard prompting to Alleviate Misery. — A brotherly disposition to alleviate the misery of men may be exhibited in cherishing feelings of compassion and sympathy; in performing actions of humanity and charity; and, where the misery of others has been caused by the agent himself, in the work of restitution and reparation. These are among the most important of the great social agencies for removing or lessening the miseries of the world, and the proper attention to them is therefore a most imperative duty.

1st. Compassion and Sympathy.— A proper regard for the well-being of men will lead the agent to cherish toward them feelings of compassion in their trials and misfortunes, and of sympathy in their sufferings. There are times when the most grateful, if not the only, offering man can make to his fellow-men, is to *feel* for and with them; and to do this becomes then a most important duty.

Compassion is grief for the distress of others. It has more of tenderness than *pity*, which sometimes implies an approach to contempt. These are feelings which all men are able and bound to cherish, whether they are liable to the same misfortunes and miseries or not. They are demanded of the agent toward all the unfortunate and miserable, whether they deserve well or ill. The sorrowing, the poor, the oppressed, and the vicious and the criminal are to be pitied.

Sympathy, or fellow-feeling, is more grateful than compassion. It implies a community in liability to suffering, if not in actual suffering, on the part of him who offers and him who receives, — a community which fits the one for appreciating and entering into the sorrow of the other as he could not otherwise do. True and heartfelt sympathy with the wretched, by bringing others to bear the burden with them, does much toward taking away the bitterness of human sorrow and suffering. The tender sympathies of man's nature should therefore be most assiduously cherished and most generously exercised.

2d. Humanity and Charity.— A proper regard for the well-being of men should lead the agent to deeds of humanity and charity, in seeking their benefit, where such deeds are called for. The feelings of compassion and sympathy find their natural outlet in such acts of relieving human suffering and supplying human want.

The Offices of Humanity include "those kind attentions which go to alleviate sickness, to soothe pain, to cheer melancholy, and to chase away the feelings of disappointment and despair." *Humanity* proves the sincerity of compassion and sympathy, by doing what can be done to remove suffering and sorrow.

The Duties of Charity find place where the sufferings of those around us admit of pecuniary relief, and are obligatory according to the ability of the agent. So frequent and strong are the demands for such pecuniary relief that the term *charity*, which was originally equivalent in meaning to *benevolence*, or brotherly love in general, has come to be almost restricted to this particular expression of it.

Principles of a True Charity and their Violations.— There are certain generally admitted principles which should guide all acts of charity:

They should proceed from sincere compassion and sympathy.

They should be performed in a kindly and affectionate manner.

They should be wisely directed to the relief of truly needy and deserving objects.

The first of these principles is violated by that ostentatious so-called

22 *   R

charity which would build its own monument under pretence of compassion for human suffering. The second is violated by all that indolent charity which attempts to supply the wants of men in a mechanical way, and without any real brotherly regard for them. The third is violated by all careless and unintelligent giving for purposes professedly charitable. It is a most important thing that charity should be dispensed wisely. All so-called charity to those who are not needy and deserving encourages idleness and beggary, and leads to moral worthlessness. Modern philanthropy seems to have demonstrated that *the true charity is that which most helps men to help themselves,*—thus preserving their sense of independence and developing their powers. Modern observation has also shown, that the results of giving to charitable objects during the life of the giver are more satisfactory than giving to such objects to take effect after his death; in other words, that *a man is his own best executor.*

3d. Reparation or Restitution.—A proper regard for the well-being of men should lead the agent to seek to remove their suffering and misery by making reparation or restitution, where he has himself been the cause of their misfortunes.

The Duties of Reparation and Restitution, so far as they involve pecuniary considerations, belong properly under duties pertaining to property; but in that wider sense, in which they involve so much more, they are properly treated here.

The Duty of Reparation consists in restoring things, as far as possible, to that state in which they would have been but for our injury. Where anything, whether it be of property or reputation, has in any way been unjustly taken from men, the duty becomes one of *restitution.* It is evident that when one sees that he has in any way injured his fellow-men, a proper sense of the injury must lead him at the same time to see that he is under obligation to repair it. The duty needs, however, to be clearly pointed out and strongly emphasized, since selfishness and a false shame often lead men to neglect it, and to seek to justify that neglect. There are various cases in which the temptation to justify such neglect is peculiarly strong:

First, where he is unable to make complete reparation. This occurs where life is taken away, or property destroyed, in which cases actual restitution is impossible. But he who has committed the wrong is bound to do *the utmost in his power* to repair the injury.

Second, where there is unwillingness to receive the reparation. The injured person may be unwilling that anything should be done toward repairing the injury. In such cases a debt, for example, may be remitted; but its remission must be received as any favor is received. "Before the duty of *restitution* can be dispensed with, the claim to it should be cheerfully relaxed on the part of our neighbor, and we should be satisfied that he will sustain no serious inconvenience from the relaxation of it."

Third, where equal or greater counter injury has been received. Injury received from others is no reason why reparation should not be made, unless it is right to return evil for evil. It has already been seen that man has a right to resist and repel wrong, and that no claim can be made for the repair of injury inflicted in self-defence, unless it is inflicted in a spirit of revenge or retaliation.

Subject 3d. Brotherly Regard prompting to Forgive Injury.

— A brotherly disposition toward those who have done injury should be exhibited by the agent, in the moderation of his resentful feelings; and in the forgiveness of the injuries.

These duties furnish a most important agency in taking out the bitterness and animosity which add so much to the miseries of the world, and are therefore of most imperative obligation.

1st. Moderation of Resentment.

— A proper regard for the well-being of those who have injured either himself, or others in whom he is interested, will lead the agent to moderate his resentful feelings toward them, and keep them within the bounds of a righteous moral indignation. Resentment, in this latter form, is one of the wise provisions of the Moral Governor to prevent injuries, or to remedy them when done.

Resentment, in its righteous form as *moral indignation*, arises in immediate connection with man's sense of justice, and from the intuitive judgment of merit and demerit. It is the assertion of the moral nature that wrong deserves reprobation and punishment. It may involve an element of ill-feeling or hatred toward the doer of the injury, and become immoral, as in *anger* and *rage*, or *resentment* in its excessive and unrighteous forms.

Righteous Resentment. — The practical questions concerning such righteous moral indignation are: *When is it warranted? What is the proper measure of it? How long shall it be cherished?* Answering these in order, the following principles may be safely affirmed:

First, such indignation is warranted only when there is injury intended, or actual injury inflicted as the result of intention or of culpable carelessness.

Second, such indignation is righteous only as it is strictly proportioned to the injury intended or inflicted. He who tamely submits to injury himself, or allows it to be inflicted on others, encourages its repetition and thus increases the injustice and evil in the world: he who repels an injustice by a greater, provokes retaliation and thus increases the evil.

Third, such indignation should cease the instant the cause is removed.

Unrighteous Resentment. — Resentment in its more violent and improper form as *anger* should always be restrained: since it is contrary to a brotherly regard for men; inconsistent with a prudent regard for our own character and happiness; and introduces the greatest discord and evil into society.

2d. Forgiveness of Injury.

— Proper regard for the well-being of those who have injured him will further lead the agent to forgive the injury which has excited his resentful feelings, and to seek to cherish toward the injurers becoming feelings of good-will.

The Nature of Forgiveness. — True forgiveness requires:

First, the remission of the right to demand justice of the offender;

Secondly, the dismissal of resentful feelings;

Thirdly, the actual revival of the feelings of good-will.

The Law of Forgiveness. — In the exercise of forgiveness regard should be had to the following considerations:

First, to the extent of the injury, as great or small;

Second, to the causes which led to it, whether mere carelessness and inadvertence, or deliberate ill-will;

Third, to the conduct of the party offending, whether for the first time or repeatedly;

Fourth, to the regret and penitence of the offender, or the absence of these;

Fifth, and above all, to the common guilt of all in the sight of the Moral Governor and the common need of his forgiveness (*Matthew* vi. 14, 15).

Subject 4th. Brotherly Regard prompting to return Favor.

— A brotherly disposition toward those to whom the agent is indebted for favors should be exhibited, in gratitude in return for benefits, and confidence and helpfulness in return for friendship.

Gratitude is the natural response of the heart to kindnesses intended or received. It implies the desire to show a proper appreciation of the favor, and to requite it if possible. Its presence is properly an indication of a generous and unselfish spirit; its absence, of a base and selfish one.

Friendship is the mutual esteem and regard cherished by kindred minds, as the basis of the mutual interchange of good offices. The only solid basis of true and lasting friendship is to be found in the mutual possession of right principles, virtuous character, and a true life. In order that it may be morally helpful to those who cherish it, friendship should lead to mutual *confidence;* to mutual *advice* and *reproof;* and to mutual *kindness* and *constancy.* Men may thus become in the largest degree mutually *helpful* in the great work of life.

SECTION II.

The Duty of Social Improvement.

As the full development of the powers of men is indispensable to the fulfilment of their moral mission, *it is man's second duty toward his fellow-men* to seek, so far as ability and opportunity allow, to improve their being and powers.

Involved in the General Duty.—The duty of social improvement is clearly implied in the greater duty: "Thou shalt love thy neighbor as thyself." It is evidently a higher order of duty than those treated under social conservation, since it has to do more directly with fitting man for his moral mission in the world.

Topic First. General Principles of Social Improvement. — Man is under obligation to do for his fellow-men, so far as possible, the same work of culture which he has been shown to be bound to do for himself. It is his duty to apply the true principles of physical culture and spiritual culture for the development and perfection of mankind. What these principles are may be learned from the treatment of *Self-Culture* under *Individual Ethics*.

The Range of Effort Limited. — Man himself is, so to speak, always within the reach of his own powers; but his fellow-men are often partially beyond the reach of his efforts. The possibilities of his improving mankind are therefore limited as compared with the possibilities of his improving himself.

The Work must begin nearest Home : although it is not to stop there. The influence of the agent in improving the powers of men varies with the intimacy of his connection with them ; being greatest over those most closely connected with him. Hence the chief work of social improvement must be done for this class. There are, however, abundant facilities for the exercise of a wider influence upon the improvement of mankind in general, and the use of these facilities need not interfere with the duties of the more intimate relations.

Topic Second. Special Principles of Social Improvement. — As man can secure the permanent improvement of his fellow-men, only by aiming at producing in them the noblest moral and religious character; and by making use of the agency of Christianity to secure it (p. 166),— it becomes his duty to govern his work of social improvement in accordance with these principles.

Subject 1st. The Ultimate Aim in Social Improvement.— The ultimate practical aim of a Christian morality, so far as it respects the improvement of mankind, is to lead the moral agent to do his utmost to develop the moral and religious nature of men, and thus to form in them the highest and best character. Any departure from this aim is fatal to their true and permanent improvement.

Character the Aim. — Character is the great thing to be aimed at in improvement, so far as the aim is to be found in the man. It has been defined to be "the present intellectual, social, and moral condition of an individual." It is in truth his great and permanent possession ; the thing which makes up the man ; the one thing which, when fixed for good or evil, he must carry with him in his immortality. The man can only be improved as the character is improved; character must therefore be the aim.

Character, how Formed.—The highest and best character can only be formed by the right culture of the moral and religious nature. This is evident, because these are the highest elements of man's being, since they alone fit him for virtue and immortality. Any culture that leaves out this his nobler nature degrades him from his true manhood, and prevents the attainment of the best character. The best and noblest character, from the moral and religious point of view, must therefore be the aim.

Subject 2d. The Effective Agency in Social Improvement.

— As Christianity has been shown to be the only hope of mankind, as a reconstructing agency, it is the duty of the man, who would compass the true and lasting improvement of his fellow-men, to seek it in accordance with the principles of the Christian system. Human experience has demonstrated that, in man's present condition of moral disorder, schemes of government, philanthropy, moral reform, and education are sources of blessing and elevation to mankind only as they have a solid Christian basis.

Christian Government. — No scheme of government can give permanent and true elevation to society without the aid of Christianity. Two things are absolutely necessary in order that society may be made and kept what it should be: a standard of absolute right and justice must be furnished and put into the hands and minds of rulers and subjects, to be the perfect guide of both; and a power must be provided to bring men in their conduct up to this standard. No merely human theory of freedom and progress has been able to bring true elevation to men; as has been shown by the experience of Mexico, the South American States, France, and other nations. That such schemes of freedom bring elevation, in proportion as they go along with and are based upon a morality vitalized by a pure Christianity, has been shown by the experience of the ancient Jews, of Great Britain, and of our own country. Hence the duty to make and keep all schemes of government *Christian.*

Christian Philanthropy and Reform. — No scheme of philanthropy or moral reform can give permanent elevation to society, except as it adopts the aims and uses the means furnished by the Christian system. In order to the actual removal of the various evils of society, the moral disorder of man's nature, in which they have their origin, must be remedied. The Christian system alone provides the necessary remedy. The great modern philanthropic and reform movements, so far as they have succeeded, have originated in Christianity and succeeded by its power.   Attempts at such movements, so far as they have been merely sentimental or humanitarian, have utterly failed, or have made merely a temporary progress to be succeeded by a greater reaction.   Hence the duty to make and keep all such schemes *Christian.*

Christian Education. — No scheme of education can lead to the permanent elevation of society, except as it is Christian education.   Education as divorced from Christianity can only develop what is in man. As man is in a condition of moral disorder, even education of the most liberal and comprehensive kind must fail to improve and purify, and may at the highest make a Lord Bacon, or a Byron, or a Burr, or a Mill.   It is the province of education to sharpen and strengthen what is in a man; but it brings no change of moral desires and furnishes no new and essentially different moral motives.   If men are good, education will make them more powerful for good; if they are bad, it will only make them stronger for evil.   Hence it is, that the profoundest of American orators has said, that "since the introduction of Christianity, it has been the duty, as it has been the effort, of the great and the good, to sanctify human knowledge, to bring it to the fount, and to baptize learning into Christianity; to gather up all its productions, its earliest and its latest, its blossoms and its fruits, and lay them all upon the altar of religion and virtue."   In the oration, on the Girard College Case, entitled *The Christian Ministry and the Religious Instruction of the Young,* Daniel Webster gives a powerful and luminous presentation of the absolute necessity of the influence of Christianity in order to a pure morality.

SECTION III.

The Duty of Social Direction.

As the powers of men are given, conserved, and developed to fit them for a high moral mission, in which all are alike interested, *it is the agent's third duty toward his fellow-men* to aid them, so far as possible, to control and direct their powers to the accomplishment of this mission.

As man's duties toward his fellow-men are determined by his duties toward himself, it follows that the general ethical principles of *Self-Conduct,* as unfolded under *Individual Ethics,* apply to the social conduct or direction of men.

General Principles of Social Direction.— In the chapter on *Self-Conduct* will be found the requisite view of the general duties of control, in aiding men to govern their active propensities and to preserve the balance of their powers; and of the general duties of direction, in aiding them to form the true and noblest purpose, and to execute that purpose.

In the present *Section* the aim will be to emphasize some of the special duties of social control and social direction.

Topic First. Special Duties of Social Control. — A Christian morality demands especially, that man should use his utmost endeavors to increase the power of the moral and religious restraints, and to lead to the predominance of the nobler moral and religious elements in his fellow-men; and forbids him, for any cause, or under any pretence, or in any manner, willingly to lessen these restraints or to degrade these elements.

Subject 1st. Weakening Restraints. — It is evident from the importance of man's higher nature, that the man who attempts to weaken the moral and religious restraints, which keep men from moral evil, is guilty of a most atrocious vice, and is one of the worst enemies of human kind.

By Example.—These restraints may be weakened by example. He who by his immoral and irreligious conduct familiarizes men with vice and godlessness helps to destroy the sense of the baseness of these evils. When the evil-doer is possessed of brilliancy or genius, he is able to give a gloss to the worst of vices, and make them appear almost virtues to men less gifted. Such men as Byron and Burr have made godlessness and licentiousness attractive to thousands of ordinary young men.

By Conversation and Writing.— These restraints may be weakened by conversation and writing. This is done by treating the distinctions between right and wrong, vice and virtue, with open scorn or covert contempt; by ridiculing "the obligations of morality and religion, under the names of superstition, priestcraft, prejudices of education;" by presenting such views of God as would lead men "to believe that he cares very little about the moral actions of his creatures, but is willing that every one shall live as he chooses; and that, therefore, the self-denials of virtue are only a form of gratuitous, self-inflicted torture."

"It is against this form of moral injury that the young need to be specially upon their guard. The moral seducer, if he be a practised villain, corrupts the principles of his victim before he attempts to influence his or her practice. It is not until the moral restraints are silently removed, and the heart left defenceless, that he presents the allurements of vice, and goads the passions to madness. His task is then easy. If he have succeeded in the first effort, he will rarely fail in the second. Let every young man, especially every young woman, beware of listening for a moment to any conversation of which the object is to show that the restraints of virtue are unnecessary, or to diminish in aught the reverence and obedience which are due from the creature to the law of the Creator." *Wayland.*

The Baseness of such Conduct. — No words are strong enough to express the baseness of the man who thus silently removes these restraints from the innocent and unsuspecting youth, and so prepares the way for the triumph of the allurements of vice and the reign of the madness of passion. All good men in all ages have agreed in reprobating and detesting such men. Benjamin Franklin, however slender his claim to be called a religious man, evidently had a clear conception of the enormity of this vice, especially as it aims to weaken the religious restraints which hold men back from evil. When Thomas Paine sent to him the manuscript of his *Age of Reason* for his judgment, the sagacious philosopher returned it, with these words: "I advise you against attempting to unchain the tiger. Burn your piece before it is seen by any other person. If the world is so wicked with religion, what would it be without it?"

Basest of all is the man who does such a work in the sacred name of religion, whether by the press or from the platform or the pulpit.

Subject 2d. Exciting Passion. — It is evident, for like reasons, that he who goes still further, and attempts in any way to excite and call into action the evil dispositions in men, incurs a guilt certainly not less enormous, and is no less to be regarded as a foe of human kind.

Through Imagination. — This may be done by viciously stimulating the imaginations of men. This may be accomplished by improper publications and actions. The opera, the theatre, and the immoral dance, exert the same influence, and have always merited and received the unanimous condemnation of the wise and virtuous. The *nude art*, which is so fashionable in certain quarters at the present day, has been shown by Prof. Bascom, in his *Æsthetics*, to be worthy of the same condemnation. It violates the law of propriety, on the side of vice; it is pagan in its origin; it sprung originally from the licentiousness of Greek and Italian society; it ignores and despises the true glory of man and exalts the baser elements of his nature; it is utterly unnecessary to a true art. "A distinguished American artist, who had resided in Rome for twenty-five years, said to me, 'The Italians are nasty, filthy, beastly, in morals as in body.' Nude art may not be the cause of this, but is certainly its concomitant. Most of the European cities have a street decency that we should term indecent, and that is quite in keeping with the exposure of their art." *Bascom.*

Through Appetites. — It may be done by an immoral ministering to the appetites of others. This is seen in the sale of intoxicating drinks, as luring men to use them as a beverage; in the sale of opiates and narcotics, as leading to their habitual use; and in every other like form of invitation to vice.

It may be done by using others to minister to vicious appetites. Both the seducer and his victim descend together into the depths of infamy; but society needs to be made to feel that to the former belongs a horrid guilt, to whose expression words are unequal.

Through Evil Passions. — It may be done by cherishing the evil passions of men. Immoral appeals are thus continually made to ambition, avarice, party zeal, pride, and vanity, by those who would further their own selfish ends at the expense of human virtue and happiness.

A most popular, and at the same time a most objectionable and deleterious, form of this last immorality is to be found in connection with the *benevolent work* of the Church of the present day. Dr. Wayland has well said concerning it: "It seems to me that no man has a right to present any other than an innocent motive to urge his fellow-men to action. Motives derived from party zeal, from personal vanity, from love of applause, however covertly insinuated, are not of this character. If a man, by exciting such feelings, sell me a horse at twice its value, he would be a sharper. If he excite me to *give* from the same motives, the action partakes of the same character. The cause of benevolence is holy: it is the cause of God. It needs not human chicanery to approve it to the human heart. Let him who advocates it, therefore, go forth strong in the strength of him whose cause he advocates. Let him rest his cause upon its own merits, and leave every man's conscience to decide whether or not he will enlist in its support. And, besides, were men conscientiously to confine themselves to the merits of their cause, they would much more carefully weigh their undertakings before they attempted to engage others in support of them. Much of that fanaticism which withers the moral sympathies of man would thus be checked at the outset."

Topic Second. Special Duties of Social Direction.—A Christian morality demands especially that man should exert himself to the utmost to lead his fellow-men to the attainment of the noblest manhood and the accomplishment of the appointed life of duty.

Man Naturally Aspires to Leadership among his Fellows, as has been already shown. This aspiration is at the foundation of this duty, as its spring. In its proper form, *leadership* is—as Pascal so admirably shows in his letter to Queen Christina of Sweden—one of knowledge and influence, and not of power and despotic authority. The best among the great leaders of mankind have had no place of worldly power, but have accomplished their mission by sheer force of ideas and character. In its improper and perverted form, the aspiration to be leaders has fashioned the ambitious conquerors and despots of the world.

It is the duty of every man, according to the measure of his influence, to be a leader of his fellow-men toward the truest manhood and the highest life. Whatever gospel a man may have for men, he is bound to aid them to the possession of it, by the use of his personal powers, of the forces of nature, of wealth and time, and of whatever else of influence the Moral Governor may have given him; and to do it at the expense of all necessary self-denial.

Man a Leader.—Every man is a leader in some degree among men, as the aspiration to be such is in every man. Those who have done most toward elevating mankind to the true manhood have not always been those possessed of the greatest genius. The very highest nobility is found in *goodness,* not in greatness; and God has therefore used the weaker things of this world to confound the mighty. Goodness is therefore the moral power in the world. Every good man, just so far as he is good, has some gospel, some glad tidings for mankind, and some power over mankind.

Duty to be a Powerful Leader.—Every man is bound to be the most powerful leader he is able to be toward the true mission of humanity. He is to present his gospel, whether it be little or great, with all his powers and with all his enthusiasm. If it be truly the "glorious Gospel of the blessed God" in its completeness, having in view the reconstruction of the world in righteousness, then no powers, no wealth, no time, no genius, no enthusiasm, can possibly rise beyond the demands of the work on which depends the moral hope of mankind.

Self-Denial in Leading Men.— Duty to men demands the utmost reach of self-denial and sacrifice in the task of leading them to the true destiny of humanity. Those who have done the most for mankind have denied themselves everything, have perilled all, even to life itself, in the accomplishment of their task. They have followed Jesus of Nazareth, the one perfect Moral Leader, through contempt and reproach and death to ultimate triumph. Without such self-denial and sacrifice and suffering, no great and beneficent moral idea has ever made its way to supremacy among men. When the moral destiny aimed at is the true destiny of the "sons of God," the sacrifice can never equal in its greatness the magnitude of the eternal results for good.

This highest social duty coincides with the individual duty; so that, in leading men up toward the true manhood and mission, the moral agent reaches his own complete manhood and highest destiny.

Harmony of Individual and Social Duty. — Thus, in a true system of duty, while it appears that the unobstructed working of the force of that true regard for mankind, revealed in Christianity as *brotherly love,* "will make the most and best possible of the individual;" it also appears that it "will bring him, like true knight-errant of old, to devote himself unreservedly to the service of the highest welfare of the world." Jesus of Nazareth, who perfectly performed all duty toward himself, gave himself unreservedly to the service of mankind, thus demonstrating practically that both forms of duty are but necessary parts of one consistent life.

Duties of Societies and Corporations.

It will at once appear obvious that, from the point of view of a Christian morality, all human societies and corporations must be bound, in their dealings with mankind, by the same principles which bind the individual in his social duties. There is required of them by the Moral Governor the same strict regard for the rights of man to life, liberty, property, truthfulness, and the offices of human brotherhood. No human conduct whatever can be righteously exempt from the moral principles which have been set forth under *General Ethics.*

23 *

CHAPTER II.

ECONOMICAL, OR HOUSEHOLD ETHICS.

Economical, or Household Ethics, is that branch of Social Ethics which treats of the duties of man toward others, as members, with himself, of the same family or household.

"*Familia* was the word used by the Romans to denote the persons collected in the house with their parents, and also with servants. The head of the house was called *paterfamilias;* his wife, in general, *materfamilias.*"

Society is the divine arrangement for bringing man up to his high mission as a social being. It results from the association of men in various relations. Man is led to such association by the natural social desires. Of human societies the family is the most important, as furnishing that school in which, by divine appointment, all men must be trained for their duties in the state and the world. It is "the foundation of the state, which is a community or society of families gathered into one organization, rather than a casual combination of individuals, otherwise isolated."

The duties of social conservation, improvement, and direction, already presented, not only hold, but become more specific, in the family relations.

The duties in the three principal relations in the household furnish the subjects of the following *Sections :*

Section 1. Duties of the Marriage Relation.
Section 2. Duties of the Parental Relation.
Section 3. Duties of Master and Servant.

Other Relations.— It will at once be evident that various other relations, such as that of teacher and pupil, employer and employee, properly fall under the second and third *Sections.*

SECTION I.

Duties of the Marriage Relation.

The duties of the marriage relation are determined by its nature, origin, and design. The nature, origin, and design of marriage, and the duties of the marriage relation, will therefore furnish the *Topics* to be considered.

Topic First. The Nature of Marriage. — Marriage may be defined to be a compact between one man and one woman to live together, as husband and wife, until separated by death.

Subject 1st. Marriage is a Compact. — Marriage is a mutual and voluntary compact entered into by a man and woman, "having for its proper basis, not mere personal respect and regard, and not merely the convenience and interest of the parties, but mutual affection."

A Christian morality requires attention to certain prerequisites to the marriage compact, and to its proper sanctioning.

Prerequisites of the Marriage Compact. — "Bodily defect and mental imbecility, hereditary disease, and extreme old age have been thought sufficient to prevent those who labor under them from entering upon the married state."

But, beyond this, it is evident that morality must require:

First, that the parties shall be capable of giving a voluntary and deliberate consent. Hence, all forced marriages are immoral, as the compact is not voluntary. All marriages, entered into before the age at which it may reasonably be supposed that the parties fully understand the conditions, duties, and responsibilities of the marriage state, are immoral, as the compact is not deliberate.

Secondly, that the relations of consanguinity and affinity previously subsisting between the parties shall not be too near. By the Roman law, marriages were declared *incestuous,* "when the parties were too nearly related by *consanguinity,* — that is, by being of the same blood, as brother and sister; or by *affinity,* — that is, by being connected through *marriage,* as father-in-law and daughter-in-law." The Levitical law corresponded closely to the Roman in its requirements in this respect. That marriages between those who are thus closely related are unnatural, and hence immoral, may be shown by the following considerations: (1) the natural affection which relatives have is incompatible with conjugal love; (2) the prohibition of such marriages is requisite to domestic purity, and to the health and welfare, bodily and mental, of the children; (3) the prohibition is necessary that the ties which bind society together may be multiplied by marriages between those who are not previously related.

Thirdly, that neither of the parties be already united in marriage, or obligated to marriage, to another. The *betrothal* is only less sacred than the marriage, and interposes an effectual moral barrier to marriage with any other person. It should be borne in mind, however, that the betrothal is not marriage, but a mutual promise of future marriage; and that it must therefore be governed, not by the *law of marriage*, but by the *law of the promise* (p. 251).

Fourthly, that there be mutual affection as the only true basis of a moral, peaceful, and happy domestic life.

The Sanction of the Marriage Compact.—The manner in which marriage has been sanctioned and celebrated has been very different in different countries and ages. It is evident that the preservation of a pure morality requires some proper public sanction at the entrance into the marriage relation, by the ministers of religion, or by authorized officers of the civil law. Laxness in this respect always tends to immorality.

Subject 2d.   Marriage is Monogamic.—Marriage is properly the union of one man and one woman, as opposed to polygamy, which is degrading and immoral.

Grounds of the View.—That monogamy is the only proper and moral form of marriage may be seen from the following considerations:

First, God constituted marriage as a union between one man and one woman. Accordingly, the number of males and females is always nearly equal, in all ages and nations.

Second, the primary ends of marriage are best secured by such marriage. The proper mutual affection, the mutual interest in the children requisite to their right training, are possible in no other way.

Third, polygamy, on the other hand, divides the affections of parents, and is ruinous to their peace and happiness; and it reduces the female sex from wives and companions to slaves and drudges.

Subject 3d.   Marriage is for Life.—Marriage can only be naturally dissolved by the death of one of the parties. The

unnatural modes of bringing it to an end are, a breach of the seventh commandment, and wilful and continued desertion, as implying a breach of that commandment.

Grounds for Permanence. — That the marriage relation is naturally a permanent one, is clear from such considerations as the following:

First, from the necessity of its permanence in order to the accomplishment of its moral ends: in benefiting the parties themselves; in the proper training of the children to obedience and virtue; and in furnishing them affectionate advice and direction, after they have gone out from the home of their childhood.

Second, from the fact that the Moral Governor has declared, both in man's nature, with its growing affection, and in Scripture, that it ought to be permanent.

Reasons for Dissolution. — The marriage relation may be dissolved by adultery, and by wilful and permanent desertion. Christ teaches, in Matthew v., that it may be dissolved by *adultery*. By this act, the parties cease to be any longer *one*, in that mysterious sense in which the Bible declares a man and his wife to be one. It is therefore a practical dissolution of the marriage bond, and a crime of fearful enormity, as striking a death-blow at the peace, purity, and morality of the family and of society. Paul teaches, in 1 Cor. vii. 15–18, that *wilful desertion* is also properly a dissolution of the marriage bond; but the whole passage shows that such desertion must be deliberate and final. It is probable, from the tenacity with which the Scriptures elsewhere adhere to adultery as the proper ground of divorce, that desertion only justifies divorce as it implies adultery, as the two doubtless always went together in that licentious age.

Indissoluble by Man. — The marriage relation cannot be dissolved by man without immorality. Says Dr. Charles Hodge: "Marriage is an indissoluble compact between one man and one woman. It cannot be dissolved by any voluntary act of repudiation on the part of the contracting parties; nor by any act of the church or state. 'Those whom God has joined together no man can put asunder.' The compact may, however, be dissolved, although by no legitimate act of man. It is dissolved by death. It is dissolved by adultery, and, as Protestants teach, by wilful desertion. In other words, there are certain things which from their nature work a dissolution of the marriage bond. All the legitimate authority the state has in the premises is to take cognizance of the fact that the marriage is dissolved; officially to announce it; and to make suitable provision for the altered relation of the parties."

All those other grounds of separation of husband and wife, which have been advocated in various quarters and for various reasons, are not recognized by the divine law of morality as adequate to warrant divorce. Especially is *incompatibility of temper* an insufficient ground of divorce.

Incompatibility of Temper.—Milton advocates this ground of divorce, pressing the argument, drawn from his own bitter experience, that such incompatibility frustrates the great end of marriage, which is the happiness and comfort of the parties, and inflicts positive misery. But it is argued on the other hand:

"*First*, if unsuitableness of temper were admitted as sufficient ground for a divorce, no attempt would be made to mend the state of matters by mutual accommodation and compliance.

" *Secondly*, a separation of views and interests would arise.

" *Thirdly*, the natural inconstancy of human affection would be encouraged.

"So that even on views of expediency, and independent of the authority of Scripture, the only ground on which divorce is justifiable is the ground of adultery in either of the parties.

" Bishop Burnet tells us that divorces were freely granted in the Canton of Berne; but any husband and wife applying for one were first required to pass six weeks together in one small room, furnished with only one chair, one plate, one spoon, one bed, and so on through the whole furniture, with the single exception of a small treatise on the duties of husband and wife, of which there was a copy for each. The Bishop adds, that, under this *regime*, the parties, finding it necessary to accommodate one another, were soon on excellent terms, gave up the idea of separation, and were never known to make application again." *Fleming.*

Topic Second.   The Origin of Marriage. — Marriage is in its origin a divine institution. It has, however, a natural basis in the social affections and desires of man; and becomes, in a sense, a civil institution from its practical connection with civil society.

Marriage is a Divine Institution. — This is clear for the following and like reasons:

First, because God himself constituted it at the beginning. He made man male and female, and ordained marriage as the indispensable condition of the continuance of the race. He commanded marriage.

Second, because God has made known the nature of marriage, the prerequisites to the marriage compact, the ground of its dissolution, and the end and duties of the marriage relation.

Third, because the husband and wife acknowledge its divine origin by making their vow of mutual fidelity to God.

Fourth, because its existence before the origin of civil society proves it to be in its origin not a civil institution.

Marriage has its Natural Basis in man in the social affections and desires which have been seen to be a part of his nature (p. 52). The divine ordinance is thus fitted to the nature of the human agent, so that the family is the natural outgrowth of his constitution.

Marriage is in a Sense a Civil Institution. — This arises from its connection with civil society, and is clear from the following or like reasons :

First, because it is, and must be, recognized and enforced by the state.

Second, because, in binding to such duties as support of the wife by the husband, it imposes civil obligations which may be enforced by the state.

Third, because it involves rights of property which must be secured by the state.

Fourth, because to the state has been granted, by common moral consent, the prerogative of determining what marriages are lawful and what unlawful; how the marriage compact is to be solemnized and authenticated; and what shall be its legal consequences.

The civil authority is therefore subordinate to a higher authority in dealing with the marriage relation. Its proper limits, in its legislation and action touching that relation, are to be found in the will of God as revealed in the nature of man and in the Scriptures. All legislation and practices based upon a false theory of the nature and origin of this fundamental social relation must necessarily tend to the degradation and destruction of society.

The Iniquitous Divorce Laws which now deface the statute-books of almost all the States, are of this nature. They have already wrought fearful moral ruin, and must work still greater. Of a still worse character is the project of vicious and abandoned politicians, originating in the licentious tendencies of the age, to legalize the so-called *social evil*. Such a project if carried out would be in this country — as it has been in France — equivalent to signing the death-warrant of social and national purity, virtue, and stability.

Topic Third. The Design of Marriage. — The marriage relation was designed by the Moral Governor to constitute the *family*, as an institution for the continuance of the race, and as the perfectly adapted sphere for the training of its members to the complete moral manhood and for the mission of duty. As the most important of earthly societies, it can therefore realize the divine idea of its constitution only by conforming perfectly to the divine law of right ordained for its government.

Subject 1st. The Family and Social Purity. — The family is an institution most perfectly fitted to secure domestic purity, perfection, and happiness. Ordered in conformity to the moral law, it controls, chastens, and elevates the social appetites; develops most powerfully the human affections and sympathies; exalts husband and wife to the highest and most unselfish manhood and womanhood; and prepares them for the true life mission in the world.

The Family a Means to a Higher End. — The family is not an end, to be sought for its own sake. It passes away, just as the state passes away. As an end it is only subordinate to the higher ends which have been enumerated, and a means to them.

The Social Appetites find here their Perfection. — Says Dr. Haven: "Those natural desires and propensities, which relate to the intercourse of the sexes, look forward to this relation as their end, and are at once regulated, refined, and chastened by it. Without such an influence, and such an end, these desires would constantly tend to the degradation of man, and the disorganization of society. Under the influence of the marriage relation, these disturbing forces are curbed and tranquillized, security and confidence are imparted, and society is established on a firm basis. The parties united in this sacred relation — joined, not in person merely, but in heart — become one in all the interests and duties, the joys and the sorrows of life."

The Development of Social Affection. — The social affections and sympathies, which give such power for good in the world, here find their very best place of development, and perfection. That union which is based upon mutual affection; which brings mutual joys, aims, and responsibilities; which perpetually calls for mutual forbearance and helpfulness; and which thus replaces solitary labors and lonely failures and unshared successes by a mutual life of love, — is assuredly adapted to exalt to the best manhood and the truest womanhood. It is fitted to lead both man and woman to regard what is distinctive in sex with reverence; to meet generously upon all that is common; to seek with the utmost tenderness each to elevate the other; and together to aspire to what is the noblest and the best for humanity.

Subject 2d. The Family the Place of Training. — The family is an institution most perfectly adapted to the protection and training of infancy and youth. When it conforms to its true law, it enlists in this work the strongest and most unselfish human interests and affections; brings to bear in it the experience, wisdom, and strength of years; and prosecutes it under the most solemn and weighty sense of responsibility.

The Intensest Interest. — That the family enlists the most powerful and unselfish human interest and affection in the protection and training of the young appears from its entire arrangement. The babe in its origin and birth; the infant in its helplessness and clinging tenderness; the child in its unfolding beauty and brightness; the youth in his promise of strength and glory, — all appeal most powerfully to the parental instinct. In the family where the right is the law, whatever can be done for the good of the children, in shielding them from danger and in training them for life, will assuredly be done. No more potent springs of interest and affection could possibly be brought into play.

The Largest Experience. — Equally important and complete is that arrangement of the family by which it secures the experience, wisdom, and strength of the mature man and woman, for the support and training of inexperience, ignorance, and helplessness; so as to render it certain that the most possible will be done for the child's good.

The Most Solemn Responsibility. — The solemn sense of responsibility resting upon the parent's soul, in view of his agency in deciding the character and destiny of the immortal being, completes the provision made in the family for securing the best possible care and direction, from the opening of the child life to the crowning with full manhood.

Topic Fourth.   Duties imposed by Marriage. — The duties of the marriage relation arise from the very nature of the compact, and are either such as are common to both husband and wife, or such as are peculiar to each.

24

Subject 1st. Mutual Duties of Husband and Wife. — Of the duties common to both husband and wife, the first is mutual fidelity; the second, mutual affection; and the third, mutual sympathy and co-operation.

The Basis of All in the Intuitive Moral Principle. — All these duties are evidently but applications of the fundamental moral principle of all social ethics (p. 231) to the peculiar relation of husband and wife. These are the special duties required by social conservation, improvement, and direction in this special relation. The same thing holds of all the duties in all the relations of the family.

1st. Mutual Fidelity. — The duty of mutual fidelity requires the faithful observance of the marriage compact; since upon such observance the welfare of the family and of society depends. It especially forbids every violation of the law of chastity.

Sacredness of Chastity. — The interests involved in preserving inviolate the law of chastity are the greatest possible, both for the family and for society. Its violation destroys at once the purity and harmony of the domestic relations; unfits the home for being the training-place of the race to all that is good and noble; and corrupts society at large. "Hence, in all ages, and by all laws of God and man, it has been treated as an aggravated and serious offence." By the Jewish law the crime of unchastity was punished with death.

Danger of Neglect. — Fidelity to the marriage compact forbids not only criminal relations, but whatever tends to weaken or destroy the mutual faith of husband and wife; such as want of mutual kindness and attention; and the preferring of the society of others to that of each other. These are often the starting-points for complete and immoral estrangement.

2d. Mutual Affection. — The duty of mutual affection requires that husband and wife shall preserve that tender regard which furnished the proper basis of the marriage compact; and that they shall deepen and strengthen that regard by constantly seeking to become more unselfish, more noble, and more lovely for the sake of each other. It especially forbids everything that would mar or lessen that mutual regard.

Sacredness of Mutual Affection. — Much of the wretchedness of the home life results from an immoral disregard of this plain principle.

The mutual affection which once existed is suffered to die out, and hatred and strife take the place of love and domestic harmony. The home loses its attractions, the man and woman become strangers in heart and life, and all the noblest ends of the family are frustrated. Every separating influence, in thought, word, or act, should be guarded against, with jealous care, as if a mortal foe.

Growth of Mutual Affection. — Where this principle is duly regarded, the mutual affection grows with the passing years, the increasing ties, the strengthening character, and the advancing life work; and as, in the strife to become nobler and better in and for each other, they "walk this world yoked in all exercise of noble end," human love is perfected and fitted to be exalted to a divine home.

3d. Mutual Co-operation. — The duty of mutual sympathy and co-operation in the work of life requires, that, in the accomplishment of the one great mission of the family, the husband and wife shall be one in interest and effort, seeking together to accomplish the most possible. It especially forbids everything that would tend to indifference or negligence in that work.

Sacredness of Mutual Co-operation. — The so common estrangement of husband and wife often begins just here. The two recognize no common mission, sympathy, and work; the man becomes absorbed in his business or his profession, and the woman in fashion or household cares; they cease to look for common thoughts, common interests, and common joys; their love loses its height and purity and unselfishness, and wedded life loses its attractiveness and grandeur and becomes a common-place and base thing, shorn of all noble aspiration and true inspiration.

Growth in Sympathy. — Mutual sympathy and co-operation in the one great work of life furnish the true preventive of such evils. In the one chosen pursuit along which the husband makes his way in the world, the wife must bring to bear her powerful aid, in the inspiration of intelligent wifely interest, sympathy, and effort; and so the two, "thought in thought, purpose in purpose, will in will," may together accomplish tenfold more than would be possible to the man alone.

Subject 2d. Duties peculiar to Husband and Wife. — Of the duties peculiar to each, it belongs to the husband to rule and defend, and to the wife to obey and trust; it belongs to the husband to provide a suitable maintenance for the house-

hold, and to the wife to see that the means and substance of the family are used with prudence and economy.

The Husband is the Head of the Family, by the law of nature and of the Scriptures. He holds the place of authority, as the one appointed by the Moral Governor to give unity to the household. Hence there arises the duty to rule wisely, unselfishly, and affectionately. Paul teaches that it is the duty of the wife, where there is conflict of opinion or choice, to submit herself to her husband as unto the Lord, since the husband is the head of the wife, even as Christ is the head of the Church. He adds, in the same breath, the injunction : "Husbands, love your wives, even as Christ also loved the Church, and gave himself for it."

The Husband is the Protector and Supporter of the Family. — For this end, in part at least, he is made the stronger of the two, that he may defend and cherish the weaker. He is to provide for the comfortable maintenance and support of the wife; to protect her from injury and insult; to do everything in his power to elevate, ennoble, and bless her. She is to confide in his strength ; to enter as far as may be into his plans; to use with prudence and economy the means of support; and to be herself the chief joy and attraction in a home made attractive by thrift and the gentle ministries of a true womanly and wifely affection.

The Two the Perfected Humanity. — In performing their peculiar duties in the spirit of a Christian morality, while cherishing mutual fidelity, affection, and sympathy, husband and wife advance toward the true unity of the moral manhood and womanhood in the family. In the rich verse of the poet-laureate :

> "—— in the long years liker must they grow;
> The man be more of woman, she of man;
> He gain in sweetness and in moral height;
> Nor lose the wrestling thews that throw the world ;
> She mental breadth, nor fail in childward care,
> Nor lose the childlike in the larger mind ;
> Till at the last she set herself to man,
> Like perfect music unto noble words:
> And so these twain, upon the skirts of time,
> Sit side by side, full-summ'd in all their power,
> Dispensing harvest, sowing the to-be,
> Self-reverent each and reverencing each,
> Distinct in individualities,
> But like each other even as those who love.
> Then comes the statelier Eden back to men ;
> Then reign the world's great bridals, chaste, and calm :
> Then springs the crowning race of humankind.
> May these things be ! "

SECTION II.

Duties of the Parental Relation.

The duties of the parental relation are determined by the nature and design of that relation, as already set forth.   They may be divided into duties of parents toward children; and duties of children toward parents.

Topic First.   Duties of Parents toward Children. — Of the special duties of parents toward their children the first is parental affection; the second, parental training; and the third, parental control and direction.

Subject 1st.   Parental Affection. — As a true parental affection is the foundation and measure of all proper care for the children of the household, and all powerful influence for good over them, it becomes the first duty of parents to cherish this affection in its purest, most unselfish, and most intense form.

Origin of Parental Affection. — The origin and growth of such affection are provided for in the constitution of the family itself.   It has its *first natural root* in the mutual affection of husband and wife, and is not to be expected in any proper measure where this does not exist.   It has its *second natural root* in the relation of the children to the parents as "bone of their bone and flesh of their flesh."   Paul presents a principle of universal application when he declares that "no man hateth his own flesh, but nourisheth and cherisheth it."   It has its *third natural root* in the innocent helplessness of the child, which makes the bosom of its parents so long its place of security and rest.   This is the most powerful of all influences for the development of the fatherly and motherly tenderness; and the parents, who turn the children over to the almost exclusive care of menials and hirelings, place themselves in measure beyond its reach, and so make the highest and purest and most intense development of parental affection impossible.   It has its *fourth root* in right and adequate views of the immortal existence and boundless possibilities of the child-nature, and of the grandeur of training it for immortal goodness and glory.   The parental love that does not strike deep root in this is of the earth and time only, and furnishes no fit motive to the training of the children for the highest mission.

24 *

Power of Parental Affection. — That such affection alone can make the parental influence most powerful for good must be admitted by all who understand the springs of human action in the child. It was a father's love that brought back the prodigal; it was a mother's love that saved the life of the great Hebrew Lawgiver: it is parental love that shapes the destinies of mankind. It is the power back of all training and control.

The Importance of this First Duty cannot then be overestimated. The character and destiny of the children depend upon it.

Subject 2d. Parental Training.

— As only the right parental training can prepare the children for the work of life, it becomes the second duty of parents to give them such training in its best available form. This carries with it the duty of making proper preparation, so far as possible, to give and direct such training; the duty of securing the requisite aid in the work from others who are fitted to give it; and the duty of suitable maintenance, at least in the earlier and more helpless stages of the life and development.

The First Teachers. — To the parents belongs the chief responsibility of the training of the children. The parents must begin the work when the nature of the child is the most susceptible to impressions, and when the most decisive and lasting impressions are made. They cannot therefore meet the demands of duty by ignorantly, carelessly, or selfishly giving over the work into the hands of any other person whatsoever, — from the uneducated servant-girl to the sage. Parents, as intelligent beings who are morally responsible, are morally bound to acquaint themselves with the great issues and duties of human life, especially in its moral and religious aspects; and with the right mode of preparing their children to meet them.

The Assistant Instructors. — In the better fulfilment of the duty of *training*, parents are morally bound to secure, so far as possible, the aid of others, as teachers of industry and art, of science and religion, who can co-operate with the parental work in fitting the young for their mission in life.

The True Training. — The true parental training is summed up in such an education, physical and intellectual, moral and religious, as will bring out the peculiar powers of the child; best fit him for his special work in his own sphere in life; and make the most of his moral and immortal being by bringing it under the control of the highest moral and religious principles.

Subject 3d. Parental Authority. — As parents are in a large degree responsible for the conduct of their children, who are without the knowledge necessary to direct themselves, it becomes their third duty to exercise a wise parental authority in controlling and directing that conduct. This involves such special duties as, that of directing them to the choice of that vocation in life best suited to the capacities of each; that of preventing improper and immoral companionships and marriages; and the *general duty* of requiring that obedience to law human and divine which is indispensable to right life, — the only safe, happy, and successful human life under the rule of the Moral Governor.

Grounds of Parental Authority. — Parental authority rests on the ordinance of God. The necessity for its exercise springs out of the helplessness and ignorance of children, as absolutely requiring the wisdom and experience and power of the parent. It is hallowed by parental affection, and finds its standard in the law of God.

Extent of Parental Authority. — The duty of parental authority is modified, in its exercise and extent, according to the age to which the children may have attained.

During the period of *infancy*, the authority is absolute, as the ignorance and dependence are complete. In *childhood* and *youth*, in short, all through the period of *minority*, it is wellnigh absolute, for a like reason.

There is no fixed rule for deciding the precise period in life at which the child becomes fully responsible, and is freed from the absolute control of the parents. The age differs in different persons and in different countries. Most nations fix upon some period by law.

Although the absolute authority of the parents ceases when the children reach the period of majority, it is still a parental duty affectionately to furnish such advice and direction as may be dictated by a larger wisdom and experience, and as may be of service in the new emergencies of life.

Authority in Choice of Vocation. — The special duty of directing the children in the choice of a trade, business, or profession in life, suited to their various capacities, is clearly binding upon the parents. As it is one of the most delicate and difficult of parental tasks, so it is one of the most important of all, and the one upon whose wise and proper performance success in the life work most of all depends. The man out of his place in the world is comparatively a cipher in his influence for good (p. 221); and the parent who puts his child out of place, or carelessly allows him to get out of place, in the work of the world, becomes responsible for making him a cipher. In the exercise of this parental duty, it is obvious that there is special need to guard against that false pride which shrinks from directing the child to his true work of life, whether it be in the forum or on the mission field, at the plough or the forge, in the commercial house or the college.

Authority against Evil Associations. — No less clear, and far more imperative, is the duty of guarding the children against demoralizing influences and vicious associations and companionships of every kind. As the marriage relation is of such vital importance, it is generally admitted that parental authority should be wisely, affectionately, and firmly used against improper marriages. This exercise of authority does not, however, extend to the power to compel marriage, and it ceases with the legal majority of the child.

Obedience to Law. — Most important of all is the general duty of requiring obedience to law. This, in fact, includes all the others. To parental authority belongs the power *to compel* such obedience. The momentous character of the duty is evident from the principle, already shown to be universal (p. 156), that transgression of law works destruction and death, and that in obedience to law is virtue, safety, and life. It is only as the lesson of the supreme sacredness of law, human and divine, is properly represented in the parents, and duly and fully impressed by parental authority, that the children are fitted for that best and noblest mission which consists in perfect obedience to the whole law of God.

Loose Views of Parental Authority. — The true conception of the design of parental authority sets in their true light the loose views of some of the most popular of the would-be moral and religious teachers of the present day. The most certain way to undermine all morality, to corrupt the family, the society, the state, and the race, and to bring in the reign of vice and crime and godlessness, is to lower the public estimate of the sacred character of parental authority, by holding up to ridicule the strictness of the parental training to which these very teachers owe everything they are that is not base and contemptible, and which was moreover in accordance with God's Word.

Topic Second. Duties of Children toward Parents. — The special duties of children toward their parents are summed up in the reciprocating of the parental duties already considered. The first duty is filial affection and trust; the second, filial docility; and the third, filial obedience.

Importance of Filial Duties. — So important are these duties of the child, in the sight of the Moral Governor, that one of the commandments of the Decalogue is devoted to the enforcement of them. Paul (*Eph.* vi. 2) calls this "the first commandment *with promise;*" since it alone is emphasized by the addition of a promise. The *honor* of the Scriptures includes the affection, docility, and obedience.

Subject 1st. Filial Affection.

— As it has been shown to be the first duty of the parents to cherish parental affection toward the child, and as a true filial affection is the foundation and measure of all right conduct of the child toward its parents, it becomes the first filial duty to cherish this affection, as love implying complacency, and as gratitude leading to requital.

Origin of Filial Affection. — Filial affection has its natural root in the relation of the child to its parents. From them it drew its being; and to them, therefore, its first human love belongs. By them it has been nourished and protected; and so by a law of its being it learns its first lesson of love from the gentle bosom and the strong arm. Richter has said truly that "Filial love can only spring up toward a heart whereon we have long reposed, and which has protected us, as it were, with the first heart's leaves against cold nights and hot days." To them the child owes everything, — life, care, training for usefulness, direction toward the noblest ends, — since the Moral Governor has chosen to make the parents his agents in the bestowal of all choicest blessings, and his representatives in his most beneficent work; the child has therefore unbounded reason for love and gratitude; and if it has in it the true and noble child-nature, the love and gratitude must become unbounded.

Filial Affection the Basis. — This filial affection is at the basis of all right conduct on the part of the child toward its parents. It gently covers their defects, weaknesses, and errors, and crowns and glorifies the true *father* and *mother* in them. It takes an interest in the increase of their comforts and joys. As *gratitude*, it seeks to make *requital* for the parental affection so lavishly bestowed; and when age comes on with its infirmity and helplessness, it generously and lovingly hastens to furnish support and maintenance. It is evident, moreover, that a true filial affection can alone prepare for true filial docility and obedience..

Subject 2d. Filial Docility.

— As it has been shown to be the second duty of the parents to train the child for the work of life, and as such parental training can only accomplish its end through the co-operation of the child in filial docility, it becomes the second duty of the child to receive the training of the parent with this docility of spirit.

True Filial Docility is Essential to the accomplishment of the highest end for which the family was instituted: to be the training-place of the child for the moral manhood and mission. It is the child's duty, therefore, to yield cheerfully to the instruction and direction which the superior wisdom and experience of the parents may dictate. Without this there can be no growth in knowledge, wisdom, and power. The stubborn and rebellious spirit, that sets up itself against the wisdom of those whom the Moral Governor has appointed for its training, and refuses to be guided by their counsels, thereby unsettles the moral order of the family, and prevents its own acquirement of any fitness for the true work of life. As this great sin is aimed at the destruction of society, under the Jewish law it was punished with death (*Deut.* xxi. 18-21).

Subject 3d. Filial Obedience. — As it has been shown to be the third duty of parents to exercise parental authority over the child, and as this authority can only accomplish its end through the co-operation of the child in filial obedience, it becomes the third duty of the child to yield unreserved and reverential obedience to its parent.

Filial Reverence for Person and Authority. — The first requisite to a right filial obedience is reverence for the person and authority of the parents. Without this there can be no true *honoring* of the *father* and *mother.* It carries with it that *respect* and *deference* which are becoming toward all superiors, and most of all toward parents. As reverence for the *person* of the parents, it bows affectionately before the *father* and the *mother* in them, whether they be high or low, learned or ignorant, cultivated or uncultivated. As reverence for their *authority*, it affectionately bows before the parents as the representatives of the divine law, and the Divine Lawgiver. It is this spirit that fits the child to take his place under law, not in the household only, but in the state and in the kingdom of God as well.

Filial Yielding to Will of Parents. — The second requisite to a right filial obedience is an unreserved yielding to the will of the parents. Such, according to the voice of mankind, and the teaching of the Scriptures, is the duty of the child.

It is not necessary, therefore, that the reasons for a parental command should be made plain, before it is the child's duty to yield obedience. Duty demands prompt and unquestioning obedience to the *authority* of the superior and wiser will. Ordinarily, intelligent and reasonable subjection to authority is doubtless a better training than unintelligent and unreasoning subjection; but one of the chief lessons man needs to be taught is, *to bow to rightful authority whenever it speaks, and whatever its requirements.*

Nor is it any more necessary that the command of the parents should agree with the wishes or inclinations of the child before obedience becomes the filial duty. In a world of moral disorder the will of the ignorant, inexperienced, and wayward, will often conflict with the will of the wiser and more experienced. It is a most important end of the training of the child to correct wrong inclinations and a perverted will. Filial duty, therefore, demands that the obedience be just as prompt and unreserved, when the requirement of the parents is contrary to the wishes, as when it is in agreement with them.

Limit of the Duty. — The limit of the duty of obedience is furnished by the moral law. The child is not bound, at the bidding of the parents, to do anything that is clearly seen to be morally wrong. No parental command can bind him to steal, or lie, or cheat, or break any law of the state, or of God. A parent has no right to give such commands. The child is bound, in such cases, to do right, and suffer the consequences.

Where, however, there is *a reasonable doubt* about the right or wrong of any requirement, the authority of the parent must prevail; since the presumption is that his larger knowledge and experience are more likely to reveal to him what is right and proper.

SECTION III.

Duties of Master and Servant.

The duties of the master and servant are determined by the nature and design of the relation. They may be regarded as including also the duties of employer and employee, of principal and agent, and other kindred relations; since the same general principles apply to these also.

Origin and Design of the Relation. — The relation of master and servant has its origin in that mutual dependence of men in society, which renders necessary mutual helpfulness. Its design is to bring mankind more closely together into a true brotherhood, in which they may the more powerfully influence and aid one another in the work of social conservation, improvement, and direction.

Forms of Service. — *Servitude* has been distinguished as *perfect* and *imperfect*. The former is more commonly denoted by the term *slavery;* the latter denotes the state of *limited and voluntary service*. *Slavery* has already been considered under the *right of human liberty* (p. 241). Only *voluntary service* remains, therefore, to be treated here. So far as slavery already exists, the law of human brotherhood must control it for the high moral and social end just stated; and must speedily work the elevation and emancipation of the slave.

The Benefits Mutual. — Master and servant are alike dependent upon one another. In a righteous society there is no conflict of capital and labor, none between employer and employee. There is a mutual rendering of indispensable service. Upon the regulation of the whole relation by the second of the great fundamental moral principles (p. 171) depends the general well-being, and especially the business prosperity of society.

The Benefits not merely Pecuniary. — A Christian morality has always tended to redeem this relation from the curse of selfishness and covetousness. It leads men to recognize the higher relations of life, and its nobler moral and social ends, and to make the lower *service* a means to these higher ends.

Formation of the Relation. — The arrangement for voluntary service is generally entered into by the parties for a limited period; often for a specified kind or amount of work; and should always be confined to right and lawful undertakings. Hence arise the reciprocal duties of *masters toward servants;* and of *servants toward masters.*

Topic First. Duties of Masters toward Servants. — Social duty requires the master or employer to make a fair return as wages for the service rendered; to control the servant or employee, during the rendering of the service, in the spirit of brotherly kindness; and to seek to make the relation a means of social, moral, and religious elevation to both parties.

Wages of Service.—The duty of a fair return for the service rendered cannot be reasonably denied. The producer has a natural right to what he produces (p. 243); and when he employs his productive powers, according to agreement, for others, he has a right to demand a fair remuneration. Hence the sacredness of the wages of labor has always been recognized. The principles which control in this duty are:

First, the wages should be a *fair equivalent* for the service. The civil law enforces the payment of the *stipulated* wages; but the moral law requires a *fair return*, according to the principle of action, "whatsoever ye would that men should do to you, do ye even so to them." The aim of every employer who is a true man must be to return for services rendered the *utmost possible* consistent with a righteous success in business; rather than the *least possible.* In the sight of the Moral Governor so much is due. The Scriptures, by the Apostle James, say to the extortionate rich: "Behold, the hire of the laborers who have reaped down your fields, which is of you kept back by fraud, crieth: and the cries of them which have reaped are entered into the ears of the Lord of Hosts." An enlightened Christian conscience agrees with the Scriptures in unmeasured condemnation of all such extortion in heaping up riches at the expense of the poor and oppressed; and in declaring that it tends to beget selfishness, inhumanity, and oppression, and to destroy all sense of human brotherhood. Wealth gained by such extortion brutalizes the man who gains it, corrupts the family that lives upon it, and destroys the society that approves it; and is thus certain to bear with it its complete penalty of evil at the last.

Second, the wages should be *promptly and cheerfully paid.* The hire of the poor man is his means of support, and is due as soon as his labor is performed. It was therefore a beneficent provision of the Mosaic Law, that the wages of the day-laborer should be paid at the close of the day. "The wages of him that is hired shall not abide with thee all night until the morning." Equally binding with the prompt payment of the wages due, is the duty of cheerful and ungrudging payment, when the service has been carefully and faithfully rendered.

Control by the Master.—The duty of exercising control in the spirit of brotherly kindness is equally imperative. Servitude, in all its forms, is humiliating and painful, and those who occupy the place of masters should spare as much as possible the feelings of those who serve them. They have a right to require the fulfilment of the stipulated task; but they have no right to be harsh and rigid in their demands. They are directed by a Christian morality to forbear threatening, and to avoid all tyrannical measures and unjust casting reproach and disgrace, knowing that they also have a "*Master* who is in heaven, and that there is no respect of persons with him." The *master* is not to be a *taskmaster.*

25   T

Elevating Influence of Master.—The duty of the master or employer to use his position for the higher ends of life is a still more important one. By his example, his principles, his authority, and his active efforts, he is to seek to elevate to the noblest moral manhood all over whom the Moral Governor has given him control. When those employed become in the strict sense members of his own household, duty and affection toward the other members help to make this duty doubly important and impressive. Upon its faithful performance, therefore, depends the highest good of all the parties concerned.

Topic Second. Duties of Servants toward Masters.—Social duty requires the servant to reciprocate the duties rendered by the master. He is to render a faithful service; to accord a cheerful obedience; and to seek to make his service conduce to the higher moral ends of life.

Faithful Service.—The duty of faithful service is the proper reciprocation of the duty of bestowing fair wages. The same principles govern master and servant alike. The servant is bound to render his service faithfully, promptly, and ungrudgingly. The civil law enforces only the rendering of a stipulated and formal service, but the moral law demands good and faithful service. The aim of every servant or employee, who is a true man, must be to render *the most and best possible service* consistent with a righteous regard for his own well-being, rather than *the least possible.* By making himself indispensable to his employer, he will accomplish the most for himself.

Cheerful Obedience.—The duty of cheerful obedience corresponds to the duty of kindly control. It greatly enhances the value of the service when that obedience is intelligent, cheerful, and unfailing. It is at the same time true that such obedience always elevates and strengthens the character of him who renders it.

Elevating Influence of Servant.—The summit of duty is reached in reciprocating the efforts of the master to make the relation conducive to higher than temporal and pecuniary ends. The servant should yield himself readily and gratefully to all efforts which have in view his true elevation, and should cheerfully co-operate in such efforts. When the servant or employee is the superior in culture and character, as is very frequently the case, it becomes his great duty to seek, so far as possible, to bring the master up to his own moral level. It was as a slave that the Jew Daniel began the moral work which brought the ruler of the greatest empire of the early ages to acknowledge the true God to be the only God.

CHAPTER III.

CIVIL ETHICS.

Civil Ethics is that branch of Social Ethics which treats of the duties of man toward others as members with himself of the same state or nation.

A brief consideration of the nature, origin, and design of the state is necessary to prepare for the treatment of civil duties.

1st. The Nature and Origin of the State. — A state is a community organized under one civil government, and ordinarily dwelling together in one and the same territory. There is essential to it, association, organization, civil government, and a common place of abode for its members. It actually grows out of the family; but it has a divine basis in man's social nature and relations; and its forms are decided by men.

Historical Origin of the State. — Historically, the state is but an outgrowth of the family, which is the unit or atom of society. The one family becomes gradually many families: the government of one family, the government of many families. The natural order is: the family, the community, the tribe, the state; the father, the patriarch, the chief, the king or president.

The State is a Divine Institution, since the Moral Governor has so made man as a social being, and placed him in such relations in this world, that association, organization, and civil government are the natural results of his development; and since the law which ought to govern it rests on the divine law.

The State is a Human Institution, in the sense, that its form of organization and government originally depend upon the choice and moulding influence of men. However little foundation there may be for the theory of *social contract*, or *social compact*, it is clear that men do actually have largely to do with shaping their political institutions.

2d. The Design of the State. — The state was designed by the Moral Governor chiefly, to widen man's sphere of social effort, and ensure freedom and security in that sphere; and to direct men, as associated in the nation, in working out a national mission.

The Wider Sphere. — A wider sphere of effort than that furnished by the family is essential to a complete manhood and work. The family has been seen to be but the training-place for this. The state furnishes this, in its larger community, broader interests, more varied relations, and grander scope for activity. In this wider sphere there is protection, freedom, and security of rights. As the states of the earth approximate to the true idea of the Christian state, the sphere of activity must be widened, through the relation of states to each other, so as to take in all the nations of the globe, and give man the whole world as the scene of his free development and effort.

The National Mission. — A national mission is the natural result of the organic unity and life of a nation. It is the accepted doctrine of the foremost political thinkers of modern times, that "a nation is not a mere conglomeration of individuals. It is an organized body. It has of necessity its national life, its national organs, national principles of action, national character, and national responsibility." It is the doctrine of the foremost thinkers in physical geography and philosophic history, that each nation has providentially given it a mission to embody some great social idea, or solve some great social problem, or push forward some great social enterprise. If this be accepted as the true theory, then one design of the state is to work out this appointed national mission.

3d. Distribution of Civil Duties. — The design of the state determines the civil duties. They may be considered under two *Sections:*

Section 1.   Duties of the State.
Section 2.   Duties of the Citizen.

SECTION I.

Duties of the State.

The duties of the state as represented by civil government, and as determined by its design, include duties toward the citizens, toward itself, and toward other states; and duties toward God.   Hence the *Topics:*

Topic 1.   Duties of the State toward its Citizens.

Topic 2.   Duties of the State toward itself and other States.

Topic 3.   Duties of the State toward God.

Ordinary View. — Of these various duties those toward the citizens and toward other nations usually occupy the chief attention in treatises on ethics; but it is evident, from the point of view of a modern Christian ethics and philosophy, that the other subjects equally demand consideration.

Topic First. Duties of the State toward its Citizens. — As one chief design of the state is to furnish man a wider sphere of social activity, it is its duty to secure to its citizens the largest freedom in attaining the complete manhood and life in that sphere.   This necessarily involves the duty and right of making use of the authority, and of providing the means requisite to the attainment of the proposed end of public freedom and public order.

Subject 1st. The State and Civil Authority and Law. — It is the first duty of the state toward its citizens, to exercise its authority in regulating their public conduct, by laws based upon the immutable law of right, so as to secure to them the most perfect freedom and order in the sphere of activity which it furnishes.   This is chiefly a duty of conservation.

1st. Necessity for Civil Authority and Law. — As man's nature is in moral disorder, his unregulated development and action must lead to unjust interference with the freedom and rights of other men. Civil authority enacting law, and

25 *

coercing obedience to it when denied, becomes therefore a necessity to public freedom and order.

Normal Development. — Were man a perfect moral being there might be no place for this duty of the state. The development and action of the individual would be governed by the fundamental principles of duty toward himself, mankind, and God; and could not, therefore, interfere with the rights of any other being whatsoever. All men would be perfectly free in conformity to moral law, and there might be no need of positive civil enactments.

Abnormal Development. — But as man is a morally imperfect being, so that his development and action are constantly running counter to the rights of his fellow-men, and perilling their freedom and safety, state authority must come in with regulating laws. It must embody the right in law, and set it before the many who do not or cannot know what is right; and must impress it upon the consciences of those who know their public duty, but do not propose to do it. It must settle those practical matters concerning property, business, marriage, and all human intercourse, which the individuals cannot settle, but upon which the proper on-going and the true well-being of society depend.

Coercive Power Necessary. — The coercive power of civil authority is necessary to give to law any certain efficacy in regulating the public conduct of men. Socialism denies the need of any coercive measures in connection with law. Man may be trusted to find out what is right, and to do it without degrading penalties and appeals to base fear; or he may be taught to do it; or he may be brought up to it by moral suasion. In the light of all human experience, and especially the experience of socialists themselves, the absurdity of all such claims is perfectly evident. Anarchy and licentiousness have been the legitimate and inevitable results of all attempts to carry out such baseless schemes.

Penalty Necessary. — State authority, therefore, must enforce law by penalty, if need be. Purely moral considerations, such as the sense of right, and the approval or disapproval of conscience, fail to reach the desired result of preventing man from interfering with the rights of others: guilt must be made dangerous, and crime must be made a source of serious evil to the criminal himself.

Penalty Essential. — That the coercive power may be most effective, the penalty must be strictly proportioned to the guilt of transgressing the law in each particular case; both law and penalty must be clearly understood by all concerned; and the penalty must, if possible, inevitably follow the transgression. The only hope of public freedom and progress, in man's present moral condition, arises from the wise combination of this coercive power of civil authority with the best moral instruction and direction.

2d. The Place of Sovereignty in Civil Authority. — In civil authority the sovereignty resides in the state itself, which is before, and therefore above, all kings and rulers. But in the actual exercise of authority that sovereignty is usually delegated by the state to one or more of its members. It is its duty to delegate it to those best fitted for its right exercise.

Sovereignty is Originally in the State, and not in any king, or in any other ruler whatsoever. This is established by the fact, that the state exists before all rulers; and by the further fact, that it has its own great ends for the accomplishment of which it is responsible, and in which rulers can, at the most, be but its instruments. The *divine right* of kings has therefore no basis on which to rest; except that it is the divine right and duty of kings, when once invested with sovereignty, to administer the civil authority as the instruments of the Moral Governor, and for the highest good of the state.

To Whom to be Delegated.— It is the duty of the state to delegate the exercise of the sovereignty to those who are best fitted to administer it for the ends to be secured. A pure democracy, or state in which all the people assemble for the purpose of exercising sovereign authority, being practically impossible, it becomes a necessity of the state to delegate its authority temporarily or permanently to some one or more of its members, who shall be competent to govern in the name of the state. Hence arise the various forms of government,— monarchies, oligarchies, republics, etc.

Qualifications for Sovereignty.—The elements of fitness for the exercise of the prerogatives of sovereignty are found in certain natural and moral qualifications. There should be a natural talent for leading men and directing them to the accomplishment of the great social ends of the state. He who has not this will make but a poor ruler. A congress of men without it may be even worse for a nation. There should be a complete understanding of the ends of government and of the means to be used in their attainment, and the largest possible ability in using these means for accomplishing the desired ends. Men who are wanting in these qualities are unfit to be intrusted with the prerogatives of sovereignty, whether as individuals or as a congress or national assembly. There should also be the moral qualifications: a thorough knowledge of principle; a firm adherence to right and truth; and an unselfish patriotism and love of public liberty. Men who have not these moral qualifications are unfit for the place of rulers. However competent they may be in other respects, they will, whether acting as individuals or as a congress, wreck the state by their *depravity*.

3d. The Basis of Civil Law.

As the state, as an organic body, is under the Moral Governor and responsible to him, its sovereignty is only a delegated and not an absolute one. It is therefore the duty of the state to base all its laws on his immutable law of right.

The Divine Law the Basis. — The only safe basis of civil law is the divine law of right. That law of right is the law which is administered in God's moral government of the world. Whatever conforms to it may continue to exist and to prosper; whatever does not conform to it must inevitably perish.

The Sovereign a Law Proclaimer. — The position of the sovereign authority in the state is therefore never that of a *law-making power* in the strict sense, but that of a *law-proclaiming power*. The state is to seek to ascertain what are the moral principles, already ordained of God, which apply to the regulation of the conduct of its citizens in their various stations and relations; and then to embody these principles in laws and apply them to secure public freedom and order.

False Idea of Sovereignty. — The modern idea that the sovereign people may make laws which violate all moral principles, if they choose to do so, is therefore equally baseless and ruinous. The true theory, as expressed in the Scriptures (*Romans* xiii. 1–15), is as follows:

First, that all the authority of law and government is *from God.*

Secondly, that the civil rulers are ordained of God as his agents to carry out *his will* in exercising authority over men.

Thirdly, that in the exercise of that authority they are to be obeyed *as a matter of conscience, and as a part of our obedience to God.*

Civil Law, in its exercise, may therefore be defined to be, the constraint of individual choice by the state acting in accordance with the moral law, for the end of public freedom and order.

4th. The Essential Mechanism of Civil Government.

Civil government comprises the mechanism devised by the state for carrying out its mission of authority for the benefit of society. Its essential functions are the legislative, judicial, and executive. It is the duty of the state to see that they are all performed in strict conformity to the moral law.

The Legislative Function is at the Foundation. — It is necessary that the state should first of all lay down and clearly define the laws which are to govern its citizens in their activities and intercourse, basing them upon higher divine principles and attaching suitable penalties for transgression.   This is the province of the legislator.

It is Obviously the Duty of the Legislator to prepare himself for his work, by seeking to understand man as a social being, by acquainting himself with the nature of the state in general and of his own state in particular, and by grasping the true nature and end of civil law; to confine his work strictly to the sphere assigned him by the state; and to be governed in all his enactments by the principles of the moral law.

The Judicial Function comes next in Order. — The law defines the various forms of transgression, but has reference to no particular case. When some case of transgression, real or apparent, occurs, it becomes necessary to apply the law to this particular case.   In order to this it is necessary to interpret the law carefully; to decide whether the case is an actual violation of it; to render the proper decision, — which involves, where the case is one of crime, the pronouncing of sentence upon the culprit, and in all cases the directing of the action of the executors of the law.   This is the province of the judge.

It is Obviously the Duty of the Judge to understand fully the nature and extent of his judicial authority; to possess a thorough knowledge of the principles of law in general and of the laws of his own state in particular; and to explain and apply these laws with absolute justice and impartiality.

The Executive Function comes Last. — After the law has been made and applied to the particular case, it needs to be carried out or enforced. This is the province of the executive branch of government.

It is Obviously the Duty of the Executive Officer to carry out the law, — as enacted by the legislator and interpreted by the judge, — in accordance with the authority vested in him by the state.   When the law requires him to do that which he believes to be morally wrong, it becomes his duty not to resist the law, but to resign.   He is not the judge of the law, but he must conform his individual conduct to the moral law.

5th. The Reach of Civil Authority.

— It is evident that the control of civil authority stops with man's outer life and conduct.   From its very nature it can regulate overt action only.

Limited to Overt Acts. — Civil government can only take cognizance of dispositions of men as they express themselves in act.   Its machinery is too coarse and clumsy to enable it in any way to ascertain and understand the inner principles of action. It takes no notice of man's *wish* for his neighbor's death so long as it remains a wish only; but so soon as the wish becomes choice and leads to the *death-blow*, it is recognized as that "malice prepense," which is the basest element of murder. It leaves it to the moral law and conscience and the Moral Governor to deal with those inward states of the soul which do not express themselves in executive action, while its own efforts are turned to the protection of life and property and to the preservation of public freedom and order by the punishment of actual evil-doers and the rewarding of those who do well.

It Permits True Freedom.— Civil government, in its regulation of public conduct, is therefore bound to leave every man free to attain to the true moral manhood and life. It must recognize the equality of men in this moral freedom; must allow freedom of thought and belief; must secure freedom of conscience; and must permit unrestrained action in everything not subversive of public freedom and virtue. In a righteous government the largest individual freedom is compatible with the largest public freedom and the most perfect public order.

Subject 2d. The State and Political Improvement.—It is the second duty of the state toward its citizens to devise and furnish the requisite means for improving and perfecting the sphere of social activity which it prepares. This includes especially the duties of increasing the facilities for intercourse, and of providing for the public intelligence and morality. These are chiefly duties of culture and direction.

1st. The State and Public Intercourse and Influence. — The importance and success of man's work in his relations in the state depend even more largely upon the ease with which he can exert and receive influence and power, and the extent to which these may reach, than upon the public freedom and order which are essential to prepare the sphere of social activity. It is therefore the duty of the state to furnish, so far as practicable, the facilities requisite for the largest and freest intercourse.

The Greater Human Tasks are only possible where this larger sphere of activity allows man's desire to co-operate with men for grander than individual and family ends (p. 52) to be brought into full play. The larger the sphere furnished, the greater the possible results through this co-operation. Ten men, by organized and wisely-directed co-operation, can often accomplish what a million could not accomplish, each working in isolation; and the power of the million so organized and directed, and aided by appliances of steam and electricity, becomes irresistible, when wielded by some master mind for some great end.

This duty involves the regulation of whatever conduces to this end of increased intercourse and influence, as, for example, the rights of property, inventions, and publications; the transaction of business and commerce; the transportation of mails; the necessary internal improvements; the care of the poor and unfortunate classes; and the right of raising the requisite means for such purposes by equitable taxation. In all such work the state must be guided by a strict and impartial regard for the public good.

2d. The State and Public Education and Morals. — The freedom, reach, and value of man's work depend most of all upon the intelligence and virtue of the people; since the greatest and best purposes can only be accomplished by the intelligent co-operation of great masses of good men. It is therefore the duty of the state to provide for the education and moral elevation of its citizens.

Education Essential. — As education is essential to all the great ends for which the state exists, — public freedom and order, wide co-operation in grand social aims, — it becomes the right of the state to regulate the popular education. This becomes an absolute necessity to the continued existence of the state where a popular form of government prevails.

State Systems of Instruction. — When the intelligence of the people is not otherwise certainly secured, it is the duty of the state to establish and direct a general system of education, that regular and systematic instruction may be insured. This includes the right to appoint the teachers, determine the text-books, and to control the internal regulations of each and every school; and the right, where the efficiency of the system demands it, to provide for its support by taxation, and to compel attendance.

Objection from Liberty. — In reply to those who object to public education as infringing upon human liberty, it need only be said that it is obvious to every right-thinking man, that liberty to remain in brutish ignorance is not one of the essential and inalienable rights of man; and no man will claim it to be so who is what a man ought to be. Moreover all such ignorance prevents the ends of public freedom and progress, and is therefore immoral.

Objection to Taxation. — To those who object to taxation for educational purposes, as being unjust and oppressive to the rich, it is sufficient to reply, that the power to acquire wealth, and security in retaining and enjoying it, depend upon the popular intelligence and virtue, and such taxation is therefore both proper and equitable, as the rich thus reap the largest advantage from such taxation.

Moral and Religious Instruction. — As public virtue is more important than even public intelligence, and as it has been shown (p. 263) that this cannot be secured by a mere secular education alone, it becomes the right and duty of the state to combine with this education such moral and religious instruction as will tend to bring men up to the proper moral elevation.

Objection and Answer. — If it be said that the conscience of the atheist, the infidel, and the free-thinker generally, will be oppressed by such instruction; it is a sufficient answer, were no other possible, that in a Christian land such as this the conscience of a vastly greater number would be oppressed by the opposite course.

But beyond this, the fact that such instruction is an absolute necessity to the highest public freedom, order, progress, and perfection, is an unanswerable argument in favor of its being used for this end.

The One True Moral System the Basis. — It is absolutely essential to the highest public good, that the state should regulate its conduct toward its citizens by the one true moral system as ascertained by the proper investigation. Individual opinion, or conscience, or no-conscience, has no weight as against the requirements of this system, according to which the affairs of the world are regulated by the Moral Governor, and according to which the affairs of the state must be regulated if its continued existence and the good of its subjects are to be secured. The thief may reason himself into the belief that his stealing is right, the murderer that the murder is justifiable, the socialist that free-love is virtuous, the infidel that there is no morality, the atheist that there is no God; but the state that attempts to regulate its course in harmony with all such vagaries will stultify and ruin itself, and so destroy public freedom and order.

Instruction in that System Essential. — That the true moral system should be somehow fixed in the public mind is therefore indispensable to public morality and public good. The very highest interests bind the state to secure the moral and religious instruction of the people along with their secular education. This does not of course necessarily involve state instruction in religion for the sake of *piety*, for that is the province of the Church; but for the sake of the *public weal*.

Topic Second. Duties of the State toward itself and other States. — As it is one main design of the state to direct men, as associated under its authority, in working out a national mission as its part of a greater world mission, this design determines the duties of each state both to itself and to other states.

The Great Plan. — The world is but one plan of the Moral Governor, a plan taking in all the nations. Professor Arnold Guyot, in *The Earth and Man*, has admirably presented this idea, from the point of view of the historian and physical geographer. The geographical march of history has brought out clearly various features in this great plan and its parts.

First, it has shown that the three Continents of the North are organized for the development of man; and that each is fitted in its physical structure to perform a special function in that development. "Asia, Europe, and North America, are the three grand stages of humanity in its march through the ages. Asia is the cradle where man passed his infancy, under the authority of law, and where he learned his dependence upon a sovereign master. Europe is the school where his youth was trained, where he waxed in strength and knowledge, grew to manhood, and learned at once his liberty and his moral responsibility. America is the theatre of his activity during the period of manhood; the land where he applies and practises all he has learned, brings into action all the forces he has acquired, and where he is still to learn that the entire development of his being and his own happiness are possible only by willing obedience to the laws of his Maker."

Secondly, it has also made it evident, that the three Continents of the South,—on which nature has bestowed her gifts with most lavish hand, and which have hitherto been outcasts in appearance,—are to be brought into the great movement of human progress. "The races inhabiting them are captives in the bonds of all powerful nature; they will never break down the fences that sunder them from us. It is for us, the favored races, to go to them. Tropical nature cannot be conquered and subdued, save by civilized men, armed with all the might of discipline, intelligence, and of skilful industry. It is, then, from the northern Continents that those of the South await their deliverance; it is by the help of the civilized men of the temperate continents that it shall be vouchsafed to the man of the tropical lands to enter into the movement

26

of universal progress and improvement, wherein mankind should share."

Thirdly, it has moreover brought the world already to that age in which the three historical Continents of the North as leaders are carrying out their beneficent mission for the three Continents of the South, which appear as their aids in the great plan of the world. "The people of the temperate Continents will always be the men of intelligence, of activity, the brain of humanity, if I may venture to say so; the people of the tropical Continents will always be the hands, the workmen, the sons of toil." "Each Northern Continent has its Southern Continent near by, which seems more especially commended to its guardianship and placed under its influence. Africa is already European at both extremities; North America leans on South America, which is indebted to the example of the North for its own emancipation and its own institutions. Asia is gradually receiving into her bosom the Christian nations of Europe, who are transforming her character, and beginning thence to settle the destinies of Australia. Lastly, the Christian missions are organizing upon a larger and larger scale in the two leading maritime countries of the globe, England and America, to whom the dominion of the sea seems granted for this end; and by engrafting upon all the nations this vital principle of civilized societies, without which no real community can exist between them, are preparing and hasting the true brotherhood, the spiritual brotherhood, of the whole human race."

The Christian State in this Plan. — In this grand plan each Christian state has its ascertainable place and part. The knowledge of that place and part has been made possible by the modern progress in comparative physical geography, the branch of science in which Professor Guyot is the brightest ornament, and in social science, and the philosophy of history. It is one of the highest offices of the true Christian statesman, to ascertain the mission of his own state, and its part in the greater mission of the world, and to fashion his statesmanship accordingly.

The Aim of the Plan. — That this plan in its whole and parts has in view the moral perfection of the race is evident at once from what has been already presented, and from the special revelation of the divine purpose in the redemption of the world.

Subject 1st. Duty of the State toward Itself. — As each state has its part in this one plan of the world, it becomes the duty of each to ascertain its own particular mission, and to seek intelligently to fulfil it.

The Mission to be Ascertained. — The nation must seek to ascertain its mission, in order that its work, for itself, may be intelligently directed. This is as indispensable for the nation as for the individual; and as much more important for it, as the nation is greater than the individual, and its mission grander.

The American Mission. — The mission of our own nation is to demonstrate to the nations of the earth the power of a free Bible Christianity to give to man the highest freedom, and to elevate him to the noblest moral manhood.

Says Professor Guyot: "Luther drew the Bible forth from the dust of libraries, where it lay forgotten, at the moment when Columbus discovered the New World. Will any one believe that here was only an accidental coincidence? More than this, for the first foundations were then laid of the edifice rising at the present day before our eyes, the actual construction of which, three centuries and a half later, enables us to see the providential connection of the two events.

"The founders of social order in America are indeed the true offspring of the Reformation — true Protestants. The Bible is their code. Imbued with the principles of civil and religious liberty they find written in the gospel, and for which they have given up their former country, they put them in practice in this land of their choice. They are all brethren, children of the same Father — this is equality, independence, liberty. They submit from the heart to their Divine Leader, and to his law; this is the principle of order. Now the union of these two terms is free obedience to the Divine Will, which is the condition of a normal development, the supreme end of the education of man."

Special American Duty. — It is, therefore, the special duty of the American nation to keep fast hold upon this its mission, and to seek to fulfil it perfectly by building all its institutions upon the basis of a Bible Christianity, and by rooting all its political and social life in that Christianity. To institutions so built, and a life so rooted, it owes all the prosperity which it has enjoyed in the past. To departures from its fundamental Christian idea, it owes all the great judgments with which it has been visited.

Most pressing of all its duties toward itself, at the present day, is the duty to guard against the danger, to which it is now exposed, of suffering this solid foundation to be removed, and of being robbed of this noblest mission of the ages. It behooves the nation to set itself as adamant against the efforts of the hosts of godless political demagogues, and of infidel and immoral subjects, who are doing their utmost to destroy the Christianity, which is the very basis of that beneficent power to which they owe all their blessings, and to unfit the state for that Christian mission which is its chief glory.

Subject 2d. Duty of the State toward other States. — It becomes the duty of each state, as having part with all other states in the great divine plan of the world, to aid them in ascertaining and realizing the true conception of their various missions.

This duty takes a special form with the intelligent and Christian nations, and increases in its obligation with their increasing intelligence and influence.

Duties of the Nobler Races. — "The privileged races have duties to perform, proportioned to the gifts they possess. To impart to other nations the advantages constituting their own glory, is the only way of legitimating the possession of them.

"We owe the inferior races the blessings and the comforts of civilization; we owe them the intellectual development they are capable of; above all, we owe them the Gospel, which is our glory, and will be their salvation; and if we neglect to help them partake in all these blessings, God will some time call us to a strict account." *The Earth and Man.*

The Special Duty of our own Nation to the other nations is seen, in the light of its mission, to be a most solemn and momentous one. It is to illustrate for them the true Christian freedom, purity, and prosperity; to arouse in them a longing for the same blessings; and to co-operate, by the gracious and benign influences of the Gospel of peace, in elevating them to the best Christian civilization. It is to bring the nations into the great forward movement toward the moral perfection of the world, along the only possible line of moral progress, — the line pointed out by a genuine Bible Christianity.

In performing this duty in the greater society of states, each state is to be guided by the same general principles of conservation, improvement, and direction, which hold among individuals. *The good of mankind is one;* and it is the duty of statesmen and states to recognize this as a first truth worthy to be placed at the basis of all state morality, and all statecraft as well. The same fundamental moral principles should control in all the intercourse of peace, and should govern and ultimately put an end to all war.

The Law of Nations. — The general principles of ethics must therefore regulate the comity of nations, their treaties, alliances, and confederations. They furnish the rules which should govern all acts of national courtesy, and all the forms of national friendship, union, and intercourse.

Origin of War.— War arises, in the intercourse of the nations, or within the state itself, by reason of some wrong or injustice of one or both the parties which become involved in it.

Righteous War. — By the law of conservation war is righteous in defence of the existence and essential rights of the nation, just as self-defence is righteous in the case of individuals. Every state is responsible for the righteous continuance of its own being. War is undoubtedly a fearful evil; but it is not so great an evil as public dishonor, and the triumph of injustice and tyranny in the world. It is, however, to be resorted to by a state only in the last extremity, when all other measures have been tried in vain.

The Prevention of Wars.— It is a part of the mission of the Christian nation to aid in putting an end to wars by helping to put an end to all forms of national wrong and injustice.

First, this may be done *by diffusing the principles of a Christian morality.* The nations may thus be led to a true sense of right and justice, and the occurrence of wrong and injustice be prevented. When wrong has been done, the true morality will lead the nation, in which its principles prevail, to the acknowledgment and reparation of the wrong.

Secondly, it may be done, as has been shown by recent events, *by the arbitration of nations friendly to both the nations* which have a just or imagined reason for war. As the nations increase in righteousness, or, in other words, as the Christian morality becomes more prevalent, *courts of arbitration* will doubtless have increasing weight and influence.

Thirdly, as the world becomes more fully conscious of its unity, a *Congress of the Nations* will doubtless become a great power in deciding the principles of international law and polity; in settling the differences that arise between states; and in protecting the weak from oppression and destruction by the strong. When the nations come to understand their various parts in the one great plan for the moral regeneration of humanity, such a congress will be one of the most efficient aids to the nobler nations in lifting all the others up to their own height of attainment and character.

Topic Third. Duties of the State toward God.— As the state is an organic unit, whose mission is just as truly wrought out under the Moral Governor as is the mission of the individual, this determines the duty of the state toward God himself and toward his law.

Subject 1st. Acknowledgment of God. — A state must have some religion, true or false; its only safety is found in holding to the true religion. It is the duty of the state to acknowledge, everywhere and in every proper way, the rightful sovereignty of God over it, and to recognize his law as its absolute standard of right and duty.

Religion Inevitable. — The state must have some form of religious faith, good or bad, true or false. Man is a religious being. He must carry his religion into the state with him. The state, if it would conserve public freedom and order, must use appeals to conscience and to the belief in God and immortality. It must have its fundamental religious beliefs. Without some well-established religious principles, it can gain no strong and enduring hold upon its citizens; and, without some fixed standard of right and wrong, it can furnish no strong and stable guiding and controlling power, and must therefore sink into anarchy.

True Religion Essential. — The only righteousness or safety for the state is found in holding fast to the true religion. If the state is to maintain public freedom and order, its ultimate standard of appeal must be the *true standard*. If there is a perfect standard of morality, and if a revelation of this is contained in the Christian system, then duty toward the Moral Governor binds the state to accept the *Christian system* as the basis of national law and life.

Christianity to be Acknowledged. — It is therefore the duty of the Christian state to embody the great moral principles of the Christian system in its constitution and organic law, and in its institutions. It is its duty publicly and officially to acknowledge God as its Governor, and his law as its authoritative rule of action. If Christianity is the only true scheme of moral reconstruction for human society (p. 166), then it is the duty of the Christian state to acknowledge it as embodying, in the highest form, the only way of righteousness and life ordained for the nation.

Subject 2d. Conformity to the Law of God. — Duty toward God requires of the state that it should actually conform its conduct to the will of God as the immutable law of right.

Actual Conformity to Moral Law. — Outward acknowledgment of God is not the sum of the duty of the state toward the Moral Governor. This world is the scene of the judgment of the nations. That judgment is in strict righteousness. It is a divine decree revealed in Providence as truly as in the Scriptures, that "the nation and kingdom that will not serve God shall perish;" and, in accordance with that decree, the nations of the earth have always been judged in strict righteousness. National departure from God has in all ages invariably gone before national destruction, and made it inevitable. The Moral Governor has in this way taught the lesson that it is the duty of the nation to conform its conduct to his righteous law. The state is morally bound to conduct its affairs in accordance with God's law, whether revealed in man's nature, or in the government of the world, or in the Scriptures.

Union of Church and State. — This does not involve any union of church and state. The state has to do with religion, not for the sake of purifying or propagating it, nor for the sake of developing personal piety and saving men, — for that is the work of the church; but for the sake of public freedom and order, in its progress toward the accomplishment of its appointed national mission.

Nor does it involve the error, into which the Puritans fell, of supposing that the *views* and *opinions* of all men must be brought, by persecution, if need be, to conform to the standard which has been set up by the government. It allows to every man the right to his own religious views, so long as these do not bring him into outward and open conflict with law and authority.

Opinion of Judge Story. — "The promulgation of the great doctrines of religion, the being, and attributes, and providence of one Almighty God; the responsibility to him for all our actions, founded upon moral accountability; a future state of rewards and punishments; the cultivation of all the personal, social, and benevolent virtues; — these never can be a matter of indifference in any well-ordered community. It is, indeed, difficult to conceive how any civilized society can well exist without them. And, at all events, it is impossible, for those who believe in the truth of Christianity as a divine revelation, to doubt that it is the especial duty of government to foster and encourage it among all the citizens and subjects. This is a point wholly distinct from that of the right of private judgment in matters of religion, and of the freedom of public worship, according to the dictates of one's conscience." *Exposition of the Constitution*, p. 260.

SECTION II.

Duties of the Citizen.

The nature and mission of the state determine the duties of the citizen. They are responsive to the nation's work for the citizen himself, and to its mission for the world.

Topic First. The Citizen as Protected in Freedom. — As the state, by its exercise of authority, protects the citizen in the enjoyment of all his blessings and furnishes him a wide sphere for development and activity, there obviously arise the duties of honor and affection for the state and its constituted authorities; of support and defence of its existence, rights, and institutions; and of obedience to its just laws.

The inherent dignity and importance of the state and the innumerable and great blessings it confers upon the citizen are the measure of his obligation to cherish sentiments of honor and affection toward it.

Civil Respect and Honor. — Respect and honor to the state and its constituted authorities lie at the basis of duties to the state. It is worthy of the highest honor as embodying a great and beneficent idea of the Moral Governor. It is therefore the duty of the subject to treat with becoming reverence its laws, its established forms and usages, and its magistrates and officers, whether legislative, judicial, or executive.

Civil Affection and Gratitude. — The sentiment of honor prepares the way for affection and gratitude to the state, as the source of the greatest personal and public good, in giving the freest scope for the widest human intercourse, connections, and enterprises. Hence arise love and gratitude, leading to that most ennobling civic virtue, *patriotism*.

The sentiments of honor and affection prepare the citizen for the duty of self-denial and effort for the support and defence of the existence, rights, and institutions of the state. This duty, like the preceding, finds the measure of its obligation in the inherent dignity and the beneficent mission of the state.

Civil Self-Denial. — Self-denial for the state has been judged a duty in all ages, since the sentiment of patriotism first found place in the hearts of men. It has led them to unlimited self-denial and sacrifice for the sake of their native country. They have been willing to peril everything to preserve it in its integrity and glory, and have judged it to be right and virtuous to do so.

Civil Support. — Active effort for the state has always been judged a duty. Men have everywhere agreed that it is the duty of the citizen to support the state in its dangers by needful supplies. Hence the citizen is called upon to submit to taxation and to the regulations of trade and commerce by which the revenue is secured for this end. With equal universality, men have agreed that it is the duty of the citizen to defend the state against its enemies by personal service, even to the extent of risking the life, in repelling foreign enemies, and in putting down domestic sedition and rebellion.

The two preceding duties prepare the way for the rendering of a hearty and complete obedience to the just laws and requirements of the state. This is the capital duty of the citizen, without which the ends of the state cannot possibly be accomplished.

Civil Obedience. — Obedience is to be rendered to the state as to God. It has been seen that the state, as a divine institution, and, so far as its laws are based on God's immutable law, embodies and represents the authority of the Moral Governor himself, — so that he who resists the ministers of the state resists God.

Limit of Civil Obedience. — The limit to the requirement of obedience to the civil authority is reached when the state requires of the citizen that which is contrary to the revealed will of God, or morally wrong. It is to be remembered that so-called *legislators* are not *law-makers*, but *law-proclaimers*. When they pass beyond their true sphere, and not only require of men what the Moral Governor has not authorized them to require, but has rather positively forbidden, the obligation to obedience ceases. For example, the state has no right to pass laws requiring man to blaspheme, or to steal, or to profane the Sabbath; and the citizen is therefore under no obligation to obey any such unjust and immoral laws, or he is rather under most solemn obligations not to obey them.

Duty toward Unrighteous Authority and Law. — When the limit of righteous obedience is reached, various courses of conduct may be open for the subject to pursue:

First, he may disobey and take the consequences. This the Apostles did, when they were forbidden by the rulers to speak and teach in the name of Jesus.   By acting in that way which he believes to be right, and so suffering in the cause of right, even to the extent of martyrdom, if need be, he avoids the evils which result from resistance by force, preserves from destruction whatever is good and wholesome in the existing civil authority, and brings to bear upon society a powerful moral influence in favor of the cause in which he suffers.   Such a course often brings better results than can possibly be attained by the violent method of *rebellion* and *civil war*.

Secondly, he may, while passively resisting, seek to effect the change of unjust or immoral laws by constitutional or legal methods: by revision or repeal of the laws through the legislature; or by review and decision upon their constitutionality by the courts of justice.   This course, where practicable, prevents that rousing of the angry passions of brethren; and avoids that disruption of society, and that destruction, bloodshed, vice, and crime, which inevitably follow upon civil war, that most horrible of all the evils which men inflict upon themselves.

Thirdly, the last resort is open resistance or rebellion, leading to civil war.   That this should be a last resort, to which recourse is to be had after the other methods have been tried and found ineffectual, appears at once from the uncertainty of the results for good and the certainty of great results for evil.   Yet it is nevertheless true that such a course may become a most solemn duty to the oppressed citizens of any state. The resistance may take the form of simple rebellion or of revolution. *Rebellion* may be justifiable where any great wrong is inflicted upon a portion of the citizens of a state, but its only aim should be to secure the correction of the evil and security against its recurrence.   During its continuance those who are engaged in it are bound, as protesting against injustice, to refrain from all approaches to injustice, and to avoid every unnecessary evil.   When the movement has accomplished its legitimate ends, they are bound to lay aside all personal and ambitious aims, and to take their places again as law-abiding citizens.   *Revolution* is justifiable where the wrong and injustice on the part of the civil authority amounts to the permanent subversion of the great ends for which the state exists.   Where national oppression and injustice and corruption usurp the place of freedom and justice and purity, and where the true national mission is made impossible by the inefficiency, or moral worthlessness and baseness, of the existing government, it may become the most sacred duty of the citizens, toward themselves, mankind, and God, to overthrow that government, and build the state anew upon the foundations of right, justice, and truth.

Topic Second.   The Citizen and the National Mission.—

As the state embraces the work of the citizens in its national mission, and as their honor or disgrace is involved in its success or failure, it becomes the duty of the citizen to do his utmost to aid the nation in understanding and accomplishing its mission.

Duty to Elevate the Nation. — The height to which the nation is to rise must always depend upon the elevation of view, character, and conduct to which its citizens attain. It depends especially upon the elevation of those citizens who have chiefly to do with the framing of its policy, the management of its affairs, and the moulding of its destiny.

Duty to Lead to its Mission. — It is therefore obviously the sacred duty of the citizen, to gain if possible true views of the part assigned to the nation in the great plan of the world, and to do his utmost to influence it in acting that part. The obligation to this task evidently increases with the breadth of view, the degree of power, the extent of influence, and the rank and station of the individual; so that it reaches its utmost sacredness in the case of those who have the gift of genius, and who occupy the high places of society, in business and instruction, in church and state.

DIVISION III.

THEISTIC ETHICS.

Statement and Subdivision.

Theistic Ethics is that division of Practical Ethics which treats of the application of the principles of the moral law to the regulation of man's conduct in his immediate relations to God.

As the requirements of the moral law toward God are summed up in supreme devotion to God, Theistic Ethics is simply the unfolding and application of this germ of the law.

The Sphere of Theistic Ethics. — This Division of Practical Ethics has properly nothing to do with the demonstration of the being of God, or with the establishment of the fundamental principles of the moral law. Its sphere is limited to the *application* of what it accepts as clearly demonstrated or established. It accepts the truth of the being of God from *Theoretical Ethics*, which again receives it from *Theology Natural and Revealed*. It also accepts the principle of the law toward God from *Theoretical Ethics*, whose office it is to evolve that germ from the moral consciousness.

As man's spiritual nature, which is in the image of God and brings him into conscious relation to God, is essentially made up of intellect, feelings, and will, supreme devotion to God is naturally considered under three *Chapters*:

Chapter I. Supreme Devotion of the Intellect to God.
Chapter II. Supreme Devotion of the Heart to God.
Chapter III. Supreme Devotion of the Will to God.

Principle of Division.—The necessity for a philosophic and exhaustive principle of division of Theistic Ethics will appear at once to any one at all acquainted with the mechanical and fragmentary treatment so often accorded to this branch of the subject.

Man in God's Image.—God, the Moral Governor, is the Infinite Intellect, Heart, and Will, and reveals himself to man, the finite intellect, heart, and will, as the Infinite Thought, Love, and Power. It is the likeness of man to God that enables him to come into conscious moral relation to God. He has a nature in some degree responsive to the manifestations of the Divine Being. He can read something of the thought of God, can feel something of the goodness of God, and can recognize and in some measure respond to the will of God as power and as law, and as an expression of justice.

Relative Importance of Duties toward God.

— Of the various duties of man, those which have immediate reference to God are entitled to the highest rank. The duties toward God performed will prepare for all other duties, and bring all others in their train; these neglected will lead inevitably to the partial or entire neglect of all others.

This View has Won the Consent of all Ages.—Plato taught that "it should never be thought that there is any branch of human virtue of greater importance than piety toward the Deity." Socrates, in the *Memorabilia* of Xenophon, is represented as speaking of the worship of the gods as a duty acknowledged everywhere, and received by all men as the first command. Cicero, in the *De Officiis*, makes those duties which we owe to the immortal gods the first in importance. This is in accordance with the teaching of Christ: "Thou shalt love the Lord thy God with all thy heart, and with all thy soul, and with all thy mind, and with all thy strength; this is the first commandment."

The Supremacy of these Duties follows, because God is the actual embodiment of the highest good for man, — the infinite thought, love, and power, in which alone the finite and progressive intellect, heart, and will can find complete development, satisfaction, and rest. The height and true glory of man's being can never be reached except as he draws light and inspiration and motive from the one Source of truth and love and power. His knowledge of God, love for God, sympathy with God's will, must measure the height and depth and length and breadth of man's life of duty in the world.

27

CHAPTER I.

SUPREME DEVOTION OF INTELLECT TO GOD.

AS man was made to know, so he was made above all to know God the source and centre and sum of all wisdom and truth. In short, it is the supreme duty of man, as an intellectual being, to strive with all his power to know God and his revelation of his infinite thought.

Activity of intellect toward God is moreover absolutely essential to the highest manhood; and all atheism and scepticism sink man below the true height of his being.

The Supreme Knowledge.—That man was made to know, and to know God has already been shown (p. 36). If it be true — as it undoubtedly is — that the objects upon which the human intellect is exercised decide its breadth and power, then atheism and scepticism, in withdrawing man from the contemplation of the grand idea of God to that of the lower ideas of man and material nature, must dwarf him intellectually. It will appear evident that the right use of the power of thought must require its exercise upon the highest object of thought, not only in order to its own best development, but also in order to the best development and direction in duty of the whole being of man.

The Key to all other Knowledge. — Says Dr. Blackie, in *Self-Culture:* "The idea of God as the absolute self-existent, self-energizing, self-determining Reason, is the only idea which can make the world intelligible, and has justly been held fast by all the great thinkers of the world, from Pythagoras down to Hegel, as the alone key-stone of all sane thinking."

Hence appears the Reasonableness of the Scriptural Requirement that man shall "love God with all his *mind.*" The true answer which every moral being should be able to give to the question, *What am I above all things striving to know?* should be, *God.*

314

SECTION I.

The Binding Force of the Duty.

The binding force of the duty to render to God the supreme devotion of the intellect is self-evident to every man whose moral nature is at all developed and by whom the revelation of God is at all understood.

Topic First. The Obligation is Self-Evident.—If God, the Infinite Wisdom, is the Source and Revealer of all truth, and the Author of all blessing, and if man's mission and destiny can only be understood and achieved in the light of God's being, character, thought, and work, then the duty of the supreme devotion of the powers of intellect to the work of finding out God and his purpose is self-evident.

Topic Second. The Obligation begins with Knowledge.—The obligation to this duty does not wait for a mathematical demonstration of God. The bare imagination, *there may be a God*, Upholder and Governor of all things and the Author of all blessings, binds man to investigate the matter at once and with all his powers; for, if there be such a God, that is the most important fact for man to know, and the nature of that God and his relations to man are the most important things for man to understand. The obligation increases with the increasing clearness of the revelation.

The Duty imposed by the Bare Imagination of a God.—Says Dr. Chalmers, in his *Natural Theology:* "The very idea of a God, even in its most hypothetical form, will bring along with it an instant sense and recognition of the moralities and duties that would be owing to him. Should an actual God be revealed, we clearly feel that there is a something which we ought to be and to do in regard to him. But, more than this, should a possible God be imagined, there is a something not only which we feel that we ought, but a something which we actually ought to do or to be, in consequence of our being visited by such an imagination. . . . . . To this condition there attaches a most clear and incumbent morality. It is to go in quest of that unseen benefactor, who, for aught I know, has ushered me into existence, and spread so glorious a panorama around me. It is to probe the secret of my being and my birth; and, if possible, to make discovery whether it was indeed the hand of a benefactor that brought me forth from the chambers of non-entity, and gave me place and entertainment in that glowing territory, which is lighted up with the hopes and happiness of living men. It is thus that the very conception of a God throws a responsibility after it; and that duty, solemn and imperative duty, stands associated with the thought of a possible Deity, as well as with the sight of a present Deity, standing in full manifestation before us."

The Increasing Obligation.—The same reasoning which makes it evident that with the first whisper of the existence of God, the obligation to search after him with all the powers of the being begins, makes it also appear that the obligation increases with all the increasing evidence of the existence of God and of his various relations to man.

Topic Third. The Obligation is Universal.—The obligation to this duty of searching God and his works is not confined to any one man or class of men, but reaches to all men of all classes. To every man is given his great moral task to work out; to this task everything else in life is subordinate; and it cannot be completed without this divine knowledge. Neither the plea drawn from the cares of worldly business, therefore, nor that from the drudgery of labor, nor yet that from the slavery of custom and fashion, can excuse from this duty.

No Excuse from this Duty.—It is clear that the Moral Governor would not require of man anything that would render impossible the performance of his true moral task, and that he has not so arranged the affairs of this world as to make it necessary for man to neglect that task. When, therefore, those engaged in the practical business of life would turn over the investigation of the great questions concerning God and duty to him, to the scholar or the theologian, and plead their own lack of time for such investigations, that very plea is proof of an entirely false view of the work of life, a view which cannot fail to degrade those who hold it. The worldly business of man is but one means to be used in the accomplishment of his life task, and must be always kept subordinate to that great end of life and made a help in attaining it. Nor does the drudgery attendant upon poverty furnish any better excuse from this great duty to God than the cares of riches. No better right has the slavery of the false and complicated customs and fashions of society to stand between man and this high duty. It is man's sin alone that puts these hindrances in the way of duty; and, in the light of the moral law, all these common pleas, which he urges to excuse himself from seeking to know God in his being, character, and works, are seen to involve the greatest moral wrong and to imply great moral baseness.

SECTION II.

The Range of the Duty.

The forms in which God has revealed himself to man are stated in the order of their increasing importance: that in the material system of the universe; that in man's own constitution; and that in the Christian system. In all these the divine thought appears in all its forms, and man's investigation should extend to them all, with a thoroughness proportioned to the importance of the revelation.

The Breadth of Investigation. — The principles laid down in the preceding *Section* make it obvious that the obligation to study God and his revelation of himself is not confined to any one form in which he has revealed himself, but holds with reference to all the forms, and increases with the importance of the revelation.

Topic First. The Study of the Material System. — Man ought to study God in the material system of the universe, because God has there revealed on the grandest scale his eternal wisdom, goodness, and power, as employed for the benefit of man as his creature, and especially in fitting up the place for the fulfilment of his mission.

The Key to the Interpretation of Nature. — He who would understand anything of the universe must remember that it is a *thought* as well as a *thing;* or, rather, that it is the embodiment of the one great and perfect thought of God. In no other way can its phenomena be interpreted. The language of the true philosopher, as he pursues his investigations, is that of a Kepler, when he exclaims, in ecstasy, "O

27 *

God! I think thy thoughts after thee!" and that of Agassiz, when he affirms, deliberately, that "all just and thorough classification is but an interpretation of the thoughts of the Creator." Starting upon his investigation in this humble spirit of the great philosophers, the plain man, intent upon his mission of duty, will read marvellous lessons of God's infinite wisdom, love, and power in constructing and fitting up the material world as the theatre of that mission; in spreading out before him everywhere blessings in lavish profusion and richness; and in placing manifold means and forces within his reach to aid him in fulfilling his exalted destiny.

Topic Second.   The Study of the Human System. — Man is eminently under obligation to study God in his own constitution, as containing God's plainest, most indispensable revelation of the divine image, and as revealing God's purpose concerning man's appointed mission.

The First Lesson. — The motto of the old Greek, "Know thyself," implied faith in man as the highest and most perfect being; hence the duty to know him was the first and highest duty. To the Christian, however, God is, in his spiritual and immortal being, infinitely higher than man. But if man is made in the image of God, and if the plainest and most direct manifestation of Deity to man is in God's image, that is, in man, — then the duty to study man has a higher reason, namely: *in order to know God.* The binding force of the duty is increased by the fact that in man's nature is found God's fundamental revelation of his own nature to man, without which revelation, as the basis and alphabet, all higher revelation would be unintelligible.

The Second Lesson. — The world may be looked upon as comprising a great system of means and ends. Every being becomes thus a means adapted to some end; and in the nature and structure of each being is declared the great end for which it was intended by its Fashioner. Man may thus be studied in his nature and structure as embodying the design of the Creator; and a true understanding of man, — as a self-active spirit, embodied and for the present bound to the earth, but linked with God and working out an immortal destiny, — will necessarily cast the greatest light upon the purpose of the Moral Governor concerning his duty.

Topic Third.   The Study of the Christian System. — Man is pre-eminently under obligation to study the Christian system of revelation, as containing God's special manifestation of himself in grace to man as a fallen being, needing deliverance and reconstruction. In view of the clear fact of the moral wreck of his being, if there be but a bare probability, or even an imagination, of the existence of such a revelation, he is bound to investigate the matter; to search the evidences; and, if these have any real weight, to study the contents of the revelation as an expression of God's wisdom, power, and grace, and as defining the forms of human duty and the entire moral task.

The Obligation from the Grace. — The argument of Dr. Chalmers, for the search for the being of God, holds with increased force when applied to the revelation of God's grace,— as in that revelation God professes to come nearest to man, and to become in the highest sense his Benefactor. The cavalier manner, in which in these days so many men of professed intelligence treat the appeals of the Christian revelation to man's moral instincts, implies a base indifference to their own highest practical interest, and involves the deepest wrong toward God. Duty to God most clearly binds man to the thorough study of the evidences of the Christian revelation. Doubt is philosophical and allowable only so far as there is a want of any satisfactory evidence, or as the judgment is suspended in the process of seeking and weighing that evidence.

The Common-Sense Principle. — Duty toward God requires that man should accept, for his guidance, in his conduct toward God's revelation, the same common-sense principle which governs him in all the practical affairs of life. Bishop Butler has shown, in his *Analogy*, that "probability is the very guide of life" for man. Man does not wait for demonstration or certainty before he acts. This would in almost all cases be impossible, from both his nature and his condition. He who would refuse to sow his seed until certain of his harvest would never sow at all. "In questions of difficulty, or such as are thought so, where more satisfactory evidence cannot be had, or is not seen; if the result of examination be, that there appears upon the whole, any the lowest presumption on one side, and none on the other, or a greater presumption on one side, though in the lowest degree greater; this determines the question, even in matters of speculation; and in matters of practice, will lay us under an absolute and formal obligation, in point of prudence and of interest, to act upon that presumption or low probability though it be so low as to leave the mind in very great doubt which is the truth. For surely a man is as really bound in prudence to do what upon the whole appears, according to the best of his judgment, to be for his happiness, as what he certainly knows to be so. Nay further, in questions of great consequence, a reasonable man will think it concerns him to remark lower probabilities and presumptions than these; such as amount to no more than showing one side of a question to be as supposable and credible as the other: nay, such as but amount to much less even than this."

The Supreme Interest. — If the evidences of Christianity are found on the whole to render the system probable, then the Bible theology, especially in its scheme of redemption, and moral reconstruction, at once asserts its claim to the supreme attention of the human intellect, as giving the clearest and highest view of man's mission of duty on earth, and affording him the only efficient aid in fulfilling it.

Topic Fourth. The Aim in the Duty. — The aim of the study of the revelations of God should be directed especially to securing clear conceptions of his character or attributes, his providence, his moral government, and his administration of grace, — as these cast the greatest light upon human duty.

Subject 1st. The Attributes of God. — It is man's duty to study the attributes of God as exhibited in his revelations of himself, — since these make up that nature and character of God which furnish the basis of the divine providence, moral government, and grace.

Moral Attributes Chief. — In this study it is man's special duty to give chief attention to the higher moral attributes of Deity, — as these show him what he ought to make his own character.

Natural and Moral Attributes. — The attributes of God have been distinguished into *natural*, or such as are involved in the very idea of a First Cause, or Creator, as personality, unity, spirituality, eternity, omnipresence, and omniscience; and *moral*, or such as belong to him as the Moral Governor of the universe, — as goodness, justice, and holiness.

The Moral Attributes have been called *imitable*, or *communicable*, — "because it is our duty and our destination to admire and imitate these perfections, as they are manifested in the works and ways of God; and by transfusing somewhat of them into our own character and conduct, to experience somewhat of that eternal peace which pervades his infinite mind," and to attain more nearly to that moral perfection which is found in likeness to his perfect character.

The Chief Duty. — It is therefore clearly man's duty to give chief attention to the moral attributes, as his manhood and mission depend chiefly upon these. This duty needs the more to be emphasized, since it is possible always, and, in these days of scientific culture and progress, easy and natural, to give attention to the natural attributes to the exclusion of the moral, and so to dwarf men and pervert their development by introducing a deadening culturism into the place of a helpful morality and Christianity.

To be Studied in Due Proportion. — Moreover it is man's duty to study the moral attributes of Deity in their proper relation and harmony; since it is only in their due co-ordination that they furnish for man a true view of God and the basis of a symmetrical character.

The Harmony of the Attributes. — *Goodness* in Deity is a goodness which is consistent with *justice* and *holiness*. Each attribute is in perfect harmony with every other in completing the perfect character of God. The man who exalts the divine goodness or benevolence above the divine justice dishonors God; and deprives himself of that firm foundation of *righteous principles* on which alone a strong character can be built. Such a man may be considered kind-hearted and benevolent; but his character is both unsymmetrical and unstable, and his influence almost inevitably goes toward unsettling the ideas of justice on which the social fabric rests. The man of genius who teaches men such views of God and forms such character is justly to be regarded as one of the worst enemies of social order, purity, and virtue.

Subject 2d. The Providence of God. — It is man's duty to study God as he has revealed himself in his providence and moral government, — since these reveal to him in some measure the perpetual and universal care of God for his preservation, and the righteous and immutable will of God for his guidance.

Nature of Providence. — The providence of God involves the divine prevision, prearrangement, and government of all beings, and all events. In the present condition of danger and moral disorder, a belief in the superintending agency of a wise and beneficent God is alone adequate to sustain man in all the varied emergencies, and all the thick darkness, through which, from time to time, he is called to pass. When all things seem to go wrong, and when evil and woe seem to prevail, faith in the providence of God is the good man's last resort, and his all-powerful support. It is his duty to seek to understand more and more of the wisdom and love that preside over the universe, that from his times of trial he may come forth honoring God, and with his strength and manhood preserved.

Nature of Moral Government. — The moral government of God is his special arrangement for encouraging virtue, and discouraging vice. According to Bishop Butler (*Analogy*, pt. 1, ch. 2): "The proper formal notion of government is the annexing pleasure to some actions, and pain to others, in our power to do or to forbear, and giving notice of this appointment beforehand to those whom it concerns." And (ch. 8), "Moral government consists, not barely in rewarding and punishing men for their actions, which the most tyrannical person may do, but in rewarding the righteous, and punishing the wicked; in rendering to men according to their actions, considered as good or evil."

Mechanism of Moral Government. — The arrangements of God's moral government for the accomplishment of its ends are very varied and complete. Its principles are embodied in the family, in which the utmost helplessness on the one side appeals to the utmost tenderness on the other for instruction, guidance in virtue, and restraint from vice; in civil society, where the public good requires the development and reward of virtue, and the repression and punishment of vice; in man's own conscience, where there is the approval of virtue, and the condemnation of vice; in man's body, where the peace and serenity of virtue tend to preserve the health and strength, while the unrest and indulgence of vice bring disease and pain and wreck; and, in short, in all the universe, where every force, from the lowest physical to the highest moral, appears as the friend and protector of the virtuous, and as the enemy and destroyer of the vicious.

Moral Government as a Motive. — A strong faith in this righteous and universal government of God is one of the most powerful motive powers in man for sustaining him in righteousness in the great crises of life, and for bringing him up to the true moral height of his being.

Subject 3d. The Grace of God.

— It is man's duty to study the grace of God in the administration of his government under the Christian system, — since here alone he can learn the divine provision for his deliverance from the moral disorder and ruin into which he has fallen.

CHAPTER II.

SUPREME DEVOTION OF THE HEART TO GOD.

AS man was made to love and desire, so he was made above all to love and desire God, as the centre and sum of all good. In short, it is the supreme duty of man as an affectional being to respond with his whole heart to God's revelation of his infinite thought of justice and holiness, of wisdom and love.

Warmth of heart toward God is moreover no less essential, than Godward activity of intellect, to the highest manhood; and all coldness toward the Divine Author and Governor sinks man below the true height of his being.

The Supreme Affection. — The objects upon which the human heart is exercised decide the character and depth of its workings. Coldness or indifference toward God, the good and lovely, must therefore degrade man affectionally. Accordingly, it will everywhere appear that the right use of the heart must require its exercise upon the highest object of love and desire, — both in order to its own best development, and, also, in order to the direction in duty of man's entire being.

The False View. — There is no falser or more pernicious notion than the so common one, that deep and tender feeling, especially toward God, is evidence of a weak and unbalanced nature. The deeper the feelings the more powerful the springs of action. In truth, *a man's force for good in the world, other things being equal, is exactly proportioned to his strength of heart toward God.*

Hence is evident the reasonableness of the Scriptural rule requiring that man shall love God with all his *heart.* The true answer, which every moral being should be able to give to the question, *What do I above all things else love and desire?* should be, *God.*

SECTION I.

Binding Force of the Duty.

The obligation to the duty of supreme devotion of the affections to God is, like that of the supreme devotion of the intellect, self-evident. It begins with the first knowledge of God, and binds all men everywhere and always.

The Obligation Self-Evident. — If God, the infinite good, is the Author of all the good, either actual or possible to man, so that man's mission is bound up with God, then man's duty to render to him the supreme devotion of the heart is self-evident. As the good for man in God is boundless, so the love and desire in man toward God should be boundless.

The Obligation begins with Knowledge. — It is moreover true of this heart devotion as of the devotion of the intellect, that the obligation begins with the first whisper of the existence of such a God of goodness, and that the devotion is due to every form of the divine goodness revealed, and in the highest degree for the highest revelation.

The Obligation is Universal. — The obligation to this duty reaches to all men of all classes. The highest impulsive forces or springs of moral action, which are essential in the working out of the great moral task, are found in man's *feelings toward God,* arising out of his views of God. If the right life is impossible without these divine springs, then the supreme devotion of the heart to God is demanded of every man.

It follows that no one can rightly allow anything to stand before God in his heart, without preventing the accomplishment of his true moral mission. When any other affections are allowed to become supreme and controlling, they blind, narrow, and debase man, and unfit him for the task of life.

SECTION II.

Range of the Duty.

The infinite goodness of God, as revealed to man, takes chiefly the following forms: infinite excellence or perfection; infinite righteousness or justice in his dealings with man as a subject of his government; and infinite beneficence and grace in his dealings with man as a creature of his bounty and a transgressor of his law. Hence arise the various duties.

First, to God as Infinite Excellence. — When God's goodness appears as infinite perfection or loveliness in himself considered, duty requires such feelings as *esteem* and *adoration; delight* or *complacency* in God; *sympathy* with God in his wise and loving plan; *desire* for God as the sum of all perfection and the only satisfying portion for a soul made in his image.

Secondly, to God as Infinite Righteousness. — When God's goodness appears as righteousness or justice in his dealings with man as a subject of his moral government, duty requires the exercise of such feelings as *reverence* and *godly fear*.

Thirdly, to God as Infinite Beneficence. — God's goodness may manifest itself as love and mercy toward man as dependent or wretched; or as grace toward man as sinful or undeserving.

God's goodness as love and mercy, exercised in creation and providence, obviously binds man to render to him *gratitude* and *love*, in view of his past blessings; to exercise *trust* or *rest* in God, including *resignation* as *confidence* in his goodness in the present; and to cherish *hope* in God, because of his assured goodness for the future.

God's goodness, as grace to the sinner, binds man — in view of that system which proposes to lift him out of his sin and death and to bring him into full union and sympathy with God — to exercise *penitence*, with a boundless *gratitude, confidence, hope,* and *devotion*.

28

CHAPTER III.

SUPREME DEVOTION OF THE WILL TO GOD.

AS man was made to lead a life of activity under law, so he was made above all to lead it under God, whose will is the true law of human conduct. In short, it is the supreme duty of man, as a voluntary and free being, to give himself to a life of obedience and service to that being whose will is his highest law and whose service is his noblest activity.

Activity of will toward God is no less essential to the complete manhood than activity of the intellect or heart toward him; and all inactivity or disobedience Godward dwarfs and prevents man from attaining to the true height of his being.

The Supreme Purpose. — It is evident, from the principles already presented, that he who fails to set before himself God and his will, as his guide and standard in all the planning and execution of the work of life, belittles and degrades himself; and, by the law-breaking which such a course involves, dooms himself not only to the penalty of wasted energy, but also to the added penalty of self-destruction. *Man's true glory* is reached when he brings his will into perfect conformity to the divine will. As all great thought is attained only by thinking over God's infinite thought, so all truly noble work is performed only by working with all our energies along the line of God's infinite purpose.

Hence appears the Reasonableness of the Scriptural Rule which requires that man should love God with all his *strength*. The true answer which every moral being should be able to give to the question, *What am I above all things seeking to do?* should be, *The will of God.*

The Obligation. — It is, moreover, self-evident that this devotion of the active powers to God is universally binding, and that the duty begins with the dawning knowledge of God.

Obligation Self-Evident. — It is a fundamental principle that the will of God as Creator and Moral Governor is the supreme law of the universe. If, therefore, he reveals his will, it becomes at once evident that every man is bound to respond to that revelation by the supreme devotion of all his active powers to the carrying out of that will in obedience and suitable services.

Obligation begins with Knowledge. — It is moreover true of this devotion of will, as of the devotion of intellect and heart, that the obligation begins with the first whisper of the existence of such a divine will and law; and that the devotion is due to the divine will in whatever form revealed, and in the highest degree to the highest and most complete form.

Divisions of the Duty. — Man's first and all-comprehensive duty, in his activity under the moral law, is the duty of obedience to God. In connection with this and in subordination to it arise certain special duties toward God: such as the appropriate outward expression in worship of the views and feelings reached by the devotion of the intellect and heart, and the diligent use of any provision God may have made for the repair of his moral ruin. These furnish the subjects of the following *Sections:*

Section 1. Obedience toward God.
Section 2. Worship of God.
Section 3. Acceptance of the Divine Scheme of Moral Reconstruction.

SECTION I.

Obedience toward God.

Supreme devotion requires, in general, that man should conform all his activities toward God — so far as they are properly subject to his own will — to God's will. The nature and grounds of this duty furnish the *Topics* to be treated.

Topic First. The Nature of the Obedience. — Obedience toward God follows naturally upon those right views and feelings, already considered, as involved in supreme devotion of the intellect and heart to God. It is utterly impossible that man should have correct conceptions of God's character, providence, moral government, and grace, and cherish right feelings in view of them, without a consequent life of obedience.

Obedience is here used in the Narrow Sense. — In the wide sense, the duty of obedience to God's will comprehends all man's duties, — those toward himself and his fellow-men, as well as those toward God: but obedience toward God, as treated in Theistic Ethics, covers only that portion of man's duty which has direct reference to God, and is performed directly toward him.

Obedience toward God, in order to be dutiful, should be intelligent, cordial, prompt, and complete.

Obedience Intelligent. — The inanimate and irrational creatures of God attain the end of their being by the working of necessary forces, or by blind instinct or appetites: man was made to reach the end of his being by the exercise of reason, and he can therefore meet with the approval of the Creator, in the highest sense, only when his obedience is intelligent. Intelligent views of duty, coming from the supreme devotion of the intellect to God, must precede obedience as its condition.

Obedience Cordial. — Obedience to the divine will must be not a matter of form merely, but a matter of the heart. The sincere feeling of reverence, regard, and love to God, growing out of right views of God, must be at the root of all right obedience to God.

Obedience Prompt and Complete. — Obedience to the divine will must neither be hesitating nor partial. It must arise from the free, spontaneous, and prompt movings of an enlightened will, and must bend all the powers of man's being — none left out — to the fulfilment of his duty toward his Maker. Complete obedience must also have respect to the will of God, not only as shown *in what he commands*, but also as shown *in what he does;* since that determines *what we are to suffer*, and since duty requires that man should suffer with resignation whatever God in his providence sees fit to inflict.

Topic Second. The Grounds of the Obedience. — The obligation of man to such obedience toward God is apparent from God's relations to man: as his Creator and Moral Governor; as his ideal of perfection; and as the end of his being.

God is Man's Creator and Moral Governor; therefore man should obey him. It has been seen that the highest right to anything, that is admitted among men, is *the right of production*. The producer has a right to what he produces, — is the principle at the basis of all human property. To God as his Creator man belongs absolutely; since God is the absolute producer of man and all his blessings actual and possible. God is therefore his rightful Governor; God's will his rightful law. The denial of the duty of obedience to God's will would involve the denial of the very principle which enables man to claim anything as his own, and which is one of the greatest incentives to all free activity. Paul therefore presents the true philosophy, when he declares that *the commandment* (or law of God) *is "just."*

God is Man's Pattern, or Ideal of Perfection; therefore man should obey him. As man was made in the image of God, the ideal, to attain to which is his true glory, is found in God. In God, in an infinite degree, are all the attributes and all the perfections, which man must possess in order to reach his true manhood. The law of God, as expressing his will concerning man, may justly be looked upon as God's direction how man may secure the most perfect likeness to himself; and obedience thus becomes the imperative duty of every man. This is in accordance with Paul's teaching that *the commandment is " holy."*

God is the True End of Man's Being; his law is but the expression of his way of giving himself in his fulness to man for his enjoyment; therefore man should obey his law. One true and original aim of the law of God was to mark out, not only the way of righteousness and of perfection, but also *the way of blessedness*. This is in accordance with the teaching of Moses when he declared to Israel that *God had given them all the commandments "for their good always."* This is also in accordance with Paul's teaching that *the commandment is " good."*

The Infinite Reasonableness of Obedience toward God thus appears from every point of view. Whether man consider God in his infinite excellence, as his Lawgiver, his pattern or his blessedness, he cannot deny the obligation without casting away right reason. It is a still more solemn practical truth that while by obedience he may reach the true manhood in righteousness, holiness, and true blessedness, he cannot neglect this duty, without inflicting upon himself the inevitable penalty which follows upon *the worst of all forms of law-breaking*, — as aimed directly at God; and dooming himself to perpetually increasing imperfection and wretchedness.

28 *

SECTION II.

Worship of God.

As God is a Personal Being, it is proper that man should express to him directly his sense of his infinite excellence and glory. That expression takes form in worship, which is properly man's recognition of God's infinite worth. It is the natural result of the supreme devotion of the soul to God. It is an instinctive principle in human nature, which has asserted itself in all places and all ages.

Worship Natural to Man. — This has already been shown (p. 36). Man finds in God the satisfaction of his being. God is of infinite *worth* to him. Worship has been as universal as faith in a Superior Being controlling man's course and destiny. The worship of the fetich and idol, of the forces of nature, of the heavenly bodies, of man himself, and of the one true and living God, all alike prove the natural impulse in man to give expression to his sense of the divine worth.

The duty of worshipful recognition of God's infinite excellence requires the reverent treatment of everything whereby he has revealed himself to men. It therefore especially forbids the irreverent and profane use of his names and attributes.

Tendency to Profanity. — "All literature, whether profane or Christian, shows how strong is the tendency in human nature to introduce the name of God even on the most trivial occasions. Not only are those formulas, *Adieu, Good-by,* or *God be with you,* and *God forbid,* which may have had a pious origin, constantly used without any recognition of their true import; but even persons professing to fear God often allow themselves to use his name as a mere expression of surprise." *Dr. Hodge.*

The habit of *profane swearing* is most useless and foolish in itself; most offensive to all right-thinking men; and most vicious in the sight of the moral law, as exhibiting base ingratitude, irreverence, and even contempt toward the infinitely good and glorious Maker and Governor of all. *No good man, nay, no true gentleman, ever indulges in the habit.*

A clear understanding of the nature and sphere of worship calls for a special consideration : of prayer, the representative act of worship; and of the Sabbath, the embodiment of the true system of Christian worship. Hence the following *Topics :*

Topic 1.   The Duty of Prayer.
Topic 2.   The Duty of Sabbath Observance.

Topic First.   The Duty of Prayer. — Prayer is the representative act of worship.   It is necessary to consider the following *Subjects:* the nature of prayer; its postulates; the grounds of its obligation; and the conditions of its efficacy.

Subject 1st.   The Nature of Prayer. — Prayer is the expression by man, either in soul or by word and posture, of his dependence upon God and absolute need of him as his infinite good.   It may express man's sense of God's infinite greatness and excellence; or of his righteousness; or of his beneficence; — and may therefore take the form: of adoration of the divine perfection; of confession of helplessness and sin; of petition for blessings needed; and of thanksgiving for mercies received.

It is against prayer as *petition for blessings needed* that objections are chiefly urged; and special attention needs therefore to be given to prayer in this aspect.

Meaning of Prayer. — In the strict and narrow sense, prayer is the supplicatory address of the creature to his Creator, in which he entreats him to bestow some needed blessing, to remove some present evil, or to defend him from some future danger which he has reason to fear.   In this sense it would embrace only the third of the four acts enumerated above.   The wider sense, as embracing adoration, confession, thanksgiving, is however the more appropriate one.

The Foundation of Prayer. — Prayer is the natural and spontaneous expression of the soul toward God.   When man knows God and has the right feelings toward him, there is an irresistible impulse to pray to him.   The starting point is doubtless in a sense of weakness, dependence, and helplessness.   "The very atheist in these days is compelled to become a pantheist, that he may find outlet to these feelings, in communion with an irresistible power."   But beyond this crying out of the helpless creature to God for help, there is evidently an aspect of prayer corresponding to each form in which God's infinite goodness is made known to men.

Kinds of Prayer. — Prayer does not necessarily express itself orally or in any other outward form.   Its fountain is in the human soul. But as man, body and soul, is one being, it is right that on suitable

occasions the desires of the soul should express themselves in appropriate language and postures of body. As he is individually responsible,
and has therefore strictly personal relations to God, *private prayer*
becomes a duty. As he is a social being, and has therefore certain
relations to God in common with other men, *social* and *public prayer*
become duties.

Subject 2d.   Postulates of Prayer. — Prayer assumes that
the Moral Governor is a Personal Being ; that he is everywhere present and able to hold intercourse with his rational
creatures ; that he has perfect knowledge of everything in the
universe ; that he has personal control over all beings and
forces that exist, including of course man himself and the
forces of nature ; that he is both able and inclined to hear
and aid and bless man in his temporal and spiritual interests.

These Postulates Essential. — Only a Person can hear and answer
prayer : blind force cannot. The God of prayer cannot therefore be the
name for some unknown force, or for the moral order of the universe, or
even for the unconscious universe itself. It is further evident that only
an *all-present, all-wise, all-powerful*, and *beneficently disposed Person* can hear
and answer prayer. The Christian system assumes all these postulates.

The Answer to Prayer especially Essential. — The Christian system
and the instincts of humanity can only be satisfied with a theory of
prayer which implies that God does hear and answer man, and does
actually bestow upon him blessings both temporal and spiritual. Says
Dr. Chalmers: " Prayer and the answer to prayer, according to the
popular understanding, according to the natural understanding, according to the Bible view, are simply, the preferring of a request upon the
one side, and compliance with the request upon the other. Man applies,
God complies. Man asks a favor, God bestows it. These are conceived
to be the two terms of a real interchange that takes place between the
parties — the two terms of a sequence, in fact, of which the *antecedent*
is a prayer lifted up from earth, and the *consequent* is the fulfilment of
that prayer in virtue of a mandate from heaven."

Prayer has a Twofold Sphere. — The view which would confine prayer
to a purely spiritual sphere, and regard it as inherently inapplicable to
the sphere of physical causation, is entirely untenable. The spiritual
and physical forces are inter-related and reciprocal, and cannot be separated in any such way. It is impossible to ascertain the exact border
line. There are *some things which ought not to be prayed for*, but such
things may lie in the sphere of spiritual forces as well as in the sphere
of physical forces.

Modern Infidelity denies the Postulates of Prayer. — It bases its denial either upon the construction and government of the universe, or upon the unchangeable purpose of God.

First General Objection. — There are some pretentious scientists who affirm that God — if there be a God — has so made the universe and so governs it, that it would be impossible for him to answer prayer without injuring or wrecking it. These men urge their objections from various points of view. Some of these will be considered.

Invariable Amount of Physical Force. — It is objected that "the amount of physical force in the universe is incapable of either increase or diminution, and only capable of endless modification; therefore prayer cannot be answered, since it requires the introduction and action of a new force." In reply, it may be denied that the Christian theory of prayer *absolutely needs* the introduction of any new physical force. The *modification by the divine will* of the forces which already exist, is all that is needed in answering prayer. The conservation and correlation of the physical forces are fully admitted. But since *man's will* so modifies and directs these forces as to produce all the varied and wonderful results of human art and industry, it is obvious that *God's will* can, by the simple shaping of the existent forces, produce the more wonderful results involved in some of the answers to prayer.

Unbroken Physical Nexus of Phenomena. — To meet this reply, it is objected, that "the *physical nexus* between phenomena in their ceaseless flux and reflux is never broken, and therefore the interposition of the divine will is excluded; so that God cannot answer prayer by modifying these forces." This is merely an abstruse and obscure statement of the simple and familiar general principle of *uniformity of causation*. It is a sufficient reply to the objection, that this law of causation, so far from being an impediment to will, divine or human, in working out its own designs, is *just the contrary*. The constancy of elementary forces, and the certainty of consequences, are the very conditions, and, so far as we know, the essential conditions, on which will works and works with illimitable effect. So far, therefore, from excluding the interposition of the divine will, this principle prepares for that interposition on the grandest scale.

Adamantine Reign of Law. — To meet this reply, it is still further objected, that the order in which phenomena appear in the universe is governed by the rigor of adamantine law, and that there is therefore no place left for the free interposition of a divine will in answering prayer. It is a sufficient answer to this objection, that the principle which it assumes is *in no intelligible sense true*. There is no such iron rule of law. The phenomena of the universe are capable of endless change and variety through the modification of the laws of nature. By the minutest differences in the arrangement of the most trivial circumstances, perhaps by the lifting or turning of a finger, results may be endlessly modified, even where the same general laws control. In short, instead of immutable rigidity, *plasticity — infinite plasticity —* in the hands of knowledge and power, is of the very essence of natural law in both its combinations and its results.

Physical Consequent of Spiritual Antecedent Impossible. — To evade the force of this reasoning, it is objected, once more, that a spiritual antecedent will not produce a physical consequent, and it is therefore impossible for a spiritual God, by the exercise of his will — a purely spiritual procedure — to produce the physical results which are often absolutely essential in answering prayer. It is an unanswerable reply to this objection, that *the principle which it assumes as true is known to be untrue by every man.* Any one has the clear proof of its falsity in his own organism, since he is constantly exercising his spiritual power, by the will, and producing physical results, in the movements and changes of the body. Man is also constantly making use of and varying the forces of nature by the action of his will through the instrumentality of the body. So far from its being true, then, that a physical consequent cannot be produced by a spiritual antecedent, it is scarcely an open question, whether any physical consequent is ever possible without a spiritual antecedent, or, in other words, whether at bottom there is any other cause in the universe than spirit. It is worse than absurd, then, to deny that the destination of physical forces can be arrested, otherwise inevitable results be prevented, and new results be brought about in answering prayer, by the exertion of the will of the Divine Spirit.

The universe has not been so made, nor is it so governed, that its Maker and Governor must wreck it in order to hear and answer prayer.

Second Général Objection. — There are others who object that the immutable decree, or one unchangeable plan, of God stands in the way of his answering prayer. Everything has been fixed from the beginning, and there is therefore no room to change it to meet the special needs of the creature as expressed in prayer. The objection has weight only upon the groundless hypothesis that God has built the world after the objector's fashion and in his small way. God's one great and beautiful plan, just because it is God's plan, and not man's, is able to take in everything and to provide for every emergency from the beginning. In order to answer prayer, "he does not require to interfere with his own arrangements, for there is an answer provided in the arrangement made by him from all eternity. How is it that God sends us the bounties of his providence? — how is it that he supplies the many wants of his creatures?—how is it that he encourages industry?—how is it that he arrests the plots of wickedness?—how is it that he punishes even in this life notorious offenders against his law? The answer is, by the skilful prearrangements of his providence, by which the needful events fall out at the very time and in the way required. When the question is asked, How does God answer prayer?—we give the same reply:—it is by a prearrangement, when God settled the constitution of the world, and set all its parts in order." (See McCosh, *Divine Government*, p. 222.) Man is wise enough to prearrange all his affairs, in even the most extensive business, so as to secure the varied results which he desires for any given period of time: God is able to do the same thing on the grander scale of the universe for eternity. If his neighbor were not wiser and more skilful in the management of his business affairs than this objector credits the Hearer of prayer with being in ordering the affairs of his universe, he would justly pronounce that neighbor a *fool*. There is nowhere evidence of any plan or decree of God which interferes with the free action of man or of God, or which does not embody the designs of infinite wisdom, infinite love, and infinite justice.

Subject 3d. The Obligation to Prayer.—This appears from its being the expression of a universal instinct; from its being essential to the development of the highest manhood; from its being God's way of conferring the most important of the divine blessings essential to man. These three points all alike indicate that prayer is a law of man's being, written in him; and it is therefore a natural consequence that, wherever the light of nature has taught men to acknowledge the being of God, there it has directed them to pray to that God.

A Universal Instinct. — Prayer is but one application of a universal principle. Man, in all ages and countries of the world, has obtained what he desired of men by entreaty. With the same universality he has made application of the same principle for securing the supply of his wants from a supernatural power. Such universal action can only be explained by a universal impulse or instinct implanted in the constitution.

Essential to the Highest Manhood. — True prayer is the sublimest act a human being ever performs. Or, as Coleridge expresses it: "Spiritual praying, in its most perfect form, is the highest energy of which the human soul is capable." It is direct communion with the infinite God; it recognizes man's high destination as immortal and linked with God; it gives expression to his highest nature and noblest life. Its exercise is therefore, by its reflex influence, a most important means of lifting the soul into conformity with the divine will and to likeness to God himself. Man's noblest life must perish without prayer as its embodiment and expression toward God. Prayer would therefore be of priceless worth to men, were there only this reflex influence attaching to its exercise.

God's Way of Conferring the Greatest Blessings. — God doubtless knows man's wants, and *one might suppose* could supply them without the asking, if he chose to do so. But the fact that he has chosen that man should ask in order to receive makes it man's duty to ask. God, who bestows the blessings without any adequate return, assuredly has the right to decide *on what terms* he will bestow them.

Moreover, a closer knowledge of human nature shows, that supplication for needed blessings is one of the instrumentalities that God uses to bring man to feel his need of the blessings, and to work in him a fuller appreciation of them when received. Were the blessings conferred without the asking, such is fallen human nature, that they would be received as a matter of course and enjoyed without appreciation and without gratitude.

Subject 4th.   Conditions of Efficacious Prayer. — Prayer, in the Christian sense, in order that it may be efficacious, or that it may be heard and answered by God, should be for things which are in accordance with the will of God and which man truly needs, and should be offered in sincerity, reverence, and humility, with importunity, submission, and faith, and in the name of Christ.

True Prayer Efficacious. — That such prayer is efficacious is proved by the indisputable facts of human experience. The Baconian philosophy can never lead men to decide against the Bible view of prayer. There are great facts which it cannot ignore: such as the fact that God has so made the human soul that the race cannot resist the conviction of the propriety and efficacy of prayer; and the grand fact, in harmony with this constitution of man's nature, that prayer has been answered and is still answered in innumerable instances. The philosopher has just as much right to deny the facts about nature as the facts about prayer, — nay, more, for the facts about prayer are infinitely more important as pertaining to the most momentous interests of the highest being on the globe.

The Experimental Test. — The experimental test is applicable to prayer in the sense in which it is applicable to all the great practical doctrines of Christianity. He who approaches God, complying with the conditions just enumerated, may confidently rely upon the divine attention and aid. He will find infinite wisdom, love, and power ready to interpose in his behalf, and to exert themselves in working out for him that which shall be in the very highest sense best for him. Each one may thus reverently put the power of prayer to the test for himself. It is at the same time manifest that any proposal *to experiment* upon God in prayer, for the purpose of arrogantly putting him to the test, receives no encouragement from any revelation he has made; but is irreverent in its character, and betrays an utter want of knowledge of the nature and conditions of efficacious prayer. The great Creator and Governor never reveals the secrets of his wisdom and power, whether in nature or his Word, to those who will not inquire of him humbly, reverently, persistently, and in faith.

Topic Second. The Duty of Sabbath Observance.—The Christian Sabbath embodies, in a special and perspicuous manner, the worship of God. Its origin, its design, its authority, and its right observance are the important *Subjects* for consideration.

Subject 1st. The Origin of the Sabbath.—The Sabbath was instituted immediately after the creation of man. Its institution was ratified, and special rites and ceremonies added when the law was given to the Israelites by Moses. The Apostles incorporated with it the principles of a complete Christianity, accepting it as the special day of Christian worship, and at the same time changing it from the seventh to the first day of the week, the day of Christ's resurrection.

The Original Sabbath. — The Sabbath was instituted at the origin of the human race. The *presumption* is strongly in favor of this view from the fact that man's need of the Sabbath began with the beginning of his existence. But the *historical argument* is conclusive. The record in the opening of Genesis does not admit of any other natural interpretation than that which makes the institution of the Sabbath coeval with the creation of man. In corroboration of the original institution of the Sabbath may be cited, the evidence that the division of time into periods of seven days was common long before the time of Moses. Noah is said twice to have rested seven days (*Gen.* viii. 11, 12). In the time of Jacob, the division into weeks was an established usage (*Gen.* xxix. 27, 28). This division of time into weeks was not confined to the

Hebrews, but was almost universal. All this is best accounted for upon the supposition of the original institution and continued observance of the Sabbath. Add to this the fact that the Sabbath, before the giving of the law, was treated by Moses as a well-known institution, in the regulations about the manna (*Exod.* xvi.); and the further fact that its being well known is implied in the very form of the commandment (*Exod.* xx. 8-11). The institution of the Sabbath was therefore *certainly* ante-Mosaic, and *almost as certainly* Adamic.

The Jewish Sabbath.—That the Jewish Sabbath was but a modification of the original Sabbath, to give it the new truths of *the covenant Jehovah* and *the coming deliverer*, and to fit it, by rites and ceremonies, for the special needs of the Jewish race as the conservers of divine revelation, will hardly be denied by any one who admits the Adamic origin of the Sabbath.

The Christian Sabbath, as observed on the first day of the week, had its origin with the Apostles and the Primitive Church. It is a simple historical fact that the Christians of Apostolic times, under Apostolic guidance, universally ceased to observe the seventh day of the week, and did observe the first, as a day of rest and religious worship. It was eminently in accordance with the nature and design of the Sabbath, as the embodiment of the true religion and its worship, that it should be changed to the day of Christ's resurrection, and so become, not only a memorial of God the Creator and of Jehovah the Covenant-maker and Deliverer from Egypt, but also a memorial of the new creation and the greater deliverance of redemption brought in by the rising of the crucified Christ.

Subject 2d.   The Design of the Sabbath.—The Christian Sabbath embodies the Christian system of worship and religion, as suited to meet the needs of man; and it aims to turn the tides of the human soul in supreme devotion Godward, in order to lift man up to the true spiritual manhood.

1st. It Embodies the Christian System.—The Sabbath has been from the beginning a special practical embodiment of the true religion, and in its changes from the original and universal Sabbath, first to the Jewish, and finally to the Christian Sabbath, it has marked the advancing stages of that religion.

Design of the Original Sabbath.—The original Sabbath was, *first,* a *memorial of God as Creator of the universe.* It was thus fitted to keep him before mankind as the Maker and Lawgiver, and as the infinitely excellent and beneficent God, worthy of the homage of all his rational creatures. It was, *secondly, a day of rest from the purely secular activities*, that man's soul might be turned in its activities Godward. It was, *thirdly, a perpetual act of imitation of God* in his resting from the work of creation, and was thus fitted to keep God always before man as his true and only pattern. ·After the fall of the race, there was probably connected with it *the ordinance of sacrifice for sin*, which should keep before man his relation as a sinner to his righteous Creator and Governor. The Sabbath was thus peculiarly fitted to keep man's soul fixed upon God, by keeping before it the facts of his creation and dependence, and the essential facts concerning the Creator and Ruler. Man could not keep the universal Sabbath and forget God.

Design of the Jewish Sabbath. — When the new revelation of God as the covenant God was made to the Jewish race by Moses, and its advanced and essential truths embodied in the ceremonial law, the substance of this revelation was added to the idea of the original Sabbath, and the institution became a *sign* between God and his peculiar people Israel. "Moreover, also, I gave them my Sabbath to be a *sign* between me and them." It was still a memorial of God the Creator, a day of rest and Godward activity, and a starting-point in the imitation of the great example; but it now became also a memorial of the deliverance of Israel from Egypt, turned men more directly and devoutly to God by the rites which kept before them the infinite grace of the Covenant Jehovah and of the coming Deliverer. The Jew could not truly keep the Jewish Sabbath and remain away from God or make fatal failure in his moral and religious mission.

Design of the Christian Sabbath. — When the Christian revelation assumed its full and final form, the Sabbath, with its worship, became again the embodiment of the essential elements as given anew, or as developed from the old. It still held all the old truth concerning God the Creator and Covenant-keeper, while, by its change from the seventh day of the week to the day of Christ's resurrection, the first day, it henceforth became likewise a memorial of that greatest event in the religious history of the world; and, by its special ordinances of preaching, prayer, praise, and communion, embodied in practical form the essential truths of the complete Christian revelation. It thus becomes apparent that the Christian Sabbath is the great bulwark of Christianity, so that the Christian cannot duly observe it and yet make a failure in his mission.

2d. It meets the Necessities of Man's Physical and Mental Nature.— Scientific observation and the general experience of men have convinced the most profound and careful thinkers, that the rest provided for by the Sabbath is a necessity of man's constitution, physical and mental; of the constitution of the beasts subject to man ; and, to some extent, even of the inanimate objects and agents under his control. (It is a well-ascertained fact that both body and mind require intervals of relaxation from accustomed toil. It is clearly demonstrable that, if this law be disregarded and the vital forces become impaired and exhausted, paralysis and softening of the brain, with physical helplessness and mental imbecility, are but too often the penalty of the continued and unremitted tasking of the powers.) By obedience to this law of remission of effort, fixed in the human constitution, more labor, of whatever kind, is accomplished with less waste of the forces of life. Moreover, experiments — such as that made in France, by the *Theophilanthropists*, in substituting every tenth day in the place of every seventh as a day of rest — go to show that the precise demand of man's constitution is for the seventh day rather than any other.

Social Nature. — It is still further obvious that the rest of the Sabbath, while conserving and adding to man's vigor, physical and mental, gives opportunity also for the development of his social and domestic nature in the home, and increases largely his social and domestic enjoyment.

Moral and Religious Nature. — But, rising above all these considerations, it can be shown conclusively that the Christian Sabbath, properly observed, is absolutely essential to the moral and spiritual development and culture of man. Such a Sabbath arrests the secular and selfish work of the world ; impresses the necessary lessons of sin, of the cross, and of Christian principles upon the minds of men, and brings them into the most intimate communion with God himself. The supreme importance of such a work is readily shown by such considerations as those which follow :

First, an unremitting worldly activity would tend to secularize man ; to confine his thoughts and energies to the narrow limits of time and the earth ; and to reduce him almost to the level of the mere animal.

Secondly, at the same time, if left without the constant inculcation of the great moral and religious principles, which should guide him in his present relations and with reference to his immortal destiny, man would soon run riot in crime and corruption, and civilized society would perish.

Thirdly, as the Christian system, embodied in the Christian Sabbath, has been shown to be the only true theory of moral reconstruction, mankind without it is in a hopelessly wrecked condition, and can never be brought up to the true manhood and the true life of duty.

Hence the Sabbath is seen to be exactly suited to the moral and spiritual necessities of man. It is one of the grandest practical ideas, fitted at once to turn man toward God and to mould him into the divine likeness.

Subject 3d.   The Authority of the Sabbath.—In both the origin and design of the Sabbath is seen the evidence of its universal authority, as instituted by God for man.   The universal need which man has for its rest; its worship adapted to man's nature and relation to God; and the Christian system of moral reconstruction which it embodies and expresses, and which its proper observance brings to bear practically on man, —are all but the handwriting of the Divine Lawgiver witnessing to its authority over all mankind.

While the Sabbath was clearly *made for man*, it is seen to be likewise true that all duty toward God is inseparably connected with its proper observance; so that a Christian nation that parts with its due observance, by so doing parts with its Christianity, its Christian morality, and its true prosperity.

National Obligation.—National obligation to Sabbath observance is accordingly one of the most important and salutary principles which can be impressed upon a people. This obligation has of late been denied by a large element of the foreign-born population of this country. "It is urged that, as there is in the United States an entire separation of church and state, it is contrary to the genius of our institutions to enforce the observance of the Sabbath by the civil law. The state has nothing to do with religion." It is further urged that, as all citizens have equal rights, irrespective of their religious beliefs, it is an infringement of those rights if one class of the people are required to conform their conduct to the opinions which another class entertain concerning a purely religious institution like the Sabbath. These objections may be answered in the light of the true view, already in part presented (p. 306), touching the relation of this nation to Christianity.

The Claim that the State must be Atheistic.—The claim that the civil government in this nation has nothing to do with religion has been seen to be utterly baseless. It is not true of any institution in the world. Says Dr. Hodge: "That is not true even of a fire company, or of a manufactory, or of a banking-house. The religion embraced by the individuals composing these associations must influence their corporate action, as well as their individual conduct. If a man may not blaspheme, a publishing firm may not print and disseminate a blasphemous book. A civil government cannot ignore religion any more than physiology. It was not constituted to teach either the one or the

29 *

other, but it must, by a like necessity, conform its action to the laws of both."

The Issue is really between the True Religion and Infidelity or Atheism. — The men who advocate the antireligious character of the state are, as a general thing, themselves antireligious and immoral, and they would give their own character to the state. In the name of liberty, these men, who owe all they have of any value to the Christian institutions of this country, would destroy those institutions and bring perpetual immorality and blight upon the land that has furnished them a refuge from oppression and loaded them with blessings. The *Sabbath Laws* furnish a convenient point of departure in their tyrannical work. Says Dr. Hodge: "It is a condition of service in connection with any railroad which is operated on Sundays, that the employee be not a Christian. If Christianity is not to control the action of our municipal, state, and general governments, then, if elections be ordered to be held on the Lord's Day, Christians cannot vote. If all the business of the country is to go on, on that as on other days, no Christian can hold office. We should thus have not a religious, but an antireligious test-act. Such is the freethinker's idea of liberty. But still further, if Christianity is not to control the laws of the country, then, as monogamy is a purely Christian institution, we can have no laws against polygamy, arbitrary divorce, or free love. All this must be yielded to the anti-Christian party; and consistency will demand that we yield to the atheists the oath and the decalogue; and all the rights of citizenship must be confined to blasphemers."

The Law of Self-Conservation binds to Sabbath Observance. — Destruction is all that these opposers of Sabbath observance can offer this nation. In order to safety, men must submit to the laws of their nature, not only as sentient, but also as moral and religious beings. "These laws are ordained, administered, and enforced by God, and there is no escape from their obligation, or from the penalties attached to their violation." To all right-minded men Christianity has been abundantly shown to be the true view of man's nature, relations, duties, and destiny, — the only reconstructing and elevating agency in the world. Conformity to its principles is virtue, prosperity, safety; departure from them, vice, adversity, destruction. In all the history of mankind, the nations have been free and prosperous as they have adhered to the principles of Christianity; they have lost their freedom and made wreck as they have departed from those principles. And this must always be so; for the fundamental principles of Christianity are the fundamental principles of the government of the universe. The freethinkers, whose understandings are emancipated from their conscience, and who consequently wish to see civil government emancipated from religion, are therefore exhibiting toward the land that has cherished them, the gratitude of the viper toward the peasant who warmed it to life in his bosom. In spite of all such opposition, the nation is bound to recognize and guard the Sabbath as embodying the great conservative principles upon which its continued existence depends. It can concede to no man or set of men the right to do that which shall destroy it.

National Responsibility to God binds to Sabbath Observance. — If the nation is under the Moral Governor and responsible to him, then if he requires the Sabbath to be set apart for his worship, the civil government, while it has no right to require of men adherence to any religious doctrine or attendance upon any religious services, is yet bound to enjoin upon them that they abstain from all unnecessary worldly occupations, so as not to interfere with those who do desire to make proper religious use of it. This *civil Sabbath* the state owes to God.

Moreover that this is a Protestant Christian Nation binds it to Sabbath Observance. — That it was Christian and Protestant in its origin and genius has already been seen (p. 303). That it is such still is established by the historical fact that Protestant Christianity is the law of the land. It was distinctly adopted as such by the early settlers, and has been repeatedly decided to be so by the Civil Courts. "From Maine to Georgia, from ocean to ocean, one day in the week, by the law of God and by the law of the land, the people rest." Here is the corner-stone in the foundation, and the citadel in the defences of our free institutions; here the key-stone in the perfect arch of the national mission.

Subject 4th. The Proper Observance of the Sabbath. —

The design of the Sabbath decides the proper manner of its observance. Man is under obligation to use it in such a way as shall best secure the end for which it was instituted. What is consistent with that design is lawful; what is inconsistent with it, is unlawful. He must evidently cease from his worldly vocations in order to secure the rest of body and mind intended; and he must devote himself to the worship and service of God in order to secure the intended development of his being toward God.

Observance for Rest. — The *natural* though subordinate reason for the institution of the Sabbath must be borne in mind. So far as is possible, consistently with the higher purposes of the Sabbath, there should be an entire cessation of the ordinary pursuits, for the purpose of resting and refreshing both body and mind. The Christian should guard against allowing even religious duties to be multiplied to such an extent as to make the Sabbath a day of weariness and exhaustion, and so prevent it from bringing the designed rest and refreshment and the intended spiritual culture.

Personal Culture, Moral and Religious. — This is the higher end aimed at in the institution of the Sabbath. It should bring men individually into communion with the God of creation and redemption. Man should aim to devote this day especially to securing his own moral and religious improvement and perfection, by seeking to know, love, and serve God supremely. As it practically embodies the great principles of duty to God, man may expect, by properly observing it, to be brought more nearly up to his duty toward God. As it practically embodies the true and only scheme of moral reconstruction he may expect, by properly observing and making use of its provisions, to be brought in the divine way up to the true moral manhood and the true life of duty.

Public Worship. — As man is a social being, the public worship of God is likewise an obvious and important duty, without which that complete moral and religious development in his social relations with his fellow-men, which fits him for the widest fulfilment of his highest mission in the world, cannot be reached.

SECTION III.

Acceptance of the Divine Scheme of Moral Reconstruction.

The duty of the devotion of the active powers to God culminates in requiring of man, in his condition of moral disorder and ruin, the practical acceptance of the divine scheme for the moral reconstruction of human nature and for securing immortal progress and glory.

Christianity the Basis of Morality. — Christianity has been shown to be the only hope of the world (p. 166) in its present moral condition. *All human duty*, no less than all the special duties toward God, culminates in duty toward God as he has revealed himself in Christianity. Without this supreme duty the others become impossible.

This practical acceptance involves personal devotion to Christ and his system in attaining the true moral manhood; and devotion of the powers to the fulfilment of his last command in bringing the world up to the same moral manhood.

Topic First.   The Personal Acceptance and Devotion.— Every possible moral consideration, from the lowest to the highest, binds man as a moral agent to the personal acceptance of Christianity and personal devotion to Christ.   The same considerations bind him to recognize, accept, and co-operate with, the Church of Christ, as the chief instrumentality in conserving his doctrine, in renovating and blessing man, and in directing him to his highest moral task on earth. In the fulfilment of these duties man is to attain to his complete moral perfection as an individual being.

The Personal Duty to Christianity.— Man finds himself in this world with a ruined being, but with a divine provision for the repair of that ruin and restoration to sonship to God made accessible through the Christian religion.   He finds himself upon the threshold of an infinite hereafter with an endless progress of being before him, which without Christianity must be an endless progress in unrighteousness and misery, but with it may become an endless progress in righteousness and blessedness.   It is therefore the first, highest, and most sacred of human duties, to secure the full benefits of the Christian system for these high ends; "to grow up into him, in all things, which is the head, even Christ" (*Eph.* iv. 15); "to lay hold on eternal life" (1 *Tim.* vi. 12). The infinite grace of God and the infinite necessities of man combine with the direct divine command to urge to this first and highest duty.

The Duty to the Church.— The existence and mission of the Church are among the most important of all the social facts that attract the attention in a Christian country.   It claims to be a divine institution,— God's ordained agency for bringing man to that higher and better moral and religious condition which is essential to the individual, the family, and the state.   It therefore becomes the duty of every man to ascertain whether it is really of God; to study and understand its mission; to cherish it and seek its progress; to find his own place and work in it and with it.

Topic Second.   The Acceptance and Devotion for Mankind. —The personal acceptance of Christ and the Christian system prepares man for the fulfilment of his highest social mission as a moral and religious being.   The highest considerations, involving the fundamental principles of Social and Theistic Ethics, bind him to the duty of holding the treasures of Christianity, not for himself only, but for his entire race, and of devoting his powers to the work of bringing all men up to its high moral standard and mission.   In the fulfilment of these duties man is to attain to his complete perfection as a social and religious being.

The Duty for Mankind. — Man finds the whole race in the same moral ruin with himself here, and with the same possible and endless destiny of shame or glory hereafter.   The intuitive moral principle, which requires that he should love his neighbor as himself, and which prompts him to share his blessings, and chief of all the blessings of his religious faith, with that neighbor, makes it imperative that he should seek to give to all men the full benefits of the scriptural provision for the moral reconstruction of the world ; and so reach the highest perfection as a social being by obeying the great commission of Christ: "Go ye into all the world and preach my Gospel to every creature." The principle, which requires supreme devotion to God, combines its authority with that of social duty in making the same demand.

As Theoretical Ethics reaches its completion in Christianity, as the only true scheme for the moral reconstruction of mankind ; so Practical Ethics reaches its conclusion in the all-comprehensive duty to God of making the most of Christianity for its great individual and social ends.   The true morality therefore culminates in Christianity, and the complete manhood is attained only in the true Christian.

In the fulfilment of his duties toward God, therefore, man is to reach his complete perfection as a religious being, and to realize his true moral manhood and life work.

THE END.